The Alchemist's Stone

BEING PART ONE OF

WAR OF THE LAST REMNANT

JOEL GILLESPIE

PUBLISHED BY JOEL GILLESPIE ● MEMPHIS, TENNESSEE

The Alchemist's Stone
Copyright © 2013 by Joel Gillespie
First Edition, 2013

The Alchemist's Stone is the first book of the fantasy fiction series, *War of the Last Remnant*.

Authored and Published by Joel Gillespie
6010 Wind Meadow Lane
Memphis, Tennessee 38115

www.warofthelastremnant.com

ISBN: 978-0-9895832-0-6

Cover designed by Duncan Long
    Manhattan, Kansas

Edited and proofread by William Mitchum
    Memphis, Tennessee

Printed in the United States of America

ACKNOWLEDGEMENTS

I would like to thank all of my family and friends who have supported me through this lengthy process. But I would like to give a special thanks to my wonderful wife, Krystal, for all her love and support through the long and grueling work I put into this book. Thank you, my beloved, for always encouraging me in my writing endeavors and for being a part of my dream. I write this with gratitude to you.

I would also like to thank my illustrator, the talented Duncan Long, for the incredible book design he supplied for me and also for his patience with me through all of this.

To my friend, William Mitchum, I am extremely grateful for the edits you supplied for me as well as your hard work proofreading my book.

Above all else, I would like to thank God for graciously supplying me with a talent and a passion for writing, and more so, I give thanks to God for saving me through Jesus Christ.

As a final word, I would like to dedicate this book to Naomi Grace, my daughter who has gone before me. Though I never really knew you, this book is written in honor of you. In addition, I devote this book to my son, Solomon, my precious gift from God.

In a world of evil wrought from malice old:
The Last Remnants of Light stand and oppose
The armies of Dragoth, their ancient foes.
The Last Remnant of Dragons awaken anew
To combat the Dark Lord, of him to subdue.
The Last Remnant of Wizards return to the fight
Against their brethren who strayed from the Light.
The Last Remnant of Men their last tales now unfold
In the struggle against Abaddon and his malice of old.

CONTENTS

PART ONE

Beginnings

It was *Vaaspar* who existed since the beginning of time—as told in the lore of the world—and He awoke all living things with a unique Magic of His own making, known as *Elúvías*. He desired greatly to create and awaken living things that slept away in the earth, and those He awoke foremost He called 'Beloved.' In His own tongue they were called *Celebhas*, the Celestial Spirits. Having awakened *Abaddon*, the Prince of the Celebhas, out of the ground where he slept, Vaaspar gave him strength, and the Celebhas took in the breath of life. Many others did Vaaspar awaken at the beginning of time, and many dwelt in his home in *Elúne*: it was known to Men as 'The White Land.' He taught them all, His Beloved, to awaken and love life.

As the days elapsed, Abaddon marveled at the beauty of Vaaspar's home; indeed, he yearned for it and alas! he lusted after it. He desired to have it for himself so much that he fell out of the Realm of Light and into the Realm of Darkness, for he plotted to overthrow Vaaspar secretly; but his plan was discovered, and Vaaspar, knowing his thoughts, cast him out of Elúne into a forsaken land of solitude and darkness. He turned from the Prince of the Celebhas and became the King of the *Draemhas*, the Infernal Spirits: they were those who loved darkness rather than light and were made black by the evil in their hearts. And many followed him.

In the years that followed, having been given immortality by Vaaspar's blessing at the beginning of the days, Abaddon studied his former master and learned of His great love for Men: for they were the youngest of all the awoken creations and in great need of knowledge and wisdom. Vaaspar dwelt amongst the Men of Gaia—the lands belonging to Men—for quite some time, and He was called the 'Lord of Light' by the peoples of Gaia. He taught them many things of the world, and how to care for the land. But through all the passing days, Abaddon had not forgotten either his anger against Vaaspar for casting him out of Elúne or his desire to be ruler of the White Land; and he longed before long to change it to a land of endless darkness. Thus, he mustered up an army of wild animals and

1

terrible beasts of old for his first assault on Elúne. In those days, time seemed to pass quickly; the days were like a short breath or the blink of an eye.

It was during those days—the Age before Men had kings—when Abaddon, the Lord of Darkness, arose from *Vexú'Nar Krja*—the Realm of Darkness—a place of great evil and shadows, and assaulted Elúne, the Realm of Light where Vaaspar dwelt; it was the year 1378 World Reckoning, during the first years of Men. He took with him many of those who were among the first awoken at the start of it all. They were called the Celebhas, an immortal and celestial race, before their rebellion against Vaaspar. Later, those who had fallen came to be known as the Draemhas, the Scourge of Elúne.

After suffering a terrible defeat at Vaaspar's hand, Abaddon retreated to his land to the far north of the Eastern Lands of Gaia across a small sea called *the Grim Deep*, for he was unable to endure Vaaspar's mighty bow and his gleaming sword of blinding, white fire. Vaaspar had the mind to end his life there, but He relented and resided peacefully in Elúne for some time, not to return to Gaia for many long years. The Men of Gaia gave the name *Dragoth* to the Realm of Darkness where Abaddon dwelt, and they feared him greatly for many ages. He came to be known as 'the Dark Lord' in those days and Men held a great sense of contempt towards him.

In the year 2567 Men's Reckoning (M.R.) of the First Age of Kings, when time still seemed to move swiftly, and the years of Men numbered more than three hundred—when *the Great Lords of Gaia* ruled their glorious kingdoms of old—Abaddon mustered a new army: this time he would attack the Men of Gaia out of spite for Vaaspar. Abaddon used the knowledge taught to him by the Lord of Light to awaken new, vile creatures and more Celebhas whom he charmed and changed into Draemhas. He used his knowledge of the land and his ever increasing power to raise a land bridge, almost four leagues wide, from Dragoth to Gaia so his armies could march upon the kingdoms of Men.

As quickly as his army grew, his blackened heart was filled with great anxiety for the plan he set before him. His conquest began in the northeastern land that would one day come to be called *Caire Thrael*. The Great Lords rose to face the Dark Lord, but his power was too great. And the swing of his mighty war maul and the slash of his black blade were too dominant for their might; and the shots of his fiery darts proved menacing. The Great Lords of Gaia retreated far away to the Western Lands across the Great River—which

2

flowed for miles wide in between the two landmasses of Gaia—named *Raumas Mílnk*: it was named by Vaaspar Himself, and its name meant 'enormous river.'

The Lord of Light, hearing word of the invasion, awoke mighty beasts from the earth and gave them each a mighty element to use as power: one was given power over the earth, another over fire, one over lightning, another over wind and the last one ruled over water. These He gave control to rule the five elements of power, one to each beast. He called them *Elúvaín*, which means 'Brood of Light,' and Men called them *Dragons*. This day began the age of Dragons, year one of Dragon Reckoning (D.R.). The five mighty Dragons flew across the Great Sea and defeated Abaddon with the help of Vaaspar, the Celebhas and the armies of Men; and so the Dark Lord and his armies fled across the Grim Deep to Dragoth on their black warships, though many also fled into the Eastern Lands finding their way back along the land bridge to Dragoth. The Elúvaín were ordered by Vaaspar to deliver Abaddon to Him; then Vaaspar banished Abaddon's spirit to the Realm of the Dead or *Shaekle* as it was called in the ancient tongue. And there after, the spirit of the Dark Lord roamed the earth seeking a new body, but there was none in whom he found favor.

Many years passed, and he discovered new powers that were previously unbeknownst to him. In the year 1654 D.R., the Dark Lord began to whisper into the ears of Men; and their minds were swayed, and their hearts plunged deeply into darkness. Many evil Men obeyed the callings of the Dark Lord, and Vaaspar was grieved by their treachery. New armies, wars and, ultimately, destruction erupted across the lands of Gaia once more. The Dragons were ordered by Vaaspar to safeguard the lives of Men, but the Dragon era was nearing its end, for Abaddon's whisperings were instilling fear of Dragons into the hearts of Men; and so the Men of Gaia sought to eradicate them.

Two ages had nearly passed since Men first appointed kings over their lands when Abaddon's full evil and rage poured forth from his northern kingdom. His army flourished anew, and it grew stronger than ever. From the Realm of the Dead, he shared his evil plots with his faithful followers. Vaaspar once again roamed the lands of Gaia until Men, poisoned by the whispers of the Dark Lord, looked at Him with evil intent. Before long, Men attacked Vaaspar filling him with many arrows and many swords and many spears. He died that day in Gaia in the year 1663 D.R. Abaddon rejoiced greatly, but Vaaspar's spirit returned to Elúne; and it was there that He found new life. Abaddon looked on from Shaekle as the Lord of Light sat once again upon His great and glorious throne and was filled with despair and ire.

Now it seemed that time slowed down, and Men were dying sooner than in the previous ages; and their years rarely exceeded one hundred. Then Men cursed and accused the Dragons for their shortening life. Thus, *the Great Dragon War* commenced in the year 1664 D.R. Vaaspar, ashamed of Men and for awakening them, remained in Elúne, and Men quickly forgot about Him. Before long, Men spoke of Vaaspar as in legends or rumors to their children. Yet, a small few upheld Him as the God of *Valor*—this was the name of the world given by Men. For the most, however, talk of Vaaspar became merely great fables told in fireside tales. Without the Lord of Light to protect them, the Dragons were slain, all but a few, and the Great Dragon War ended in the year 1670 D.R.

After the Great Dragon War—though it was not so great, for only a few Dragons retaliated, since it was their purpose to protect and not harm humans—Men saw the scars of war on the world around them, and they cried out in despair. They now suffered deeply to mend a broken world ruined by their own doings and mischief. After the decimation of the Dragons, humans were filled with confusion and easily fell astray to join evil powers, for the Dragons were responsible for teaching and protecting as were Vaaspar's orders. It seemed to Abaddon that he had won against Vaaspar at last, and he planned, before long, to destroy the last of Men. He was thus called 'the Great Destroyer,' and Men were, for a time, filled with contempt towards the Dark Lord once more. Following the Great Dragon War and the destruction of the Dragons, the Second Age of Kings began.

In the years that unfolded, Men established fewer kings to rule their new lands, for in ages past, the lands were governed by many rulers and the hearts of Men were easily corrupted. And so, in the beginning of the Second Age of Kings, in the year 83 Post Dragon Era (83 P.D.E.), Men established the new kingdoms of Gaia. In the Western Lands, there were three powerful kingdoms: Alterash, Vash'ala, and Bolteras. In the Eastern Lands, there were eight mighty kingdoms: Caire Thrael, Sanctum Anthropolis—consisting of the three realms known as the Guole Sector, the Vexica Sector, and the Grimora Sector—Scipherius, Xiphoria, and the Bestial Lands.

Since Abaddon raised the land bridge, called *the Dark Lord's Pass*—or *the Serpent's Pass* as Men began to call it, for they considered Abaddon a cunning snake—Dragoth became a part of the Eastern Lands and loomed ever ominously to the north of Caire Thrael. This was the eighth and last of the lands considered a part of the Eastern Lands. These lands, eleven in all, formed the world of Gaia. Many of the inhabitants of Gaia began to wonder if the White Land still existed to the west or if it was simply a fabricated tale of old, for none now dared venture across the Great Sea ever since the rise of the terrifying *Sea Serpents*. And only a few wise and powerful knew whence they truly came. And so Elúne—whether it still existed to the far west or whether it faded into ancient memory—was long forgotten to Men.

The years passed, and the countries merely existed, ostensibly peaceful, for a long period of time until the year 1332 P.D.E. Unexpectedly, Abaddon's army in the north stirred and descended into Caire Thrael to the south where they met little opposition. The Men of Caire Thrael, the descendents of the only race of Men who once defended the Dragons during the Great Dragon War, were now eager to accept the Draemhas into their midst. They welcomed them with pride in their hearts because they desired to do battle with them and prove their might against them. As time elapsed, the Men of Caire Thrael and the forces of Dragoth forged an alliance in 1348 P.D.E. The Dark Lord had found favor in the Caire Thraeleans' strength and planned to use it to his advantage.

Before long, war revisited the Eastern Lands, and evil was awakened amidst the kingdoms of the East. Rumors were heard of an evil arising also in the land of Vash'ala to the west. How the forces were reaching the Western Lands, none knew; and there were none of Men in the Eastern or Western Lands that ever saw the forces of Darkness passing through to the Kingdom of Vash'ala. However he had done it, Abaddon now had influence in both the Eastern and Western Lands of Gaia; yet he halted his advance for he was still a spirit banished from his mortal body, and he desired fervently to conquer the world of Gaia by his own hand. And so small battles were fought here and there, but the Dark Lord never sent his armies in full force.

More time passed, and the rumors of Draemhas existing in the West were confirmed by many. But there arose from amongst the Keshians in the land of Bolteras a few brave people who came to be some of the most vital characters during the war in the Western

Lands, for they would inspire many to rise to arms against the threat of evil. The year was 1363 P.D.E. when Victor Perigas, son of Valent the Alchemist—whose prowess was unmatched—set forth with his adoptive father, Arthur Grause, and a band of travelers to the glorious capital city of Vallicore in Bolteras to learn of their destiny in the chaotic happenings of the world.

Chapter I

Unwelcomed Guests

When springtime had begun in the Western Lands of Gaia during the year 1363 P.D.E, the village of Kesh in the land of Bolteras was enjoying a season of growth and prosperity. Being a small village of less than two hundred inhabitants away to the far eastern edge of Bolteras near to the Cold Stone Mountains, they often felt cut off from the rest of the world and even their own brethren, but they were quite fond of the tranquility and simplicity of their lives. Their closest countrymen resided in Balas, a sturdy fortress only five miles to the west and south some from Kesh, but they were not too fond of the busyness of city life. The people of Balas were also recognized in the land for being discourteous drunkards, so the people of Kesh rarely made relations with them.

The *Keshians*, as the villagers called themselves, lived a simple life: they farmed in the plains about the town and hunted for food in the Grey Forest to the north; they also practiced archery—more for fun than for battle—made their own clothing, and enjoyed eating their fill with ale to accompany. There were hardly any who traveled from other towns or cities in Bolteras to visit; in fact, they had no family ever visit as all their family lived there in the village. Visitors were a rare sight since the departure of the *Alchemists*, maybe once or twice a year if ever they came at all. But they were glad to be left alone to mind their own affairs, for they rarely had to prepare food and lodging for travelers. And it was uncommon for any of the villagers to ever travel far from the town unless they were hunting or tending to their fields.

They were a humble people who despised complaining and bickering, unless someone was foolish enough to insult their kin, which was considered an 'unforgivable offense.' There were even times when they abandoned their way of thinking and traveled to Balas to quarrel over insults to their kin. Yet, this was an infrequent occurrence and most of their insults stayed between family members; and they tried always to mind to their own immediate family affairs. Thusly, they remained a fairly peaceful tribe compared to the rest of the world.

It was always in their best interest to resist fights and battles except to protect their own. They wished to be left alone to mind

7

their own affairs and to enjoy their own parties, and they were content with only themselves with the exception of a few villagers who were often called 'wayward souls' or even 'dotards.' These few would often visit Balas and even Pilias to the south and were often scoffed at by their fellow kin. Even with these few odd characters from Kesh, many of the other Boltian towns and villages considered them to be a selfish tribe of 'outlanders,' but the Keshians did not care for the opinions of others.

Quite often, they would throw parties in celebration of birthdays and weddings and anniversaries—which was always an excuse for them to overindulge in food and to have their fill of ale. Their favorite drink was a brew of their own making which they called Mayle's Ale: for it was named after Mayle Bradeur, a famous Keshian carpenter from a few generations old. He was responsible for constructing many of the fine shops and houses of Kesh, and he skillfully crafted them out of rich cedar, smoothed and cared for with the utmost consideration. He was a brilliant mind in his youth, but his brilliance altered in his old age, for his love was given to the brewing of rich tasting beers—the best of them all was named in his honor.

There were many shops and houses in Kesh: the village stretched about two furlongs long from north to south and about six furlongs wide from east to west. The village was built in a simple fashion: two crossroads ran through the village, one north to south and the other east to west. On either side of the roads were buildings as far as the roads stretched, and only a few structures—a mill, a well, and a lonely house to the southeast that once belonged to Mayle Bradeur—were built away from the road. But along the crossroads there were barns full of provisions from the harvests and storage huts for their hunting gear and stables full of animals: they raised chickens, turkeys, cows, several donkeys and mules, and a small host of horses. They desired to have additional oxen for the plow, but they never could afford to buy more than the two they already had: there were not many in all of Bolteras, and the majority was owned by the prosperous farmers of Vallicore—the capital city of Bolteras. To buy more oxen proved an impossible feat for the poor peasants of Kesh, and they stood a better chance of crossing over to the Eastern Lands where oxen lived in abundance than they ever did buying from the wealthy inhabitants of Vallicore. But, as was their habit, the Keshians did not often leave the village, for they loved their charming, little homes. Still, they found contentment with the oxen they had, and still their harvests were plentiful.

The Keshians were particularly fond of deer, turkey and chicken when it came to eating meat and their healthy farms yielded a great harvest of corns, taters and an assortment of other vegetables which they added to their festive meals. Their favorite vegetable, besides their beloved taters, was peas. They ate peas almost every meal as long as they had supply. But it was more common for them to enjoy their potatoes year-round, and they never grew weary of doing so.

To the south of Kesh, about three furlongs from the southernmost building which belonged to Mrs. Boris, who was an expert tailor, was a grove of an assortment of fruit trees. From the boughs of the trees grew apples and bananas; some grew oranges and pears; and on others still there grew peaches and figs. It was a tradition for the children in the village to go out once a week and pick the most appealing fruits to their little eyes. The Keshians were quite quaint in their traditions yet exceedingly high in spirits.

To the east of the grove of fruit trees across a small, shallow stream running from the *Grey Forest*—the woods ran from the northwest around to the east and to the south of Kesh—along the eastern border of Kesh was a dale full of rolling knolls. The stream diverged from the *Roaring River*, which flowed from the *Cold Stone Mountains* in the northeast, and trickled back down through the valleys to the south emptying into the Great Sea beyond the stronghold of Pilias. Atop one of the larger knolls, only a couple stone throws away from the fruit tree grove, there rested a single cherry blossom that rose higher and more majestic than any tree in the land—to the Keshians, it was a beacon of hope. The villagers named the tree *Ole Faithful*.

Its blooms were bright pink and gleamed brilliantly in the rising sun. In the eyes of the Keshians, this was the most beautiful sight in all of Bolteras, though very few knew anything outside of Kesh. Much further to the south and east some across a stone bridge leading over one of the streams that poured from the southernmost peak of the Cold Stone Mountains, near to the ocean before the grass turned sandy and full of shingles, was a great mass of mounds, some with memorials and some barren. It was enveloped by a great ring of stones much taller than a man. It was a monument for all of the Keshians' departed. From the inside of the circle, which they named the *Burial Grove*, after every interment, they turned around to the north and saw the large, bright colors of pink from the cherry blossom and were encouraged anew. It appeared to them that the tree grew brighter and taller every time a villager passed away. It came to pass in their telling of legends that the tree was filled with all the souls of the deceased Keshians, and that is why the tree appeared to grow taller and brighter with every death. Whenever visitors came to Kesh, some would boast, 'The tree is a beacon of hope, for with every death, there is life anew!' The villagers loved that tree as one of their own and would often go and speak to it, as with a friend, in their moments of difficulty.

* * *

The day was March the thirteenth, and it was Arthur Grause's birthday. Arthur was the village elder, and all the Keshians held the greatest respect for him even though he was considered one of the wayward souls as he often traveled to other villages and some of the Boltian strongholds. He was a friend of the king and an amiable old man. He was also the adoptive father of a boy named Victor Perigas whose parents withdrew with two other Alchemists from Bolteras fifteen years ago to help the Vash'alans in the northwest recover from plague and famine that resulted after the war with Bolteras twenty years prior. They were well known Alchemists—people of great power who knew the ways of Magic, especially the arts of healing—and their gifts of healing were unsurpassed in all the lands of Gaia. They were also responsible for using their Magic to grow the cherry blossom which brought much joy to the Keshians. It was told of in the tales about Ole Faithful that the Alchemists used their alchemic prowess to enchant the tree with the ability to house the souls of their lost loved ones, and many believed the stories despite their fabled origins. And Arthur also helped to look after a boy named Hildegard Gruff, the son of the other two Alchemists who went to Vash'ala.

The morning was just beginning for Arthur, as he had just awoken, but the village was already in much ado. Villagers were running to and fro through the lawns of neighbors' houses and in and out of alleys between the buildings in preparation for Arthur's sixtieth birthday. Tents were pitched and food was gathered away in the woods to the north; and wood was brought along with flint and steel for fire making and torch lighting. The whole village was excited.

'No one throws a bash like Mr. Arthur! He is the finest of Men, yes indeed that he is!' they would say in likeness as they

10

scurried back and forth. Arthur never failed to deliver a great banquet, and he constantly made his parties more about the guests than himself. 'Most importantly,' one villager liked to say, 'he brings enough Mayle's Ale to last us half a year, if we are being polite that is.'

That day Arthur woke late: it was his second favorite pastime to wake late on his birthday. He resided in an upstairs bedroom above his shop where he smelted many fine crafts of metal. He was the village's finest smithy and was even regarded as one of the finest in all of Bolteras. Often times, he would travel to the strongholds of Bolteras with carts full of weapons for the armies of the king and would stay for days in the company of soldiers and drunkards. He was one of very few Keshians that found favor with and was even welcomed by Boltians everywhere, including the unpleasant townsfolk of Balas. Often times, his kin would say things like, 'He is an adventurous man, but a loveable one if you can believe it.'

He arose from his bed and stretched his arms above his head as he looked out his window to see the many bustling figures passing back and forth. He smiled and a light gleamed in his eyes. His bedroom window looked out to the north, and he observed afar, slightly off to the west, the sight of targets still full of many arrows aloft the hills of the *Rolling Vale*. Now his smile grew ever wider with the thought of archery: it was his favorite pastime to hold an archery competition on his birthday, to which he always won as he was the most skilled archer in Kesh ever since the departure of Valent the father of Victor. He stood there looking out and drifted into a daze with excitement in his heart wondering how he would fair in the competition this year. A few minutes later he stirred from his reverie to the sound of hammer on metal. *Clank! Clank!* The sound seemed sudden, though it had been going on for several minutes, but he was simply unaware, trapped in his thoughts and daydreams. Below, in his workshop, Victor, his adopted son, was pounding away at an unkempt, notched blade.

'Oi! Victor, my lad, hearken to me! Come now, boy, I do not have all day to wait!' Arthur cried out from the top of the stairs. The sound of scampering footsteps answered his call.

'Aye, sir!' returned Victor at the foot of the stair. There stood his fifteen year old adopted son, his golden locks hanging loosely on his shoulders. 'Begging your pardon, sir, but I was working on your birthday present.'

11

'Oh? Were you now?' laughed the elderly man. He ran his hand through his snow white beard and ran the other through his bushy white hair; he peered at the boy at the edge of the stair and chuckled. 'You look more like your father with every passing day, my lad. What an extraordinary man that Valent was.' He paused and sighed deeply thinking to himself. His face appeared troubled as his brows began to wrinkle and his cheeks drooped as did his lips. 'My boy, I certainly do miss those folks of yours…that I do.'

'Aye, as do I, sir. But believe you me, they will return one day! And it is a good thing they are doing for those Vash'alans. Poor chaps! Suffering from all those plagues and famines, they are. We have no reason to be missing my folks when their task is so noble…no, none at all!' Victor stood there at the bottom of the steps looking up at his adoptive father with a smile upon his face. He was content living there even though his yearning for his parents was great. He had no regrets living with 'Uncle Arthur,' as he called him.

'You are such a courteous lad. I am proud of you, my boy. Yes indeed, very proud. Go on, now! You have much to do ere the start of the party, of that I am confident!' Without a word, but with another smile, Victor sped off, and the loud clanks of hammer against steel echoed below once more. Back in his room Arthur threw open his window and breathed in the warm spring air. As he was basking in its warmth, he saw old Mrs. Boris scuttling across the fields next to Mr. Cradger's farm crying out 'Thread! Thread! Where have I placed my thread? Oh, how will an old woman finish weaving a fine tunic and finer leggings without some thread?'

Again, he chuckled; he was simply amused at the vitality and high spirits of the villagers. This was without a doubt his favorite day of the year and not only for the celebration of his birthday but because of how he celebrated: always on his birthday, he danced with one girl of his choosing, married or not. 'And no one is allowed to complain,' he would tell them with a laugh. Usually, the villagers were already too drunk by that point to even mind. Arthur always scanned the gathering of women admiring their beauty, but he chose to dance only with the woman whom he deemed to be the loneliest and most downcast of them all. At that time, Arthur was the town's most beloved man, for he cared more about others than himself.

Victor's favorite day of the year was also his uncle's birthday. He had called him his uncle, even though they were not related by blood, ever since the day his parents left Kesh; and all the while he believed that his parents would return some day. But still he felt, at times, that Arthur was the only family he really had. In fact, he loved no one more than Arthur. This is why he enjoyed his uncle's birthday more than anything, for it reminded him always that he still had family; and he was simply glad to enjoy yet another year with his uncle. Victor did not care about petty details; whether by blood or not, family was family, and he loved Arthur as such.

As he beat away at the old, notched blade that had clearly seen many battles, Victor wondered if he would ever be able to restore the sword to its former glory. It was a fine blade of sharp steel, but it had become dull and rusted on the hilt. The grip of the hilt was made of iron and clothed in raiment of worn leather that revealed the iron underneath. The cross-guard was golden and oval-shaped, but the gold had faded beneath a moss green hue. He took a brief respite from his hard labor and stared at the sword, contemplating how to mend it. He was eager to find a way to restore it for he had often seen Uncle Arthur holding the blade and crying over it. Whenever Victor asked about the sword, Arthur always replied, 'Perhaps I will tell you tomorrow, lad.' He sat there a moment wondering about his uncle's obsession with the sword. At long last, he stirred and decided to strip the leather from the grip; and he found beneath that there were bright green gems of jade embedded in its make. 'Why would Uncle Arthur cover such a beautiful grip with such ragged leather,' he said aloud.

'I hid its beauty,' answered the voice of Arthur as he descended the stairs, and Victor leapt with alarm. The old man chuckled and continued, 'from those who would seek to pilfer it from my possession. It is a great sword passed down to me by my father and before by his father. It is not an item I would so quickly wish to yield. It is very precious to me because my father gave it to me upon his deathbed. You take good care of it now! And if anything were to happen to it, if you understand my meaning lad, then I ought to make something more terrifying *happen* to you!' He spoke harshly, but his face revealed a silly grin; the twinkle in his eyes showed he was proud and quite honored by the sentiment behind Victor's gift.

Arthur turned and walked out of the stable muttering 'Very proud I am of that boy, oh, yes indeed.' He turned right out of the stable and headed west out of the village, and then he turned north until he came to the Rolling Vale. At the bottom of a slope leading down from a series of mounds were bows made of yew already prepared for the competition and leather quivers full of arrows were lying beside them. Away to the northwest were targets, about twenty fathoms beyond, still full of arrows. He picked up a bow and, fitting an arrow to the bowstring, he bent it back. He took his aim carefully, but before loosing his dart, he relaxed the bow and laid it on the ground again. 'I ought to spare my strength and energy for the competition. And it is not right that I should practice while the rest of the village prepares for the festivities. I suppose I will go rest under the shade of Ole Faithful for a while.'

Arthur spent much of his leisure time under the tree's shade, for he considered the tree to be a dear friend to him. So off he went back around to the southeast passing through the village and past his stable. He turned onto the southern road and followed it past its end beyond Mrs. Boris' tailor-shop, and he continued on his way across the grassy valley to the south until he reached the grove of fruit trees. He turned east and strode to the edge of the shallow stream of water trickling down from the Roaring River to the north, and he paused for a moment to cool his feet in the fresh waters of the stream. After a moment of soaking his feet, he pressed on further to the east; it took him only a few minutes to reach Ole Faithful just as the sun was approaching noon.

'I wish that you were able to speak in my language, old friend,' he said aloud to the tree. 'If it were that you could talk, I imagine we would have many long, fulfilling conversations. Often times I wonder where the future leads me and my kin, and I think you would have much to say about the matter, for you are more learned in the lore of the world than me or so I like to believe. I thank you, my comrade, for remaining with us all these years— twenty-two it is now, I think; but my memory fails me of late. You are our greatest source of hope! Never does it fail that when we are cheerless and bitter, we can look afar to the south and see your warm blooms ascending towards the clouds. You warm our beings down to our very souls.' He stood there silent for a while staring at the pink blossoms and then spoke again. 'I do not think you will care enough to answer me, but would you mind if I rested against you for a time? I am an old man, you see, and I need to lie down. I grow weary easily.'

He moved towards the tree and a gust of wind blew; Ole Faithful's leaves and branches swayed in the wind, and it appeared to Arthur like pink waves rolling across the seas. 'Were that there existed more creatures of beauty liking to you, these dark days would not seem so hopeless!' He sat silently under the boughs of the tree at

14

the foot of its enormous, grey trunk, appearing in the sunlight to be bright, glistening silver. Arthur yawned and sleepily he whispered to the tree. 'I feel my days are drawing to an end, but you are not to speak of this to any of the villagers, you hear? Of course you do not hear...but if you do,' he exclaimed while closing his eyes and shaking his fist at the tree, 'and *if* you speak of it, then I vow that I will cut you down myself and throw you to the fire!' Whether what happened next was Arthur's imagination or not, he thought he heard the tree laugh tenderly. Confused yet exhausted, he fell asleep feeling as though he rested in the arms of a loved one. As Arthur slept peacefully under the shade of the cherry blossom, a troubling dream took hold of him.

* * *

He saw across a wide, flat wilderness an approaching army with crimson armor. On their shields and red banners were the images of black entwined snakes: their heads pointed upwards with their blood-red tongues jutting from their mouths, and their bodies converged into one tail. Above the heads of the snakes was the image of the sun. He knew as he looked on that this was the army of Vash'ala, the worshippers of the god Vash'alari: the idol the Vash'alans claimed to be the god of the sun. Amazed he stood there in the void of the wilderness as a ghost watching history unfold, and he was unable to interact with those around him, though he still tried. He turned around and saw the banner of Bolteras: a white flag bearing the image of a red Dragon breathing forth fire both green and terrifying.

Arthur was overjoyed at the impressive sight of the Boltian army, his kin, in all their array of glory led by the mighty King Haus, former King of Bolteras. Suddenly, arrows twanged through the air. The Vash'alans' darts were black and some aflame, and so great a number filled the sky that the sun was for a moment hidden from sight. Boltian warriors were slain by the hundreds, but they fitted arrows to their bows and opposed their enemy. Many brave men lay dead upon the field of battle; time seemed to shift forward, and the Boltians were nearing victory when, suddenly, the King of Vash'ala stepped forth to do battle. He carried a mighty, spiked flail and wore a distinct helm: it was a helmet of crimson with a black plume on top; two horns of black rose upward two feet from the sides and converged in the center to hold together a yellow orb liking to the sun. King Haus rose to oppose him but fell in an instant. A moment later there stood before him a young man clothed in a silver cuirass

15

with the symbol of Bolteras sketched into it. In his hand was Arthur's sword. 'Threngol,' Arthur shouted to the man. 'Threngol, my boy,' he wept, but there was no reply. He stood there, amidst the ruin and chaos of battle, a lonely figure witnessing a past war he never partook in.

The King of Vash'ala stepped forward and swung his flail at Threngol son of Arthur. Threngol swung his fearsome sword, and, to the Vash'alan King's dismay, the chain was broken; and Threngol charged forward and leapt upon his enemy. Approaching from the west, Arthur beheld the image of Lord Edgar, the current King of Bolteras, in his youth before he was crowned king; he was a sturdy twenty-eight years of age, dashing to the aid of Threngol, but he was too late. As Threngol raised his mighty sword to cleave down his enemy, the Vash'alan King drew a long, curved dagger from a sheath concealed beneath his cloak and thrust forth. He drove the dagger deep into Threngol's heart and blood gushed forth; Threngol's hands could no longer grasp his sword, and so he released it.

The blade trembled on its path to the ground, and Lord Edgar, now drawing nigh, released a mighty roar. Edgar wielded a mighty war maul, and he slung it with full force at the enemy king. The hammer smashed through his dagger and shattered his cuirass, and the Vash'alan King fell lifeless upon the ground. Edgar held Threngol, one of the brave captains of the Boltian army, in his arms and wept bitterly. Threngol gasped violently for air and relief but found none. Arthur stood there filled with sorrow crying out his son's name, but he was never heard. He watched in despair as Threngol barely held on to his life…

* * *

Arthur awoke to the dropping of rain on his face or so he thought; but as he sat up and looked at the sky there was no rain cloud to be seen or rainfall to be felt. He looked around curiously noticing now that he had tears streaming down his cheeks. He stood and looked behind him at the tree. From the leaves of Ole Faithful, drops of water like dew fell to the earth. 'You cry for my sorrow, old friend? I declare this day that I have never met so great a tree and so great a friend as you in all my life. It is an honor to have befriended you! I know the end of my life is drawing nigh; yes indeed, I can almost taste it. Look after this village and its people for me when I am gone, will you? May Vaaspar's Light shine brightly on you for many hundreds, no, thousands of years! Alas! I must go. Lo! I reckon the villagers have nearly finished arranging for the festivities and dusk draws ever closer. I think you ought to be ashamed of yourself letting me sleep so long under your shade! I nearly missed my own birthday. Oh, but how I do wish you could come with me wherever I go. Then, I imagine nothing could make me sad! Bah! Farewell my friend.'

Arthur was unaware that this would be his last day spent resting under the boughs of Ole Faithful for quite some time. He took one hard look at the tree, smiled and returned to the grove of fruit trees across the stream and then went northward to Kesh. As he walked he counted his steps for a while, but then began to hum to the tune of an old drinking song. He then lifted his voice and sang loudly:

All along this beaten path I think,
There is no greater a brew I drink
Than Mayle's Ale, the mightiest of beer
So good it is; it wipes away fear!

Skillful Mayle of carpentry olden
Your greatest skill is one now golden.
All throughout the vast plains I will hail
So that all will know of Mayle's great ale!

His voice faded, and he began to hum once more. The village was quiet and vacant when he entered Kesh as all the villagers had already moved to the large coomb in the Grey Forest to the north of the village. The sun was now falling to the west and the villagers were awaiting their guest of honor. The coomb was surrounded by the trees of the Grey Forest on the west, north and east sides, but on the south side there was an opening, a wide path of turf that ran all the way from the forest to the village. Above the grassy path leading to the coomb, the trees hung over, their branches intertwined, like an archway leading to a great hall of a king. The archway of trees resembled a tunnel, and its length was about sixteen fathoms long. It was a beautiful sight, and the Keshians adored holding all their celebrations in the grove beyond the overhanging trees.

The edge of the forest was nearly five furlongs to the north of Kesh, but Arthur did not have to travel deep into the woods to reach the coomb. He strode forward leisurely toward the banquet and could see fires glowing dimly through the veil of trees ahead. He saw through gaps between the branches of the trees the tops of vast tents looming high into the graying sky. There was much chatter coming from within the grove as though the party had begun without him. He halted a couple fathoms away from where the arched trees ended and the shadows of the woods concealed his presence. He took a deep breath and emerged from the veil of trees into the light of many torches. His eyes had grown accustomed to the increasing darkness of the night, so the light blinded him as he stepped forward.

'*Here, here!*' the villagers shouted as the elderly man appeared. He was still tired from his nap but the welcome was enough to rouse him quickly. 'Our guest of honor comes at last,' said a man at the foot of an elongated table made of fine pine. An unblemished white tablecloth was laid atop of it and foods of all kinds were laid on platters of silver, and goblets were filled to the brim with rich red wine. Arthur passed to the right of the long table where forty of his guests sat already and were very clearly, as it appeared to Arthur, full of much drink. His seat was at the north end of the table at the head, and Victor sat at his right hand beside him. All around the long table were smaller, rounded tables scattered about with equally clean, white cloths laid atop. At one of the small tables a woman cried out, 'Do you like the linens I made for the tables, dearie?' It was Mrs. Boris; she stood up proudly and smiled gaily at Arthur with a goblet of wine in her hand—she was red in her cheeks with drunkenness. Arthur acknowledged her with a friendly nod and passed to the head of the table and plopped down onto his chair. He raised his hand as a gesture of silence, and the crowd was quick to end their cheering and chattering.

'Fair-skins and roughnecks,' he called out to the men and women, 'Lads and lasses... welcome to my birthday banquet! I am truly glad in my heart that each and every one of you could come today. And I thank you for always celebrating with me on my birthday! Let us eat!' The whole crowd cheered loudly, and the feast began. At once, hands were reaching and grabbing, and faces were being stuffed fat. A young boy grabbed several biscuits and gobbled them up as quickly as he could, and he choked briefly on his food; and the whole lot roared with laughter. The lad was quite embarrassed, and his face turned a bright pink. A half hour or so later, Arthur ordered the hosts to bring out his supply of Mayle's Ale. A shout louder than before was let out by every person present, for this was their favorite part of the festivities. Within the hour, all of the adults were seemingly drunk! Some of the children tried to

18

sneak a mug or two, but Arthur was ever watchful and prevented them from succeeding.

Arthur took his time to choose a woman to dance with, for he could choose any woman he desired, married or not; but he chose, as was his custom, one who appeared the most troubled and lonely that night. He chose a young girl with brown hair; she was pretty but sat with her hands folded upon her lap with her eyes downcast. When he drew near to her, her face lit up for she knew he had chosen her, and she was honored to dance with the old man. They moved to an open grassy area to the east of the tables where a ring of torches was placed to give light for all to behold their dancing. The crowd clapped and cheered and some even began to play music to accompany the dance. After a few minutes, they stopped and bowed before the party guests and the crowd applauded their performance. The woman's face had turned bright pink, but none had seen her happier all year. Arthur kissed her affectionately on the cheek, and she returned to her seat with a bright smile stretching upon her rosy cheeks.

As another half hour went by, the last light of the sun faded, but there were torches enough to light up the whole area of the coomb. Arthur received his gifts in turn, all but Victor's—which the lad hid under his chair as he was afraid his uncle would not be impressed with it. He received a fine tunic and finer leggings from Mrs. Boris. Though he already overheard her surprise earlier that day, he reacted as shocked as he could manage while being full of much drink; Mrs. Boris was thrilled and could not tell the difference being quite drunk herself. He also received more clothes from other guests, some dinner ware and a pipe. Some of the children had picked beautiful shells from the ocean shore and gave them to Arthur, and it cheered his heart greatly. 'But the greatest gift of all,' he told them, 'is to have your company on my special day!' With that statement he received many *Here, Here's* and shouts of endearments. There were many party guests who neglected to bring gifts, and they excused themselves for their 'hard work' of setting up the party. But Arthur was content, gifts or no gifts. 'Mayle's Ale is enough to keep me happy,' he shouted and the guests cheered, 'but I thank you for my presents. And I thank those who worked hard to prepare this special occasion for me.'

At the end of the second hour, the crowd cried out in sync, 'Toast! Give a toast!' Arthur smiled and staggered to his feet. He raised his hand and said, 'my friends and family, I want t—' but

19

silence overtook him; he stood agape with his eyes fixated at the entrance to the coomb just under the archway made by the trees. 'Friends and most honorable guests, welcome to our humble gathering!' he hailed after a moment. All those assembled—that had not passed out from their fill of ale—turned in their seats and beheld the presence of Lord Edgar, King of Bolteras, and lord over the capital city Vallicore; he was now forty-eight years of age, yet he looked still fair and gallant. From the shadows behind the King of Bolteras, a large, brawny man of dark skin stepped forth. He was bald and appeared enormously tall, perhaps eight feet from head to foot. He was called the 'Ogre of Bolteras' because of his mighty size. There were none of Men in Bolteras or in all of Gaia who could compete with his might. The two newcomers stood abreast for a moment before Edgar addressed the people.

'Fair Keshians, how goes this magnificent evening?' he asked standing erect and appearing glorious though he was dressed in simple clothes, for a king at least. He wore raiment of fine, leather leggings and a blue tunic; he had also an elegant red cloak with a hood though it rested loosely upon his back. Atop his broad shoulders, his wavy, silvering locks dangled down. The crowd let out a few sounds of alarm followed by an amiable *Here, here* and *welcome*. All who were still able rose and bowed before the king, but he waved his hand and beseeched them to take their seats.

'Tonight is not about me, fair Keshians, though the honor you show me does not go unnoticed! I have come simply to celebrate with an old friend. Come now, Arthur, I believe they asked for a toast!' Again the crowd cheered and turned their gazes eagerly upon Arthur; there were still a peaceful few who lay face down on their tables asleep and full of much food and drink. A couple of the children had now fallen asleep on the turf away a little to the east of the tables, but others ran about now pretending to be knights in Lord Edgar's army.

'Aye, a toast I shall give. But first! Give these men food and drink to their fill. Bring out more Mayle's Ale!' Slowly, several people jumped from their seats and lurched about trying to obtain food and drink for the king and his companion. As the two stepped forth, many guards—thirty in all—arrayed in leather armor also came forth. 'And get those brave soldiers something to eat! They must be weary from many days of journeying. Bring much food and drink for Grinshawl; he is the large, dark-skinned man beside the king. He is a big eater that he is!'

20

The large, black man laughed cheerfully and said, 'Aye, this is true! No man eats more than Grinshawl, the terror, no, the Ogre of Bolteras!' He threw both of his arms in the air and flexed. His muscles bulged, and the people found it very entertaining, for he appeared to them an unusual character. 'And there is none who can compare to his strength and his muscles! I introduce you to my most trustworthy friends: *Bolt and Hammer*! There are no arms mightier than these, and they require much food and ale, yes, ale indeed!' Many laughed and soon the feasting and celebrating continued once more, and the king and his company were greatly pleased.

At last Arthur began his speech. 'To my fellow Keshians and also to my lords from Vallicore, I thank you for attending my special celebration of my sixtieth birthday! There are many here that I would like to recognize but ever do I grow tired; and there is still the archery competition to come!' A few *hurrahs* were heard in the crowd. 'Many fine gifts have I received this day, but the greatest now is being in the presence of our great king and my friends and family! None are kinder than all of you, and I am honored now to be in the presence of a man as honorable and valiant as Lord Edgar! Aye! But there is one gift that I have yet to receive, and I imagine it will truly be the greatest gift of the evening.

'Victor, my lad, arise! It is now time for you to present your gift to me.' Victor rose from his chair and knelt before Arthur, lifting up a folded cluster of cloth. Arthur took it and unveiled the hidden sword within its sheath. Drawing the sword he said, 'Lo and behold! Victor has wrought my sword anew! This is the same fine blade that once belonged to my father and to his father before. Alas, so it was that I passed it down to my son, but he is no more. As you all know, Threngol died around this time twenty years ago, and I did not find out about it for weeks after that terrible battle in Vash'ala. I would that I never had to be a father to bury his only son...that I had gone to battle with him. Maybe if I had, he would be here to celebrate with us. But you do not want to listen to the sad ramblings of an old, reminiscing man. Here, here! A toast to Threngol!' He raised his goblet in honor of his belated son. 'To Threngol!' the crowd replied. 'May his soul find rest in the White Land of Elúne, if he is welcome there.

'And now, I behold this restored sword that my adopted s— no, my son, Victor, carefully mended for me. It was once notched and beaten, but now it shines new! Fine craftsmanship went into the forging of this blade, and there are not many amongst Men who could refurbish it so elegantly. Thank you, Victor my lad. And thank you for training as my apprentice and for learning much. I hope that you will carry along my crafts as a smithy as long as you have life. I am honored to have adopted so great a boy as you. I do wish that your parents could be here to see how great a man you have become.' Victor and Arthur smiled at one another and drank to his words. 'But let us not dwell on sadder things. I love you, my boy. To Victor and the brave Alchemists of Kesh!' he cried, and the crowd echoed his words.

'Sixty years of life have taught me many things—both good and bad—and all throughout my long journey my kin have honored me greatly, though I do not think I deserve such kindness. I am old and I have many regrets in life—most of all of my cowardice that led me to avoid the war that took my son's life—but I have come to believe that I have been blessed with a great life. And now I wish to give one last toast to Ole Faithful, if only he could be here with us. He is as much a part of Kesh as any of us!' *'Hurrah! Hurrah!'* the crowd called before drinking in honor of their beloved tree.

'Forgive me, kind guests. My thoughts race one way to the next. I suppose this is a sign of old age!' he chuckled and others laughed with him. 'And now let me finish this prolonged speech. Let us toast to Kesh, the loveliest of villages in all of Bolteras, though I am quite biased in the matter.' The crowd laughed. *'To Kesh! To Bolteras! To Lord Edgar, great King of Bolteras! And to Arthur our village chieftain! Here, here!'* the crowd shouted in accord. This was the last toast of the night, and the last one Arthur would ever give in honor of his birthday. 'And now let those who wish come with me to the Rolling Vale and compete with bow and arrow!' One last, loud *hurrah* rang out, and then those who were still able and willing rose and went out to the Rolling Vale for the competition. The rest stayed behind and rested for a while or else helped clean up the mess left in the coomb.

The night was waxing quickly and the moon was high in the eastern sky when they came to the vale. Countless stars twinkled in the sky above and the moon was half full and shone a dim yellow; but the light of the heavens was not enough for the archers to compete, so torches were placed all about. Some of the villagers went to the targets and removed the arrows still stuck within its woodwork, and, after twenty minutes, all was ready for the competition. Arthur was given the first shot, so he picked up his bow and fitted an arrow to the bowstring. He took his aim carefully and loosed the arrow. It whistled as it flew through the air and struck the target with a loud thump. The dart had pierced the target directly in the center. The crowd was amazed and applauded for their chieftain. Many had carried their mugs of Mayle's Ale—freshly filled to the brim—with them and were drinking throughout the competition, so there was often excessive clapping and cheering; but the competitors paid them no attention.

After the noise died down some, Arthur called for Lord Edgar to take a shot. The king's arrow also struck the middle of the target right next to Arthur's. Then it was Victor's turn, but his hit a little to the right on the upper edge of the mark. The next contender was Hildegard, who was Victor's best friend—he too was fifteen years old, though a couple months younger than Victor. He shot and hit slightly to the right of the center. Victor was jealous of Hildegard, for his friend was more adept with a bow, and he greatly desired to beat his uncle in the competition. Grinshawl laughed and cheered during the competition but refused to partake in the games claiming, 'The Ogre of Bolteras needs no skill with bows! His weapons of choice are maces and axes and his mighty arms could shatter an arrow!' He roared loudly and Edgar laughed and shook his head at his friend's inane behavior.

A few other villagers took a try with the bow and even some of the soldiers of the Templar Guard—the elite imperial soldiers of Vallicore and Edgar's personal guard—took their tries. All were eliminated from the competition one by one—and to his dismay, Victor was the second eliminated where Hildegard nearly made it to the end—until only Arthur and Edgar remained. The crowd was full of cheerful and drunken clamor. As was the Keshian custom, the last two remaining archers would take aim and fire their arrows simultaneously at the same target to decide the champion. The owner of the arrow to strike the closest to the middle of the target would be declared the winner.

Grinshawl was honored as the unbiased judge of the competition. As was the custom in Kesh when only two competitors remained, the judge tied different colored ribbons around the shafts of the arrows: he tied a red one around Arthur's arrow and a blue one around Edgar's. The two stood there, their arrows fitted to the bowstring. Upon a count of three, they loosed their arrows and the audience watched and listened as the arrows loosed with a sharp twang and struck the target with two loud thuds. The people cheered loudly due in part to their overconsumption of ale. The arrows

23

seemed to be joined together, hitting at precisely the same point, and the shafts of the arrows were broken. Neither one could be named the victor.

So yet again, the two fitted arrows to the string with new ribbons and fired. *Plink!* Arthur's arrow—distinguished by the red ribbon that glistened in the light of the torches—had hit Edgar's! Edgar's arrow flew away to the right of the mark, and Arthur's barely hit the target. Arthur was claimed the champion. The two men shook hands, and Edgar bowed slightly to him, showing him great honor. The audience cheered and began to retire to their homes, muttering as they lurched their way back to the village. The king rose and embraced his friend and then whispered to Arthur saying, 'I wish I could have saved your son long ago so he could be here to share in this moment with you, my old friend.' A few tears ran down Arthur's face, and he hugged his friend even more firmly. The rest of the contenders strode about grabbing each others' arms and shaking in good sport before returning home. But Victor and Hildegard remained with Arthur and the king while Grinshawl ran off to retrieve the arrows used in the competition. After a brief respite, Edgar pulled Arthur to the side.

'Friend, tomorrow I have need of word with you: it is a matter of the utmost urgency. I am sorry, but I have reason to speak with you soon and in private.'

'Then, we ought to speak of it now!' Arthur replied enthusiastically.

'May it not be so! I shall not be the harbinger of ill fortune on such a joyous occasion! Enjoy this night! We will speak of ill news upon the new morn.'

'Friend, do not take me for a fool. Your face reveals great troubles. What news from Vallicore? Are the rumors I heard from Balas true? Are there happenings in our side of the world that involve the Draemhas? That would be most urgent, indeed! The morn cannot wait for such news!'

'Aye, my news is of the Draemhas. But listen; it shall wait! I am king of this country, so by my leave it will wait. I will not burden you and ruin this occasion.'

'Friend, hear my supplication! If the Draemhas have come to our lands, then we should not be enjoying occasions like this. I beg of you, speak to m—' as he spoke an arrow whined across the plains and struck Arthur in the back, and he fell to the ground upon his stomach with a great crash.

Chapter II

Heir to the House of Grause

Immediately the king and his royal guard drew their swords and swung their shields from their backs, forming a phalanx of defence around the body of Arthur. 'Stay your ground! Move not from this place! Grinshawl, take some men and pursue the criminal. Discover his motive and, if you deem it just, bring him to swift judgment! But if he is not worth executing, then bring him back to me!' Ten in all guarded the body of Arthur, whilst the remaining score of soldiers advanced in the direction of the forest, whence the arrow came. Grinshawl led their procession with a small battle hammer and axe which, in his large hands, seemed exceedingly feeble.

'Victor,' Edgar shouted to the wavering boy, 'today you become a man! Arise and shake off your fears. You and Hildegard go to the village and wake all the able-bodied men and protect the village lest an assault is upon us and we are all brought to ruin! If there are any who have not yet found their way home, then be their guide! You must secure the village and bring the women and children back from the coomb at once if they still remain in the forest. We will protect Arthur with our very lives if we must. Confirm the safety of the village first and establish guards from your midst for its protection; then, if any are willing, return here and bring us your report!'

Without a word, Victor and Hildegard sped off to the southeast towards the village and followed the king's commands precisely as he instructed them. At once, Edgar turned and fell to the ground alongside Arthur. The ten guards stirred and filled the break in their wall of defence. He placed his hands on the old man's back and watched for a moment, and peace welled up inside of him as Arthur started to breathe.

'My friend, I cannot think of words great enough to express my distress! I am truly grateful for your many years of friendship and counsel, but I still have need for your friendship and wise counsel. So, I appeal before you now: do not die, Arthur!'

'Victor,' he returned, 'where is my boy?' He choked and coughed up a small amount of blood. But he turned his head with a smile upon his face and said, 'I have something I must say to him...oh yes, that I do. You will see to it that I have that chance, yes?'

'Aye, I give you my word. I sent the lad to the village just a moment ago to secure its safety. I would not leave you under these circumstances, so he was most fit for the task. He is an obedient young man. You must be very proud.'

'Aye, he is an obedient son, that Victor. Yes indeed, I am very proud of him. Let me rest for a while, for I have something of the utmost importance to speak with him about. And do not use your power until he has come to me. I want him to witness it!' He closed his eyes but seemed to be breathing softly and steadily. Edgar sat on the ground beside him with Arthur's head resting carefully in his arms. The king grabbed the shaft of the arrow and broke it in half so as to ease the weight and pain from Arthur's back. Away to the north, the light from the torches carried by Grinshawl and his men faded into the shadow of the woods, and the soldiers guarding Arthur relaxed and lowered their guard.

* * *

In the forest, Grinshawl sprinted after the shadowy image of a man in the grey light of dusk. The light from the stars and the moon barely shone through the branches and leaves of the trees: the forest was very thick, full of many cedar and oak trees. The hour was nearing midnight when Grinshawl and his company passed into a small treeless grove, hardly large enough for all of the pursuers to stand within. The grass was grey in the moonlight, and the shadowy figure was nowhere to be seen. An arrow whistled past one of the soldier's face; the shot came from the forest to the east. Weariness came over Grinshawl and his men: many in Bolteras were doubtful of the Grey Forest, for there were a great number of rumors that spoke of great evils lurking in its shadows. It was said by some that ghosts and monsters dwelt in its woods, though nothing was ever confirmed of the tales.

Reluctantly they dashed back into the wood to the east. Their path was leading them to the foot of the Cold Stone Mountains. Before long, they saw the shadowy figure ahead of them, but this time he was not alone. Now it seemed that there were ten forms running away instead of the one. Signally to his men for an ambush, Grinshawl sprinted ahead to the flank of their attackers: his speed was so great that it seemed none could rival. In an instant he overtook his enemies, and they never saw him coming. Terror overcame his enemies as he roared loudly and leapt upon them, but they fled at a greater pace.

He caught a quick glimpse of them in the light of the moon and perceived that they were not soldiers or Draemhas or even ghosts. He saw, to his surprise, that they wore rags upon their brows and old, beaten garments over their trunks; and their leggings were filled with holes and slits. They had not even a shoe upon their feet. 'Bandits,' Grinshawl said to himself and signaled for his company to halt. 'What poor fortune for us that a man as great as Arthur should be felled, and by bandits at that!' He darted forward once again and overtook his enemies, and the Templar Guard followed in swift pursuit. Some of the bandits turned and drew their daggers—they were dull and short, mere knives to the eyes of the Ogre of Bolteras—while the others drew their bows and arrows.

As Grinshawl closed in, one of the brigands leapt forward and slashed, but Grinshawl raised his hammer up and guarded against the blow. The giant then grabbed the man and threw him against a tree, and the bandit fell unconscious. At that moment, the rest of the company of thieves fled in panic and distress. A few released their weapons as they ran, but the archers in their ranks quickly loosed their arrows before sprinting away. One of the warriors of Bolteras, named Hamben, was killed instantly as an arrow pierced him in the heart. The Boltians countered the attack with full vengeance. They loosed a volley of arrows at once, but only two of the bandits were struck and fell whilst the rest disappeared into the shelter of the trees. Grinshawl commanded his men to halt, and they all wept for Hamben, for he was an honorable man. After a quick view of the situation, Grinshawl turned his eyes upon the figure lying upon the ground. He peered at the bandit for a while and perceived him to be the same person responsible for bringing harm to Arthur.

Then the figure rose and jumped with alarm as he beheld the soldiers. 'Spare me!' he shouted as he knelt down before the giant. His voice was whiny, and he seemed rather small, only a boy. 'I beg of thee, good sirs, spare a poor beggar!'

'And why should I spare the life of a beggar who fires upon an innocent man at his birthday party?'

'Sir, we were hungry! From afar, we saw fire through the woods and knew those villagers were throwing another party as is

27

common amongst them; we knew there would be much food and drink and hoped to steal some for ourselves. But when we arrived, there was not even a scrap left for us dogs. We j—'

'Aye, you are dogs; that much is for certain! Come with us; I do not deem you worthy of death, so the king requires an audience with you! Pray to Vaaspar that he has mercy on you. That man you attacked has been a great friend of his for many long years!'

The boy was filled with grief and began to cry. 'The king? You cannot mean the King of Bolteras?'

'Aye, Lord Edgar is his name. And he will be the one to judge you.'

'Forgive me, sir, and let me go. Surely he will put me to death!'

'Whatever he chooses, he is just in doing so!' The soldiers tied the hands of the boy and veiled his eyes before they made their way back to the Rolling Vale.

* * *

Edgar's guard felt the presence of danger was far from them, but still they began to pace back and forth vigilantly as they awaited the return of Grinshawl and their brethren. From a distance to the southeast, lights like fires flickered. They were torches carried by Victor and Hildegard; but the rest of the villagers had stayed in Kesh to protect their own. Victor was ahead of Hildegard by several fathoms running as quickly as he was able. He stopped at the maimed body of Arthur with a sword in hand.

'Is he dead?' he asked forlornly.

'Nay, he lives by a thread of his life. We have tended to the wound as best as our human abilities allow us, but I fear the wound is much deeper than our eyes can perceive.' Victor wept loudly and knelt down beside his uncle, who appeared strangely at peace.

'Fret not, my boy,' answered Arthur's soft voice. 'Do you know in whose presence you stand? I need not fear and neither should you, my son! Do I speak truthfully, my liege?' At that time, Hildegard arrived at the group gasping for breath.

Edgar smiled. 'You do speak justly indeed! Victor, have you ever heard of *Magic?*'

'Magic? Of course I have. What does that have to do with my uncle's life?'

'Magic is very powerful, but it is mastered by only a few elite, for it requires intense training and a great amount of *Mana,* that is Magical power; and only the great Mages of old have retained the knowledge and control of Magic in its highest sense. But we Boltians—or rather all the lines of Men who hold true to the Light and good will—have been blessed with a Magic that transcends the five elemental Magics of the Mages! Behold the gift of Vaaspar! Witness a true miracle!' Edgar forcefully removed the remains of the arrow out of Arthur's back. Blood flowed out like a small stream running down from the top of a mountain.

'This is madness!' Victor shouted. 'He will surely die!' But to his amazement, he saw something that his eyes had never before known. Edgar's right hand rested over the open wound, and a dull white light emanated from his hand. The king fixed his eyes upon Victor and said, 'Lo! this is the power of Elúvías, the strength of Light!' Pulling his hand away, he revealed Arthur's back, and the flow of blood had ceased. The wound was healed entirely, and not even a scar remained; then life returned to Arthur's face, and he smiled lightheartedly at Victor.

'Elúvías?' Victor said slowly and questioningly, but he could not bring himself to say anything else.

'Aye, it is the power of Light passed down to us by Vaaspar himself,' returned the king. 'There is much in this world that you do not know! But all your questions will be answered soon enough.' Victor and Hildegard stood so perplexed that they had not yet had the chance to calm their minds and process the chaotic events of that evening. Arthur rose from the ground and opened his mouth to speak to Victor, but he could not find the words and so said nothing.

They waited for half an hour before Grinshawl and his men returned, and they carried behind them the body of Hamben. Two soldiers leading the bound bandit by a rope removed the boy's blindfold and pushed him forth, and he fell to the ground in front of Edgar. He lay prostrate and looked up at the king. Edgar's eyes were red like fire, and they revealed a great wrath from within him. 'Stand worm!' The man, appearing now in the firelight to be only a young boy of twelve or thirteen, struggled to his feet, which proved to be a difficult task as his hands were bound and he was weary from much travel. 'Of what house do you belong to and what land?' Edgar yelled with every word he spoke, and his voice echoed with authority and power. The boy quivered before him. The king stood now erect, and Victor noticed for the first time how frightening he could be. He looked fearsome but still more kingly than when they first met; and he now seemed to Victor a mighty warrior full of intense vigor.

'I b-belong t-to no house, sir. I am a vagrant, you see, just a poor lad looking for food. I belong to no land neither, sir. I simply roam the lands of Bolteras. If there were a home a beggar like me lives in then it is these old woods.' He answered frantically and stuttered often, for he was afraid for his life.

'Tell me your name, lad, and enlighten me as to why you are traveling with marauders at such a young age.' Edgar had calmed down, and the boy felt at peace for the moment.

'Well, sir, it all began many years ago when I first began to travel. My kin were wanderers, always have been, so they tell me. Begging your pardon and forgive me my manners, but my name is Pakko son of Elko; I am thirteen now, and not so very young, sir, by my thinking. But as I was saying, a larger group of thieves attacked our caravan nearly five years ago, and my parents were killed. The survivors were all older than me, sir. You see, I grew hungry, and they told me they would feed me if I was willing to work for it. I was desperate, you see…very, very desperate, yes indeed. I am not a' liking to going hungry, no sir, I am not. But believe me; they have never done such a wicked thing as long as I can remember. Please, do not punish them too harshly.'

'How I punish them is up to me, boy. From the bottom of my heart, I am truly sorry for the loss of your parents. But being an orphan and a starving bandit does not excuse your behavior! Tell me, what drove you here, Pakko son of Elko? And why did you attack my beloved friend? Understand this now: I have a good mind and a clear conscious to cut your head clean off your shoulders! But know this also: I do not like to hurt my fellow man, if I can help it,' he said with a wink that brought only slight comfort to Pakko.

'P-please s-sir, I be begging your pardon, sir, ah yes! Please do not cut off my head…a bloody mess that would be, oh yes indeed! I am thinking my shoulders would, ah, be very lonely without my head around, you see!'

'Answer me!' Edgar snapped, but he was tempted to laugh at the boy's rambling.

Pakko now seemed to become oddly somber. He spoke now softly and remorsefully. 'I killed him as I was told. My leader commanded me to do it. He had no knowledge of the presence of soldiers and even more the King of Bolteras!'

'Does that justify your actions?' Edgar shouted at the top of his voice. 'You fool! This man's son stands before you! What would you say to him? Should I allow him to shoot an arrow through your chest as I know he desires to do?' He asked waving his hand towards Victor whose eyes were bloodshot with rage and his hand was shaking whilst fingering the fletching of an arrow fitted loosely on his bow.

Pakko's face grew long and grim. 'Forgive me,' he cried in anguish. 'Please let me go! I beg of you! I did not mean to hurt anybody!'

'Take him to the village and keep watch over him through the night. We shall cast lots on what to do with him in the morning.' As he finished speaking, Victor widened his stance and pulled back the bowstring. He nearly let loose the arrow, but Edgar grabbed the bow and threw it to the side; the weapon nearly hit Pakko, but he dodged at the last second. Edgar placed his hands atop Victor's shoulders. 'There will be no vengeance tonight, laddie!' Victor jerked his body away from the king's grip, picked up his sword from the ground and walked angrily away to the east. While he was off a ways, he turned and shouted, 'You are a foolish king!' He then turned about and kept walking and disappeared into the night.

Edgar placed his hands over his face and wiped away the sweat from his brow. He looked at Pakko, angrily at first, but a smile slowly crept on his face. Suddenly, Edgar laughed, and the boy cowered in fear before him, halfway expecting the king to go mad and kill him.

'Am I a jest to you, good sir?' asked Pakko, son of Elko while grinding his teeth. 'Do you plan to kill me now?'

'Not so!' Edgar laughed. 'That boy just has plenty to learn. He witnesses a miracle and then turns to kill a wretched, deprived bandit, and a polite one at that!'

'What miracle do you speak of, sir?'

'Ah,' Edgar replied sternly, 'you do not know yet. Listen to me closely now. Fear not, boy!' he chuckled. 'The man who you thought to be dead is alive. Behold!' He pointed his hand to his left to Arthur who stood unharmed before the young thief. Pakko stood agape for a moment, but then breathed a sigh of relief.

'How is this possible? Surely he should have died, but here he stands completely unharmed! You have amazing vitality, sir! I cannot believe my e——' He paused and fell to his knees. 'Forgive me, good sir! I have not even taken the time to apologize for my crime against you.'

Arthur stepped forth and looked in the boy's eyes, and he pitied the boy as he discerned great tribulations in his life's walk.

'Stand boy! Why do you call me good? There is only one who is truly good, and I am not that man! Only the Mighty Warrior who saves is good, and by Him I live—by Vaaspar the Lord of Light. Relax now; I have discerned great troubles and weariness in your eyes. So come! Tonight you stay in Kesh, though you must be restrained against your will! I hope you understand.'

At that moment, Grinshawl threw a bag over Pakko's head and tied it loosely about his neck to veil his eyes from his whereabouts. But Pakko complained that he could not breathe, so the giant cut a hole in the sack near the boy's lips. They traveled back to the village, the soldiers of Grinshawl's group carrying the corpse of Hamben: two stood at his feet carrying one leg each, two more at his head carrying him by the arms. They had stripped him of his armor and abandoned it in the woods where he was killed to ease the burden of carrying him back to Kesh. Edgar noticed the dead soldier for the first time and wept alone for a few minutes before returning to the village.

As they approached the village, the Keshians mistook Hamben for Arthur—as Victor had informed them of the attack— and wept loudly calling out, 'Arthur, finest of folk! May Vaaspar's Light guide you to Elúne!' But Arthur came forth and called out, 'You are mistaken, my beloved kin! I live by the healing of Lord Edgar, no, the power of Vaaspar. The might of Elúvías lives on! But alas! This man is Hamben, son of Dramben of the Templar Guard from Vallicore! Weep not for me but rather for this heroic and honorable man.' The villagers ran out to meet them, weeping instead for the fallen soldier of Edgar's company. Arthur, Grinshawl, and Hildegard led the thief-boy into Arthur's workshop; there they tied the arms of Pakko behind a post. Edgar joined them a few moments later. They cast lots and the first watch fell on Grinshawl who, though he was weary, willingly accepted the task.

The soldiers of the Templar Guard carried the corpse of their fallen comrade to Mrs. Boris' house. The soldiers removed the dart that was still in Hamben's heart and cleaned the wound, stitching it closed. Mrs. Boris grabbed a beautiful white cloth and laid it upon a large, wooden bier. The warriors laid Hamben upon the cloth, and all helped to anoint his body with oil and preservatives brought from Tom Hahn's oil shop. After the preservation was complete, they carefully wrapped the white linen around his body leaving only his head to be seen. And they adorned his head with a silver circlet and combed his hair so Hamben showed his former glory even in death.

The yellow moon waned quickly as the night had already progressed much. Grinshawl was drifting off to sleep when he felt the grip of a hand on his shoulder. 'Get up, greatest of friends. You need sleep,' said the voice softly and gently. 'I will take the watch now.' Grinshawl lifted his head and smiled at the king and made his way to the rooms on the second floor of the shop. There were several beds full of the exhausted bodies of Hildegard and Arthur and even some of the Templar Guard who had come there after preparing Hamben's body for his funeral. Since there was no bed left or even big enough for the Ogre of Bolteras, he laid a blanket on the ground and slept upon it that night.

* * *

The sun rose over the eastern horizon early the next morning. The villagers proceeded to the Burial Grove where a grave had been dug by several villagers during the night. Hildegard willingly guarded Pakko while the others were away at the funeral for Hamben. Carefully, the Boltian soldiers lowered the body of Hamben into the grave, raised their swords in honor of him and then withdrew to the village: it was their way of showing honor to their fallen comrades, and it signified that Hamben would still march on with them in spirit. Arthur paid his respects to Hamben by tossing a few of Ole Faithful's blooms, which he had plucked earlier that morning, over the body. Some of the villagers tossed some flowers into the grave while others stood and watched from a distance. Edgar and Grinshawl were the last to approach the grave. Grinshawl knelt down and placed his beloved hammer and axe across the chest of Hamben and said, 'You are an honorable knight even in death, faithful Hamben.' He then rose and stepped aside as the king drew close to the edge of the grave. Edgar sung a dirge that was well learned in Vallicore. It went in part like this:

> *Far away from the West Land they call,*
> *'Lonely soldier, o how did you fall?'*
> *But see now the Lord of Light's mighty hand*
> *Reach out from your home in the White Land!*
>
> *Do not worry for your friends and kin*
> *They may cry and wail, 'No, not again!'*
> *But go in peace, warrior once so great*

To your new home and keep your path straight!

Follow the light coming from Elúne
Forget us not, we will see you soon
Now go at once and enjoy the view
And cry no more, o soldier born anew!

He stopped singing though there seemed to be more to the song, but he was overcome with sadness and wept for his fallen companion. Everyone who was still gathered grabbed a handful of dirt and tossed in into the grave as their way of saying farewell. Then they turned and walked solemnly back to the village where Mrs. Boris and a few other women had prepared a meal for the mourners in their grief.

* * *

Since the night before, Victor had not returned to the village, and he did not attend the interment for Hamben. After his attempt to slay Pakko was thwarted, he disappeared into the woods to the coomb where the party had taken place and sat in the seat of honor that belonged to Arthur. Although he was relieved that Arthur was healed, he still felt indignant towards the thief-boy. He sat there in the middle of the night devising a clever plan to accomplish his revenge until far off he saw flickering lights drawing near. At once, he rose and fled, not wanting to be seen by anyone, for he was still overwhelmed with embarrassment. That night he withdrew to the plains north of the archery competition grounds. He lay down atop a hillock not far from the targets that were still pierced with several arrows. The sky was clear and stars glimmered in the sky, and the sight of it calmed his mind. He lay upon the turf with his head on his hands and marveled at the beautiful array of stars. 'I wonder how they all got there,' he thought aloud. As the moon waned on and turned to a light blue, he fell fast asleep.

He woke with the cool breeze of morning just as the sun began to rise. He rubbed the sleep from his eyes and glanced about the ground; to the south he saw his bow atop the grass with a stray arrow close by. Descending the hill, he picked his weapon up and turned towards the targets. Fitting the arrow to the string, he aimed carefully and released the dart. It whistled through the air and struck the target precisely in the middle, and Victor was overjoyed, for it was the first time he had struck the center. Over and over again, he continued practicing until the sun loomed directly above his head.

'Last night was not your finest moment, Victor. No indeed, it most certainly was not,' he said to himself.

'I would reckon not, but I have never seen such keen eyes from you, my boy!' Victor turned and saw Arthur standing before him. 'Perhaps last night was a bad moment indeed, but today is your finest one yet! Go on, shoot another!' Victor smiled and fitted another arrow to the string and released. It whirled at the mark but missed the middle by an inch. 'Try again, lad. I believe you get nervous when others are watching.' Again he fired, and he missed the mark by several inches. 'I appear to be correct. You are a nervous lad under watching eyes. You have a mighty good aim when you are alone, but that will do you no good on the field of battle,' Arthur laughed.

'Did you simply come to mock me, uncle?'

'Of course not, my boy...I came on behalf of Hamben. I believe you ought to pay him your respects, Victor. But that is just the opinion of an old man.'

'I wanted him to die last night, uncle,' Victor responded solemnly. Arthur answered with a distressed look. 'No, you mistake me, uncle! I meant that thief-boy who hurt you. I am sure Hamben was an honorable man and needed not to die.'

'Aye, I know, but lo! I am not hurt. Take a look! I am healed, and that boy does not deserve death either, lad. If I, who was injured by him, do not judge him, then why should you?' He smiled, but Victor's eyes still showed intense anger. 'I wonder, lad, if you are just eager to kill,' Arthur said sadly and walked away without another word.

'Why would you say that, uncle?' Victor shouted in response. There was no answer, which caused Victor to become even more irate. He threw his bow to the ground violently and sat upon the ground with tears in his eyes.

* * *

Back in Kesh at Arthur's workshop, the king and his men, along with Arthur and Hildegard, discussed their plans regarding Pakko, the thief-boy. It seemed in the light of day that Edgar had become older, for his hairs were greyer than they were the night before. There was much clamor, and words were hurled back and forth. Half of those gathered, it seemed, wanted to kill the boy immediately as punishment. The other half, perhaps, wanted to figure out an alternative form of punishment. Grinshawl—who was at this point sitting down on a large stool—rose and towered above

35

the company and grunted. Instantly, they all turned and listened intently, for Grinshawl was revered for his wise counsel.

'I conclude that there are just arguments for both sides from what I hear, for indeed the boy deserves death for harming a man as great as Arthur. If punishments were not dealt to criminals, then we would be a land of rebels and murderers. Yet, I believe there is always room for grace and mercy. But hearken to me, for this is what I have to say: let the king decide as of now, whether it is judgment or compassion. He has received enough wise and helpful rede in this matter; but, if I know him as well as I think, then I am certain he has already put forth much thought late into the night to make his final decision. As it was when I was on my guard over the thief-boy, Lord Edgar came and roused me from sleep. I discerned that he had spent much time in thoughtful consideration of the thief-boy's fate. As I have said, let us hearken to the just and fair King of Bolteras!' All the men looked around and nodded in silent agreement.

'You speak rightly, Grinshawl. Here is what I have to say, then,' Edgar addressed them. 'Grinshawl, Arthur, Hildegard, and I along with Victor, if he is able to swallow his pride, will lead the thief-boy back to his abode in the woods. If the boy cooperates, then it is only this small company that I desire to attend me on my way. If he wills it, this Pakko will take us to his leader and peace will be made! I give you my word in this as your king. Are there any who would oppose my will?' None spoke though doubt was apparent in some of their eyes. 'Then I will understand your silence to mean all are in agreement with my plan.' All nodded in accord. 'Then I say, bring me Victor, for I much desire to speak with him.' The soldiers of the Templar Guard left the presence of the king and, an hour later, they presented Victor who was found at the grave of Hamben paying respects to the fallen warrior. 'Welcome home, Victor son of Valent! How do you fare this fine morning?'

'I am well. Forgive me, Sire, for my actions last night. I acted rashly and foolishly, but Uncle Arthur rebuked me as he quite often does.'

'I am sure any of us in your position would have done the same since you love Arthur more than any other. Forget the matter! We now have a new issue to speak of.' He told Victor of their meeting and the decision that was made to return Pakko to his home in order to make peace with the bandits.

'Is this mere jest? He deserves death, does he not? Yet you desire peace? Surely, this is the folly of a king!' Victor responded in his anger.

'Folly you say? And I thought your uncle's rebuke had rid you of your stupidity!' the king returned angrily. 'No, my boy,' he continued calmly after a heavy sigh, 'it would be folly to continue a quarrel that needs to be put to rest. Silence your hasty tongue on matters you do not understand! We will make peace, for they live within the boundaries of Bolteras; therefore, they are Boltians with whom I desire peace. It has already been decided, lad, but will you come?' Anger was still in Victor's eyes, but he consented at last.

'Now that it has been decided, I have a matter of my own to address,' Arthur added. 'Victor, my son, listen to what I have to say. After the events of last night, I have had much to consider. First, you must put away that anger, laddie, or else use it against the Dark Lord and his forces of Darkness. You worry me with that anger of yours, and I would hate to see you overcome by that rage and lash out against your fellow countrymen. Secondly, I am alive now, but I will not be forever. That is why, in your absence last night, I thought long and hard about choosing an heir for my household, of the house of Grause. Victor, my lad, I would be honored if you became my heir and carried on the name of my household, the line of Grause in the place of my late son Threngol! I addressed all the villagers of my wishes last week, and they agreed that this was a prudent decision. I intended to wait a while before I asked you, but after I nearly died I knew I had to ask you now while I still have the chance. You are an obedient young man, Victor, and I would not ask any other to carry on my name. What say you?'

Tears filled Victor's eyes, and he leapt forward wrapping his arms around Arthur. All the anger welling up within him vanished, and his heart softened at last. 'Sir, it would be an honor!' he shouted joyfully. 'Forgive me for my folly! I will put this anger behind me and be a man you will be proud to call your son.'

'But I am already proud to call you my son! So be it! On this day of March the fourteenth of the year thirteen sixty-three of the Post-Dragon Era, I name thee, Victor Perigas, heir to the house of Grause!' Those present clapped cheerfully and shouted many *Here, Here's* and *Hoorahs*. Then, Edgar added, 'Hail! Long live the heir of the house of Grause!'

After they rejoiced for a moment and congratulated Victor, the attention turned to the bound boy who was off in the corner of the shop tied to a wooden post. Edgar approached him and removed his binds.

'I cannot…no, I *will* not betray my comrades! I w—'

'Silence boy!' Edgar retorted. 'Lend me your ear, for I am no enemy, least of all to a small band of hungry thieves. All who live within the boundaries of Bolteras belong to my people, and I will bring no harm to you or your people, Pakko son of Elko. Hence, I give you my word that no sword or bow or arrow or any other weapon shall be carried among us. I give you my word, wanderer-thief!' Pakko peered deeply into Edgar's eyes and found no deceit within them. Reluctantly, though feeling oddly comfortable, he agreed to lead them to his home in the Grey Forest. 'Good! We leave in one hour. Knights of the Templar Guard, bring food and other provisions as an offering of peace, and clothe the boy in finer clothes to show we value their worth!'

The king's soldiers obeyed their orders at once as the five men quickly prepared for their journey. They scurried to and fro amongst the shops and houses packing food and clothing. Pakko gave them a headcount of the thieves and mentioned that they lived in forts made in trees. The travelers were amazed that a place existed so close to Kesh, and they were thrilled to be able to witness what the thieves called home. Grinshawl purchased ten empty grain sacks from Farmer Cradger to use for packing food and clothing, though the old man tried to refuse selling anything to him as he was the famous Ogre of Bolteras. But Grinshawl insisted on paying and in much abundance too. Each carried on their backs a pack with their own provisions, only about three days worth, so their packs were fairly light. Also, each one was to carry two additional sacks—one full of food and one full of clothing—provided to them by Grinshawl to be given to the thieves upon arrival. One hour elapsed, and the sun was hanging slightly in the western sky. When their packing was completed, they all assembled back at Arthur's workshop once again. They were now heavy laden with all the goods for their travels. Edgar had even packed an additional bag with several smaller bags of gold and silver inside for the thieves, and he gave it to Pakko to carry.

'Tell me, how long is the journey to your home, Pakko son of Elko?' Edgar asked excitedly.

'It is nearly five or six miles into the Grey Forest to the north and eastward some. Considering the difficulties of the journey, what with all the hills and brushes and clusters of trees along the way, it ought to take no more than a day or two to journey to my home. It would not take so long if I did not need to guide a company untrained in the woodlands.'

'We are not as untrained as you think thief-boy,' Edgar responded. 'But be it so, it would prove best for us to arrive in daylight where no arrow can strike us blindly. Let us press on during the light of day; then we will rest once the sun has gone down and upon the next morning, we shall put this issue to rest as quickly as we may. We have more urgent affairs to deal with.'

'Why then, my friend, do we go into the woods chasing starving thieves? Are we not simply wasting our time if time is truly of the essence?' Arthur asked skeptically.

'Aye, so it would seem from your outlook. I am afraid, however, that we shall need all the able-bodied men we can spare for this type of urgency! There are not many who would dare to cross swords with the Draemhas.'

'Draemhas?' wondered Hildegard. 'The rumors are true then? Alas! They come to the Western Lands and even to the great Kingdom of Bolteras?'

'Quiet your voice!' Edgar interjected. 'We must not speak of this too loudly. One can never know for certain when the Enemy's spies are listening, and I do not wish to wherrit those whose concern is not of war. Aye, there are rumors, and I would that the elderly and women and children continue to believe them to be *only* rumors. But alas! the rumors are in fact true. As I said before, many will not willingly cross swords with the Draemhas, so we must make haste to find those who will. Thus, we need to seek those of Men who are brave and who can inspire others to rise to arms. Help is scarce, but perhaps we will find friends in the shadows of the forest! But fret not, young Hildegard, for the Draemhas have not yet invaded the borders of Bolteras. We can be certain we are safe as long as the archers of the Lonely Forest keep watch on the borders of Vash'ala. But come now! We will speak more of this in the days to come.'

'I will fight the Draemhas, Your Majesty!' Victor exclaimed confidently. Arthur stirred uncomfortably, shook his head and muttered, 'what a foolish boy.'

'Good, good,' Edgar responded seeming only to be half listening, 'but let us resolve the issue at hand first, and then we will converse more about the problem of the Draemhas.' Pakko stared at the king and his face turned white. 'It appears that you have knowledge of these tidings, young thief-boy, or are you simply afraid?'

'Now I know more than ever, sir…I must take you to Treehouse, our home in the woods. I feel you are a people we can trust and surely we must if the days are as evil as you say!'

'Let us make haste!' cried out Edgar, and at his words the company hurried along onto the crossroad leading north out of Kesh. The road ran to the north and rounded to the west along the edge of the Grey Forest, but they continued further north into the coomb. From there, Pakko led them northeast and proceeded deep into the forest. The hour was now past high noon when they came upon the place where Grinshawl intercepted the thieves the night before, but the bodies of the thieves were gone.

'This is the place of our encounter last night,' Grinshawl said noticing arrows still scattered upon the ground. 'But there were two, I believe, that were slain, yet they are not here.'

'Maybe they returned to bury my brethren,' Pakko responded sarcastically. Grinshawl had the sudden urge to punch the boy, but he refrained.

Taking notice of Grinshawl's annoyance, Edgar firmly said, 'Lead the way and be silent! I will have no more of your snide tongue!' Pakko winced and gave a nod, and they pressed onward to the northeast.

In the Grey Forest, the trees were gathered in great numbers. Carefully, they followed their guide as there were many branches sprawled upon the ground and leaves veiled the presence of massive tree roots. The large cedars and oaks seemed to grow closer together as they traveled deeper into the woods. Suddenly, tall brushes appeared before them maybe a mile from the coomb. The copses were thick and impenetrable so Pakko led them around to the west. Their path cut through many smaller thickets until the land plunged downhill into a stretch of land with many gnarled trees. They continued this way for nearly a mile, and the land rose and fell with many hills adorned with the twisted trees. The sun was passing to the west, but it was veiled and dimmed by the trees and the many leaves on their branches.

They turned from the west and headed northward where there were squat trees spread amongst many more great thickets. As they pressed on through the thickets they caught eye of a group of harts darting away, some to the north, others to the west. As they passed through the thickets, they were elated to see many gossamers floating in the thick air of the forest. The branches of the trees were now splayed and stretched high and long, and the leaves were full of various colors. They traveled further to the north for about three furlongs and climbed to the top of a treeless hill flourishing with bright green grass—it towered above many of the surrounding trees. From there, they looked outward to the east and saw the Cold Stone Mountains: its peaks were hidden in a thick layer of fog, but the foot of the mountains stretched far to the south toward the shores of the Great Sea and also far away to the north into the lands of Alterash. The trees of the Grey Forest spread almost to the foot of the mountains but stopped nearly half a mile short of it. They rested for a while on the knoll, and Victor was glad, for he was growing weary, although he had quite enjoyed the journey thus far.

'Here is a landmark my people use to guide us to our home,' said Pakko. 'We call this place the King's Summit, though we do not have a king amongst ourselves. It is a name our leader picked, and I suppose he is the closest thing we have to a king. We will head due east from here, but we will not approach the Cold Stone Mountains within a mile or two. There are said to be great evils that lurk within those mountains. But lo! my home lies just to the northeast!' The travelers looked afar and could see a wooden fence stretching around a large section of trees, but they could not see much else.

'Aye, we are not far now, I see,' Edgar chimed in. 'As you mentioned, I too have heard many tales of great fiends in those mountains. But tell me, what is the name of your leader? I will call upon him when we arrive.'

'We simply call him Leader, but his real name is Rolo Longleaf. I do not know much more about him except that he is a brave and capable man.'

'Very well, I will call upon Rolo Longleaf when we arrive. Lead us to Treehouse right away, young guide!'

At once, they sped down the hill, and Victor reluctantly followed still tired from the journey thus far as he was not accustomed to traveling long distances, especially over many hills and through the terrain of the forest. At the bottom of the hill, they crossed a shallow and narrow stream that ran southward branching off from the Roaring River and entered the forest once again on the other side. The sun was now sinking far away to the west and their trail began to turn grey. 'Let us travel just a bit further,' Pakko called out keeping his eyes carefully fixated on the trail, 'then we will set up camp and sleep through the night. We have only about two more miles to reach Treehouse, and the terrain will be much lighter from here. Also, you did say you want to arrive during the day, yes?' he asked turning to Edgar, and the king nodded with a weary smile. They continued eastward for nearly ten minutes, but the sunlight was fading quickly, and all the land about them was turning grey from the light of the moon. The light of the heavens was not bright enough to guide them further, so they decided to halt and set up camp for the night, making certain to light no fires for fear of being discovered. Pakko was bound and tied to one of the trees so he could not run away in the middle of the night.

Chapter III

Servant King

In the night, Victor stirred to the sound of a loud, howling wind. The eastern air from the Cold Stone Mountains carried a chill breeze down into the woods where they lay fast asleep, and he awoke; and the tree roots digging into his back were no help as he struggled to find rest. He was convinced when he woke that he heard the sounds of tormented shrieks coming from far away to the east, and the noises chilled him to his bones. As he began to drift off into sleep once more, he caught a glimmer of light like fire coming from the direction of the shrill cries. None of his company noticed as they were still fast asleep; but he saw it, though he began to wonder if he was simply imagining it.

Victor rose and walked to the east but did not stray far from the campsite. As he drew closer to the light, it seemed to move as if flying through the air. Whether it moved on its own or something made it move, he could not tell, but he was frightened and withdrew back to the campsite. As he made his way to his stiff bed of leaves on the ground and covered himself with a blanket, Hildegard roused.

'Oi! What were you doing now, Victor? You ought to have a good reason for startling me in my sleep! Come now, what was it?'

'Nothing at all, I just thought I heard a noise.' For the time being, he did not speak to Hildegard or any of the others in his company about the mysterious fire he saw in the distance.

'Get some sleep, friend. We shall not have you slowing us down on the journey tomorrow. I want to see this *Treehouse* they call their home. It sounds like a child's game that it does, but all the same I am eager to see it.'

'As am I, friend…as am I. Goodnight then.'

And at that, sleep overtook them, but their sleep was interrupted gallingly by the Ogre of Bolteras. 'Wake up my merry, young lads! A quick breakfast we shall eat and off we shall go—to Treehouse! It sounds quite thrilling, does it not?' he said laughing excitedly and clapping his hands in an absurd manner. 'A house in a tree! How did they think of that? That is the mind of a true mastermind, I say!' He chuckled again and then swiftly devoured his food, not stopping even to chew or so it seemed to his companions. Edgar was rubbing his lip obsessively as though he was trying to clean some left over food from his face, though he had not yet eaten, and Arthur was pacing back and forth ostensibly in deep thought. Victor and Hildegard realized that most of the company was already well fed and prepared to leave at a moment's notice, so they leapt to their feet and quickly prepared their breakfast.

The sun's rays broke through the leaves of the trees, and the two boys squinted as their eyes were still heavy from sleep. After his eyes had adjusted to the morning light, Victor looked away to the east, but there was no flying fire to be seen; and since he also heard no more sounds of shrieking, he felt very much at ease. The two boys ate their food at a swift pace, almost as quickly as Grinshawl, as they were eager to press on and bring their journey in the Grey Forest to an end.

'Slow down, lads! There is no need to eat so hastily, not if it kills you to do so!' Arthur called. Suddenly, a loud trumpet was heard. The sound of it was shrill and deafening like the sound of a battle horn. The blast sounded from the north. Pakko stood suddenly and gazed ahead into the mass of trees.

'That is the sound of our Leader's horn! Rolo blows it when there is trouble. I reckon they spotted us from afar!'

'Let us make haste and present ourselves as friends before we are slain as enemies of the tree-dwellers!' Grinshawl cried.

'I agree,' said the king. 'Let us depart as soon as we have gathered our belongings. But stay calm. If they have seen us from a distance, then surely they know we are unarmed. And perhaps they know the face of their king and have refrained from attacking.' At this point, Victor looked at Edgar and was filled with amazement: he was finally struck with the reality that he was in the presence of the King of Bolteras, a man he considered now to be wise and noble. The party swiftly finished collecting their goods, and Pakko continued to lead them north towards Treehouse.

'Lord Edgar, Sire, there is something I have wanted to ask you since this morning,' Victor said suddenly whilst staring at the king's face.

'Do I look older to you today, Victor?' Edgar asked perceiving the question in Victor's mind.

Victor stared at him agape and perplexed. 'So you are aware?'

'It is the outcome of using the mighty Elúvías that was given to us by Vaaspar. The bodies of Men are yet too frail, and thus there are consequences to using the Lord of Light's power. It would take far too long to explain, so for now let us leave it at that. All you need to know now is this: by using the gift of healing, our bodies will age, for the art of leechcraft drains much of our spiritual energy, which is the very essence of Mana. Obtaining and using Elúvías, though it has many benefits, weakens our bodies in the end, for mere Men cannot control the full power of Vaaspar. There is a price to pay for using the powers of Light, though the price is greater for those who use the powers of Darkness! However, there are powers within Vaaspar's blessing that have no price such as the power of courage—yes indeed, the power of Light can bless one with courage, wisdom and things of the sort. But you will certainly learn more of these things as your journey progresses. Be patient, Victor son of Valent and always be willing to learn!' Hildegard listened on with curious ears; Grinshawl, who was well-trained in the lore of Elúvías, merely smiled and laughed at his ignorance; and Arthur trailed behind them lost in thought and did not hear their conversation.

They strode forth for nearly an hour as the land rose and fell through the great woods of the Grey Forest. Pakko stopped as if frozen by a sudden icy breeze. Edgar felt the presence of watchful eyes and stirred uncomfortably as the cool eastern breeze fell upon them. The trees of the forest had now become wide and tall and soared high in the sky like the mighty towers of the ancient eras. The company looked all about their position and up to the treetops, but there was no fortress or any sign of habitats that could be seen— Victor and Hildegard were greatly disappointed. The party grew anxious, and the burden of their packs only weighed them down and increased their nervousness.

Suddenly an arrow whistled at the band of travelers: it was aimed at Pakko. Grinshawl dashed in front of the boy and blocked the arrow with a sack full of food. The arrow struck deeply into the sack, ripping it and spilling its contents onto the ground. Pakko was saved from injury thanks to the Ogre of Bolteras. Grinshawl threw the sack on the ground and picked up the arrow and held it high in the air; then, he broke it so the attackers would know he did not fear them. The giant stared down at the bits of food scattered on the ground, though it was mainly bread crumbs, and let out an angry groan. He peered at the bag and stomped his mighty foot upon it, and the ground shook beneath him. 'That was a perfectly good supply of food gone to waste! And your arrow nearly hit one of your own kin! Explain your act,' he shouted so his voice could be heard far and wide.

'So...it seems we have a traitor in our midst, eh fellas?' a voice echoed from deeper within the forest to the north. 'I have a good mind to slay the whole lot of you. And what reason do I have not to? After all, killing a king and his guard would bring me great renown. Perhaps then I could be King of Bolteras and live the gluttonous life of the imperials. What do you say fellas?' The sound of men laughing preceded his voice.

'I call upon the name of Rolo Longleaf, also known as Leader by his people!' Edgar responded.

'Then you call upon the man who holds your very lives in his hands. If I give the word, my company and I could fill you with a thousand arrows!'

'I am not fond of embellishments, Leader of Treehouse!' Edgar roared in response. 'And we come not as enemies but as messengers of peace. Behold! we carry no weapon for a counterattack and no shield for defense. Will you not hear my request?'

'What days are upon us that a king should call upon a band of vagabonds?' He laughed loudly as if mocking Edgar. 'Come away to the north! Just a little more than a mile away you will find our fortress, Treehouse! There we will speak.' The king looked about at his company and all nodded as consent to continue; but they halted for a moment to rest and to ease their minds. After fifteen minutes, Pakko led the group northward once more, and they descended a long slope nearly a furlong ahead. The remainder of the journey was close to seven furlongs from where they encountered Rolo Longleaf, but it lasted more than an hour as the last stretch of land was a long, steep incline.

But the land leveled off and they came at last to a section of the woods where a large fence was built around many of the trees; and it appeared to be a fine stronghold to the travelers. Within the fenced area, the trees rose high into the air. There were walkways built across the boughs and bridges connected to the trunks of the trees. The abodes were finely crafted and surprisingly large, and the thieves were safely guarded from any chance of an assault. The company stared at the fortress amazed at the workmanship that was put into making such a stronghold. As they drew nearer, there was a small gate at the front of the fence, but it was barred from the inside to keep strangers from entering.

A man stood atop a walkway built upon the inner side of the fence—like that of a parapet—with his bow in one hand and an arrow in the other. The bandit was easily distinguished as the leader of the fort by his dress and demeanor. He peered down doubtfully at the foreigners and then turned an angry glance at Pakko. He opened his mouth to speak but before he said a word, Edgar knelt on the ground with his eyes facing the ground. The thief leader was baffled as were Edgar's companions.

'Why does one as *great* and *honorable* as you kneel before a band of poor-folk?' the man called out derisively. 'Is this the image of a king? Has Bolteras truly fallen so low that her ruler humbles himself so?' As he awaited an answer, Arthur too knelt before the man. The sight of two men bowing shocked him further.

'Leader of this group of bandits, I beseech you, hear my words,' Arthur called with his head lowered.

'Speak old man,' Rolo answered skeptically.

'Forgive us! I beg of thee. Forgive the people of Kesh and me, their chieftain.' Both groups were even more amazed at this request than they were of Lord Edgar kneeling before a thief. Edgar rose and shook his head at his friend's words. 'If we had only been more aware of you, our neighbors, then we would have known of your poor state and had food to spare for you! Woe is me to find such anger in the hearts of hungry thieves at my doorstep!'

'And who is this man who makes such an outrageous plea for forgiveness even after years of injustice shown to my people?'

'Rolo, this is the man I hit with my arrow!' Pakko cried out. 'He is very kind and fully of mercy!'

Rolo laughed. 'How can a dead man stand before me? Your arrow must have killed him! So why then does he kneel before me now? Do you know, old man, that I gave the order to kill you out of hatred of you well-fed folk? Tell me then, how do you live?'

'Yes, yes, calm yourself,' Arthur replied with a slight raise of his head. 'Pakko son of Elko already informed us of your intentions the day before yesterday. But I begrudge you not! For if your circumstances were mine, I reckon I might do the same. And I have been healed by our just king, so I will not be bitter towards you. You see, I have never been poor, so I am only trying to understand things the way your eyes see them.'

'Get up, old man! We are strong and able people. Do not pity us! Be gone from my sight!' Rolo yelled with spit thrown from his mouth. Arthur rose despondently and mumbled, 'Forgive us,' as he turned his back on the bandit. Rolo, though he would not admit it, was moved by his mercy and bravery.

'Rolo Longleaf,' returned the voice of the king, 'much have your people suffered while those of us before you have suffered little indeed. This is an intolerable injustice for you and your people, of that I will agree! But war is upon the doorstep of Bolteras, and we have need of aid in the war against the Draemhas. Bolteras would benefit greatly from your people's strength and bravery! This is the true reason we have come. Will you join us?'

Rolo laughed hysterically. 'Will we join you? This war is not for thieves to fight! Nor would we so quickly forget the greediness of Bolteras! Where are the king's servants and all his glorious warriors now? Have the forces of Bolteras all been dispersed? It is madness to ask a band of outlaws to assist a king in a war and against Draemhas all the more!' He laughed again more loudly than before, though his voice revealed a hidden fearfulness.

'Aye, it is madness. But there are few Men who are brave enough to stand before the demon-folk of Dragoth! We seek heroes who would fight against this great evil. Hear you me, if we fail in this war, then all the lands of Bolteras, no, all the lands of Gaia will fall to darkness. For if they conquer the Western Lands then what will stop them from pressing against the kingdoms of the East on two fronts? If we do not stop them here, then all hope is lost! What say you?'

'We cannot trust the word of the rich and the fat!'

'O, come now, fat is a harsh word; I prefer well fed!' Edgar replied sarcastically out of his annoyance. 'Then I propose to you an offer that I hope you will not resist, my friend. Join us and wages will be given to you equal to that given to any of my soldiers. Also, your kin, if women and children you have, may live in Vallicore at no cost to you! Now, what say you?'

'So you think you can charm us with wealth? I have heard enough! For insulting my people and for discovering our hideout, I sentence you to captivity and death!'

Edgar stepped forth, and he seemed to increase in size. His eyes flickered as with fire, and he was terrifying to behold; and the man called Leader cowered behind his wall. The king appeared young and vibrant for a brief moment as he did in his youth, but then he suddenly seemed to shrink back to his usual stature.

'You need not force me into captivity. I offer myself to you freely, Master Longleaf! Pakko will be returned to you if you give your word that no harm will befall him, and you may lead my company blindly to any part of the forest you wish and abandon them there; but you must not harm them. If after one week you cannot trust me and come to peace with me, by my leave you may throw me into the darkest caverns of the Cold Stone Mountains to die and loose your fiery darts upon my men! But I beseech you, do not act hastily!' Rolo looked curiously at Edgar and smiled.

'You are a bold man, Edgar King, or at least a fool. But still, I have yet to meet a man as brave as you! It is agreed then. I will accept your challenge! You will stay as our captive and servant, and you must obey whatever it is we ask of you.' He glared at the king awaiting a response, and Edgar nodded. 'If we are not pleased with you by the twenty-second day of this month, you shall be slain and your head sent on a spike to Vallicore. But we will not harm young Pakko or your companions in any way. These are my rules. What say you now?'

'As you have said, let it be done! Send my companions away wherever you would.'

'This is madness!' Victor shouted. 'You call yourself a king? You are a fool! If I were king, I never w—'

'Victor, be silent!' Arthur rebuked. 'Show some respect for your king and his wishes. No man leads a king but rather a king leads his people; so whatever he wills, we shall obey without a complaint.' Victor grinded his teeth and scoffed at the absurd idea of a servant king.

'Victor, listen to me lad,' Edgar demanded with great authority; there was no sound of fear or doubt in his voice. 'You confuse the role of kingship. A king is not chosen to be served by his people, laddie! No, a dignified and just king comes to humbly serve those under him. A leader who only pursues his own interests puts his people's lives in peril and becomes a tyrant! A true king will always put the interest of his people before his own unless their interests seek to do evil in his sight. Remember that well, boy, and fret not! I will return. I give you my word.' Victor felt embarrassed from Edgar's reproach and spoke no more.

'Bind the king and lead him through the gates,' Rolo commanded a group of bandits, 'and then cover the eyes of his company and lead them far away. Go at once!' The order was given, and the gate to the stronghold swung open. The rest of Edgar's company took one last glance at the figure of the king before he disappeared with Pakko within the fortress Treehouse; then their eyes were veiled, and they were led by eight bandits back into the forest to the west.

Ropes were tied around their wrists, and their captors led them at a swift pace, ignoring the difficulty the travelers had to endure as they traversed through the forest blindfolded. For what seemed to be an hour, they ascended and descended many slopes as they were led deeper into the woods. Soon, they began to grow weary and distressed as they were uncertain how far away they were from Treehouse and the king. Their thoughts constantly wandered into worry as they tried to determine the conditions of Edgar's captivity. At first, they attempted to identify their course but their minds were clouded with anxiety; yet Grinshawl alone took careful consideration of their path, for he was not in the least worried about the king. He counted their steps and remembered each turn and hill so they might find their way back to the fortress in the trees if the need arose.

An hour and a half into their journey—though it felt to them like many more hours—Hildegard stumbled upon a tree root and fell to the ground dragging his guide down with him. The thief cursed and raved furiously to himself. He violently picked the boy up and set him on his feet, and their journey continued. Filled with despair and worry, Victor and Hildegard soon lost knowledge of their setting, and Arthur only maintained that they were still heading west from the stronghold of the thieves; but they soon came upon a familiar landmark: their feet splashed in the same waters of the stream they crossed the day before, but the water was stagnant and made no sound. Still, Grinshawl never lost sight even for an instant, for he was well trained to handle such circumstances even while blinded. All along their journey he remained calm, wanting only to laugh at his companions for their incessant fretful behavior and excessive groaning.

Suddenly, they halted and were spun around by their guides many times until they felt dizzy; but Grinshawl was not fooled and turned slowly as the thieves could not move him easily, and he still kept track of their course. After a brief respite, their escorts turned to the south and proceeded down a long hill. The slope proceeded into a long wooded dale. They came upon a dirt path that ran westward through the dale with thickets overhanging and followed it. Along the trail, the sun and sky were visible, but the sun was beginning to fall to the west. They felt the warmth of the sun on their faces and knew they had left the thickness of the woods for the time. Several minutes later, many howls of wolves echoed through the small valley, and the travelers were terrified, all but Grinshawl. They treaded onward for a while and turned to the right and then headed down another long slope. Branches and leaves struck them like a slap on the face as they proceeded down the hill. Before long, they heard the sound of rushing water ahead of them, though it still sounded far away—Grinshawl perceived that they were now close to the Roaring River. The hill rose to a flat stretch of soft turf, and the trees began to dwindle as they drew nearer to the rushing water. Then, the land changed abruptly to rough shingles leading to a shoal at the foot of the once grandiose waterway known as the *Roaring River*.

The source of the ancient river began high up in the Cold Stone Mountains to the east and descended west into the midst of the Grey Forest continuing through the Lonely Grey and even past the Lonely Forest. From there, the waters split in two directions: one led to the north into Vash'ala where the stream turned into a dry ravine from the scorching heat of the land, and the other led west to the foot of the Sage's Mountain where it gathered into a large lake. Noticing the arid ravine formed by the northern stream near the borders of Bolteras, the archers of the Lonely Forest built a dam to stop the flow and began to use the newly made ponds to fill their flasks with fresh spring water.

Their feet became sore from the rocks and shells that dug deep and hard into the soles of their boots. *Splash! Splash!* They met the water unexpectedly, and Victor slipped upon a moss-covered rock. He plunged backward into the gradually flowing river and cut his cheek on the surface of a coarse stone in the riverbed. Blood ran out from his cheek, and his escort quickly lifted him up and patted him on the back. The cut made him wince, but he grinded his teeth and said nothing. They reached the other side of the river and turned right, back to the east as Grinshawl discerned it. On this side of the river were willows and elm trees scattered abroad, but not as thickly as the southern portion of the forest. They followed the river east along its northern edge, and the rapids grew louder with every step. After walking along fairly level ground for half an hour, the land suddenly rose with a steep incline, and they continued upward for what felt to them to be an hour or more. As they walked on, the rushing water began to sound more like the crashing down of a great tower or the continual crackling and roaring of thunder during a terrible rainstorm, and they discerned that a waterfall was looming ahead on their right.

They traveled further until the sound of the waterfall was directly to their right; one blunder—they feared—and they would plummet to their deaths upon the rocks beneath the crashing waters below. The falls were fierce and booming, and the weary travelers felt that its end was far below them. They had traveled far up the incline to a point of smooth land, and it seemed to them the waterfall fell for miles. A great anxiety overcame Victor, for he feared his captors would ignore the agreement made with Lord Edgar and thus push them into the falls to their miserable deaths. But it was not so; and while they were still trapped in their wandering thoughts, their guides unexpectedly pulled them away from the falls to their left, back again to the north. They hardly strayed far from the cascade when their ropes were released by the bandits, though still left tied about their wrists. They could hear the sounds of footsteps upon the leaves of the forest as they faded down the slope to their left. It seemed they had been released and abandoned by their captors.

Grinshawl waited patiently for the steps to completely fade away and then he pulled his arms apart snapping the bonds about his wrists. He removed the cloth from his brow and looked at his companions who seemed gravely troubled. He smiled and slowly removed the cloths covering their eyes and untied their hands. 'We are free at last,' the giant proclaimed. The voice of the Ogre of Bolteras was deep and frightening yet oddly soothing to his shocked companions. 'We stand midway up the Mithras Falls! I imagine we are directly north of Treehouse, though those cursed trees block my sight.'

'How did you free yourself of your bonds, great warrior?' Arthur asked raising an eyebrow in alarm.

'I used my strength,' Grinshawl laughed. He raised both arms above his head and flexed. His muscles bulged, revealing great power. 'Behold the might of Bolt and Hammer!' he roared with a loud *Hoo-ha!* His companions laughed and clapped their hands as they marveled at the Ogre of Bolteras' great might and wit.

'What do we do now? Shall we return to Treehouse and rescue Lord Edgar?' Victor asked.

'Rescue?' Grinshawl laughed. 'Edgar needs no rescue! He can certainly hold his own if only bandits dwell in that fortress. It will not be long before he befriends the whole lot of them! Besides, lad, do you know where we are?'

'W-well, I know we went west and maybe south, but I lost my sense of direction after a while.' *Bwa-ha-ha!* the voice of the giant man chimed in with laughter. Thinking himself to be clever, Victor swiftly replied, 'I know! we are at the Mithras Falls!'

Grinshawl paused for a moment in shock and then laughed again. 'What a clever boy you are! I mentioned the name just a moment ago, and I nearly forgot! So you are indeed lost and confused! How then shall we return? No, lad, I think it is best that we wait. Look! the sun appears to be falling and the light is retreating. I imagine nightfall will soon be upon us, but these tall trees veil the presence of the sun from my eyes. All the same, we shall rest tonight near the shade of the trees. I am just grateful that our escorts did not loot our goods as I am quite hungry!' he laughed again.

'Perhaps Uncle Arthur knows the way back!' Victor replied not wanting to spend the evening in the forest. 'He is the best tracker in all of Kesh, though he is the only tracker in Kesh. But he can lead us back, of that I am sure. Besides, I am not fond of the idea of sleeping in a forest that houses wild wolves!'

'Alas! I know not which way is back, or front for that matter. I lost my way some time ago—too many distractions you see—but you forget in whose presence you stand. The Ogre of Bolteras is no fool as his epithet implies. Lord Edgar chose him as his right hand for more than just his brawn! His mind is brilliant! Surely we have no need to fear, my boy.'

'You speak too highly of me, my kindhearted, little friend,' Grinshawl returned enthusiastically. 'But indeed I know the way, wise Arthur. I never lost sight of which direction we went or what terrain we crossed. Though we were blinded, I knew every step and turn we made. Listen close; we will rest here tonight, and we will not return, not until six days are spent! Edgar put me in charge of this group, and we will return on the seventh day.'

'I never heard him say a word about *charge*!' Hildegard interrupted with a laugh, revealing Grinshawl's guile.

'Then I put myself in charge,' Grinshawl snapped and flexed his muscles once again. 'Or do you wish to challenge the might of Bolt and Hammer?' The giant's gaze was fixated on the shrinking form of Hildegard. They stood there staring into each others' eyes for a while until Grinshawl suddenly burst out in mirth. 'I jest, my young friend,' he said patting Hildegard on the back; the young boy fell to the ground. 'But you serve yourself best to listen to my counsel. Would you rather travel alone with no weapons in the company of wolves? We heard them some time ago, as Victor mentioned, and I have kept their scent in my nostrils for many miles as it seems. They are prowling about as we speak, so we will each take our turn keeping watch during the night. I will take the first, so rest your weary bodies!' The group hesitated with a fearful and doubtful look on their faces. 'Go now and be at peace. You have my word that no harm will come upon you. I can see the weariness in your eyes, so tarry no longer! I advise you to stay near to the falls away from the shadows of the trees. There the moonlight will fall upon us, and our line of defense will be greatest and our vision keenest.' The party reluctantly prepared their beds on the ground and fell asleep within the hour.

As the last light of day sunk away and night fell upon them, dark formations of clouds passed across the sky. Soon the stars and the moon were shrouded by thick billows and Grinshawl could hardly see; so he built a fire close to his companions and set about it a ring of stones. For the first half hour of the watch, Grinshawl heard no noise besides the sounds of crickets and the crashing echo of the waterfall. He paced up the length of the hill to the summit of the waterfall and saw the river stretch all the way to the foot of the mountains, and it glistened curiously with the resemblance of dazzling silver in the darkness of night; and it was peculiar to him as all light was blocked by the thick clouds above. It seemed to Grinshawl that the river emitted a light of its own, and he believed that either some ancient Magic had been used to enchant the waters or perhaps that silver covered the surface of the riverbed. Whatever the explanation, the giant was fascinated by its beauty.

He turned around at the top of the hill and saw, by the light of the fire still blazing strong, his companions resting peacefully at the edge of the waterfall. A moment later, he perceived a shadowy figure emerging from the forest. It walked on all fours, and he recognized it as a wolf prowling quietly and ever closer to his slumbering friends. His suspicion was confirmed when the beast snarled and howled.

He leapt down the hill and sprinted toward his companions, and the wolf sprung forth. Grinshawl ran as fast as he was able and then saw some five or six more wolves emerge from the forest, barking and howling, but they did not yet advance. The company stirred and scattered at once, all but Victor who cowered as the first wolf pounced at him. At the last moment, Victor dodged the attack only by an inch or less; but the wolf scratched his leg, and he screamed and hobbled closer to the edge of the path near to the cliff. He was nearly about to fall into the cascades below when Grinshawl suddenly tackled the wolf. The two fell to the ground and rolled to the edge of the slope. The wolf leapt to its feet quickly and stared at Grinshawl with fierce, burning eyes. The wolf was extremely large, nearly the size of Grinshawl if it stood on its hind legs, yet it was not as powerful as the Ogre of Bolteras.

The beast lunged forth at Grinshawl, but he quickly eluded and grabbed the wolf by the head; the other wolves now darted towards the giant man. Grinshawl roared and, swinging the creature high into the air, hurled the beast into the rapids below, but he received a painful bite on his arm just before releasing the beast to its death. The wolf squealed on its way down and the shrieks were quickly drowned out by the sounds of the deafening waterfall. The other, much smaller wolves as they were, after witnessing the defeat of their leader, screeched and fled down the hill never to return. The company recuperated from the confusion and reconvened by the fire at their campsite.

'Is anyone injured?' asked Grinshawl while holding his wounded arm. Arthur and Hildegard scanned their bodies but were unscathed.

'I have a scratch on my leg,' Victor responded. 'That mangy wolf's claw hit me when he pounced earlier or else I scraped it on the ground. I am not sure which it was. But how are you? You received a nasty bite on your arm!'

'We are blessed that it was no worse than a mere scratch!' Grinshawl answered. 'Those wolves appeared very hungry and would have eaten us all if I had chosen to sleep first. Do not concern yourself with me, lad. The Ogre of Bolteras has endured much worse than a simple wolf bite.' He spoke confidently, but his face revealed agony. The company was elated to have such a brave and powerful guardian as a companion, and they thanked him accordingly. But Grinshawl simply smiled and urged them to rest insisting they were safe, that the wolves would not return. Trusting the giant's strength more than they feared the wolves' bites, they fell asleep once more. Grinshawl remained vigilant all throughout the night without relinquishing his watch to any of his company. In the morning, Grinshawl ate breakfast with the group and then retired under the shade of the nearby elm trees. While he slept, Arthur carefully cleaned and bandaged his wound but was surprised to find the teeth had hardly sunk into the giant's skin.

For four days, they stayed at the edge of the woods beside the waterfall Mithras. They passed the time eating from the sacks of food that were meant for the bandits of Treehouse—they had forgotten to present their gifts during the hasty encounter the day before—and occasionally explored the surrounding area. But they were glad for their forgetfulness, for they had no weapons with which they could use to hunt. Several times Grinshawl went to the river to try and catch fish—which was his favorite of foods—but he never caught even one. So the days passed with little activity except the telling of tales and rumours; and though they were easily bored, they were merely glad to be free from the threat of the wolves. Each night just before they fell asleep, Grinshawl told tales of *the Order of the Magus*, a group of Wizards who used great and powerful Magic said to be passed down or taught by the Dragons of old. Victor scoffed at the idea, but they all listened to the tales curiously and elatedly as they were full of adventure and great battles.

He spoke particularly of the many journeys of an old Mage named Alastair and described him as a mighty Wizard and a beloved hero. Arthur seemed to be reminiscing as he listened to all the tales of Alastair the Wizard. Grinshawl even mentioned that Alastair and one other Wizard—whom he would not name—were alive and fought during the Great Dragon Wars that were recorded in the history books of Bolteras. On the fourth night of camping in the woods, Grinshawl continued his story. 'Many story books and legends were formed from those days but few knew the whole truth of it all,' he said. 'But perhaps there will come a day when the truth will be revealed to you. As it was though, Alastair was a mighty Wizard. He attained the rank of *White Mage* before he disappeared from the world. His magical prowess was especially strong in the arts of leechcraft, though his other Magic was not something to be trifled with. He cared for the world, and he loved using his powers for good. He was an honest man, very wise indeed.'

'You speak as if you knew him,' Victor chimed in.

'Aye, I did at one time,' he said with great sadness in his voice and spoke no more that night. The others watched Grinshawl intently hoping he would have more to say, but he remained silent and fell asleep; so they too retired for the evening dreaming of life during the age of Dragons and Wizards.

On the morning of the fifth day, the twentieth of March, the company became weary and anxious from waiting. They thought little at first of Edgar and his fate in the hands of the thieves but now it was the only thing on their minds. No one spoke to each other that day. Mostly, they just paced back and forth around the area of the camp and into the forest some, but Victor spent much of his time at the pinnacle of the Mithras Falls. He sat upon a large stone looking down at the water crashing below and drifted into deep contemplation. The hours passed slowly and Victor grew weary as he listened to the soothing sound of the falls.

'Hullo, lad,' spoke a voice from behind him after a tiresome period of silence. Victor jumped and spun around to witness the face of a man he did not expect to see. 'I do not suggest you stare too long into the falls or you might fall in!' the voice exclaimed with a laugh. There stood Lord Edgar fully clad in his simple yet kingly garments with a large, unusual smile upon his face.

'B-but how?' Victor asked. 'How did you escape from those horrible bandits?'

'Horrible? Escape? You use such awful words, young Victor! Nay! They are not horrible folk but rather strong-willed and cautious, as they should be in days such as these. And I had no need to escape; no, in fact, I came here freely, as did they.' He waved his hand behind him and pointed to a group of thieves—about fifteen in all—who suddenly emerged from their hiding spots behind the trees. At the front of their group was Rolo Longleaf—Pakko had remained in Treehouse with his kin—and a strange smile, as it was to Victor, was on his face. Victor reddened with embarrassment. 'You see, I come with friends! Did I not tell you to worry not? And returned I have, moreover with newly acquired friends! The only way to truly gain the respect of your people as king is to lead by example. I say the humble way is the most efficient. Remember that well, boy,' he said with a smile on his face: it was warm and pleasant and greatly inspired Victor. 'Come let us join with the rest of our companions!'

'Where is Pakko?' Victor interrupted with an anxious expression on his face.

'Pakko?' Edgar questioned. 'Do not be afraid! He is quite safe. No need to worry.'

'I was not worried,' Victor replied quietly. 'I just wanted to see to it that those bandits kept their word.'

'Aye, kept it they did!' Edgar laughed. 'But come now. They are no longer bandits! They are our fellow kinsmen.' Victor bowed before the king and then they descended the slopes; the others quickly caught sight of Edgar approaching with Victor, and they ran to the foot of the hill to greet him.

'My liege, welcome back!' hollered Grinshawl. 'I knew all was well. It was in your eyes, and you needed no counsel from me. I see we have new friends!'

'Aye,' said Rolo, 'we come now in peace and as brethren in arms! If Draemhas are mustering their forces in the Western Lands as the king says, then we must act quickly and put this to rest. That is my counsel.'

'And I would agree with you, Rolo Longleaf,' Grinshawl replied. 'I am Grinshawl, commander of the Boltian army, second in command to Lord Edgar King of Bolteras. I am the king's chief advisor and the mightiest man, as they say, in all of Gaia. They call me the Ogre of Bolteras on account of my size,' he said with a boisterous *Bwa-ha-ha!* 'And these are my companions—Victor you have just met—and here is Hildegard, Victor's closest friend, and the other is Arthur, Victor's uncle as he calls him, though they are not blood related. And do not forget my mightiest friends, Bolt and Hammer!' he exclaimed showing his arms to the band of thieves which they deemed an odd gesture. 'Pardon me, I speak with much haste. I am merely glad to see the king alive and well and to see you now as friends. You have my most sincere apology for the deaths of your brethren,' he said bowing his head.

'Well met, friends, especially to the latter two!' laughed Rolo clapping his hands cheerfully. 'But raise your head, great Ogre of Bolteras! I will have you know my kinsmen are safe.' Grinshawl raised his head and looked curiously at Rolo. 'Aye, they live, though they were badly injured. But they have recovered now thanks to Lord Edgar. There is something I must say now before you all! This day in the company of friends, family, lords of Bolteras and the king himself, we, the thieves of the Grey Forest of the fortress Treehouse, openly declare allegiance to Lord Edgar King of Bolteras for proving his might and trust. Though we agreed to seven days, he proved his worth in five! He is a great king, not like the ones we thieves hear of in stories, for he is a servant king, born not of nobility or royalty but poverty and made nobility by the fruit of his labor! He is the first king my ears have heard to sit on a throne though he was not the rightful heir to do so! King Haus was a noble man too as the stories go and must have seen great worth in you. Forgive my rambling; let me explain what took place these past five days.

'At first, we were cruel and beat the king until he could stand no more; then, upon the next day, we forced hard labor upon him, this Edgar, but he never once quarreled or grumbled. We had him hunt deer, under watch of course, and he never failed to bring us the meatiest of the beasts and even removed the antlers for our collection of treasures. And when we tested him and offered the best meat he said, "Not for a servant but only for the lord of the house and his kin." Never have we thieves met a man of such high status act so humbly before a poor people. We were astounded, and we discussed it amongst ourselves. Pakko confirmed that he was an honorable man, yet we were not fully convinced.

'Several of my men suggested that he was trying to deceive us for dishonest gain, so we truly put him to the test. We had him clean away all of our excrement, that of our men and our fowl. After he completed the task and bathed himself, he washed our feet by his own free will! And out of his bag he pulled finely scented oil and washed our feet with it. This type of oil was meant for kings and other important peoples, and yet he anointed us with it and declared us his brethren. Neither I nor any of my kin have ever been so highly exalted! And what is more, he gave us gold and silver as homage to our people! Lastly, he willingly healed the wounds of our injured brethren who were struck by the arrows of his own soldiers upon the evening of March the thirteenth. He approached them and paid them proper respect, apologizing for the harm done to them; and they simply smiled and forgave him. It was that night that we put our trust in Lord Edgar and opted to join the Boltian army as archers. And here we are now, recently treated as lords by a servant king and now willing servants to the lord of kings!'

Edgar's companions were full of joy and all had smiles upon their faces. Victor was amazed at the trust Edgar had gained from the thieves in so few of days and the trials he had to endure. He rubbed his eyes as if he expected it all to be a fanciful dream. 'They exaggerate the tale!' Edgar exclaimed humbly, his cheeks turning red. 'I will not have my friends boasting so highly in me! Such respect is deserved by Vaaspar alone! Now come and let us discuss our next course.'

Chapter IV

The Road to Vallicore

The entire party sat around a large campfire prepared by Arthur and warmed themselves as the sun faded and the coolness of night overtook them. Edgar's group opened up their sacks of food and handed out enough for all to be full. After their meal, they discussed their next course of action. At Edgar's request, all agreed that they should travel to Vallicore at once for the gathering of the Boltian Council.

'Rolo, you and your men should return to Treehouse and bring your women and children to Kesh. The rest of my guard awaits there for our return. I have brought with me thirty-three horses, one for each of my men, including Grinshawl and myself, and the last for Arthur, for I intended to have him return with us to Vallicore for the Boltian war council. But alas! we now have an extra steed, for Hamben our beloved brother has fallen by one of your arrows. I admit that I was beyond angry at first, but my desire for peace amongst my people proved greater than my rage; so I will carry the burden of my loyal soldier's death upon my own shoulders. You are our brethren now, and Hamben would not be pleased to know a war was waged amongst us on his account. I think it best, former thieves, that you pay tribute to him at his grave. He deserves that much, I believe.' Rolo and his men nodded in agreement. 'With the death of Hamben, we have a rider-less horse, aye, but we have need for many more horses or else many must walk all the way to Vallicore on their own two feet! That would prove an exhausting journey indeed if women and children are in our company!'

'We have many horses in Kesh,' answered Arthur. 'Mr. Manor, the stable master—or Egberd as we call him by his first name—will gladly supply the king and his company with many fine steeds, the swiftest and strongest Kesh has to offer! But where have you kept your steeds, my liege? I never saw them in Kesh.'

'We took the liberty of leaving them at the stables when we arrived in Kesh. I spoke with Mr. Manor at your birthday party, and he was rather polite about it, though I reckon it was the ale speaking for him. If Mr. Manor is so kind as to lend us his horses, then he shall be rewarded kindly. This is good; it seems we have a plan then. Rolo, go back to your people and meet us in Kesh in three days time. We will stay one more day in Kesh once you have arrived and then embark the following day on March the twenty-fifth. Do all agree?' The entire group nodded and then prepared their beds for sleep.

On the following morning, Rolo revealed a path to Edgar and his company on the southern side of the Roaring River before returning to his people; the path, as he told them, ran southward and led out of the Grey Forest just to the northwest of Kesh. The journey from there to Kesh was slightly more than a mile.

The journey as a whole lasted the entire day before Edgar and his companions returned to Kesh, but the way was smooth and easy as the dirt path was mostly free of twigs and roots. They came upon the town as the last of the sunlight sunk into the west. The king's men—who had remained ever vigilant for their return—ran to greet them, and some of the villagers scurried about to prepare a warm meal for them. There in Kesh, they waited peacefully in the comfort of much food and drink for Rolo and the band of thieves to arrive; and it pleased them greatly to rest as they had not done so since they departed with Pakko to Treehouse on the morning of March the fourteenth.

* * *

As they agreed, Rolo and his men withdrew to Treehouse to gather their belongings and on the third day came to Kesh bringing with them a small host of people—there were forty-three in all. Edgar had already informed the villagers of their deeds in the woods, and the Keshians joyfully welcomed the former bandits by giving them an abundance of food and drink. Egberd Manor had tended to the horses day and night and kept them well fed in preparation for their journey to Vallicore. He kindly offered to give his horses free of charge, but the king insisted upon payment. Edgar had no gold with him but gave Mr. Manor his word that he would reward him kindly. Several weeks later, Mr. Manor came to receive such a large cart full of gold that he fainted from the shock of seeing it.

Edgar refused to inform the villagers of Kesh of the impending war, and he did not permit any of his companions to speak of it; and so there was no farewell party or any sort of special gathering in honor of the travelers' departure. When asked of the purpose of their trip, Arthur simply smiled and said, 'The main reason we are going is to escort the vagabonds of the forest to their new homes in Vallicore. But for reasons of my own, I wish to go and

61

take Victor and Hildegard to see the great capital city of Bolteras and home to our noble king. Fear not, caring people, we will return when we are able.' But the villagers were confused and muttered many curses. One muttered, 'foolish dotard,' while another said, 'a bunch of wayward souls those are.' Each of the Keshians grumbled in their own way as they went back to their homes. And so it was that the king and his companions finished gathering their belongings and then left Kesh upon the twenty-fifth of March. As they climbed upon their steeds to depart, the villagers of Kesh returned briefly and cordially waved them off, not wanting the travelers to leave without a proper goodbye; then they returned once again to their little homes completely unaware of the happenings in the world. Arthur turned to Victor who seemed sad and confused and said, 'It is better this way, laddie. Now they can continue to live their simple and peaceful lives free from the burdens of war and malicious death. They will be happier not knowing, my boy.' Arthur looked behind him to the southeast and saw the leaves of Ole Faithful shining bright pink as the branches stretched high into the air, and he became saddened, for he had forgotten to say goodbye.

Arthur had almost decided to turn his steed and race off to say farewell to Ole Faithful when Lord Edgar began to march forward. And so the company marched after him along the road to the north just as the sun had reached high noon, and Arthur missed his chance to say goodbye to his greatest friend. Victor and Hildegard were eager and joyful to be involved, especially when Edgar mentioned that they might learn swordsmanship in Vallicore. Arthur was reluctant to take the boys with him as the war appeared to be mere sport to them, and he was greatly troubled by their elated demeanor. But he perceived great potential in them and knew in his heart that Victor and Hildegard would never agree to stay behind in the simple life of Kesh, particularly after their exciting adventure to Treehouse.

Before they had marched far from the village Kesh on their journey westward to the capital city of Bolteras, Edgar sent out his remaining twenty-nine soldiers ahead of them to rendezvous with members of the Boltian Council and summon them to Vallicore. Grinshawl explained that they were commanded to meet in secret with men of Edgar's choosing and escort them to the king's castle in the city; the sudden news confused and worried Arthur, for he was not fond of secrets. Edgar and Grinshawl refused to abandon the travelers and so stayed with the rest of the company—Arthur, Victor,

Hildegard, Pakko, Rolo and his band of vagrants and their women and children. In all, their company was two score and eight.

Though they had departed much later than Edgar originally hoped, the company set out at last upon the long journey to Vallicore, but they felt less burdened and more at ease with the aid of Mr. Manor's horses. The most difficult part of the journey was the tending to of the women and children, but they maintained a good pace all the same. They took the northern crossroad out of Kesh which connected to the most commonly used road in Bolteras. The main path ran to the northwestern parts of Bolteras, passing by the mighty fortresses of Eordil, Bram and Cayrngras, before turning south to Vallicore; but Edgar planned to take a more secluded path home, one that ran along the southern edge of the land—the length of the journey from Kesh to Vallicore on that path was nearly forty leagues. Accounting for the women and children and much to his dismay, for he desired to arrive much sooner, Edgar concluded that the trip would take around ten days or perhaps seven to eight days if they maintained a steady pace.

'We shall arrive in Vallicore about the fourth of April at the latest, I should think,' Edgar said to Grinshawl, 'so let us not tarry. There is much to do, and we are already later than I hoped. Let us hope our enemy is not yet formidable against our might. It is only a three day journey riding swiftly on the great steeds of Vallicore, but we need not hasten on our way, above all with a group of women and children. Taking them into account, our journey will be slowed by two or more days.'

'Sire,' Grinshawl responded, 'it would be best if we rode ahead and made ready for the Boltian Council. Surely these good and reasonable people would understand and be able to find their own way, especially with Arthur in their company. Besides, they should travel at a pace of their own, and I imagine you should arrive at Vallicore before your counselors. The meeting would not get far without the guidance and leadership of the king.'

'Nay, greatest of friends, let us take it easy for a time. We certainly must arrive as quickly as we can, but I will not abandon these people to travel alone. We will be forced to make haste soon enough, but for now I should like to travel slowly while I am still able.' Grinshawl glared at the king doubtfully for a moment but conceded to his will. Edgar seemed greatly troubled as if he had foreseen some gloominess in his future and was not eager to embrace it.

The party stayed upon the open road trotting along atop their horses in a long line. There were many in the group unaccustomed with riding and had to be lead on the road as they were not able to control the direction of their horses' gaits. Edgar rode in the front with Grinshawl on his right and Arthur on his left. The vast land of Bolteras was bright green and full of rolling knolls and tall grass, and the springtime yielded many flowers for their eyes to enjoy. Victor and Hildegard rather enjoyed galloping from one side of the road to the other and up and down the rolling vales; they were the only ones who galloped and the only ones who seemed excited about the long journey ahead of them. And their horses appeared to have vitality liking to theirs.

The road continued northward out of Kesh for a mile and then curved to the west and ran along the edge of the Grey Forest for more than five miles. About an hour into their journey as the path crossed over a series of tall hills, Edgar pointed out a lonely fortress with tall wooden walls to their left. It was a fairly large town called Balas—one of many defensive towns in Bolteras—and the tall wooden posts of the walls were distinct, even at a distance. Though the stronghold was more than six miles away to the south, they could see that the posts were finely crafted into sharp, jagged spikes that rose high into the air with banners waving from the tops of them. The Keshians were quite familiar yet callous toward the peoples of Balas as, in their experience, they were unreasonably rude and outlandish, but the members of Treehouse were simply amazed to behold such a magnificent looking fortress far greater than their humble fort in the woods.

At their slow but steady pace, they came nearly an hour later upon a bend in the road at the end of the lush hills and plains of the Rolling Vale and continued on the path as it turned to the south. There were trees scattered about the plains near to the road but never in large amounts and the grass was shorter now than it was at the beginning of the journey. To their right, a small valley ran from the bottom of a long hill for about a mile before running into a narrow stream—the Boltians called it *the Wayside Stream*—that poured from north to south and emptied into the Great Sea. The valley on their left sunk deep below at the bottom of several large hills, and it opened up to a wide meadow filled with flowers of all colors and of various sorts. Edgar pointed out a large sycamore tree nearby the Wayside Stream some four miles down the road to the southwest: it was the largest tree in all the land of Bolteras, ascending higher even

64

than the boughs of Ole Faithful. The travelers marveled at its height and were eager to see it up close.

About twenty fathoms to the south of the tree, there was a bridge running over the width of the stream connecting the road from one side to the other. They strode on towards the river as the road curved to the left and headed straight toward Balas. Less than a mile ahead, it turned back to the south and later split into two paths. The one they took kept south toward the bridge over the Wayside Stream while the other turned southeast to the gates of Balas. Arthur scoffed, turned his head and said to Lord Edgar, 'I am angry with Bory and Grob. They forgot to come to my birthday party! But I suppose I will forgive them…eventually. After all, if they came, my kin in Kesh might have tortured them for their rude behavior. I suppose holding a grudge is too much work for an old man.' Edgar smiled but Arthur discerned a troubled look in his eyes, but he did not question the king about it.

After a brief respite and another hour of traveling, they came at last to the Wayside Stream and stood at the foot of the great trunk of the sycamore tree. Some of the children climbed onto the branches as though they were back in Treehouse, and they smiled for the first time since they departed from Kesh. Edgar was pleased to see their happiness, so he ordered the company to halt for the day. The sun was now slowly sinking into the western horizon, and the sky turned orange and pink, which was pleasing for them to behold. The children played for a couple more hours as the older men and women ate under the shade of the sycamore. Once the children were all fed, they set up camp and quickly fell asleep; but before they lay down to sleep, they tied ropes to the reins on their horses and also around their bodies to keep the horses from wandering or abandoning them. Some of the travelers were roused abruptly as their horses dragged them around in their sleep. But eventually the horses too were eager to sleep, and the night was peaceful for the most part.

They woke late the next morning and ate a quick breakfast before departing again. By the time they crossed the river in full company, the sun was already climbing high into the eastern sky. The path from the bridge continued to the northwest for about three miles before it ran into a crossroad which was linked to the main road of Bolteras. Far away to the north, a great stronghold rested across an immense dale, and many wished to see it; but Edgar turned their course to the south across a great open plain that ran for many miles. A forest, called *the Wooded Gorge*, was before them, more than three leagues in the distance to the south. Arthur was once again confused and became irritated as well, for he desired to visit the stronghold to the north.

'Oi now!' he called and Edgar turned his head. 'Where are you leading us? The road is to the north!'

'Yes, yes, but that is precisely why we are heading south,' Edgar replied whimsically.

'You confuse me, Your Highness.'

'It is quite simple, noble Arthur. We came by a subtle, more secretive way so we might remain more…well, secret if you will.'

'You speak in riddles, Edgar. Come now and speak clearly! This old man has no time or patience for these irritating ruses.'

'Calm yourself, friend. A king does not travel so easily through his own land, I will have you know. If I were to pass through the land by way of the main road, then I would have a great host of people after me. There are always problems in the land; yes, many disputes and offenses. But my business must be guarded until we hold the Boltian Council. That is why I have sent the Templar Guard ahead of us to summon my counselors in private. They are well equipped to handle such a task. If I were to march in to one of the great towns of Bolteras, then it might be weeks before I left! Hear you me, Arthur, we have not the time for any more delays. With the Draemhas gathering in the north, we have no time to spare. Does that answer your question?'

'Aye, it does, but I have another one.'

'Speak, friend.'

'Why are you here with us now? Go ahead as the wise Grinshawl has advised you!'

'I will not! Even a king needs to travel on a tranquil road at a calm pace from time to time. Soon I will be forced to go each day with haste in my steps until the threat of the Dark Lord's armies is gone from the Western Lands. I just wish to remain calm for now. Please do not be harsh with me or consider me a fool.'

Arthur tilted his head back and breathed in deeply. 'You are no fool, my liege. Forgive my intrusive behavior. Where you go, I will go, for I know you are a fine warrior of the Light! Lead on, my most patient friend!' Edgar smiled, and they strode on without another word.

The sky thus far had remained clear with the exception of a few white clouds looming in the sky above. They pressed on and drew ever closer to the forest to the south. The sun now rested high above their heads, and its heat made them grow weary. They rested for a while and drank water until they felt cool and relaxed. Many miles to the west, across a long, open field of grassy plains, they could see an immense wold climbing up to the southern road that split from the crossroads to the north. After their brief rest, they continued onward to the south and climbed a tall hill that revealed much of the land. Edgar turned and pointed to the north to the town beyond the crossroads: it was the same fortress the travelers wished to visit earlier that day. The travelers halted and peered across the land to the north. 'That is Eordil, one of the mighty strongholds of Bolteras! It is a good town to visit, but alas! we have no time. If ever you have time to travel and the days are happier, then I suggest you go there. They have many games and competitions that will always keep you cheerful.' He spoke with a large smile on his face as though he was dwelling on some past memory of his time there. 'Aye, I desire that we could go to Eordil for just one taste of Borgon's Beer! It is the finest beer in all of Bolteras; yes indeed, that it is.' Arthur took great offense to the king's comment, for he believed Mayle's Ale to be the finest of brews. He grumbled a quiet, 'fool of a king!' but Edgar did not hear him. 'Regrettably, we have no time for leisurely drinking and games of merriment,' Edgar concluded solemnly.

After staring into the distance for a few minutes, Edgar continued on, and the rest of the company followed in line. They rounded the hill as it descended far into a valley below which ran all the length to the forest ahead. 'Let us reach the Wooded Gorge by nightfall,' Edgar called out, 'We can rest under the shadow of the trees, and there we will be veiled from the sight of the peoples of Carg and Poleden. The hunters in Carg only track for food at the eastern edge of the forest, so our presence will be concealed.' His companions were already exhausted—all except Victor and Hildegard who still galloped all about, though their horses were growing weary—and they moaned and bickered along the way.

Some four hours passed before they came to the edge of the forest, for the land was long and the sun was scorching. They rested several times along the way at the request of the women in the group and were glad to reach the edge of the woods when at last they arrived. The sun had now faded fully and the moon was beginning to appear in the northern sky. One by one, stars began to twinkle up above, and they provided the travelers much comfort. Soon after they arrived, the party set up camp and ate. It was only their second meal of the day as they hoped to shorten the duration of the journey by halting as seldom as possible; and so, many of the company simply ate as they went along. The night was peaceful, the sky clear, and the air was cool but not cold. After tying their horses to the trunks of the trees, the company quickly found sleep. They slept rather peacefully upon the beds of leaves in the woods, but their peace was short lived: Grinshawl woke full of great vigor before the rising sun and roused them with the sound of his mighty roar.

Upon the onset of the next day, Edgar led the company through the woods to avoid being spotted as they traveled secretly to Vallicore. The forest stretched for eleven miles from north to south; but they left its shelter eight hours later still a mile short of its end and traveled southwest to a small mountain range called *Bolteras' Jaw*—the journey to the foot of the mountain range was nearly five leagues from the edge of the woods. As they traveled, Edgar pointed out the town of Poleden—though it was hard to see—many miles to the northwest near to *the Canyon of Gold*, which was a famous landmark in Bolteras, and it was well known in all the other lands of Gaia as well. Then, he pointed to the east and introduced them to the town of Carg running along the eastern border of the Wayside Stream. The host gazed to the right and to the left admiring the two fortresses from a distance and wondered what kind of life the people of fortresses lived.

Once emerging from the shelter of the forest, the land began to fall steadily, providing an easier passage to the foot of Bolteras' Jaw. But as they trudged along, clouds suddenly began to loom overhead, and it began to drizzle. Many of the women and children wanted to stop and find shelter, but Edgar insisted that they press on. The further they progressed, the greater Edgar's desire to return to Vallicore grew. Though at first he longed to travel slowly and enjoy the countryside, he now desired to press on as swiftly as they could manage. He sensed an eerie darkness, a feeling of evil, coming from the north, and he grew ever more uneasy, for it seemed to him that a shadow was upon him or a being of great malice was watching his every step. The company increased their pace as the king increased his and came to the foot of the mountain five hours later just as the sun was beginning to fall in the western sky.

Though they drew ever nearer to Vallicore, Edgar was unable to disencumber the thoughts of the awful terrors that lurked about in the north. He continued more swiftly and led them upon the road once again as he headed west. They passed the foot of Bolteras'

Jaw half an hour later and came upon a large gulley laden with thistles. Continuing further down the path beyond the mountain range, they came upon a thick blanket of mist surrounding a large bog, and Edgar ordered the party to halt for the evening. The rain finally ceased its light but constant dripping, and the clouds rolled back shortly after they finished setting up their camp. The moon and stars shone brightly above, and Edgar felt at peace once more. They fell asleep, though they were deeply troubled by the presence of the marsh before them. Many of the children whimpered about ghosts and swamp creatures, but their parents consoled them, assuring them there were no such things. But the bog, known to the Boltians as *the Misty Marshes*, contained any eerie presence, and even some of the mighty warriors of Vallicore refused to travel near it.

The next morning, the party awoke, but they were too disturbed and anxious to eat their breakfast. 'We have reached the Misty Marshes,' Edgar called with a troubled look upon his face. 'We will meet a path on the other side just before it runs into a spinney. If time allowed, we would travel around the swamp but passing through is the quickest way to Vallicore; moreover, it will completely conceal our presence. Let us press on with wariness, for it can be a very dangerous place. Follow in a line lest you accidentally plunge into a large pool, and the swamp swallows you up! These marshes are filled with impenetrable fog, so stay near to the person in front of you. We will make it out alive if you listen to instruction. These are dangerous parts I am afraid, not a place for strangers. But once we pass through the fen, we will be more than halfway finished with this journey.'

The people began to gather their belongings, but Edgar withdrew to the south near to the northwestern edge of Bolteras' Jaw. Grinshawl pursued him.

'My lord, what bothers you?' the giant called. 'The people can see distress in your eyes, and they grow fearful. You must console them.'

'Do you remember the war twenty years ago?' Grinshawl nodded. 'It was horrible, and I hoped in my lifetime to never see such war again; but alas! war comes to me and my kingdom once again. I was only made King of Bolteras after the battle that took King Haus' life, the same one that claimed Threngol's life as well. Both were great men and Bolteras suffered deeply without their leadership. It was my first war to partake in, and I failed to deliver Threngol from the clutches of death. I feel I am to blame for much of

69

Arthur's pain today. If I had known you then, I think you would have been able to prevent his death. And the strong and noble Threngol was to be released from the king's armies following that war so that he might return home to be with his family. Anguish belongs to me, Grinshawl! Even after the people made me king, I knew nothing. I gave poor counsel and led my people to an age of greed and darkness. I was young, not only in age, but in zeal, in wisdom and in leadership. I was a fool…a c—'

'Aye, you were a fool then,' Grinshawl interjected, 'but you are different now! You are wise and strong, and all your people love you. No one in all of Bolteras regrets crowning you king. Furthermore, you saved my life from the prisons of Gorgonash in Vash'ala, and I owe you my very life. I will follow you until I die to help you accomplish your goals, and all will fear the Ogre of Bolteras and the might of Bolt and Hammer! Aye, I remember that war and this war will likely bring far more anguish, but there is always hope, my liege! There is evil in the world, but you must be strong for your people. Did you forget already that you befriended marauders and earned their trust and respect in a mere five days? Your people will rally to you when the time comes, but war may be far from us yet. Be at ease, my friend, and go to your people now with a clear conscience. Many died before but that blood is not on your hands!'

Grinshawl's words comforted his friend. Edgar smiled and went away to the worried group of travelers and comforted them, for he no longer feared the growing shadow in the north. The company climbed upon their steeds with new assurance and pressed on. But suddenly, the fog grew thick about them as though a vile spell had been cast, and the people began to panic once again, though Victor and Hildegard still found the events to be amusing and delightful. All they could see was the darkening image of Grinshawl soaring high into the air.

'Line up behind the Ogre of Bolteras,' Edgar cried out, 'We must follow him through this smoggy marsh!'

'Fear not, worried travelers,' Grinshawl answered, 'for you will not lose your way and your feet will not stumble with me as your guide! Grab your horses' reins and lead them beside you on your right and *only* on your right. Heed my words if you want to come out of the swamp safely. There are pools so deep and foggy that, once you fall in, you can never find your way out again. It is a terribly frightening place if you do not know the way. But I know the way, so stay close!' Edgar desired to be the one to lead his people safely through the swamp, but he knew Grinshawl's size and booming voice were more aid than he could supply at the time; and he knew also of Grinshawl's skills in navigation. One by one, the company lined up behind the Ogre of Bolteras. Edgar was directly behind him followed by Hildegard and then Victor. Arthur was at the rear near to Pakko and Rolo. They took their place in the back to help keep an eye on the children. Each of them moved their horse to their right and awaited their orders. In the meantime, Grinshawl reached into his pack and pulled out a long rope and passed it down the line. Each of the people grabbed hold of it as commanded, and Grinshawl slowly led them through the swamp.

None knew how long they were in the marshes, but it felt like days, though the marshes only stretched for two miles ahead of them. There was no sun or light as all the outside world was shrouded by the dense grey of the fog, and the women and children cried out in distress. There were ten children in all including one infant who was carried always by her mother. The thick smoke instilled fear in their hearts and minds but every once in a while Grinshawl would shout, 'Fear not! When you are led by Grinshawl the mighty, you shall be safe! No marsh or dense fog can overcome me! Fear not, my brethren; fear not!'

As they strode forward, the ground sunk more than a foot, and the marsh waters seeped into their boots and soaked their leggings up to their knees. There were times some of the children were nearly covered up to their heads in water, but the rope helped them stay afloat. There were deeper and deadlier pools further to the left and also to the right, but Grinshawl knew the way well and strayed far from them. As they pressed on, they became weary as their dampened clothes became a burden to them, and the swamp seemed to have a power over them that made them desire sleep. 'The fog will make your eyes heavy, but this is no place to sleep!' cried Grinshawl from the front. 'Keep your eyes open and stay vigilant!'

The journey through the bog was long as they turned many times to avoid deep and deadly pools. In all, the trek through the swamp took more than six hours. They were exhausted and many wanted to give up, but at long last, the fog began to thin as they neared the end of the bog. As they emerged, the sun shone before them: it was bright red, and the sky was colored with oranges in some parts and pinks in others. Nightfall was close at hand, but Edgar advised them to press on further. They left the marsh behind them and with it also they abandoned the hopeful and peaceful feelings they had experienced on the journey thus far. As they trudged along, there was not a single person in the group with a smile on his face. One by one, the travelers released the rope that Grinshawl led them by and relaxed for a moment. But just as Arthur was about to release the line, he felt a tug on the rope.

At that same time, a woman shouted, 'Where is my boy? I cannot find my son!' The company halted, and Edgar sped away back into the marshes without a word. Faintly, he heard the cry of a young boy followed by a splash. He came to the edge of a pool where the sound seemed to come from and reached into the waters; he felt the boy's hand almost at once and quickly pulled him onto the solid ground. The boy wailed and moaned, but Edgar comforted him and carried him safely back to the arms of his mother who was cursing and blaming herself for losing her son. After the woman had hugged and kissed her son for a few minutes and excessively thanked Edgar, they continued on sluggishly. Edgar decided that they should remount and continue to the edge of the spinney ahead, which was just an hour away at a slow pace. Reluctantly, the party agreed, and they marched onward, leaving the cold, miserable marshland behind them.

They decided to continue traveling slowly, though they were anxious to set up camp for the sake of the women and children. They arrived an hour later and immediately dismounted and prepared for sleep. They tied their horses to the elms and maples of the spinney and made many fires to warm themselves from the cold of the marsh water on their clothes. Most of the company fell asleep without eating as their eyes would not stay open any longer. It was not long before sleep overtook the rest of them, and they all relaxed peacefully on the soft grass under the shadows of the trees. Edgar and Grinshawl extinguished the fires and made certain every member of the group was warmed with a blanket before finding rest for themselves.

The morning sun came like a flash of lightning, and the company stirred nearly all at once, though unwillingly. Edgar called for all to eat their breakfast and be ready for a long march—he planned to ride long, if all were able, and get as close to Vallicore as they could by nightfall. 'Four or five more days of travel, I should think,' Edgar said to himself as he pulled out a pipe. He filled it to the brim with a fragrant weed—*Bosh-Nosh* it was called by the Boltians. He released a puff of smoke from his mouth in the form of a ring, and Grinshawl knew him to be greatly troubled, for Edgar never smoked unless he was distressed. 'We shall travel four or five more days to Vallicore if all goes smoothly, and then the council will be held on the third or fourth day of April, if all my counselors arrive promptly.'

'Sire, are you well?' Grinshawl asked out of concern.

Edgar's face drooped despondently. His eyes were gleaming as though he desired to weep. His voice quivered as he spoke. 'Aye, I am just, well, distracted you see. I hope ever so greatly that Vaaspar's blessing shines on us in this war. We would need much time to ready my army and to train new hires. It would take more than a month for all my current armies to assemble and many more days to convince them to go to war! Aye, I am deeply troubled, friend.'

'These days are evil indeed,' Grinshawl empathized. 'Great troubles now lie on your shoulders, but you need not carry this burden alone, my liege. You are still young, and there is strength in you. You must rally as many as you are able, but you must not show your people fear or else you will teach them that fear. They need strength now more than ever; let me be your strength! I fear no man or beast, not even the devilish folk. Be strong and fret not; Vaaspar's light will shine on you yet!'

'You always speak such powerful words to me, friend! Behold! I feel refreshed now! Let us press on and bring courage and hope to these people.' The two returned to the camp and mounted their steeds. The company took notice and quickly gathered their belongings. The sun rose from over the horizon but its light was hindered by the trees of the spinney. The rest of the group mounted their horses and strode on slowly but steadily after the king. Leaving the spinney, the road led up a long hill and rolled down into a vast vale on the other side; the land was flat and open with only a few scattered trees abroad. The plains extended for almost twenty leagues or more and appeared endless to them, for it spread as far as the eye could see. The Boltians named this stretch of land *the Weary Vale*, as none ever crossed it without growing fatigued, for the sun burned with no shade to hide under and the vast plains extended seemingly with no end. The ostensibly endless vale proved exhausting just from the sight of it, and none were eager to continue.

They paced for hours as the sun slowly moved overhead. The party was growing weary of travel as the scorching sun beat upon their heads, and many begged to halt for a while. Edgar persisted that they continue until nightfall but he relented after another hour of ceaseless grumbling. They rested in the hot spring air in the open fields of the Weary Vale and sipped on their water slowly, for their flasks were running dry. The wind began to blow southward and brought with it dark clouds from the north. It seemed to them that rain was imminent. As the dark billows drew closer, the weary travelers became greatly discouraged at first, but then they yearned to feel the coolness of rain and escape the heat of the sun.

After an hour, they began to gather their sacks and climb back upon their laden horses. Before long, darkness filled the vale with only faint glimmers of sun rays peering through the clouds. Far away to the northwest, Edgar saw a gleam of light flickering. He looked more closely and saw the light from the sun was gleaming off of the armor of approaching riders. He perceived a great host of horsemen, perhaps forty or fifty in all: they were Boltian knights of the Templar Guard. Edgar halted and dismounted, but the rest of the company stayed upon their horses and watched with curious eyes. The clouds were now directly overhead and a heavy rain fell upon them, and they were glad, for it cooled them greatly. As they eagerly awaited the soldiers, some pulled the hoods of their cloaks over their heads to shield them from the rain. It seemed time moved slowly as the riders approached, and the company grew even wearier than before. But the riders arrived half an hour later carrying banners of Bolteras that were soaked and hanging low from the rain.

'What news do you bring from Vallicore, fair Balan?' Edgar asked unaware of their purpose.

'Sire,' said the knight leading the battalion, 'Vallicore requires your haste, for your guests of honor are nearly all assembled. As soon as we were able, we traveled through the Weary Vale knowing your journey to be one of secrecy. And you should know that a man arrived two days ago, one you were not expecting! We also came for reasons of our own to assure ourselves of your safety.'

'Lo! I am safe, but I am with great company. Two score and eight is our count, and we are weary from travel; but I shall not leave my new friends, for they are now men in my army. They shall be great archers in our ranks.'

'Sire, it is urgent. Alastair the White has returned!' Edgar stood agape, and Victor and Hildegard gasped: they were amazed at the news as they did not believe any of Grinshawl's fireside tales when they were away in the Grey Forest. 'He calls for the king.

74

Indeed, he has come to forge an alliance with the Kingdom of Bolteras!'

'This is marvelous news indeed!' Edgar exclaimed with a joyful gleam in his eyes. 'His discerning mind must have seen the demonic work at hand, and thus he has returned to aid his old comrades! But my soul is in anguish as we must fight once more in the same dreary, arid country of Vash'ala lest they destroy and pillage the lands of my people! But still, this is news worthy of celebration! I am elated to be given the opportunity to see the White Mage once again.' He paused and looked back at his companions who now looked gloomy as the rain fell upon their displeased faces. By the look in their eyes, they feared Edgar would abandon them in the vast, open fields of the Weary Vale with no guide.

Discerning their thoughts, he spoke, 'Rest assured, devoted people of Treehouse, that though you are wanderers, you shall not wander alone! I must ride ahead for urgent matters await me, but you will continue this journey with the knights of the Templar Guard! Though they are not my personal guard, they are mighty Boltians indeed! Hearken to me, soldiers of the Templar Guard, for these travelers are friends of mine and kin of Bolteras. Lead these people through the long journey to Vallicore at whatever pace is best for them. Treat them as though you were guarding me.' The soldiers placed their right hands across their chests as an oath of agreement to the king—to them it meant they would stake their lives to protect the travelers.

'Good! So the matter is dealt with. If I am to go, I require Grinshawl, Arthur, Victor, Hildegard, Rolo Longleaf and Pakko son of Elko to travel ahead with me. You are all hereby summoned to the Boltian Council as counselors in this war. Balan, I also require you to return with us, but the rest of your men will stay with these friends of ours.' Victor and Hildegard looked up delightedly to the sound of their names being called upon, and their vitality was renewed.

At the king's call, the men summoned to the Boltian Council said their goodbyes to the rest of their company and galloped away as swiftly as they could to Vallicore. Those left behind looked on sadly as Edgar and his band of counselors sped away into the distance just as the sun began to shine through the clouds once more. The dark billows rolled back suddenly as though a spell had been broken, and the rain ceased. The heat returned upon the land and filled the travelers with greater sadness as they were rather enjoying the coolness of the rain. With the return of the sun and the departure of Lord Edgar, only discomfort remained with them. As he rode away with his counselors, Edgar felt guilt for abandoning them, but eagerness quickly overtook his thoughts as he imagined seeing his friend of old, Alastair the White Mage.

Chapter V

A Great Host Arrives

Edgar and his men rode as swiftly as they could across the colossal plains of the Weary Vale. Victor and Hildegard were glad to ride at full speed, as the slow pace of their journey thus far had brought them no solace or joy. No one spoke a word but only rode with determination and swiftness, pressing their heels to their steeds. It took them two hours even at full flight and without rest before they crossed the remaining length of the vale, for their horses were weary from travel. At the edge of the vale, a small wood stood before them, but they did not pass through it; instead, Edgar turned his steed to the right and led them north along the edge of the wood.

They passed the end of the forest several miles away from the edge of the Weary Vale as the last of the sunlight faded. The moon and stars slowly appeared in the sky as they rode on and a cool breeze fell upon them from the south. A few miles later, they arrived at the eastern side of a stone bridge that led westward over a grassy ravine. It appeared as though a stream once ran under the bridge but was long dried up and overgrown with weeds. As they strode across the bridge, their horses' hooves clanked loudly against the stone; the sound carried through the air and beyond the meadows on the other side of the bridge. As they rode forth, a large hillock rose before them with many mounds following it on the other side. Edgar led them to the top of the knoll, and they peered out into the distance. The travelers marveled as they could see wide and far, perhaps five leagues or more in each direction, but the land was grey in the light of the moon and much was hidden from their sight.

The mighty city of Vallicore stood far away in front of them to the west. It was broad and vast, and they saw it clearly as there were many lights shining all throughout the city. The moon shone bright red and rested above the crest of the mountain at the back of the glorious capital city of Bolteras. Large, white walls stretched for leagues about the borders of Vallicore, for the city was immense and extended for many miles in every direction. Along the walls were many defensive towers with embrasures designed for archers in its work, and they soared high into the air. Behind the walls, buildings and houses filled the large expanse, and many lights shone from within revealing a vague picture of the splendor of the enormous stronghold. Victor imagined there to be thousands of houses and hundreds of shops and a myriad of people living within. He was amazed and filled with wonder as though he were in a delightful dream.

At the back of the city was a tall mountain peak, and the walls were built into its frame. It was not long or wide, but it stood at Vallicore's back as an impenetrable wall of protection resting between the city and the Great Sea. The capital of Bolteras was a strong, defensive city as the peak behind and the walls around provided a great defense; and the Great Sea provided a further advantage if war ever came upon the city, for it ran near to the southern and northwestern borders of Vallicore. 'From the walls, one can see far across the land and spot an approaching army while it is still miles away,' Edgar spoke. 'Since the walls of Vallicore were erected, this mighty city has never been taken. Many wars have been waged on Bolteras throughout its history, and yet not a single army has conquered Vallicore or even stepped foot behind her walls. There were darker ages in the history of Bolteras when this great city failed against the might of its adversaries, but that was before the walls were formed. Now, not even the Draemhas could defeat us unless Abaddon emptied the lands of Dragoth and sent his full force upon us.' He smiled and the others looked once again at the city, and it appeared now more bright and majestic than before. The mere sight of it gave the travelers hope and relief from their worries for a time.

'If it looks this big from afar,' Victor responded after a moment, 'then it must be massive on the inside!' He was filled with excitement and a huge smile was upon his face, for he had never even seen so large a city before and soon he would step foot in it. He felt honored and was filled with great joy. Hildegard too marveled at the city; but his vivacity had faded, and he yearned to return home to his kin in Kesh.

After admiring the city for a time, the party descended the large knoll and crossed over the rolling hummocks down into a glade of soft, even turf. They rode two miles further, and the road passed along the southern edge of a large body of water called *Lake Serenity*, which extended nearly two leagues from one side to the other. The road followed alongside it for more than a mile, and the group admired the reflection of the stars upon the lake's smooth, dormant waters.

78

'In Vallicore, we call this Lake Serenity,' Edgar shouted as they galloped forward. 'Aye, I have spent many a tranquil evening by her waters, as have many others too! The children of Vallicore often travel here in the afternoon to cool themselves during the hot days of late spring and summer. It is also an accessible pool for thirsty beasts.' They galloped onward past the southern edge, only several fathoms from the water, and followed the road as it bent around the edge of the lake and continued northward along its western rim. The path from there ran north for less than a mile before it converged at a crossroad: the road from the south met the main road of Bolteras from the north and then split to the west, forming a single path leading to the gates of the city. Edgar steered his horse along the westward road, and the others followed closely behind.

Less than ten minutes elapsed before they arrived at the gates of Vallicore. As they approached, a horn sounded thunderously loud above them. Each of the travelers looked up in shock and saw a young man, regal in appearance, standing atop the white walls high above. The man held a horn in one hand still pressed to his lips and a lantern in the other hand. Peering down from the parapet at the king and his companions, the man lowered his horn and called out, 'Lo and behold! See here, your excellencies.' As he spoke, he motioned with his arms as if an audience was listening, though there was none to be seen; then he continued, 'a king, though he is, arrives promptly late, never early, especially when gatherings of great lords and counselors have come!' He shouted loudly so they could hear his voice below, and he giggled like a child after speaking. 'Well met, Uncle Edgar!' the man exclaimed after a slight pause.

'Did he say uncle?' Victor questioned. 'Who is this noisy lout?'

'He is a noisy lout indeed,' Edgar replied with a laugh, 'but as foolish as he may be, he is still my beloved nephew. Tristan is his name.' Edgar paused and chuckled again. Then he raise his head and called out, 'Oi! lad! Order the guards to open the gates and come down from the parapets. We have guests!' Tristan jutted out his tongue and pointed it at Edgar with a ridiculous smile on his face and then turned and descended a long stair that ran behind the wall down to the foot of the gate.

The company rode closer to the entrance and heard the obnoxious voice of Tristan shouting, 'Oi! Oi! Open the gates, fools, you fools! The king has come, so get off your bum. Open the gate, for the good king is late! Oh yes indeed, very late he is.' He then let out a strange laugh, a loud *Mwa-ha-ha!* The wooden door swung open slowly, as it required a great amount of strength to push, and the company realized now how large it really was. As the gates opened, they saw ten soldiers—five on each door—pushing with all their might. Grinshawl roared loudly and ran forward with great zeal to aid them, leaving Edgar to guide the giant's horse alongside his own.

They trotted into the city and dismounted, giving their mounts a much needed rest. A couple guards with the emblem of Bolteras etched upon their cuirasses approached them and led their horses to the nearby stables. Edgar turned and held out his arm toward Tristan. At once, Tristan grabbed Edgar's arm near the elbow and Edgar did the same; and they gave one mighty shake of their arms and afterward embraced each other with a hug.

'Good to see you again, dear nephew,' Edgar declared as he embraced Tristan, 'I trust you obeyed me and kept careful watch on the city while I was away.'

'Yes indeed, good uncle. I did much watching, and I found that there are many fine beauties to be found in Vallicore,' he chuckled. 'And, oh, the city is looked after as well. Things became much easier and I had less work to do once that Alastair arrived. He is a respectable man and many listen to him, but he seems to have a nasty habit of ordering others around. However, it has been very orderly in the city thanks to him, not much like when you have your way with it,' he said with a grin. Victor snickered and wondered if Tristan always showed such disrespect. Tristan glanced over at Victor, whose face was now somber and stern, and laughed boisterously. 'Ah, cheer up, laddie! Why the angry look? Does this one ever smile, uncle? When we get back to the king's chambers, we ought to give him a draught of ale; that ought to loosen him up!' Victor's face became more stern, and he grinded his teeth angrily: he was much angrier now than before, for he was greatly irked by Tristan's constant rambling and tomfoolery.

'Tristan, my boy, these are our guests,' Edgar interjected. 'Give them a moment before they see all your unruly conduct. It is time you begin to understand the seriousness of matters if you are to be king one day.'

'King?' Victor muttered softly. 'What an absurd idea! A fool like him has no right to be called a king!'

'Edgar, my old friend,' Arthur interrupted, 'might we make way to your chambers? These old limbs of mine could use a much needed rest. Surely there was no deceit in mind when the naming of the Weary Vale came about!'

'Ah, yes of course, my dear friend; please accept my sincerest apology. Tristan, my boy, go ahead and have my servants prepare a place for our guests to recline at my table. We will eat first, good friends, and then we shall retire for the evening. And Tristan, do not forget to prepare their chambers with warm blankets and soft pillows. Go at once and without a word!'

Tristan did as his uncle requested of him, without a word, though each of the travelers saw the difficulty it posed for him. Off he ran down the main road of Vallicore: it ran west into the heart of the city for more than a mile before steadily rising up a vast slope. The path was made entirely of fine-cut, white stone and continued all the way to the middle of the city and even beyond to Lord Edgar's chambers. After greeting some of the local guards, Edgar led the company after Tristan. They passed many houses and shops along the level road leading to a gently climbing slope, which ran for a furlong or more and then evened out once again at the top of a wide, flattened hill.

All along the pathway to the middle of the city were buildings—houses or shops of some sort—that rose with the hill and spread off in every direction as far as the eye could see; and they seemed to rise and fall as though the city was built upon a great series of enormous hills. Once they reached the top of the slope, the stone path curved and ran in a circle around a large fountain; from there it branched off in all directions throughout the city. Four stone soldiers arrayed with swords and shields were standing at the base of the fountain and were equally distanced from one another. As they drew nearer to the fountain, they perceived the four pathways leading to different portions of the city: one north, one south, one west, and one east, whence they came. But they stayed upon the path leading to the west, and the path ascended steadily once again. The paths to the north and south rose and fell like waves tossed in the sea and continued for miles to their ends at the city's walls; and along the way, many other paths converged with them running both east and west. All along each side of the roads were many more houses and shops as far as the eye could see.

The King's Hall rested at the top of the long incline and was known in Vallicore as *the Silver Vestibule* as it was lined, walls and all, with traces of silver. They were exhausted by the time they arrived at Lord Edgar's bastion, for the path ran two more miles uphill from the glorious fountain to the King's Hall. Edgar's citadel was carved into the stone of the tall mountain peak, named *the King's Crown* by the people of Vallicore, and appeared to be wrought by some ancient masonry, for the style of it was more unique than anything else in all of Bolteras. At its front was a large archway upheld by large, finely crafted pillars of white stone. The pillars rose three fathoms high and in its framework were carved many elegant figures of Dragons. At the top of the archway was an emblem: it looked like two hands clothed in golden-white gauntlets, one atop the other, holding a white orb that shimmered as though it was enchanted with Magic. The images were majestic and beautiful to behold, and Victor and Hildegard stared at them ceaselessly until they passed under the projection of the arch.

Passing beyond the archway, they emerged within a large room with torches hanging from metal rafters on the walls. The room was dimly lit with the glow of fire but enough still for all to see. The room was empty except for a few chairs lined along the walls and a single table with a large bowl atop. The silver-lined walls flickered stunningly, and the exhausted travelers suddenly felt a surge of energy well up within them. They were elated and felt honored to be in the hall of their great king, and they felt a soothing peace for the first time since they left the dreadful Misty Marshes.

In the first room along the western wall, a tunneled stair stood before them and climbed to the second floor above. The bastion climbed many tiers high—ten in all counting the roof of the citadel—with Edgar's bed chamber on the fifth floor. Grinshawl's bedroom was just below the king's on the fourth level. To their left, there were two doors which Edgar informed them led to sleeping chambers; the stairs in front of them also led to many more floors and bedrooms including the king's and his servants' who slept on the higher levels. To their right, there was another passage that led into a large room that contained a series of steps leading up to a dais where the king's throne rested: it was a large chair brilliantly fashioned from ivory with images of Dragons etched into it.

They strode forth through the right passage and stood at the bottom of the short stairway of the dais. To the right, there was a large, round table of wood with many large chairs of white stone encompassing it. Food was prepared for them: there were fruits and vegetables and a large supply of chicken as well. They filled their stomachs and were rather content and at ease. 'This is where we will hold the Boltian Council before long,' Edgar exclaimed. 'But for now, let us retire. I will summon you when the council is ready to commence. I suggest you go and see the city tomorrow and enjoy yourselves until I call upon you. This may be your home for a while, though only time will tell.' Edgar paused noticing the distressed looks on Rolo and Pakko's faces and continued, 'Do not worry of your friends, Master Longleaf and Master Pakko. There are many inns with room enough for your families, and the citizens of Vallicore are kind enough to make room for them. Look now; here comes Tristan to show you to your rooms. Rest well and sleep as long as you like!'

Tristan came running down the passage and halted at the entrance to the king's throne room. 'Oi! Welcome fair country folk! Enough has been said; now let us go to bed. Tomorrow morning, Tristan your friend will give you a tour of the world's greatest city! Oh, right, yes I am Prince Tristan, nephew of Edgar, son of Bristan and Olivia the belated. And who might you all be?' He spoke in his usual, rapid speech. The mere sound of his rambling annoyed Victor. 'It seems I forgot to properly introduce myself earlier, and I have yet to learn of your names. Come now; tarry not!'

Edgar introduced his nephew to his weary companions and briefly spoke of their journey thus far. 'Victor,' returned Tristan, 'that would be the man with the unpleasant face, eh? I assure you it is my utmost pleasure to meet you!' he said in a tone that made Victor feel he was being mocked. 'Uncle, I will take them to their rooms. Go now and get some sleep! I will take care of them.'

'I know you will, lad. But tell me, where is Alastair the White? I wish to speak with him before I sleep.'

'Oh yes, about that; well, he left you see. He has come and gone many times since he arrived, but rest assured, he will return!'

'How long ago did he first arrive?'

'Nigh to one week and three days as my memory serves me. But worry not, good uncle! Burden yourself no more tonight. Go and sleep!'

Edgar rose and withdrew sleepily, lurching as he strode away, and Grinshawl followed. The two men eagerly found their way to their beds and swiftly fell to sleep. Tristan excitedly led the remaining group back to the front room and continued straight through the right door on the southern side of the room: it led to a series of bedrooms and other various rooms. The left doorway on the southern wall led to more chambers, but they were occupied by the king's royal guard and their families. As they walked through the door, Tristan handed them each a lantern which he had removed from some of the rafters on the wall. They turned right into a hall past the door and saw before them many more doorways along the left side of the corridor. Tristan informed them that the rooms were left uninhabited for Edgar's guests and also for ambassadors from other lands.

As he led them further down the hallway, they passed at least ten rooms on their left before they came to a stairway that descended to another chamber below. At the foot of the stair they arrived at small cellar with two doors: the one on the northern side of the chamber led to a massive storage room with stockpiles of food. The other door led south to another series of quarters, some on each side of the passageway. Tristan led them down the hallway and into the third room on the right.

'Victor and Hildegard will be staying here tonight. Goodnight friends!' Victor and Hildegard entered the room, and Tristan slammed the door behind them. The rest of the company then proceeded down the hallway and stopped two doors down on the left. 'Here we go, Arthur old chap! You will sleep alone, but fear not! the rats will keep you company. Sleep well!' And off he went again past a few more doors and led Rolo and Pakko through a door at the end of the passage. 'Last, and quite possibly the least, is the room of Sir Rolo and Master Pakko,' he said sarcastically. 'I jest, my friends. If my uncle likes you, then I suppose I have some reason to. I wish you pleasant dreams!' With that, he pulled the door to a close behind him and scurried off to his own bedroom on the fourth tier beside Grinshawl's room.

They awoke the next morning and were alarmed by the amount of light on their faces. The night before, they were much too tired to realize the windows in their rooms. As they looked out, it seemed as though their lodgings were impressively built into the side of the mountain within the basement of the Silver Vestibule, and they had a fine view of Vallicore. There were two windows in Victor and Hildegard's room, and they quickly rose from their beds and thrust their heads outside to breathe in the warm city air.

The city was noisy and chaotic as a great host of people were going to and fro carry goods in their arms or transporting them by carts. By the look of it, every trade and practice of commerce was available within the city walls as though Vallicore was a country of its own. Even with all the ruckus, there was a strange peace about the city that could only be explained by one thing: the presence of evil was far from the lands of Bolteras at the present time. In fact, they felt a strange sense of protection around the city, like a life force keeping watch over the people.

After glancing about for several minutes, the two boys turned to leave the room, and as they did, Tristan kicked open the door with a loud thud. 'Hullo chaps! I traveled all this way to wake you bums up, but awake you are already! I see you have taken to the view. This is a beautiful city, is it not?' Victor and Hildegard nodded; they carefully watched Tristan but something was rather different about him. They noticed that he was much calmer and more courteous than before.

'Come, good friends! There is much for you to see; oh yes, much, much, much to see indeed!' He ran out of the room, and the boys changed their clothes. Tristan returned a moment later and said, 'Well? Are you coming? Follow me! We do not have all day.' Though Victor and Hildegard could not see it, Tristan was happy to have met them. He never had many friends, so he was filled with joy to be around people near to his age who did not find him completely repulsive.

'How old are you lads?'

'Fifteen for the both of us,' Hildegard replied with a yawn.

'Fifteen you say? Aye, I suppose you do look fifteen. You are just a few years younger than I am. I am eighteen a month from today on the thirtieth of April. When were you born?' He began to walk out of the room, and the two boys followed.

'My birthday is September the twenty-first,' said Victor.

'And mine is November the third,' replied Hildegard.

'Good, good. Well, as you know, the high council meeting will be held before long. It will be quite a sight for the two of you considering you will be in the presence of the king and many great lords, such a host that your eyes have never seen! Ah yes, I am truly excited! For many years I have longed to go to war.' He paused for a moment and appeared now troubled. 'I suppose I wish to prove my worth is all,' he said with a faint grin. He then turned and ran down the hall and out of sight. Victor and Hildegard walked out of the passage and made their way back to the first room of the King's Hall; Tristan was there waiting and panting. After catching his breath, he led them up the staircase to the second tier. At the top of the stair, they continued forward to a door, and Tristan violently flung it open. Beyond the doors was a large room with many wooden tables and chairs, and there was a great host of people feasting upon a delectable breakfast. At once, Tristan abandoned the two boys for a moment and sat at a table amongst a group of soldiers. Victor and Hildegard looked at each other doubtfully and felt rather uncomfortable.

The room was filled with loud chatter. Many servants ran this way and that preparing a variety of breakfast foods for the tenants of the Silver Vestibule: there were fruits and vegetables, meats and eggs and buttered toast and biscuits. Victor was overwhelmed and considered following after Tristan, but then he saw Arthur reclining at a table with Rolo and Pakko and feasting upon a rather delicious looking meal consisting of eggs and bacon and buttered biscuits. Hildegard shot forth at once with alacrity and Victor followed. After conversing with the soldiers for a minute, Tristan approached their table with a plate full of food and sat with them.

'Victor, my boy,' Arthur called, 'sit down and eat! The two of you took your time getting here this morning.'

Victor smiled and responded, 'Did you see the view, Uncle Arthur? It was simply magnificent! My eyes have never seen such a splendid place!'

'Aye, laddie, I saw it,' he laughed. 'But I am more concerned with what I do not see, and that brings me great troubles.' He paused with downcast eyes and continued, 'They have not a single tater or pea in this whole place! What a terrible thing to discover!'

Victor chuckled and began to eat. Midway through his meal, he turned to Arthur and said, 'Will you go with me to see the city today, uncle? I want to explore the whole place!'

Arthur smiled and patted Victor on the shoulder. 'Calm down my boy and get your fill of breakfast. I will not be seeing anything but my bed and a few draughts of Mayle's Ale, if this dreadfully magnificent city has it to offer. I am weary from the journey and require rest if I am to be present at the Boltian Council.' Victor appeared now downcast and disappointed. 'But I think you ought to go and see it all, my boy. Go with Hildegard and Tristan if he is willing.' Tristan's face lit up with joy when he heard Arthur's words. 'Aye, I will even give you a pouch of silver coins; perhaps you can buy yourself a fine blade or shield.' Arthur removed a sac from his leather belt and held it up for Victor to see. 'There are one hundred thirty coins in here, lad. This is my life's savings, so spend it wisely!'

Victor sat upright and a smile stretched across his face. Arthur laid the pouch of coins upon the table and Victor quickly devoured his meal. He had hardly chewed his food before he grabbed the pouch and ran off with Hildegard and Tristan at his tail.

* * *

In the city, Tristan showed them a great variety of shops: some were filled with weapons of the finest make, others with armor, others with trinkets of various kinds, and still others were filled with seemingly magical items, but the boys questioned the supposed magical properties the charms were said to have. They decided after some debate to begin searching for new weapons. At that time, they were at the southern rim of the city, but Tristan led them north to an area full of fine weapon shops.

After an hour of searching, they came up an armory called *Vanot's Finest Craft.* Inside, Victor found a bow finely crafted from white wood and desired to buy it at once. There were no designs crafted into making of the bow, but it was smooth and extremely sturdy, capable of shooting an arrow with great speed and strength. The shopkeeper, Vanot Helmsworth, saw Victor eyeing the bow and approached him. 'Your eyes are good, my boy,' he said from his counter. 'That there is the finest bow I own. It would take years for a bow of that make to break; yes indeed, it is the finest bow I have ever made, but there have been none yet who were wise enough to buy it. All my customers ignore it since there are no carvings or elegance in its work. Thus far, they all come buying bows with intricate designs, probably for the looks of it more than the quality of the bow. But this is the greatest bow I have ever made, that it is.'

'How much will it cost to purchase?' Victor asked.

'Two hundred silver coins, or twenty gold ones. I will not accept bronze here. I do accept gems and diamonds, but few ever posses those and when they do, they never trade them.'

'Alas!' Victor cried out in disappointment, 'I do not have enough! My uncle only gave me one hundred thirty silver coins.'

There was a long pause. Vanot stood there silently for a moment glaring at Victor as if he was trying to read his mind. After a moment, he chuckled and placed his hands on his head, pulling at his hair. 'My boy, you have gone and done it! Not only were you wise enough to desire my strongest bow, but your heart is good! I have a gift, you see, of discerning the good from the rotten! But rotten you

87

are not. It would be an honor to have you wield my bow, if you promise to treat it kindly.'

Victor replied, 'I will, kind sir! I give you my word!'

'Aye, and I believe it, lad. I will sell it to you for the low price of one hundred and thirty silver coins. You seem to be a fine man, so I will toss in a nice sword for you too!'

Victor stared at him with a perplexed expression on his face. 'Sir, I do not understand. Why are you so generous to me?'

'Let us just say I am in a good mood today. Besides, war is at our doorstep, you know, so there is no need to be greedy! Come now, give me the money and go before I change my mind.' Victor handed the bag of coins to Vanot and received the bow and a fine sword with it; and he was filled with more happiness than he ever had in his whole life. At once, he and Tristan ran outside before the old man could change his mind, but Hildegard remained inside and looked about the shop. After some consideration, he purchased for himself a fine spear with a bag of coins he brought from home. The wooden shaft of the spear was light brown with smooth, white snakes carved into the wood as if they were slithering up the length of the spear. The tip of the javelin was made of bright, flawless steel, and it was jagged. Its appearance was terrifying, and Hildegard was proud to wield it.

After Hildegard rejoined his companions, they made way to the main gate where they first met Tristan. It was Tristan's favorite place to visit, for he loved to stand atop the parapets and keep watch on the land: it made him feel as though he was a great king keeping watch over his land and people. As they left the shop and turned onto the road back towards the middle of the city, Victor collided with a young woman, and both fell down with a crash; and Victor dropped his new weapons as he smacked the ground. Quickly he leapt to his feet and aided the young girl to hers. As he looked into her eyes, he observed that she was perhaps his age or slightly older.

'Begging your pardon, milady, I did not see you there.'

'Are you in the habit of bumping into women wherever you go?' she replied as she brushed the dirt from her dress. Victor stared at her blankly. 'But you were kind enough to pick me up, so I will forgive your transgression.'

Victor stared at her for a moment and noticed that she was exceedingly beautiful: she had bright blue eyes and long brown hair that was braided quite elegantly. 'A-again, I sincerely a-apologize.'

The girl took notice of his nervous response and smiled favorably. 'You are a polite one, I see. Tell me, good sir, what is your name?'

'I-it is Victor,' he said with an anxious gulp.

'And where are you from? This may be a large city full of many people, but you seem different from the city folk.'

'Yes, I am, uh, from a village in the east called K-Kesh.'

'Kesh you say? Well I see the rumors are false then,' she said with a large smile on her face.

'What rumors?' Victor replied sharply.

'Oh, just the ones my father tells me. He often says, "Those Keshians are an awful folk. They are outlandish and quite rude!"' She spoke in a deep voice imitating her father's, and Victor could only smile in response. 'But I find it humorous as my father has never been to Kesh. All sorts of people speak ill of your village, but I reckon they merely wish to know your people better.'

'Well I am not outlandish or rude!' Victor retorted.

'Indeed you are not,' the girl replied again with a smile on her face. 'And I can see that the other rumors are false as well.' With that, she turned and began to stride gracefully down the road leading north.

'What other rumors?' Victor called, but the girl did not answer. 'What are the rumors you have been told? And what is your name?' he shouted with one last desperate cry. He began to follow after her, and even took a few steps forward, but he relented, feeling suddenly nervous and afraid. He imagined chasing her down and spending the rest of the day with her, but his feet would not carry him forward. He sighed and lowered his head in disappointment.

From a distance, the girl turned around and placed her hands about her mouth and shouted, 'My name is Naomi, but my friends call me Grace!' Victor raised his head curiously and smiled. 'And I have been told that all Keshians are ugly folk, but that is certainly not true either!' She giggled and darted away. Victor blushed and stared as she disappeared into the distance.

He turned to his friends and said, 'Was that a goddess I saw just now?'

'My, my, I see you do know how to joke!' Tristan replied cheerfully.

'No, I was quite serious,' Victor answered back, and Tristan frowned.

89

'Do you think she is pretty, Victor?' Hildegard questioned playfully.

'Aye, she is the most beautiful creature I have ever laid eyes upon.'

'Eh,' Tristan wheezed, 'you are either exceptionally droll or extremely stupid. I tell you, I have seen much prettier!' At that, Tristan laughed and then darted away up the road leading north towards the fountain. Victor scoffed and hollered angrily at Tristan and then quickly picked up his weapons to pursue the unpleasant cad. All the while, Hildegard shook his head and snickered at their vivaciousness before he too followed in pursuit. Victor and Hildegard met Tristan at the foot of the fountain where he sat smiling: it was a queer sort of smile as though he was trying to appear stupid to them.

'Victor is in love, I do say!' he said as he mockingly blew a kiss in Victor's direction. 'Oi, now!' he snapped as Victor charged forth, 'I only jest!' Victor halted abruptly in front of the snide nephew of the king and smiled. 'Can you forgive me, lad?'

'Aye, I can indeed,' Victor answered with an even larger smile. He then pushed Tristan, and the boy fell backward into the fountain.

'Oi! What was that for?' Tristan called as he pulled himself out of the water. 'That was a mighty rude thing to do just now!'

'My uncle always taught me to be kind to women, so I will hear no more vile insults out of you. But I suppose we are even then, yes?'

Tristan smiled and laughed. 'You are a good friend, Victor! I think we shall get along nicely! You are the bad-tempered one, and I am the entertaining one, you see. We are the perfect pair.' He looked beyond and saw Hildegard, who looked gloomy and isolated. 'And where would we be without good Hildegard, the quiet one? In every group of friends, there needs to be the calm and quiet one who is more a man of action than of words.' Hildegard smiled, and the three went at last to the gates of Vallicore.

As they stood atop the parapets, they played around with their new weapons. Tristan borrowed Victor's sword to play with, and they acted as though they were fighting Draemhas. They imagined vast armies down in the plains below and climbing atop the parapets, and they slew the lot of them. The guards below watched them as they pretended and found great enjoyment in observing the creativeness of the three. After an hour of play, Tristan offered to

90

teach them swordplay to which Victor and Hildegard responded with glee. For more than an hour, they learned the art of swordsmanship, but as they practiced, two horse riders approached in the distance from the northeast bearing with them banners on tall, wooden poles. The three boys gazed on trying to make out the marks on the banners but the riders were too far away. Tristan disappeared for a time and reappeared with a quiver full of arrows for Victor's bow. They each wielded a weapon and patiently waited for the riders to draw near, as they were still engaged in their war fantasy and hoped to fight a real battle; and so they did not inform the guards below of the approaching riders.

It was half an hour or more before the horsemen arrived at the foot of the gate. They looked hard at their flags and saw that the riders bore banners from distant lands. The one on the left wielded a spear and carried a grey flag with a brown horse with a white-tipped nose on it; it was the flag of Alterash. He wore leather armor except for a shirt of chainmail under his leather cuirass. The rider on the right bore the flag of Vash'ala with the image of snakes and the sun; a sword was sheathed at his side, and he was arrayed in crimson panoply.

Tristan peered down at them and said, 'What business does a traitor from Vash'ala have with an Alterashian; and furthermore, what business do you have with Bolteras? These days may be strange and full of evil, but this is the oddest sight I have ever seen! Have not Vash'ala and Alterash been at odds for over a century?'

The Alterashian spoke, 'Aye, it may be so, but the days are changing. I am Gibraltar from Alterash. The two of us met upon the road to Vallicore bearing ill tidings. At first we fought, not with fists but with words, until we realized our motives were the same. No longer am I from Alterash, at least while evil rules my land.'

'And no longer am I from Vash'ala,' the other declared. 'I am Delitas, former warrior of Vash'ala. We have great tidings to bring to the King of Bolteras. Where is Edgar the brave?'

'He is away in his castle resting before the Boltian Council that will likely take place tomorrow morning. But tell me; are we not at war with Vash'ala? We have heard rumors telling of great evils arising within your borders.'

'That is why the news we bring is vital,' Delitas returned losing his patience. 'Armies are stirring in the north and war draws nigh!'

Tristan sat pondering their words. Victor held his bow at his side with an arrow loosely fitted to the string, his hands trembling. Hildegard held his spear firmly by his side, the shaft pressed against the stone of the parapets. Finally, Tristan stirred and ran down the staircase to the gate. 'Oi, you guards! Open the gates! Come now, we do not have all day. Slow as turtles you are! Ah, never mind you, I will do it myself.'

Tristan went to remove the wooden plank that barred the door shut, but he was not able to lift it. He stood there embarrassed before the guards with his head lowered; then, he suddenly erected himself as tall as he could and said, 'The heir of Bolteras has no need to open gates himself! Guards, come now and open these gates for your crowned prince!' Victor and Hildegard chuckled at Tristan's scheme to appear strong and regal.

'Too weak to open the gates I see!' Victor shouted.

'Quiet you! I would love to see you have a try at it,' Tristan retorted. The guards swung the doors open, and the riders marched in. 'Come now; leave the horses here for the guards to take to the stables.' The guards looked warily at the foreign men but allowed them passage by Tristan's command. Without delay, Tristan and the other two boys quickly led the two strangers to the entrance of the Silver Vestibule. Some of the gatekeepers became worried and followed them with swords drawn.

'Uncle Edgar,' the prince called loudly from outside, 'two guests have come to see the king!' He then turned and whispered to the boys, 'I hope he is able to stand. When there is food and drink about, the king becomes fat and jolly!' The guards with them began to laugh suddenly. Turning again to the entrance of the King's Hall he yelled, 'Come now, ye fat and gay; come and hear what these men have to say! Oi, I say! Uncle Edgar! I have seen a snail emerge from your great hall. In your old age, has a snail become swifter than you?' His company laughed even louder; and though he thought he was the object of their amusement, they were not laughing at his dimwitted remarks.

'Hullo, lad,' Edgar said from a bench to their left. Tristan jumped and turned to his left with bright redness in his cheeks, for he had not even noticed Edgar's presence. 'Are you having a merry time entertaining our guests?'

Tristan simply lowered his head shamefully and said, 'Forgive me, Sire.'

'Never mind that; come in my friends. It is odd during these days to welcome outsiders as guests, but we will make the proper arrangements.' Edgar led the group into the Silver Vestibule and turned right into his throne room where the council was to be held. Edgar took his seat on his throne atop the dais and bid his guests and company to sit at the round table, which was large enough to seat thirty people. Next to Edgar's throne on the right was a large chair: it was Grinshawl's seat, though the giant had not yet arrived.

'Speak good travelers; tell me your news, for I am sure you did not come simply to explore the great city of Vallicore.'

'Sire, the two of us met along our road here. We are sworn rivals by bloodline, but we agreed to overlook our heritage for a greater good. I am Delitas of Vash'ala and this here is Gibraltar of Alterash.'

'Ah, good fellows, allow me to interrupt your speech for a moment. Lo! good counselors have arrived outside my bastion,' Edgar said peering out the window at the back of the room. All of the men in the room turned to look out the window and saw a small company of men, four in all. 'Let us sound Deephorn, the beloved horn of Vallicore and call forth the great counselors. I had originally planned to hold the council tomorrow, but it seems the plans of Men are frail. Behold! a great host now assembles at my doorstep; though small in numbers, they are great men of honor. With the arrival of a Vash'alan and an Alterashian, it seems tomorrow is too long to wait. Tristan, sound the horn at once! The Boltian Council is about to begin!'

Tristan sped off obediently. He ascended the staircase in the first room and rose past the ninth tier to the roof of the Silver Vestibule, which was a flat path of stone jutting out from the mountain. He inhaled and breathed as hard as he could into the great horn that rested there on a pedestal: its sound was heard all about Vallicore and even in the plains below. Tristan sounded the horn only once to call forth the Boltian Council. If he had blown a second time, he would have indicated an approaching army, calling all the soldiers to arms. After fulfilling his duties, the prince quickly returned to the council room.

All who had gathered thus far stood and awaited the entry of the company of great lords. A moment later, Grinshawl rushed in with Arthur following slowly behind. Behind them were Rolo and Pakko, and they were now dressed in fine clothes instead of their former rags. Victor and Hildegard stared at the doorway eagerly and wondered who the other counselors might be. Suddenly, three men entered wearing chainmail and fine tunics with the mark of Bolteras imprinted on them. They wore also cloaks of dark blue and had the appearance of high ranking warriors. Victor figured they were leaders in the army or something of that sort.

Next, a man walked in alone wearing a green cloak, and the hood was pulled over his head so his face could not be seen. He stepped forth into the assembly hall and removed his cloak and let his brown locks loll on his shoulders. He carried with him a black longbow with shimmering runes etched into it. The next man to enter was a short, old man whose back was hunched, and he had a long, crooked nose. He had also white, bushy brows and a long, white beard. On his head rested a brown, brimmed cap. Following the old man were two men who appeared to be knights, and they were large in stature. They wore sturdy panoplies and carried their helms under their arms. Attached to their pauldrons were red capes that ran down to the floor.

The last man to enter was a willowy, old man wearing a long, white robe with a tall, pointy hat of white upon his brow. The whole of him was white from his hair to his skin and from his hat to his boots; and he even carried with him a long, white staff. Rooted in the top of the staff was a pale crystal with a faint white light shimmering within. His very body seemed to be surrounded by a faint white glow, like an aura protecting him. Though he looked old, he stood erect and appeared rather vivacious.

And so, all the members of the Boltian Council had assembled quickly, as though they were already waiting just outside the king's throne room. In all, the entire host consisted of eighteen men, though others were expected. Edgar charged the counselors to take their places at the table. He then rose from his throne and sat amongst them, forsaking his high seat to be in a more lowly position near to his advisors; and the Boltian Council began.

Chapter VI

The Boltian Council

Edgar stared at his counselors for a moment and then rose from his seat. 'Fewer men have come than I wished to see. This is grave news, as they must have known for what ill fate I have called them or have otherwise been swept up in some conflict of their own. Let us hope that the Dark Lord has not sent his minions upon our brethren. Yet if they are safe, then I am discouraged in their absence, for they should have arrived two days ago.' Edgar returned to his seat with a despondent look on his face.

'Forgive me for speaking out of turn,' Delitas interrupted, 'but why does the King of Bolteras wish to recline at a simple table instead of sitting upon his high throne?'

'Bah! I insist you speak in turn as you are a foreigner to this land,' Grinshawl retorted angrily. 'Edgar is not a king of pride or conceit but one of humility. He only sits upon his throne when there is no more room left at his table, and he has always been that kind of king.'

'Begging your pardon, sir, I meant no jest or insult to you or the king! Rather, I am quite amazed and fascinated. You see, as I have always known, a king exalts himself upon his throne and never joins the lesser folk at a mere table. I have always known our king to exalt himself as a god.'

'I am no god, Delitas of Vash'ala,' Edgar replied, 'No indeed, it is my will to be a servant rather than a god, and there exists only one worthy of that title. Furthermore, it is not to my liking to sit upon my dais looking down on my counselors. Each of you deserves my utmost respect for your vast wisdom and sound advice.'

'Lawks! If you speak as an honest man, then you are a magnificent king! I wish only that Alterash had such a man to sit upon her throne!' Gibraltar exclaimed enthusiastically. 'Might I speak first, Your Majesty? Will the counselors excuse my interruption and hear my tale?' Edgar smiled and nodded. 'Then I shall begin, but I lament the news that I must tell. My name is Gibraltar, son of Wallace of Alterash. Our king, Bormann son of the late King Aramon,' he paused noticing the alarmed expression on

Edgar's face, 'Alas! the great king who once aided Bolteras in their battle against the Vash'alans twenty years ago has fallen to a strange disease!'

'Tell me, Gibraltar,' Edgar interrupted solemnly, 'what kind of disease claimed his life?'

'Your Highness, it was a mysterious and hidden disease with no outward signs, so it was years before anyone noticed. But one day, the king woke up coughing blood from his mouth. The amount of blood was little at first. But as the years went on, the blood increased until one day he died while coughing violently in his bed. I knew it at once to be some sort of hex from the Dark Lord.'

Gibraltar halted, and Edgar appeared deeply troubled. After a moment, Edgar replied, 'That is the same disease that took from me my wife and my unborn child.' Tears filled his eyes, but he wiped them away and kept his face stern. 'Now, what more do you have to say?' Grinshawl affectionately placed his giant hand upon Edgar's shoulder, but Edgar remained still.

'As I was saying, Bormann has become the new King of Alterash, and he is a nasty man. For years, we lived under his oppression as nothing more than slaves. After the death of his father, he found great pleasure in filling his stomach, and he became very fat. As he grew in size, he began to create absurd laws: he banned the growth of vegetables and the harvesting of fruits, and before long, he forbade all of Alterash from being involved in the war against the Draemhas in the Eastern Lands. This was the first thing that troubled me. And upon the passing of that law, many of my comrades fled eastward and abandoned our people. I thought at first that he was simply grieving the loss of his father, but it became much more than that. I soon discovered that great evils were at work in Alterash. We knew that Vash'ala was mustering their forces for war against Bolteras but later discovered that they allied themselves with the Draemhas! I took my concern to the king, and that fat fool told me to ignore it! He said we would never again be involved in war—I think the Enemy intended for him to become passive and callous. Furthermore, he was convinced that his father was plagued only after returning from the battle with Vash'ala twenty years ago, so he forbade any of our people to go there.

'Bormann feared disease and the power of the Draemhas, so he withdrew his support in the war against the forces of Darkness, the selfish fool! After a few more years, he became so fat that he could not even move from his bed without the help of many slaves.

Then, he issued a decree that any outsider was to be killed before they could come within a stone's throw from any of our fortresses. Years later and just before I deserted my country, he ordered that all become fat with food and enjoy what he called "the tranquility of solitude;" the saddest part of my story is that my brethren did as he said! It was as though his words had some magical power over them, an evil influence. I saw the full force of the Dark Lord's hand at work. Our king's words were like evil curses straight from the mouth of Abaddon, but for some reason beyond me, I was protected.

'A year before I decided to leave, King Bormann ordered all the people of Alterash to move to the capital city of Kainor; all who refused were to be killed and left to be eaten by the wild birds and beasts of our land. At this news, there were many who surrendered and now abide in Kainor. There were others who took up horses for themselves and departed to the Eastern Lands to be with the rest of our kin who departed long before. Others tried to flee, but they were too slow, for they took their families and a large supply of possessions along with them. At this time, strange wolves with a poisonous bite appeared in our lands: we call them *Hellhounds*. They obeyed the will of Bormann and hunted down my kinsmen. So now there are few who are left in all the lands of Alterash, and they reside now in Kainor. After the slaughter of my kin, the king, by some foreign evil, destroyed part of the great bridge that crosses over Raumas Mílnk. That was the only passage other than the Great Sea that could carry Men from the Western Lands to the Eastern Lands.

'We have been cut off from traveling east, and I fear I will never see my fellow Alterashians again. And to make matters worse, the rumors have been confirmed that the powerful sea creature known as *Leviathan*, aye, the same one of ancient lore, has arisen from the depths of the Great Sea! And none now dare to venture across her seas. And alas! it has been heard that many great sea serpents, though smaller than the ones of the Great Sea, now roam even the waters of Raumas Mílnk! My heart is in anguish for the road to my kin was cut off from me. Having no peace or direction, I fled from Kainor and put my sole hope in the mighty land of Bolteras, our allies of old. Traveling as secretively as I could through the woods along our borders, I brought with me only the banner of Alterash, my spear and armor, and two horses, one as tribute to Lord Edgar. This is my tale in brief. And I sit here now amongst you seeking aid in my country's time of need. This is the purpose I have come, Edgar King of Bolteras. What say you?'

'You have revealed many secrets. I must reflect on your words for a time.' The council room was silent, and all dwelt on the words of Gibraltar. After some time, Edgar spoke, 'Will there be no aid from Alterash then?'

'There will be none, Your Highness.'

Edgar hung his head despondently. 'This is ill news indeed. I know not what to say.'

'I suggest we let the Vash'alan speak,' Grinshawl added. 'Perhaps we can discuss this further after he has spoken.' Edgar nodded and motioned for Delitas to speak.

'Well then, I am Delitas of Vash'ala. I was abandoned as an infant and was raised as one of the king's servants. I appreciated it, however, for I was always well fed, though the work was never easy. But once I was twenty years of age, the king put me into his army, and I was trained harshly for years. But I suppose these are things you need not know. Let me tell you of our country's descent into Darkness. Fifteen years ago, four people—two men and two women, husbands and their wives—came to Vash'ala to aid us in our fight against disease and to help stop the spread of famine and drought. I was seventeen at the time. These people were extremely powerful Alchemists.' Victor and Hildegard raised their heads and their eyes gleamed at Delitas' words, believing them to be about their parents. 'And indeed they helped us greatly! For a few years, their abilities transformed our country, and we grew vegetables and fruit trees for the first time in ages!

'Moreover, they had the power to cure us of our diseases and claimed to come in the name of Vaaspar with the power of Elúvías. They explained that each one of them could heal only one person every day and said something about an inward energy. I understood better once they mentioned Magic and how they used it for healing, but I learned that the healing required a large amount of magical power. Though few of us understood at that time, our hearts were filled with hope and joy, even knowing it would be a long process to recovery. And even King Marxas was thrilled or so it seemed. There was a time when Marxas was a good king by my standards. After the war twenty years ago, Marxas succeeded Ramox, the cruelest ruler in Vash'alan history, and began to change our country for the good. I was always away during the days of the Alchemists, training and running errands for the king. Before long, about eight years ago I believe, Marxas appeared suddenly—as it was to us in his army—to be full of evil intent, and his heart was overcome by Darkness. Then, we were reminded of the cruelty of Ramox. And I knew something evil had crept within our midst.

'After a time, some evil stirred in the ancient prisons of Gorgonash. These prisons, if you are unaware, run deep into the earth and stretch from Osceroth, the capital city of Vash'ala, to the far borders in the south near the Sage's Mountain. Other passages run eastward towards Alterash while others still run northward towards the Great Sea. I was sent regularly to deliver reports to the prison guards. One day, I went to the southernmost passages of Gorgonash and many of the prisons were emptied. I questioned the guards, but all they said was, "It is of no concern to a servant of the king." So I returned to Osceroth and questioned Marxas, but he simply smiled and laughed: it was an awful shriek of a laugh, a coldblooded shrill. I knew then that evils were spreading all throughout our borders, but I seemed alone, unaware of it all. I went all about the land seeking answers from the people, but I was shamed and ridiculed. I felt as though all my brethren had bended their wills to Abaddon, and I was the only one disturbed by it. For fear of my life, I pretended to be like-minded to them, for the presence of evil grew quickly. And I knew without a doubt I might be killed for even lesser things, as I saw many slain before my eyes, and so I lived as they did. But still they hated me. No harm came to me, and I knew that I, like the Alterashian, was protected, but as to why I do not know. But I feel the rest of the land was aware and shunned me for it.

'As my last resort, I sought out the Boltian Alchemists who had come to our aid, but I was unable to find them. I looked all about, desperately, for any sign of them, for I began to believe in the power of Elúvías. For months I looked and asked about, but I discovered nothing of their location. It was as though I was blinded to the world around me. I was told lies wherever I went. Then the king sent word to all the corners of Vash'ala stating that the Boltian Alchemists were dead!' Victor and Hildegard jumped from their seats.

'They are dead?' Edgar asked solemnly. 'Hear you me: these two boys, Victor and Hildegard, are the children of those Alchemists. Tell us plainly what has become of them.'

'Well, my lord, I know little of the truth, but I believe it all to be a lie. I reckon they live on as servants to the king.'

'Explain your words,' Edgar responded. 'Do not give us false hope!'

Delitas sighed. 'Perhaps a month or two after the announcement of their deaths, King Marxas made a sudden declaration before the great city of Osceroth. He said to the crowds, "This day I have ascended with great power and have surpassed human limitations! I have slain the sun god and have obtained his powers; and great wonders beyond the understanding of Men have been revealed to me. Behold!" Suddenly, great bursts of black flames shot forth from his hands! It was a sight that I have never seen or even heard of before. He continued, "No longer will you refer to me as Marxas King of Vash'ala but rather Sol'Czar, the Sun King!" With those words, the entire city bowed before him and worshipped him. I was away at the bottom of the great stair of Osceroth near to the gate watching, but I did not bow.

'He then called out, and I saw four figures appear clothed in dark robes with the hoods pulled over their heads. He introduced them to the crowd as *the Harbingers of Good Fortune* but later renamed them his *Acolytes of Darkness*. I was astonished to see my kin bow before such unconcealed evil! Many days passed, and then the king introduced a more horrible evil. He brought forth from the shadows of his throne room one of the Draemhas; his name was *Korvash*. Marxas affirmed the rumors that Draemhas were abiding in Vash'ala, and he spoke highly of them as one would of friends or family. My people cheered for the demons of Dragoth! They cheered!' Delitas sneered and then paused for a moment. 'I knew at that moment that all the good I once saw in Marxas was a lie. And I suspected that the Acolytes of Darkness were truly the Alchemists of Bolteras, as their number was four.

'I took flight with no intention of ever returning to Vash'ala. My homeland had become a country of brazen wickedness. I am ashamed of my people and also of King Marxas. It seems as though there is no more hope for my people. That is why I fled Vash'ala and descended into the valley at the foot of the Sage's Mountain; and it was there that my eyes caught sight of a band of Draemhas. I hid quickly and quietly behind a nearby stone and listened to them speak. They spoke mostly in a tongue I was unable to comprehend, but suddenly they spoke in the tongue of Men. Briefly I heard them discussing an approaching war against Bolteras. They scoffed at the alliance between Vash'ala and the Draemhas and spoke of the destruction of my people.

'I heard them say many times something about a secret way to Vash'ala and of the impressive skills of the Boltian Alchemists.

100

They spoke also of Alterash as being a *tamed country*. "One year," one of them said, "one year before the war on Bolteras will commence; and with the conquering of the Western Lands, we will overcome the wretched Men of the East and all their might!" I was alarmed and tried to slip away, but I was discovered.

'There were ten in all, each enormous in height. Their bodies were black and shadowy like a wraith, and they were fearsome to look at. They charged at me, their fangs dripping with large drops of saliva and blood. In their hands were long, notched blades which they swung at me, but a man wearing a strange cloak appeared suddenly like a flash of light and protected me. He was hooded and carried a magical sword that shone a cool, blue color when he swung it. In an instant, all the Draemhas were slain, and the hooded man was gone before I was able to speak. Afraid he might return, I fled for my life, believing the man to be an enemy who merely spared me for the time. I ran south through the pass between the Sage's Mountain and the Lonely Forest; and I was alarmed that I passed through with no harm done to me. When I came to the great plains of Bolteras, I saw away to the east a rider who led beside him an unladen horse. He halted before me, and I was surprised to find him bearing the mark of Alterash. We exchanged angry words for a time before coming to our senses. He lent me his horse once we established that our goals were the same, and we sped away as quickly as we could to the great city of Vallicore. It was luck, I think, that led us to meet when we did. That is all to my tale.'

'There is no such thing as luck,' Edgar replied, 'rather truth simply has a way of expressing itself at times without an explanation. Nothing is fortuitous; rather, there is a plan for everything. The only thing to ask is what that plan may be. Forgive my ramblings! I thank you both for your tales and for providing clarity in the happenings of the world outside our borders. Now then, I would like to hear the reports that Hauffa, Paladin and Ragnok bring.' At that time, the three soldiers in panoply rose from their seats.

'Sire,' Paladin stood and spoke. He was a tall man with flowing, golden hair. 'For those who do not know us, I am Paladin from Cayrngras, mightiest of the strongholds in Bolteras, besides the glorious city of Vallicore, of course. Beside me here on my right is Hauffa who comes from the fortress Bram.' There to his right stood a tall man: he had black hair and a pipe in his mouth that he never smoked. 'And on my left is Ragnok from the fortress Eordil.' He pointed to the other man beside him who also had black hair, but he was much larger in size than the other two. He was rather burly and had a bushy beard upon his face.

'We are the three captains of Edgar's army. It is a pleasure to meet you all.' The rest of the company introduced themselves formerly, exchanging names and shaking hands, for the first time since the meeting began. In their haste, they had forgotten to properly introduce themselves. 'Well now, I should think this to have been more appropriate at the beginning of the meeting! Edgar, my liege, your manners have faded as of late,' he laughed. The rest of the men smiled at Edgar, who was now red in the face. Feeling embarrassed, he covered his face and laughed at his absentmindedness.

'I would that I had some rousing tale of bravery and might, but alas! I have meager yet still ill-fated news. Bory and Grob from Balas have refused to go to war, and they simply encouraged their citizens to peacefully enjoy the last of their days. Hombag of Poleden also withdrew his support along with Teles of Carg and Enren of Pilias. As agreed, we have withheld the happenings of the outside world from the villagers and their families. Only the Boltian warriors have been informed of the war, but many have refused to join our cause, wishing only to be with their families.'

'These are sad days indeed!' Edgar exclaimed slamming his hands upon the table. 'Who can rule as king in this evil age of Men? Who can rally an army against such fearsome foes?' He sighed deeply. Turning to the man in the green cloak, he said, 'Now tell me, Meridas, what news you bring from the archers of the Lonely Forest?'

'There is little to tell, Your Majesty. We beheld the events explained by Master Delitas, but we knew his protector to be trustworthy. His guardian was Seymour Gallinger, so we let him pass safely. My scouts always keep watch in shifts over the borders of northern Bolteras, and we have seen no army stirring in the north. Rest easy, Lord Edgar! When the time comes, the archers of the Lonely Forest will support your cause and send word of approaching danger with all swiftness.'

'That is the gladdest news we have heard yet! I thank you for your report, Meridas. Elder Bowman, what would you say of all these things?'

'Hullo all,' said the old, hunched man. 'Sire, I live safely in Vallicore, and my time passes away with little knowledge of the outside world. I have nothing to say that you do not already know; however, I have many questions about the tales of Gibraltar and Delitas. There is much about their stories that makes me curious; indeed, there is much we still do not know. If it is true that war is a year away, then how will we rally your men to arms? Will Bolteras have the might to defeat such fearsome foes as the Vash'alans *and* the Draemhas? And how many Vash'alans still live on? What of Alterash? Will they turn their eyes upon us in war too? There is much I would like to know, yet I do not even know where to begin. But I will advise you all in this: forget the past mistakes of the older generations and look on to the lads who will one day take our place! They are our future and our hope. Raise your head, noble king! The might of Elúvías lives on! I have dreamt many dreams of late, but not one has foretold the end of Bolteras; and I have been known to have prophetic dreams, if that is any consolation to you, Sire.'

'Indeed it is! I thank you, wise one, for your kind words. And I desire to have these questions answered as well. But let us wait for a moment. I ask now for Balan and Langol, brave knights of the Templar Guard, to report our numbers. How many men are willing to fight for me in this war thus far?'

Balan rose and said, 'With the support of Cayrngras, Bram and Eordil we have nearly ten thousand men. If you are able to rally all the men of Vallicore to arms then we may have closer to twenty-five or thirty thousand.'

'Counting the Templar Guard,' added Langol, 'we would make for three thousand and five hundred. Meridas, how many archers do you hold in your midst?'

'Three hundred archers are under my command, but there are others who might join us with proper persuasion. Do not forget about Eagle-Eye Zoro and his band of misfits! Surely there must be others too.' Victor sat in the crowd listening to all that was said. His mind raced with confusion and worry, and he felt small and insignificant compared to the great lords of Bolteras. Hildegard was lost in wonder over the fate of his parents and did not stir for quite some time. Tristan continually tapped his fingers upon his knees, uninterested in all the ceaseless ramblings of the older men. All the older counselors sat discussing the numbers of the Boltian army, except for Arthur.

'Might I speak freely?' Arthur asked calmly after a moment; his voice quieted and soothed the counselors as he spoke with a clear mind. 'I think you all forget that there is a mighty presence here with us, namely that of Vaaspar through the blessings of Elúvías that were given to us. Aye, the forces of Dragoth, those fiends of Abaddon's making, are a formidable enemy, but you act as though there is no hope! Darkness will always be dark until it is met by light, and the Light will always overcome the Darkness! No matter how mighty Abaddon's armies may become, Vaaspar is mightier still! Now then, I advise we turn our ears to Alastair, for it seems to me he has been itching to speak.'

Alastair chuckled. 'You are more than a thousand years younger than me, yet you speak with great wisdom and insight, good Arthur. You speak truthfully indeed, yet I have another tale that I should like to hear first! Edgar, I believe you have yet to tell us your tale of how you rid Bolteras of her curse! It was about two months ago, was it not?'

The entire host turned their attention to Edgar who looked severely distressed. Edgar stirred in his seat and then rose. He walked about to the top of the dais and stood beside his throne with one hand on the arm of the chair facing away from his counselors. A moment later, he returned to his seat at the table and sighed heavily.

'Aye, it was more than two months ago on January the twenty-ninth that a horrible truth was revealed to me concerning our great country. I was asleep in my room when it all happened. But,' he digressed, 'I must first explain something. The mysterious Magic known as Elúvías was bestowed upon the people of Bolteras before the war with Vash'ala twenty years ago. Before we were blessed with its strength, the power was trapped deep within the earth where humans could not reach it. An old friend of Bolteras, whom you will all meet before long, delivered it to us by Vaaspar's command. This power once belonged to Vaaspar alone, but he graciously bestowed it upon Men as a blessing against the forces of Abaddon. Ever since the Lord of Light returned to his home in Elúne, there have been some who were able to draw upon the powers of Elúvías as they were blessed with a deep understanding of spiritual awareness, that is the knowledge of the flow of Magic.

'Thusly, with all the forces of Bolteras blessed with Vaaspar's Light, we were able to quell the armies of Vash'ala in the war twenty years ago. And the one who brought us the Great Stone from the depths of Gaia is called, in the tongue of Men, Seymour Gallinger. He is mysterious and powerful, and I knew at once that the man Delitas saw—the same one who slew the band of Draemhas and then vanished in a flash—was indeed Seymour, as Meridas also confirmed. And ever since he delivered that orb of power to us, it has remained in a sacred place in Vallicore, the *Cathedral of Light* we call it. Since it is the very essence of Vaaspar's power, Men cannot own it, but we can certainly draw new strength from its power.

'Ah, I am afraid there is much to explain. Elúvías we sometimes call the *Orb of Light*, and it is the force that protects our great land. Alastair can explain this all in more detail later, but enough of my ramblings! It was more than two months ago as I was asleep in my chambers that something awful occurred. As I slept, a vile creature of the Draemhas crept into my room like a shadow passing through the night. Grinshawl stirred in his sleep as he felt an icy chill run from his head to his foot. You see, a flow of Magic from Elúvías stirred within him and woke him, and at once he became aware of the presence of evil. My faithful friend came to my aid as swiftly as he could, but the enemy came more swiftly upon me and pressed against me like a mighty weight upon my chest. He sat upon me, and the pain I felt was unbearable. I was trapped, unable even to open my eyes. He spoke to me in a menacing voice with spurts of laughter to accompany it. He said whilst I slept, "Edgar King, behold what lies ahead!" Then, I saw in my sleep dreadful visions of death and despair. I saw Vash'ala in ruins: there was much death and destruction, and I feared the vision to be an omen of what is to come. He also showed me my own death, though I am not certain that these things are true; and yet, he revealed to me something of my past, of which I will not name. This was the most troubling of my dreams, for it made the other visions seem more truthful.

'Still I do not know what to believe. The demon may have simply held the power to bring one's fears to mind; so, I do know what the truth is. But either way, he sat atop me and mocked me while I was unable to counter his evil. I was trapped in sleep like a prisoner trapped in his sad and lonely cell. Suddenly, I saw the Eastern Lands and great fires spread across them. He spoke again saying, "I am the Alp called Greed. I am a servant of the Dark Lord. Long have I influenced your people and long have they obeyed me willingly. You store up for yourselves treasures in your mighty kingdom from the abundance of your gold while your neighbors are at your doorstep crying out for relief! Your country has fallen under my spell, and now you have no power over me, imprudent king!"

'I tried to rouse myself, but still I was trapped in nightmares forced to hear his voice taunting me. Suddenly, I heard the door of my chamber crash open and heard the voice of Grinshawl calling out

105

my name, though it was faint like a whisper. I saw then one last vision that came and went as quick as a flash of lightning, yet it was easily perceived; and then a soothing voice spoke to me. In the vision I saw a white lamb wearing a golden crown atop its head, and it was surrounded by six lions. The beasts viciously assaulted the lamb and thrashed it in a pool of blood. Suddenly, there came another white lamb, but this one was different: there was no crown upon his head, and he had bright blue eyes. The lions fled in terror at the sight of him, and the slain lamb returned to life.

'It was then that a voice spoke to me. It said, "Fear not the Alps of Darkness! Seven exist, but their end draws nigh. Greed is this one's name, for his power lies in swaying the minds of Men to greedy gain. His targets are the Boltians, but fear not, for his influence is meager and feeble. Again I say, fear not! Draw once again upon the might of Elúvías and slay the demon!" In my dreams now I appeared within the walls of the Cathedral of Light, and the Orb of Light entered my body. At once, I was filled with great strength. In my room, in the realness of the world, Grinshawl attempted to slay the brute, but his weapons and body passed through the demon. My eyes opened at long last, and I watched as the Ogre of Bolteras fell upon the ground on the other side of my bed.

'It appeared that the demon had the ability to change his body from physical to ethereal in an instant, but this gave me the opportunity to counter his power when the weight was lifted from me. I pushed him from my body and Grinshawl pulled me from my bed. Greed erected himself and revealed his black, blood-stained fangs. His body was dark grey, shadowy in appearance, and his hair was white like decay. He leapt upon us with murderous intent; but the strength of Elúvías proved true, and we slew the beast. With the power of Elúvías, I was able to strike the Draemhas, even in his ethereal form. It was that day that the curse of greed was lifted from the people of Bolteras. That is my tale.' He finished and stared downward awaiting a response, but the room was silent for a time. All pondered the words of the king, and some found them a difficult thing to grasp.

'So Abaddon has resorted to the use of the Alps again?' Alastair spoke after a time. 'It is just as I expected. Well, if there is nothing left to be said, then I shall speak, for there are many loose ends that must be tied together for this riddle to make sense.'

'First, old friend,' Edgar interrupted, 'we should all like to know where you have been all this time.'

106

'Ah, I see,' the Wizard replied stroking his long white beard. 'You are unaware then? I am afraid the Order of the Magus has been broken!' The room was hushed, and the counselors set their eyes intently on the White Mage. 'And I have come to restore it in these dark days. But as to why the Order was broken, well that is a long tale; so I will tell it in part. The last news the Men of the Western Lands received of the Order was that we had gone away to aid the Eastern Landers in their war against Dragoth. We of the Order held back the Draemhas in the capital city Portrinath in Caire Thrael for many long and tiresome days. The Men of Caire Thrael were mighty champions, and they required little aid from the Mages; so we came and went throughout the Eastern Lands fighting the forces of Dragoth, returning only occasionally to aid the brave and mighty of Caire Thrael.

'Let me inform you of our history. The newest Order of the Magus consisted of seven mighty wizards, and we were the Dragons' apprentices. There once existed five great tribes of dragons, and their powers derived from the five elements of life: earth, wind, water, fire, and lightning. We of the Order were trained by the Dragons to use Magic, but to them it was not a magical ability but rather part of life, like breathing. They foresaw their destruction long before the Great Dragon War commenced and trained noble Men to become their successors in the arts of what is known today as Magic. I see from the looks on some of your faces that you doubt the existence of Dragons, but they did once exist at large. In fact, a few still exist, though they were long asleep and hidden throughout the lands! The Mages were trained by them for the purpose of protecting the world in their stead. This was the way Vaaspar designed it.

'And it was planned that two of the seven Wizards would be taught all five elements and would one day ascend to the rank of White Mage. Upon achieving this rank, the two chosen Wizards would learn to combine the five elements of Magic to form the power of Light—Elúvías as you know it. This teaching was once passed down from Vaaspar to the Dragons, and then the Dragons passed it down to us. Long ago, there once existed two Celestial Dragons who kept order and peace throughout the lands of Gaia. Their story is much like my own. Vaaspar gave the Celestial Dragons the power to control Elúvías and bestowed upon them two unique powers. Originally the powers were both called Elúvías, and their power existed as twofold. Like two branches connected to the same tree, their power sprung from the same source, that being

Vaaspar Himself. But one of the Dragons betrayed his kin in the days of the Dragon slaughter, and thus, the dark power Vexúvías was born. And the evil one became the Infernal Wyrm of Dragoth whose power was so ruthless and filled with disdain that he reaped much havoc on the Men of Gaia.

'I will explain more about the Dragons later, but for now you must know of my death.' The room was filled with whispers and gasps of surprise. 'Yes, I did in fact die once, but I have returned. In the eastern warfront, I fought alongside my comrades of the Order. My greatest friend, Beredor, was a White Mage and had been for many years. He was the first one amongst our Order chosen to become a White Mage, and I was the second. It was nearly four years ago that I had finally mastered the five elements and ascended to the White rank; but Beredor seized the opportunity and betrayed me, for he desired none to rival his magical prowess. And so our story was much like the tale of the Celestial Dragons.

'Through the whisperings of Abaddon, Beredor had learned of an ancient secret: it was a vile act of treachery that gave one the ability to attain the rank of the *Black Mage*, a level of Wizardry that is known by its sinister Magic. A Black Mage, as one can reason from his title, is the opposite of a White Mage, and his Magic reveals itself as the Darkness that opposes Light. Now Beredor the Black receives his power from the wellspring of Vexúvías and from the hand of Abaddon himself! His heart is blackened, and his mind is set on fury and destruction. I fear the Light can no longer reach him, but not because the Light is too weak; no, rather he has set his heart against Vaaspar, and thus Vaaspar has set His heart against him. So now he is yet another servant of the Dark Lord. It pains me to say it, but Beredor has chosen his path and will never return to the Light.

'And yet Beredor was not the first to follow this path. No indeed, for there was another Black Mage who once existed, but he was slain by the Dragons long ago. The first Black Mage, named Aramyst, only became one after slaying his closest friend, Elior the White. They were both White Mages at the time and members of the former Order of the Magus. Aramyst talked of whispers in those days—the voice of Abaddon I presume—that revealed to him a mysterious rank of Wizardry existing in contrast to the White rank. He learned that if one White Mage kills another, then he ascends—or descends I should say—to a new rank of evil, that being Black. In reality, the change happened due to the condition of their hearts, for they loved Darkness rather than Light. Do not exalt us because of our title; all Mages are capable of evil, but a Black Mage is only born for his love of evil. And one can only become a Black Mage after first becoming a White Mage. It is a complete transformation from the highest good to the greatest evil.

'But I digress. You see, Beredor began to believe the lies of Abaddon and gave up hope for Gaia's future. I was slain in Portrinath four years ago by my closest friend, and my spirit roamed the lands of Gaia for many days. I watched from the realm of Shaekle as the Caire Thraeleans welcomed the Draemhas into their country and even began to host friendly sparring contests with them in their large battle arena. The two armies lived amongst each other as friends do, and the Men of Caire Thrael became full of pride. And it was that pride that led their king to cut ties with the Tri-Kingdom of Sanctum Anthropolis. And by doing so, the forces of Sanctum Anthropolis withdrew back to their homes and abandoned those prideful people to their impending fate.

'Soon, Caire Thrael was overthrown, and the forces of Dragoth dwelt within the walls of Portrinath, which became a new and mighty stronghold for the Draemhas. Before long, all the lands of Caire Thrael were overrun by the Draemhas, and their defense was fearsome. Soon their influence spread into Scipherius and the Bestial Plains of the Eastern Lands and Sanctum Anthropolis was surrounded on all fronts. None of the Eastern Landers were able to oppose the forces of Abaddon. To make matters worse, the Draemhas allied themselves with Beredor the Black; and in his betrayal, Beredor took with him two more of the Order: Maldrad the Red, the Fire Mage, and Raven the Gold, the Lightning Mage. With my death, the remaining three Mages of the Order fled into hiding and wished, I think, never to return to the Eastern Lands again. Once the Order was scattered and broken, my soul departed and my influence in Gaia faded into memory.

'I passed from this world to the next where my spirit found rest in Elúne. I saw Vaaspar, the Lord of Light, in all his radiance and glory and suddenly knew things that were once hidden from me. He is real indeed if any of you doubt! And He is extraordinary—that is the best word I can use to describe Him. But just as I arrived, He told me that I still had much left to do and pleaded with me to return to Gaia; but He left the choice up to me. I accepted, though not without regrets, for the White Land is marvelous beyond all understanding! All is white, as bright as can be, yet somehow distinguishable. There are trees and grasses and rivers and pathways of white, liquid gold. Some areas were paler or brighter in some places, but all was equally distinguishable. And Vaaspar was the Light that gave forth light. Forgive me; I cannot explain it well enough to give it justice. But with my leave, He returned me to Gaia in Men's time of need to seek out the strongest in all the lands of Valor, the true and upright. And I have come to restore the Order of the Magus that was shattered upon my death years ago. And I have set before me the task of gathering the Dragons' Stones which are hidden now. That will mean seeking out the ancient race of Dragons and begging them to aid us in this war. Perhaps their hatred toward Abaddon will be enough to fuel their desire to fight!

'I still have much to say, but you have heard the tale of my absence. Upon my return, I was amazed to learn that four years had already passed, for it seemed to me to be but a small breath of time. And now, knowing what I know, I wish I had never been slain, but there is no point dwelling on the past.' Alastair paused for a moment and cleared his throat. 'And now, there is still much from the other tales that I must explain. Gibraltar of Alterash, I believe I know many of the answers to the riddles from your account.

'The Alp of Darkness that attacked Edgar in his sleep was called Greed as you all know now. As Edgar mentioned earlier, there are seven in all, and each holds a mysterious and evil power over Men. Thus, the seven were named after a human weakness that they were able to draw their power from. The Boltians' weakness was greed, for you are a plentiful, flourishing country that was once unconcerned with the sufferings of your neighbors. But hear me, friends; I have not come to condemn you for your weakness, but to help you in your time of need. Even the Wizards of the Order have many weaknesses, so do not be discouraged. And lo! the Alp is now dead, and the weight of the curse is being lifted from Bolteras' shoulders. Soon, perhaps, all of Bolteras will carry arms and go to war! And such is the case with your land, Gibraltar son of Wallace. King Bormann and the rest of Alterash have been overcome by the power of Gluttony, the Draemhan Alp who preys upon Men's desire for much food. You see, he manipulates humans so that they never stop desiring the pleasures of eating. But you, Master Gibraltar, I am glad to say, denied the urges, though there were few in your country who did. Thus, you have escaped the Enemy's grasp for now. But the Dark Lord is roaming the lands in spirit and no doubt knows of your existence. Certainly, he will not let you escape his influence a second time!

'As for the matter of the disease, there are many from the war twenty years ago who were cursed by that dreadful spell. It is a power unleashed by the Alp, Envy. His power allows him to emit an invisible aura from the pits of Shaekle, and it plagues those who are in its presence for too long. The Vash'alans were protected from its power, for they had already given themselves over to Abaddon's will. King Aramon did indeed become sick in Vash'ala as Envy plagued him and many others from the shadows, and I am afraid the Alp has been present in Vash'ala for many generations wreaking havoc in the Western Lands. The reason Bolteras did not suffer much from the war is due to the power emitted from Elúvías: it has the ability to cure disease, but not all escaped the perils of the plagues.' He glanced at Edgar piercingly from the corner of his eyes as though he knew some sort of secret about the king.

'Is that then why Lord Edgar's wife suffered and died?' Gibraltar interrupted. 'Was it from the disease? But surely she was not present during the war!'

'I will not speak of the king's personal matters,' Alastair responded looking upon the heartrending face of Edgar, 'that is for Edgar to know and those whom he trusts with it. As I was saying, the plague continued for quite some time, and King Aramon brought with him only a few small battalions to war. Those of his army who were not slain in battle eventually died from the disease.

'Now regarding the legendary bridge of Raumas Mílnk, it has been remade! I was sent back at first to the Guole Sector of Sanctum Anthropolis and took flight to Valor's Bridge, which was once built by King Valor, the first of the Great Lords of Gaia. The bridge was destroyed, but I have remade it with the power of Light! The water serpents you mentioned are the guardians of Leviathan, the last remnant of the Water Tribe Dragons. She is mighty and ferocious, and none now cross her waters, not even the Draemhas. Her guardians—who are also her offspring—swim across the waters of the Great Sea and the river Raumas Mílnk to instill fear into Men and the armies of Dragoth so that none will threaten the great Water Dragon again. I fear Leviathan is angry still from the great slaughter of the Dragons from ages ago, but she has not yet conceded to evil. I was once her friend before she went into hibernation and disappeared for many centuries, so I know her heart is good. More importantly, her Stone of Power is protected, so the Enemy cannot use it for his benefit.

'Concerning the story of Master Delitas, I have much to say. You said that Marxas was a good king at once, but I must deny that claim. He deceived you all, I am afraid, and not just outsiders but even his loyal subjects. He could not risk being found out even by his faithful followers. At the start of his dynasty, Envy persuaded him to join the forces of Darkness. It was an easy task for him to accomplish as his influence began with Ramox. Envy slipped in unnoticed to the land of Vash'ala, for he disguised himself as a crow and appeared before Ramox during his rule. He made known the prosperity of the Boltians to Ramox, who then informed all the peoples of Vash'ala. It was an easy task for the Alp to sway their minds, for the Vash'alans already worshipped false gods and had given their hearts to the Darkness. Furthermore, Abaddon had long been whispering in their ears, and their resolve was too weak to resist his will.

'When the Alchemists, Valent and Lelane Perigas along with Bombus and Vaylene Gruff, the parents of young Victor and Hildegard, appeared in Vash'ala claiming to have great power from Vaaspar Himself, the Enemy felt greatly threatened! And the Alchemists' journey was successful at first, for they carried the radiance of Elúvías within them. They set off to work at once curing ailments and restoring the health of the land. Their abilities fascinated the king, and Envy became enraged as the curse upon the land had no power over them. Envy seized this opportunity and had the king beckon them to his castle. They were slow to arrive in Osceroth as they spent many days restoring vegetation to the arid ground and healing the sick as they went along.

'When they came at last to the king's throne room, Envy appeared and convinced them of a great power that Alchemists alone can obtain, saying that they were blessed with unique, inward power from the day they were born. The one thing he asked of them was to relinquish their control of Elúvías. At first, they refused, but Envy asked them if they had ever heard of the Alchemist's Stone. They had, but they believed it to be a fanciful legend. But it is real indeed; yes, there was a Stone forged long ago, but it has long since been banished from this world. It was created during the reign of the Dragons to be used against them, for the will of Abaddon had no power over them and his might could not compare to theirs. And so, evil Men corrupted the Alchemists and used them for Abaddon's purposes.

112

'Envy and the whisperings of Abaddon, as I have come to believe, at last reached the ears of Victor and Hildegard's parents, and they renounced the power of Elúvías. Once they did, their hearts became black, for they had abandoned the Light! Just as Beredor my former comrade, they loved the Darkness rather than the Light and joined the forces of the Dark Lord. I believe the reason they relinquished Vaaspar's ancient power was due to their yearning for the Alchemist's Stone, which is said to contain the abilities to grant immortality, to heal any disease and to even bring the dead back to life! But alas! these are only half-truths! The Stone does contain these powers, but it requires human sacrifice!' The room was filled with noise of dread and alarm. Victor and Hildegard trembled in their seats and were whispering to one another in disbelief. 'Whatever good is said to come from the use of the Alchemist's Stone is a lie! Each of its abilities comes with a painful price to pay, and I imagine the good Alchemists were deceived and felt it was a pure and noble Stone of Power. But none of you should be deceived: Elúvías is the only Stone of Power without flaw.

'And the reason the prisons of Gorgonash were emptied, Master Delitas, was for the sacrificial ritual to create the Alchemist's Stone! If you are unaware, Grinshawl here was once a prisoner of Gorgonash; and it is a good thing he was set free, for he may have been counted amongst the dead by now! Hundreds if not thousands were slain for the creation of the Stone and its power has been used to open a portal, or a bridge if you will, connecting Dragoth to Vash'ala. Abaddon's strongest Draemhas are using their powers to open the portal in Dragoth, but it is the Alchemist's Stone that creates the bridge between the two lands. And the ones responsible for creating the Stone are the famous Alchemists of Bolteras who departed fifteen years ago to the aid of Vash'ala.'

Victor jumped from his seat but remained silent. At the same time, Hildegard slammed his fists upon the table. 'This is madness! You speak lies! The Mage speaks lies!' Hildegard exclaimed frantically. 'I will not believe it!' In his head, he now heard the whisperings of Abaddon speaking doubt into his heart and mind, and he became angry towards his companions.

'Silence boy!' Alastair snapped, perceiving the mind of the Enemy at work. 'There is much you do not believe that indeed you should! Did you forget that I said they abandoned the Light?' Hildegard retorted with curses and angry words, but Alastair remained ever calm and held back his tongue. After Hildegard vented his anger at the Wizard, he stormed out of the King's Hall. Victor was filled with anger as well and was even tempted to leave with Hildegard, but Arthur grabbed his arm and held him back. Victor groaned and sighed angrily at first, but his admiration and respect for Arthur quelled his rage. Seeing Arthur remain calm helped Victor quiet his nerves, so he sat down obediently beside his uncle once more.

'Forgive me, Uncle Arthur, but I am angry. I simply do not know what to believe.'

'Yet your patience and willingness to listen first is what makes you wise, young Victor!' Alastair responded in a soothing voice. 'I have examined the mind of Edgar, and he has esteemed you highly in his thoughts; and now I understand clearly! There is great potential in you. Though you are only fifteen years old, you have attained wisdom and peace!'

'Where will Hildegard go?' Victor asked dolefully.

'I cannot say for certain, but I reckon he will head to Vash'ala and seek out his parents. Alas! my words have only angered him, and he has left before I had the chance to fully explain the forces at work. His heart has already been filled with hatred and resentment, and I fear the Enemy will use that to his advantage. I perceive that he has much bitterness towards his parents, and if he ever comes to find my words are true, he will only grow to hate them more. Or perhaps I have been wrong all this time. Though I am more than a thousand years old, and even as I have stood in the presence of Vaaspar and had great mysteries revealed to me, my understanding of things is still imperfect. Alas! this is what it means to be human!'

Chapter VII

Broken Ties

The Boltian Council continued despite Hildegard's sudden outburst, but the counselors grew weary. The room was silent for a while, and none knew what to say. Alastair paced back and forth about the room for a few minutes in silence and then halted in front of the window at the back of the king's throne room. It was dark outside now, and the moon was shining brightly above the city surrounded by a vast array of stars. He saw the figure of Hildegard illuminated by the light of a lantern in his hand heading down the long slope to the gates of the city. After a long silence, he sighed and spoke again. 'The Acolytes of Darkness that Delitas spoke of before are in fact Victor and Hildegard's parents. It is a sad fate indeed, but this is the conclusion I have come to. I would not lie about something so grave, and, moreover, I have no reason to.'

'Why?' Victor questioned. 'Why would our parents give themselves over to the Dark Lord so easily?'

'It is as I have said, boy; they traded the Light for Darkness, believing it to be more fruitful for them. But that decision became their greatest mistake. Now they are trapped inside their former bodies as slaves to Abaddon's will, never to return. You see, young Victor, your parents, and Hildegard's too, were once honest and kind people. They had the seed of Light in them, but they had not allowed the proper time for that seed to grow properly. In their hastiness, they sped off to help others without first considering the costs. O, how they should have helped themselves first!

'They were right to overlook the greed that was plaguing Bolteras and their hearts of compassion were commendable; but alas! they were too hasty, only infants in their knowledge of the Light. They still had much to learn, and as I said, the seed of Light had not yet grown fully. When the whispers of Abaddon came to them, they were tempted and enticed; then, in the weakness of their hearts, they abandoned all things good and true. Their seeds grew as seed tossed upon stones, for the roots grew but a little. Eventually, the roots cracked upon the stones and died. And when the heat of day came upon them, they were burned up by the fires of Darkness and

115

consumed by the evil in their hearts. Had they planted that root in good soil first and cultivated it, then perhaps they would have been fine men and women able to handle any task! Your parents were the seed upon the rock and Abaddon snatched them away. This is the conclusion I have come to. Given these things, what will you do now?'

Victor thought for a moment and then shouted, 'Fight!' with a large grin upon his face. 'I will fight and rescue them from Abaddon's grasp! I will give my life if that is what it takes! If I must, I will plunge into the depths of Darkness, into the dark land of Dragoth, and by the Light of Vaaspar, I shall rid the world of evil! And if they are slaves as you have said, then I will break the chains that bind them and destroy the evil in their hearts forever!' A large smile crept across Arthur's face, and he clapped excitedly.

'Fool!' Grinshawl shouted with joy and laughter. 'He is a fool!'

'What a bold statement and what a fascinating boy!' Edgar added. The rest of the counselors laughed, not mockingly but as they were full of new hope and courage from Victor's valiant declaration.

'Well then,' Alastair responded with a laugh, 'Edgar, and Arthur too, you have not deceived me when you spoke so highly of this magnificent young man!' Alastair bowed before Victor, and then the rest of the company rose and followed the Mage's lead, all but Tristan who frowned jealously at Victor. Victor had never before been so honored, above all by such a great host of Men. And in that moment he was quite happy, happier than any other moment in all his life.

'I would like to know how it is you came to know all of this, Alastair the White,' Tristan spoke and disrupted their merriment. He had a sly grin on his face as though he had caught the Wizard in an elaborate ploy of deceit.

'I imagine you consider yourself quite clever now, Tristan fool!' Alastair retorted. 'Have I not told you that I was slain and reborn in the land of Elúne? And did I not state that great mysteries were revealed to me in the presence of Vaaspar that were long hidden from my understanding? And listen further, child of tomfoolery; if ever you seek to be King of Bolteras, then you will start to humble yourself and show others proper respect! If you must know, I was informed by a friend, one whom I have known for more than a thousand years!' The company took their seats once again, annoyed by Tristan's discourteous interruption.

116

'More than a thousand years you say?' Tristan scoffed. Edgar peered at him furiously and banged his fist upon the table. Ignoring his uncle, he continued, 'And who can live so long? And how do we know this mysterious man is trustworthy?'

'Those with vast spiritual prowess can live for many ages if they are willing! Mages use a portion of their Mana to retain their youth.' Alastair returned. 'Do you know of your spiritual life force?' Tristan looked confused. 'I see. Perhaps you have not yet been informed. To be physically strong, one must train their body, correct?'

'But of course,' Tristan exclaimed proudly, 'every fool knows that!'

'Then a fool you are, for you appear weak still, Prince Tristan! Now how do you suppose Wizards use Magic?'

'You were trained by the Dragons! It is written in all of our books of lore,' he returned boastfully.

'Yes, but where does the ability come from?'

'Is it not a gift? One from Vaaspar I presume!' Tristan stated boldly, yet he was puzzled and did not speak again for a time.

'Fool! Silence your tongue! I will teach you all now.' He glanced over at Edgar with disappointment. 'I thought the king would have informed you by now, but perhaps he meant not to trouble you with the complexities of it. Mages use Magic by drawing upon their spirit's life force. Think of it like this: just as the body requires training to lift heavy objects or to run long distances or to endure lengthy battles, so the spirit requires training to use Magic. The Mages once learned through the lessons taught by the ancient Dragons.

'But how did the Dragons learn, you may ask? They learned to draw upon their spirit's energy, or Mana, through the power of the Dragon Stones that were given to them by Vaaspar's making. So the Dragons' learned as the Stones' powers drew out their energy, and they became familiar with the flow of energy and learned to control Magic even without the aid of their Stones. Unless one is taught by the Dragons, however, I am afraid the Stones are necessary to comprehend the elemental Magics. Though Mages are ancient and well-trained, they are not the only humans capable of Magic. Elúvías is inside each of you, curiously, as it is the combined strength of the five elemental Magics! But hear me; the blessed Orb of Light exists in this city, in the Cathedral of Light, waiting to be used properly

117

against the forces of evil. And Vaaspar has blessed all Men who hold fast to good with the ability to draw upon His unique power.

'But you must be taught now how to use it, as I taught Edgar and many other Boltians more than twenty years ago during the war against Vash'ala. The Templar Guard is already capable of using Elúvías, as its ways were taught to them as well. Of all Men that I have taught, Grinshawl here is the most unique! He has used his Mana to enhance the power of his body, thus increasing his strength, speed and even intellect! But do not be fooled, he has trained his mind and body apart from Magic, more so than any before him. One cannot rely on the spirit's energy alone. If you exhaust all your Mana, whether in training or in combat, you will die. Yet, the more you train your spirit's energy, the more it will grow, as does one's strength through physical training! If you are weak, however, the use of Magic will damage your body, so use it cautiously until you have developed mind, body, and spirit!'

'Aye,' Edgar interrupted, 'this is why my body ages when I use healing Magic. And the same is true of most aside from the Alchemists. The power of healing consumes the largest amount of Mana, and my body is weak—for reasons I will not say—so I age slightly every time I heal a comrade. This is why few use leechcraft in battle.'

'You should not have,' Arthur answered with regret in his voice, 'you should never have healed me, O king!'

'Do not be a fool, Arthur,' the king retorted. 'Your part in this tale has not yet ended. You still have a role to play!'

'Agreed,' Alastair continued, 'and indeed, healing is the most exhausting! When the time comes for the might of Elúvías to shine forth from each of you, make sure you have trained your bodies well! Soon I will be instructing the soldiers of Bolteras to harness the power of Elúvías, if time allows. This approaching war is ill-timed, for many of you are unaware or else ill-trained in the arts of Elúvías. Yet in the Eastern Lands, they have already discovered this power and employ it against the forces of Dragoth! If they had not learned its ways, then I fear Abaddon would have conquered them many years ago. But Vaaspar has long blessed the Men of Sanctum Anthropolis, and their strength has not yet faded! Hope still exists for the Men of Gaia, if we act quickly!'

'Begging your pardon, good Wizard,' Tristan interrupted. Alastair peered at him with a fiery look in his eyes. 'I apologize for my earlier insult. I would honestly like to know who told you of all the happenings in the world. And how do the Eastern Landers use Elúvías if we have the Orb of Light here in Vallicore?'

Alastair sighed. 'You are forgiven, child,' he answered with a smile. 'The Men of the East use Vaaspar's power freely for the reason that Elúvías is not bound by chains! You cannot tame it. Nor can one seize it as though it were a possession. It can always be used against evil, but it can never be owned. Yes, Bolteras contains the Orb of Light that helps to draw the power from within, but the power exists for all who believe in it to use. Every person has spiritual energy and the capacity for Magic; yet, the problem exists in whether they shall use their powers for evil or for good. If it is used for evil, it becomes Vexúvías, the power of Darkness. Dreadfully, the ancient Orb of Darkness, which was once wielded by the Infernal Wyrm of Darkness, still exists, and the Enemy has found it. But his armies cannot use it fully, for it is trapped deep beneath the earth where no creature can dwell. Not even the Draemhas can venture where it lies. But still they draw upon its power, and it is being used to aid the Dark Lord in his plan to recover his original form. Now for those who use their Mana for good, then the power becomes Elúvías, the power of Light, and they shall be greatly blessed by Vaaspar! Though great power exists in all of us, there are many who are unable to draw upon its source, for they either doubt or simply do not comprehend its ways. And this is why Bolteras is blessed! With the Orb of Light that once belonged to the Celestial Dragon in your midst, many in Bolteras will be able to both comprehend and utilize the powers within them.

'I will tell you now who revealed all the happenings of Gaia to me. He is the very same Seymour Gallinger whom Edgar spoke of earlier. And here is something most of you never knew: he is one of the Celebhas!' The counselors began to whisper to one another and were in awe at the news, all except for Edgar who already knew of Seymour's true identity. 'Yes indeed,' Alastair continued after the noise died down, 'he is one of Vaaspar's own, his Beloved; and better yet, he is our ally! He met me along my way to Vallicore and informed me of many things so that when I came to Vallicore I could reveal these secrets to you. He sent me with other news that I will share in a moment, but I must tell you this: Seymour lives atop the Sage's Mountain. Long ago the mountains were known as the Eagles' Mountains, but he renamed it when he claimed it as his own. And the eagles that dwell there are now his loyal servants, and they spend their time scouting the lands of Vash'ala for our sake. The

119

wise Celebhas keeps watch vigilantly upon the borders of Bolteras and Vash'ala, and his eyes are keen. He is able to see great distances and discern things from afar. If any forces were to assemble in the distance, he would be able to inform us weeks before they reached the borders. Furthermore, we have the eyes of the bowmen of the Lonely Forest. I assure you that Bolteras is quite safe for the time being.

'Now for other news: the last remnant of the Dragons has awoken! Seymour has requested that we seek out their hiding places and recover their Stones. Of the five ancient tribes of Dragons, there exists one remnant from each clan. Seymour has already discovered two: the Earth Dragon named Uras, and the Wind Dragon named Fujin. They have been awakened from their sleep in the recesses of the earth, and are now his allies, prepared to fight and die for Men once again, though they are currently fighting in the war in the east.

'The Enemy, I am afraid, has awoken the Lightning Dragon—Anu I believe is his name—and is using him as a weapon. Anu was one of the Dragons who began to hate Men after the Slaughter of the Dragons centuries ago. We spoke of the Water Dragon earlier. As I said before, she has yet to join a side in this war. She hates Draemhas, and she hates the race of Men too. Thus, the oceans roar and the waves quake from the depths to keep her protected from any who would do her harm. Her sea serpents, her offspring, roam the seas causing havoc to all who dare venture upon her waters.

'Ages ago, when the Celestial Dragons still lived, I was trained by the Fire Dragon Asura. He was my mentor when I was still a young Fire Mage. After I mastered the element of fire, I then learned from the other tribes of Dragons. At the end of my training with the elemental Magics, I learned the power of Light from the Celestial Dragon of the Western Lands, who was once called *Elú Aramos*, which means "Bred from Light" in the tongue of Men. Beredor, my ancient friend, was being trained by Anu as he was a young Lightning Mage at that time. When he had completed all of his elemental Magic training, he was taught by the Celestial Dragon of the Eastern Lands, who was once called *Elú Porthos* in the ancient tongue; his name meant "Protector of Light" in the tongue of Men. When the Dragon succumbed to evil and became the Infernal Wyrm, I fear Beredor fell with him. But lo! I have rambled on long enough. There is still much more for you to learn, but your journeys ahead may reveal greater mysteries than I have to offer.'

'We have many things to consider now,' Edgar added, 'and I should like to sleep before we decide upon further action.' Just then, a guard ran into the room and halted at the door.

'Sire,' the soldier called, 'a man has arrived and desires to speak with you.'

'Is he a member of the Boltian Council?'

'Nay, Sire! He has come from the Guole Sector of Sanctum Anthropolis, sent by King Izen as a messenger. He is one of the legendary Sigma Cain!'

'Let him come, quickly now!' Alastair insisted.

The guard looked curiously at the White Mage and then glanced over at Edgar awaiting a response. Edgar smiled and said, 'This man deserves more authority than has been given to me, loyal soldier. Go at once and bring the messenger!' At once, the soldier withdrew.

Moments later, a tall man with short black hair came in arrayed in panoply with a long, red cape attached to his pauldrons. As he entered, he removed his helm and placed it under his right arm. He had a long sword sheathed at his side and a shield hung upon his leather baldric. 'Edgar King, I bring urgent news to Bolteras. I have traveled many long days, and I am weary. Might I rest for a moment at your table?'

'Of course, good knight; sit and rest. Tristan, bring our guest some food!' Tristan sped off at once and returned minutes later with a plate full of food, and the soldier received it gladly.

'I thank you, Your Highness. It seems Bolteras is the only country in the Western Lands to maintain any good sense! There have been many from the lands of Alterash to come to our lands seeking refuge from the evil that plagued their country. They claimed great evils had befallen their people and their king. Not long before I departed, more riders from Alterash arrived to aid us in the war, but I did not stay to hear their tale. I hoped the stories would prove false, and so I sought out the aid of Alterash upon crossing through; but there was an eerie presence about that land. I had hardly stepped foot in the land before vile creatures chased me down. At first, they appeared to be ordinary wolves only slightly bigger, but then I saw poison dripping from their fangs. I took flight at once with no hope of aid from that country. It was then that I understood why so many had come seeking refuge in the East. My horse galloped away as quickly as it could. The wolves seemed to never grow weary, and I began to fear for my life; yet, as we passed the borders of Bolteras, the beasts suddenly halted. But I was glad for my horse collapsed from exhaustion, and I was given a chance to rest.

'I strayed far from Vash'ala after hearing all the rumors of Draemhas in that land. For fear of my life, I avoided them at all cost. I feared that all the kingdoms of the West had fallen to ruin but remembered the rumor that Seymour Gallinger, the hero of old, was in the land. So I have come to bring news and to call on the aid of Bolteras to do away with the threat of the Draemhas once and for all. Sanctum Anthropolis requires aid or else we will all fall to the power of Darkness!'

'Forgive me, but what is your name, good knight?' asked Edgar.

'My name is Edward of the line of Baltheim, Your Majesty.'

'Baltheim, you say? Aye! You are indeed a famous member of the Sigma Cain. We have heard many tales of your heroic deeds.'

'I am honored, Sire. But honor will not ensure my family's safety. The longer war wages on, the larger our Enemy's strength grows, and he is ever nearing his rebirth. He is powerful even in spirit, but we dread the day he returns to his former self. If Dragoth is not defeated ere he is reborn, then all of Gaia will plunge into darkness. Bolteras must end the war here and come at once to aid the Men of the East!'

'Aye, I have already considered that,' Edgar returned. 'And I am assembling my mightiest warriors to banish the Draemhas from Vash'ala. But it seems we will be delayed further, for a battle may be imminent against Alterash as well. It seems that is a fight we cannot avoid or else tragedy may befall our country.'

'Do not be rash, Edgar of Bolteras! You have heard, I am sure, of the Alps?'

'Aye, we have just been informed of their nature.'

'Then I urge you to slay the beast that haunts Alterash and rid them of their curse. Upon that day, I am certain there will be many who will join your cause! The soldiers of the Guole Sector in Sanctum Anthropolis were once haunted by the threat of the Alp named Lust. Many of our warriors—aye our king as well—were swayed by her beauty, and we withdrew our aid in the war against Dragoth for a time. But a mysterious man appeared, though none knew his identity, and he slew the harlot. Before long, our sanity was restored to us, and we once again aided our comrades in the Vexica and Grimora Sectors. Balance can be restored to the peoples of Alterash if you will only lend them a helping hand.'

'But they have grown fat and idle,' Alastair added, 'and it would be some time before they are any use to us in the war. Behold! I have already formulated a plan. War is to come to Bolteras in one year's time according to Master Delitas' tale, which has also been confirmed by Seymour Gallinger. In fact, his eagles have scouted the lands and learned of many of the Dark Lord's plans. Now, if Bolteras can muster their armies and be ready, then we can attack our enemies before they are assembled for war. I have already prepared counsel for this group, but it is good that a messenger has come from the Tri-Kingdom of Sanctum Anthropolis. Inform King Izen and also send word to Vexica and Grimora that the last standing armies of the Western Lands will come to your aid in one year's time. Let us worry about the war in these lands while Sanctum Anthropolis attends to its own matters.'

'So we can expect your aid in one year? I hope the forces of Darkness will not have conquered us by then.'

'Aye, you have my word,' the Wizard continued. 'Worry not! Abaddon is too prideful to conquer the lands of Gaia until he has been reborn. There is hope yet, Edward of the Baltheims; there are those in the next generation who have special gifts, powers unique to them. These powers have come to be called *Light Gates*. Others have called these rare abilities *Dragoth's Bane*. Fear not and always lead your family down the path of Light! Aid will come to you.' Edward nodded and forced a smile upon his face, but Alastair perceived the doubt in his eyes. Edgar bid the weary traveler to eat, and so he did. After Edward had finished his meal, they agreed to let him rest in Vallicore for the evening before departing back to his home the following morning. Then the room grew silent again.

'Uncle Arthur,' Victor said after a moment of thought, 'I am worried about Hildegard. He must be far beyond the city walls by now, and it is dark!' Victor was deeply troubled, and Arthur had compassion on him.

'Go Victor. See if your friend will listen to your counsel. Bring him back to us, if you are able!' A smile crept on Victor's face, and he looked to Edgar for approval. Edgar nodded and Victor darted away without delay. From away down the hall, Victor's voice echoed back to them, 'I am going to borrow a horse!' Edgar chuckled.

'That is a fine boy you have there,' Edward said as he lapped up the last bit of meat on his plate, 'Arthur, was it? Yes, he seems to be a fine boy indeed.'

'Aye, he most certainly is! What of you, Sir Edward? Do you have offspring?'

'Aye, I do! I am very fond of them both and proud too. My eldest is named Siegfried, and he is a skilled swordsman, far more adept than his classmates at the Academy. He just had his twenty-first birthday before I came here. My youngest is Venatras, and there is something very special about him, though I have not yet learned what it is. Perhaps he has what the Wizard calls Dragoth's Bane. Whatever it is, he is becoming a fine swordsman as well, though he is not as skilled as Siegfried. Venatras is seventeen years old now and will be eighteen in less than four months. This is his first year at the Academy. Siegfried also joined the Academy when he was seventeen, and I reckon he will soon join the ranks of the army. In less than four year's time, my eldest has surpassed even those in the ranks above him.'

'Pardon me, but what is this Academy you speak of?' Arthur questioned.

'It is a training ground we have built where we train young fighters in the knowledge of Elúvías, and we have been doing so for the past ten years. It took some time for me to enlist my children as the cost is great; and soldiers do not make as much money as we deserve. But I reckon they will be great captains of the armies one day, so I am glad to spend the money!'

'What more can you tell us of the happenings in the East?' Edgar asked.

'For now, I will not burden you with much. I can see you have enough to worry about already. If I may, I would like to retire for the evening.' Edgar consented. 'Thank you, great lords, for your generosity.' He bowed and then withdrew from the Silver Vestibule.

'I suppose this will end the council for now. I figure it is nigh to midnight now, and we could all use a little sleep,' Alastair concluded. 'I suggest we meet again in the morning, as there is still more to discuss. Shall we meet at the break of dawn to organize our strategy?'

'Hold on now!' Arthur interrupted. 'What shall we do about Hildegard?'

'Have we not sent Victor to bring him back?' Alastair answered.

'Yes, but what if Victor cannot convince him to return?'

'Speak your mind clearly, Arthur? Get to the point already!'

'If Hildegard does not return and Abaddon sways his mind, then we are all in grave danger! He carries great knowledge from this council that the Enemy will surely use against us! And the Dark Lord will come to know of the knowledge we have acquired: that he plans to wage war on Bolteras in one year's time. Learning of our knowledge, he will surely wage war sooner than we expect!'

'You speak reasonably, wise Arthur,' Alastair answered while plucking at his beard. 'But rest assured, Abaddon will not send his forces to attack until he has mustered enough strength to be certain of his victory. For him to be assured of victory, he needs to conquer the Western Lands so he can attack the Tri-Kingdom on all sides. Then, he will truly be victorious. I am doubtful that he would be so reckless as to hasten his assault. Besides, you know not the power of the Dark Lord! Surely he is among us now listening as we speak. Even holding a council is a risk to us and an advantage to the Dark Lord. All we can do now is prepare the armies of Bolteras and quell the forces at bay!

'Forgive me, wise one. Surely you are full of great insight! Yet, I still hope that Victor can convince the lad to return. I would rather not have another enemy to worry about, especially one of our kin.'

'I hope for the same, but we cannot force him to return. He will now have to choose for himself which path he will take, whether for good or for evil.

'Well then,' Edgar interrupted with a yawn, 'If there is nothing more to be said, let us sleep for tonight. I thank you all for coming. We have all heard great revelations today but do not be overwhelmed! Relax for tonight and sleep well. We will discuss our plans in the morning. Goodnight!' With that, Edgar withdrew to his chambers and the others followed, except for Arthur who stayed in his chair awaiting Victor's return. As he sat all alone, he dreamt of Victor returning peacefully with Hildegard.

* * *

At the bottom of the long slope near to the gates of Vallicore, Victor ran to the nearby stable and chose for himself a strong stallion. He begged the Head Groom to lend him a steed promising to return it. The stable master recognized him as one of Edgar's counselors and gladly lent him a steed. He led the horse to the gates and approached the guards. 'Open these gates, good knights! I beg of you!'

125

'Another one?' asked one of the guards. 'How many of you will be departing this evening?'

'You saw another? What did he look like?'

'About like you, only slightly taller; and he seemed rather upset to me. He was cursing and shouting, but he did not seem a threat to us. We let him pass through not too long ago.'

'Please, open the gates! It is urgent; but I beg you, keep watch for me. I do not know what will happen. The one who left is my closest friend, but his heart is troubled with evil. I fear he may seek to do me harm!'

'Is that so? Then I will accompany you,' said one of the guards. 'My name is Huseff. Jergon, guard the gate while I escort this lad.'

'Please, there is no time! I will ride ahead! Come after me if you wish, but I must depart at once!' The guards reluctantly opened the gates, and Victor galloped away into the night. He saw faintly in the moonlight signs of footprints on the ground. He followed them along the road leading northward towards the Lonely Forest and scanned the area for his friend.

Victor rode swiftly yelling, 'Hildegard! Hildegard, where are you?' After riding for nearly a mile, a long wooden rod flashed dimly before Victor's eyes, and he was knocked from his steed. The horse neighed and darted ahead into the grassy plains at the edge of Lake Serenity. Hildegard stood there holding his newly acquired spear with a cruel smile on his face. Victor was lolled upon the ground in agony from the fall.

'Why did you come after me? Have you come to join me, *friend*?' he said with a sneer.

Victor coughed and wheezed trying to regain his breath. 'I will never join the Darkness, Hildegard! I came to bring you back!'

Hildegard laughed. 'The Wizard lies, Victor! I can see it in his eyes. He wants us to give up on our parents, probably to use us for his benefit. Wizards are crafty folk, full of great knowledge of Magic! Surely we were all charmed, but I saw differently! I saw beyond his ruse, and I will not be swayed by his soothsaying any longer! Come with me, Victor, and we can fight the forces of Darkness ourselves!'

'You are a stubborn fool, Hildegard! There was only truth in his eyes. I do not want to believe what he said any more than you do, but we never even knew our parents! We had hardly been born before they left us! I hope as much as you do that they are still good

126

and will one day return to us, but they did not even love us enough to care for us! Who knows what they are capable of! I have relied on Arthur my whole life, and he has helped you as well. Our true family is in Kesh, no, in all of Bolteras. Our parents are strangers to us, and so we have no right to argue with the wisdom of Alastair! I want to believe our parents would never betray our country and turn to aid the forces of Darkness, but we simply do not know them. They are capable of good and evil, just as you and I are! Be careful that the Dark Lord does not sway your mind in your anger!'

'What are you saying, Victor? Are you accusing *me* of evil?' Hildegard yelled with tears in his eyes, those not of sadness but of fury. 'Our parents are not wicked, and neither am I! I am going to Vash'ala to prove the Wizard wrong, and I will fight in my own way! Now you have a choice to make since you have followed me: join me or else be killed!'

'I will not join you, nor will I be killed!' Victor retorted.

'Then it is time to sever this useless bond we call friendship!'

In his haste to pursue his friend, Victor had forgotten his sword and bow in the throne room of the king, but still he erected himself with courage and peered keenly at Hildegard. 'I will never go with you, not if it leads down the path of Darkness! I will not make the same mistake our parents made, and I vow to bring you back even if I have to knock you out and drag you back!'

Hildegard laughed. 'Now we will finally see which of us is stronger!' He threw his spear to the ground and charged at Victor. Victor readied himself, but Hildegard was too quick; the crazed boy tackled Victor to the ground and began to punch him ferociously where he lay. Victor pushed him off, and Hildegard fell to the right of the road and rolled down the hill towards the lake. Victor darted towards him, but Hildegard jumped to his feet. Victor relented. The two stood there in the plains near Lake Serenity facing each other only a foot or two apart. Victor then struck Hildegard in the face, but Hildegard answered with his own fist. They exchanged blows for nearly five minutes straight, one after the other, until Hildegard fell to the ground. Their lips and noses were bloodied, and their cheeks were battered and cut. Neither one could see clearly as both of their eyes were puffed up and bruised.

Victor jumped on top of his friend and grabbed him by the tunic. Hildegard's head leaned back from exhaustion and blood ran from his face onto the grass. Victor stared into Hildegard's eyes and saw only emptiness in them; and they appeared now black as the night. Victor finally understood that his closest friend had chosen to follow the path of evil, and there was nothing he could do to stop him. As he looked into the emptiness in Hildegard's eyes, Victor took pity on him, and his heart was filled with compassion for his friend. Then Hildegard began to laugh: it was shrill and maniacal. Victor was instantly roused by its cruel and piercing tone. 'You finally understand,' Hildegard spoke after a moment. His voice was deeper and angrier than before. 'You cannot stop me!' He laughed again, and Victor slowly loosed his grip. Without any sign of regret, Hildegard struck him to the ground. Victor stood and lowered his guard, but Hildegard refused to relent. He struck a final blow upon Victor's brow, which forced him to the ground. Victor crashed violently onto the grass of the meadows and lost consciousness. Still far away, the guard Huseff was approaching, holding a lantern to light his way. Alarmed suddenly by the sound of the approaching horseman, Hildegard grabbed his spear and aimed it at Victor, but he yielded at last and did not slay his friend. One last faint glimmer of light shone within him, and he was filled with grief; but he hardened his heart once more and stole away on Victor's wandering horse before Huseff could stop him.

The soldier halted beside Victor and dismounted, resting his lantern on top of the grass. 'Wake up, lad; you cannot die here! Please do not be dead!' He shook Victor gently several times before Victor opened his eyes. 'Praise, Vaaspar! Are you hurting, lad?'

'Yes, I am, but I will live. Please, take me back to the city. I must speak with my uncle.'

'And what should we do about that boy?'

'He has made up his mind and has chosen to give his all to the service of the Dark Lord. There is nothing more I can do for him. Our bond has been broken.' The guard took pity on Victor and led him slowly back to Vallicore, allowing the beaten boy to ride on his horse while he guided it on foot. When they arrived, Arthur was already standing at the entrance, and he ran forward to embrace his adopted son. Victor wept fervently in the arms of his uncle. Arthur was shocked and angry to see his son's injuries.

'I know, lad; I know. Cry as long as it takes. Things of this nature are never easy, and all of this occurred after you just heard the dreadful reality of your folks.' Arthur began to weep loudly with Victor. 'I am deeply sorry, lad!'

128

'Do not apologize, uncle. I am going to save them all one day! I am going to save mother and father and Hildegard too! I will even save his parents so he will never have to live in Darkness again!'

'I know you will, my boy. I know you will.' They returned to the King's Hall, and Victor slept in Arthur's room that night. As he lay on Arthur's bed, he wept bitterly for an hour or more before falling asleep from exhaustion. Arthur stayed by his side through the night and fell asleep at the foot of the bed on the cold, hard stone of the chamber floor.

The following morning, Arthur and Victor woke to the sound of their door crashing open. The light of morning was pouring through the window, and it blinded them as they rose from the rude awakening. Suddenly, Tristan walked into the room. 'Oi! Oi, I say! O-oh! What do we have here?' His noisy entrance was both bothersome and unpleasant to Arthur and Victor, and they were in no mood to entertain the prince's bizarre behavior. 'I do say! Do I behold a young lad afraid of the dark and sleeping in his uncle's bed? Victor, my friend, I never took you for a coward! But I must say this sentiment is quite heart-warming!' Victor grabbed his pillow and tossed it at Tristan's head, but the uncouth lad dodged it. 'Ho now! is that any way to be treating your friend, Victor? Vicky? Vick? I like Vicky! Do you like that name, Vicky?'

'Stop calling me that! My name is Victor! I should like to throw more than a pillow at *your* head, trifling Tristan!'

Arthur laughed tenderly and rose from the floor. He stretched his arms high above his head and looked back at Victor. He was filled with disbelief and amazement as not a single injury remained on the boy's face. It was as though he had been healed or else his body healed itself. Whatever the reason, he was glad to see his son free of bumps, bruises and cuts.

'Now there is no need to be rude, Vicky!' Tristan continued with a laugh. Instantly, Victor leapt from his bed, and Tristan ran off. The two ran down the halls with such a ruckus that Arthur heard the yelling for quite some time even as they vanished down the long halls of the corridors. After the noise died down, Edgar crept into the room with a glum look on his face.

'My, my, he is quite the lad,' Arthur called as the king walked into the room. 'After everything that he has been through, he is still able to find enjoyment. That Tristan, though a fool he is, is a magnificent boy. You should be proud. Victor needs a light-hearted friend like him in his life. It pleases me to see him smile the way he does in the presence of the prince. But alas! I fear that smile will inevitably fade in time, as the war will cause him to grow up much quicker than I had hoped. I wish these young ones could have been born in happier times, but, ah, what is the use of longing for what cannot be.'

'You simply want what is best for your son, and I admire that in you,' Edgar replied. 'Tristan is indeed a foolish, foolish child, but he is remarkable all the same. He has been through much himself, and I think it was the hardships in his life that gave him the strength and vivacity you see today. If he had not gone through the furnace of affliction, then he would not be the marvelous man I know and love today. It is a curse for a child to grow up without ever meeting his parents, but he endured, though it was not always easy for him. My nephew has a gift for bringing cheer to others in the gloomy hours of life. He even helped me greatly as I recovered from the loss of my wife and child. But I digress.'

Edgar paused for a moment and then sighed heavily. 'Before I went to sleep last night, Alastair came to my chambers, and we spent much time talking. It was decided that we must train the soldiers of Bolteras in the uses of Elúvías, and Victor will be amongst those trained. I believe with proper guidance and understanding, both Victor and Tristan will become vital soldiers in our army. It is apparent that Victor will be a great warrior one day, but I believe in Tristan too, though he is still a noisy lout. I am amazed that these young ones rely on influences other than the frail might of Men. They are still innocent and full of faith, and I confess that I covet that in them. For too long, the lines of Men have relied too heavily on their own strength, which has failed us time and time again. But in these dark days, I am glad that at long last we will call upon the might of Elúvías! We should have used its powers long ago, but I fear we were too foolish and stubborn. And we should have recognized the inspiration of our youths long ago, but we were too arrogant. Pride goes before the fall, as they say. I am glad that we have been humbled at last. Perhaps now we may avoid the fall.'

'I am glad as well. We have spent too much time denying the influence of Elúvías in our lives, but no more! And there is much indeed that our youths can teach us if we will only open our eyes to see it. My dear friend, I still have doubts. Can Men truly prevail against the Dark Lord and his armies? I ask out of hope that one day Victor will be able to live a free and fulfilling life.'

'Alas! I do not know if Men will prevail against the Draemhas.' While the two were talking, Victor and Tristan had secretly crept back near the doorway and were now listening to the conversation. 'But we must try! If we give up now, then all the lands of Gaia will fall under Abaddon's rule, and that is a fate that must never transpire. If that were to happen, he may even raise greater armies than the armies of the Celebhas, though he will never defeat Vaaspar. Men may have many weaknesses, but we will show the demons of Dragoth the true strength of Men! And that strength is not our own; no, it is a gift from the Ruler of the White Land, who gives all things graciously. Abaddon knows he will never defeat Vaaspar, so his plan is to destroy the very ones Vaaspar awoke ages ago, those he loved greatly—the race of Men! At least that is what Alastair believes. I simply do not know what to believe. My mind is clouded, and all understanding is hidden from me. But what I do know is that our children can live free and fulfilling lives now, even in this darkened age. All one must do is rely on Vaaspar for strength.'

'Sire, you are much too hard on yourself. You are a king, yes, but you are human! Even still, you are a wise man amongst Men. Do not fret in these evil days. The brave warriors of Bolteras may yet rise to your aid and hear your call. But come; let us meet with the rest of the council as Alastair requested of us.'

'Yes, this is no place for discussing our plans further. Neither is it a place for *eavesdroppers*!' Victor and Tristan jumped in front of the doorway with large grins on their faces. They both jutted their tongues out at the older men and ran away. Then Tristan's voice echoed back to the room saying, 'You are late for the council, Uncle Edgar! You are promptly late, never early, as I say!'

131

Chapter VIII

Alastair's Proposal

As Edgar and Arthur entered the throne room, they saw that that the room was already filled with the members from the day before, with the exception of Hildegard—Edgar was embarrassed by his tardiness. At that moment, Alastair was pacing back and forth with a pipe in his mouth and was fingering the brim of his hat in his hands. When he looked up, he quickly glided across the room and grabbed Edgar by the shoulder and led him to a quiet corner of the room. The counselors looked on as the two whispered in secret. Edgar's head nodded up and down as though he was in agreement with whatever Alastair was saying.

They halted for an instant, and Edgar called for Grinshawl to join them. The Ogre of Bolteras, who was still rather tired, rose reluctantly and paced to the corner of the room. He also seemed to agree with the words of the Wizard by the nodding of his head. At one point, Grinshawl looked back, and Victor swore the giant's eyes met his; then he turned back and nodded again. Alastair talked some more, and Edgar and Grinshawl replied with a couple *Ayes*. After another minute or so of talking, Grinshawl stood tall and flexed his arms and released a proud roar. 'Yes!' the giant shouted, 'now I am invigorated!' Still the others were kept in the dark, and many began to stir with their growing impatience. A few more minutes later, the parley ended, and the three returned to the table. Arthur stared at the secretive three with a disgruntled look and scoffed as they sat down.

'It has been decided,' Alastair spoke. 'I will seek out the Order, my brethren, and bring them to Vallicore if they are willing. Others will seek out the last attainable Dragon Stone, the Stone of Fire. Edgar and Grinshawl will travel about rallying the warriors of Bolteras to arms. Still yet, some must go to Alterash and slay the Alp Gluttony, for we will require the aid of Alterash when the time for battle comes. I fear there are many tasks to fulfill; even the masses of vagrants and thieves from Fort Leaf must be called upon. If all comes together before one year, then Bolteras will go to war early! After the Draemhas and the evil Men of Vash'ala are swept from the

Western Lands, we will travel east to lend aid to the Tri-Kingdom of Sanctum Anthropolis.

'Once I have assembled the Order, I will steal away back to the Eastern Lands where I am much needed. The rest of the Order will be enough to eradicate the armies of Darkness in these lands. If we can slay Gluttony, perhaps Alterash will support Bolteras in the war—that is if they are not too fat to fight! Unfortunately, we do not know the enemy's numbers; thus, we must take extra precautions and secure the Stone of Fire, wherever it may be.'

'And how will we find such a thing in so vast a world?' Arthur asked with annoyance in his voice.

'Well, I knew the Dragon Asura for years. He was my first teacher when I was still a young Fire Mage, and he particularly loved the Western Lands for some reason. That ought to narrow down our search.'

'And what if he is within the borders of Vash'ala? What if they have already found him and taken his Stone?'

'Then Bolteras will be in great trouble. I—'

'Excuse me, sirs,' Rolo interrupted. 'I beg your pardon for the interruption, but I have kept my voice quiet too long, as did young Pakko here, for we are lowly wanderers, once vile thieves in the land. Yet I have something I must say. For years now, as we lived in our fortress Treehouse, we saw afar at the foot of the Cold Stone Mountains a strange sight: it was an image liking to a cloud of fire that flew low to the ground!' Victor gasped, as it was the same thing he saw in the Grey Forest on the night before they arrived at Treehouse. 'It never soared high, and we only ever saw it briefly through the gaps in the trees when we would hunt. We never ventured near to the Cold Stone Mountains, for there are terrible rumors of fearsome monsters and wraiths and other vile creatures living there. I have no deep knowledge of the world, so I cannot confirm the rumors. I am only knowledgeable of forests and archery, but I wanted to mention this ere you decide something too rash, my lords. Perhaps this mysterious sight is some sort of clue.'

'I saw the fire too,' Victor exclaimed nervously. The others peered at him curiously.

'When did such a thing happen?' Arthur inquired.

'It was during our journey to Treehouse on the night we slept in the woods. I woke from my sleep and saw a fire flying through the trees. Immediately after, I heard the sound of beasts shrieking in pain, or so I thought. I was afraid to tell anyone at the time for fear that I had dreamt the whole thing! But Rolo's account has shown me that I did not imagine it at all!'

Alastair stared at Rolo and then glanced at Victor with a raised brow. 'Well then, I see there are great men of knowledge even in the midst of marauders, and humble ones too!' the Wizard laughed. 'This is good news indeed! Come, Edgar and Grinshawl; we must revise our strategy.' Once again, the three withdrew to a quiet corner of the room and stood close to each other as they whispered. The rest of the room was quiet again, and Arthur, feeling excluded, was quite displeased with their rudeness. For a moment, it seemed as though the three were in obvious disagreement, but a few minutes later their heads were all nodding in concord again. They returned to the table, and Alastair addressed the group.

'I will be leaving this afternoon for a time,' he said rather abruptly. 'I will be investigating the fire Rolo mentioned near the Cold Stone Mountains. I believe that fire is connected to Asura. Dearest Arthur, I have a special request of you.'

'And what does the great leader of secrecy ask of me?' Arthur replied jutting out his lower lip.

Alastair chuckled ever so slightly and said, 'Send your dear son, Victor, with me on my quest!' At once, Victor's eyes gleamed when he heard the request. The idea of journeying with the mighty White Mage filled him with joy and excitement. Arthur glanced over at the boy, who was now smiling, and sighed heavily.

'Why wait until the afternoon?' he said with a wink of the eye.

Victor leapt from his seat and shouted, 'Thank you, uncle!'

'Promise me this, though, Wizard-friend,' Arthur returned. 'Give me your word that you will explain Elúvías to Victor and train him to use it. I am afraid I do not yet know how, so he has much to learn.'

'But you do know how, good Arthur! You have been using it all these years in the way you treat those around you. Elúvías has uses other than for fighting and Magic! Look at the village Kesh, how it flourishes. It is full of happy villagers who love their chieftain. And you raised Victor, who is now a fine young man. I tell you the truth; the power of Light is great in you! You are a man who does much good for others, and that is one of the signs of Elúvías within you! And hear you me; I will indeed teach the boy. Worry not! He is in good hands.'

'But why have you chosen me?' Victor asked doubtfully.

'Why you say? I chose you for reasons of my own, and that is all you need to know. Now leave it at that and stop doubting yourself!' Victor smiled and looked around. All the counselors smiled at him, except Tristan who appeared rather jealous of Victor again. Alastair noticed the prince's jealousy and cleared his throat. 'And fear not, you who remain! I have special tasks for each of you. Edgar and Grinshawl will be going on another special errand to meet with Seymour Gallinger, whose Celebhan name is Elorén! Remember that name well! He will assist them in seeking out the members of the Order who remain yet good. His eagles will keep watch on the borders, but they are not enough to do the job themselves.

'Thusly, I request of you, keen-eyed Meridas, to take your archers and increase your watch along the borders.' Meridas nodded and placed his right hand over his heart. 'The captains of the Boltian armies, by order of the king, will go about to all the strongholds and villages of Bolteras enlisting soldiers and rallying the Boltian warriors with courage. You will bring them to Vallicore if they are willing and have them train under the Templar Guard to learn the ways of Elúvías. Be diligent and stay ever vigilant! As for Rolo Longleaf and Pakko son of Elko, you will seek the aid of Eagle-Eye Zoro at his home in Fort Leaf, wherever it may be. He is a brute of a man as memory serves. But he is mighty and many follow him, though mere paupers they may be. If he and his band of misfits joined the Boltian army, then our victory will be ever more assured I should think. With proper training, even paupers can become great soldiers!

'Elder Bowman, I would charge you to maintain order in Vallicore in the king's stead. Your wisdom and renown are well-known and the people respect you.' As Alastair proposed each plan, the members agreed willingly, and were filled with excitement and high spirits. 'Fear not, Elder Bowman, the wise Arthur will help you with this task, for Vallicore is a large city, and Bolteras requires unyielding focus. Do your best for all our sakes!' Arthur and Elder Bowman exchanged glances and smiled cordially, as is the habit of elderly folk. They warmly shook one another's hands, not realizing at that time that they would soon become close friends. 'Furthermore, Balan and Langol of the Templar Guard will remain here with you for the task of training the warriors for battle.

'And lastly, but certainly not the least, I have a special task for Tristan and the two foreigners.' Tristan's eyes gleamed with excitement. He was eager to receive his quest, hoping that his task would be as noble as Victor's. 'Your task will quite possibly be the most heroic and perilous of them all! I charge you to take with you Delitas from Vash'ala and Gibraltar of Alterash and a few battalions of soldiers from Vallicore. Your task is to find a way into Kainor in the land of Alterash. No matter what it takes, you must slay the Alp called Gluttony, though that will be no easy task; then you must wait for the curse to be lifted from their shoulders. If you succeed, the Alterashians will be confused and weak, and they will need your aid in recovering. It is likely you will experience much opposition, so stay on guard and do not fail me!'

Tristan was especially elated and eager now. He had never been given so great and noble a task and he was thrilled to be trusted after waiting so long to prove his worth to his uncle. 'I will do my best, sir!' he shouted proudly. He stood and saluted the Wizard. Alastair placed his hat upon his brow and secretly rolled his eyes. 'Such arrogance,' he mumbled under his breath. He then placed his pipe between his lips and inhaled deeply. He then blew out three large rings of smoke and laughed cheerfully.

'Well, are there any complaints with my proposal?' Each of the counselors took their weapons and laid them upon the table: this was the sign that they were in agreement, that they would not bicker and fight over the decisions made during the Boltian Council. 'You have responded wisely, fair counselors! Let us not tarry any further! It is my advice that we begin our separate journeys as quickly as we may. I suggest you all pack for many days of travel. We do not know what evils await us, so be ready and always on guard. When each of you has succeeded in your task—and I suggest you do not return until you have succeeded—then we will reunite here in Vallicore. All of you must learn the secrets of Elúvías, so I suggest you stay diligent and finish your tasks quickly.'

The council ended at long last, and its members scattered to their rooms to gather their belongings for travel. Alastair withdrew from the King's Hall into the courtyard outside, and there stood Edward Baltheim leaning against one of the pillars of the archway at the entrance to the Silver Vestibule. He was smoking an aromatic weed, and the smell was sweet to Alastair. The Wizard took a deep breath and inhaled the aroma to his delight. Edward heard the Wizard's footsteps and turned around. He was nervously fingering the hilt of his sword.

'Good Wizard, have the counselors made their final decision?'

'Aye, we have indeed. Tell me, what is that lovely weed you smoke? I have never smelt a finer scent in all my many years!'

'It is unique to Xiphoria, my homeland. We call it *Frost Weed* for Xiphoria is a land of snow and ice. It is a curious plant, as it grows abundantly and survives the harsh cold of the land, and one must sift through the snow to find it. But I sense you did not come to speak of pipes and weeds, Alastair the White.'

'You are wise as you are brave, sir knight of the Sigma Cain! Tell me, how dire is the situation in the Eastern Lands?'

'Every day a great host of Men go to do battle with the Draemhas and hundreds are slain, or so it seems. And all our attacks fail. Not long ago, we discovered something of the Draemhas that we never knew before. There are new ranks of enemies rising within the armies of Dragoth, unlike any we have seen thus far. Most of the demons we have fought were just figures of black, like shadows, though bodies they have. We are all accustomed to those Draemhas; but recently, there have been others who appeared. We discussed already the Alps, and they are fearsome enough!

'But there are higher ranks even beyond them! The Alps are the strongest of the Draemhan *Grunts,* as we call the weakest of their kind, but they are not the greatest. We have gone to battle against the Draemhan Grunts on many occasions, but others have appeared before us bearing wings: some have two, others four, and some even six. We do not know how many wings the strongest have, but it seems the more wings, the stronger the enemy. And their power is ferocious and full of malice! We do all we can to hold them back, but of those with wings, we struggle just to defeat a small band! In our lands, they each have been given a name. The ones with two wings we call *Brutes*; the ones with four wings we call *Hellions*; and the six-winged beasts we call *Devils*.

'There is something I would not say in the presence of the others, but the Tri-Kingdom of Sanctum Anthropolis is failing! You know already, I am sure, of the power flowing forth from the ancient and evil Stone Vexúvías even as it remains trapped beneath the earth; but its power is far greater than we could have ever imagined. We believed it only to be rumor at once, but its power has been made clear, as though these winged beasts have been drawing their power from the Stone. They grow stronger with every passing day, Alastair. And we greatly dread the resurrection of the Dark Lord! I fear it will not be long before he is reborn. When that happens, all of Gaia and the last lines of Men will be destroyed.'

'Alas! the world will be darker than ever before if Abaddon is reborn,' Alastair said despondently. 'I am deeply troubled by the news of the winged Draemhas. They are the same as the Celebhas, though corrupted by the evil in their hearts. I mean not to frighten you, but you must know that there exists more powerful Draemhas beyond the Devils of Dragoth. Higher than the Devils are the *Archfiends* of eight wings and the *Archdemons* of ten wings. I once fought against Draemhas of that level in my earlier years, and they are not an enemy I should like to face a second time. The only rank higher than those belongs to the Dark Lord Abaddon who is rumored to have possessed twelve wings. One can only imagine the full extent of his power. I must, however, correct you on one point: the Alps were once stronger than the winged Draemhas, but their power has waned greatly. But no matter what enemy comes our way, it is only with the power of Elúvías that we will stand a chance; and so hope still remains! Fret no more, Edward of the line of Baltheim. When the time comes, we will come to your aid. Until then, wait for us and oppose the armies of Dragoth with all your might.'

'I fear the hope I once held on to is dead. There is more to my tale. Since your death and after the fall of Caire Thrael, many Men have joined Abaddon's forces and have been blessed with great power. The Enemy bribes and entices our soldiers every day, and alas! many turn to join the Dark Lord. The people of Scipherius, though they have always been a brutish clan, have willingly devoted themselves to the Enemy. Furthermore, a new breed of enemy has emerged. The Draemhas, those accursed fiends, have found a way of breeding Draemhas together with humans. In the Draemhan tongue, they call themselves the *Unsentane*, which we learned to mean *Half-Breeds* in the tongue of Men; and their power is greater even than some of the winged Draemhas. They are humans blessed, or cursed rather, with the strength of the Draemhas and the powers of Vexúvías. I have very little hope now, White Mage. How will we, the mere race of Men, stand against such feral hatred? Is there any hope still to be had?'

'There is always hope, Master Baltheim! Rest assured, we will win this battle in the Western Lands, and some day soon, Sanctum Anthropolis will find relief from Bolteras and her allies! Go now back to your people and be rid of your anxieties. Though Vaaspar no longer dwells amongst Men, He has given us His great

138

power! Trust in Elúvías, for there is no power that can stand before it! You must hold on to hope no matter how great our Enemy becomes.'

'I have little hope these days. Still, you give good counsel and insight, and I am encouraged by your words. May Vaaspar's Light shine on you, and I pray the kingdoms of the West find strength in these troubling times. I bid you farewell for now, for I must return to my fellow warriors. I simply wish that my boys were able to live in happier times. It is my greatest regret that they were born in times of such unyielding peril and hatred!'

'Aye,' Alastair replied solemnly. He perceived doubt and trouble in the eyes of Edward, and he knew not what to say. 'Farewell, brave knight. Stay strong!' Edward gave no response but simply waved his hand and withdrew slowly down the great hill to the gates. Alastair watched as the soldier mounted his steed and took flight. And he watched with sadness in his heart until the image of the man faded in the distance. A moment later, Victor appeared behind him.

'Hullo there!' Victor shouted, and Alastair jumped with alarm. 'Are we ready to depart?'

'Have you made all the necessary preparations? We may be gone for quite some time.' Even as Alastair spoke, his mind was filled with the troubling news of Edward's report, but he smiled tenderly at Victor and tried to hide his troubles from the boy.

'Aye, sir, I am ready and willing!'

'And where is that uncle of yours? Have you said your farewells?'

'I am not one liking to goodbyes, and I will see him again, very soon I imagine. Come now, let us go!' Alastair shook his head in disapproval, but just then Arthur appeared under the archway of the King's Hall.

'So you have decided to leave without saying farewell now have you, laddie?'

Victor stood motionless for a moment and then hesitantly turned around. 'Uncle, I—'

'Go, lad. You need not say goodbye if you do not wish to do so. But hurry back! Do not make an old man worry for long.' Victor smiled and nodded and then gave a wave of his hand, and Arthur mirrored his motion. Victor turned around as if to walk away. Tears welled up in Arthur's eyes. Before he had taken two steps, Victor suddenly turned around and ran into the arms of his beloved Arthur. The two embraced for a moment and said their proper goodbyes.

'I love you, Uncle Arthur!' Victor shouted as he hugged the old man. 'I will return as soon as I can!'

'I know, lad. I love you too.' Arthur released Victor from his arms and pushed him back gently. Looking him in the eyes, the old man smiled and patted him on the head.

'Well then,' Alastair interrupted after a moment's silence, 'shall we be off?' Victor gave no response at first but only darted down the hill; then he turned his head and shouted, 'I will race you to the bottom!' Alastair sighed and then laughed. Arthur, on the other hand, began to cry as he leaned against one of the pillars of the archway and watched his adopted son disappear down the long hill.

'You take good care of him now, brave Wizard, or you will answer to me!' Arthur snapped.

Alastair chuckled and bowed before Arthur. As he rose, he gave Arthur a tip of the hat and a wink of the eye and said, 'With my life, I will keep him safe.' With that he departed and met Victor at the bottom of the hill by the gate. Victor had already prepared two horses for their journey and was waiting eagerly for Alastair. The sun now loomed overhead and the day was nearing high noon. 'We have a long journey ahead of us, Victor, and I reckon we will ride swiftly and through the night with little rest along the way. The sooner we finish our task, the quicker we may return and possibly aid the others in their tasks. Are you well prepared?'

Victor smiled and leapt upon his horse. 'I have never been more prepared in all my life! Our journey to Treehouse in the Grey Forest was the first adventure I have ever been on. Then I came to Vallicore on my second journey, but we were in such haste and excitement that I forgot to properly observe the land around me. This time, I reckon I will breathe it all in and admire every tree, shrub and rock along the way. Though these times are evil, I do not think I have ever been happier than I am now! But I am determined as well. I must become stronger so, when the day comes, I may save my father and mother from the Darkness!' Alastair rubbed his chin curiously for a moment and then his face lit up with hope.

'My boy, I believe you have an even more unique power than I imagined. You will bring great hope to many people; I believe that with all my heart. Perhaps one day you will make a great king!' He laughed with a curious look on his face and climbed upon his steed. The guards—one of whom was Huseff—opened the gates and bid them farewell. But just then, someone appeared that Victor was not expecting.

'Will you be leaving without saying goodbye, Sir Victor?' It was the voice of a woman, and Victor knew at once to whom the voice belonged. He turned, and there stood Naomi. Her brown hair was flowing and her beautiful blue eyes were glistening. Victor blushed and climbed down from his steed. He turned to Alastair with a look on his face that seemed to say, '*May I go for a moment?*'

Alastair discerned his anxious mind and said, 'Go, lad, but make it quick. We have much to do.'

'How long will you be gone?' the girl asked before Victor had a chance to approach her. 'And will I see you again?' She was always smiling, but there was sadness in her voice.

'I do not know how long I will be away, but I give you my word that you will see me again,' Victor responded with a large, nervous smile on his face. 'I will be going away on a secret mission and may not return for some time. But I will come back!'

'But you have only just arrived...I am afraid your word is simply not good enough! You must promise me,' she insisted.

'I will not. I never make promises, for they can easily be broken. But my word is good, unless death bars me from seeing you again. You will just have to take my word, Naomi.'

The girl placed her right hand over her mouth and laughed. She then brushed her hair behind her ears and said, 'You are an endearing man! I can see you are both noble and honest, Sir Victor, for you travel in the company of Wizards. Whatever your purpose, work at it with all your might. I will await your return as will my father.'

'I beg your pardon?' Victor stuttered.

'My father wishes to meet the polite and handsome boy from Kesh. Those are my words not his, of course,' she responded with a nervous giggle.

'Then it shall be as you have said,' Victor said trying to appear confident. 'I will meet your father when I return, if you are still waiting for me when that day comes.'

'I am fond of you, Victor; can you not see that? Of course I will wait for you!'

'I am confused. Why have you taken such a liking to me?'

The girl paused for a moment as if searching for the right words. 'How should I put it? There is something different about you. There is a light within you, and I enjoy being near to that light. I do

141

not know what the days may bring, but I will wait in hopes of feeling that warmth again. Furthermore, you are a handsome man, Victor. Maybe one day you and I can spend more time together?' She winked and smiled as if awaiting a response, but Victor did not respond; he was far too nervous to say anything further.

After gazing into her gorgeous eyes for a brief moment, Victor leapt on his horse without a word and galloped out of the gates of Vallicore, only looking back to see if Naomi was still watching him. Alastair shook his head and followed after him. The girl waved and watched as long as she could, even climbing upon the walls to see the image of Victor until he faded behind a thick haze of mist far away to the north.

But as he left the glorious capital of Bolteras, Victor guided his horse upon the path to the south, the same road he entered Vallicore from just days before; but Alastair called out, 'No, lad, come this way! We go north then east!' Victor was embarrassed for a moment, afraid that Naomi saw his foolish mistake, but he quickly turned his steed about and darted northward across the plains near to Lake Serenity.

Alastair shook his head again and rolled his eyes. 'What remarkable vitality! Now how will an old man keep up with such youth?' The two rode ahead into a thick haze of fog that was descending upon the land. In a swift moment, Alastair passed Victor and took the lead, but Victor did not mind, as he was more concerned with observing the land than being in the lead. And so began the journey of Victor and Alastair the White.

* * *

Away back in the city, Tristan joined Naomi atop the parapet, and the two watched as Victor and the White Mage vanished in the distance. He was sad to see Victor leave, for he had no other friends near his age since Hildegard abandoned their company. Tristan had always felt alone as the other boys his age looked down on him for his uncouth behavior and untamed energy and wits; but Victor never judged him except in friendly jest.

He watched for a moment, and tears ran down his cheeks. He wiped his eyes frantically, alarmed by the fact that he was crying. 'Come now, Tristan ole' boy, this is no time to be crying. Now that Victor is gone, you ought to have more popularity around here. Yes, this is a good thing…a good thing indeed,' he said though the tears kept flowing. Although he looked forward to his own journey, he knew that he would be separated from Victor for a long time, perhaps the whole year; and that was a good enough reason for him to feel sad. After drying his tears, he looked to Naomi who was still gazing afar with hope in her eyes as if Victor would return riding through the fog calling out her name. After a moment, she looked up at Tristan, and he smiled at her.

'My name is Tri—' but just as he spoke, the girl turned and walked away. She descended the stairs of the parapet and traveled westward up the long slope to the fountain, leaving Tristan to stand there alone. 'Well that was a rather rude thing to do! Now how did Vicky catch her eye? But he deserves a girl like her, I suppose. A beautiful girl always deserves to be with a heroic and respectable man. And that is the kind of man my good Victor is.' he said with a salute. 'You had better not go and get yourself killed! One day, we will be equals!' He stood there a moment longer in deep thought and then said, 'Farewell, most excellent friend!'

A moment later, Delitas and Gibraltar arrived at the foot of the gate. 'Oi, Tristan,' Delitas cried out, 'Edgar King placed you in charge of our company during this perilous journey. Gibraltar and I simply want to see the evil purged from our lands, so we will put our trust in your leadership. What do you require of us?'

Tristan sat down at the top of the stairs of the parapet and pondered for a moment. 'I do not know what to do,' he said gravely after a while. 'Honestly, I have never had to take such great responsibility upon myself. I am not sure if I am capable of handling this, even with soldiers to accompany me. I am afraid of dying, and I have always let Uncle Edgar do everything for me. What should I do? Surely I cannot handle so great a task!' In the short time of knowing the Prince of Bolteras, Delitas and Gibraltar had never witnessed the genuineness of Tristan. They only knew him to be an arrogant, witty fool, not timid and humble. Gibraltar took compassion on him and tried to offer him encouragement after a long, silent break.

'Cheer up, lad! Delitas and I are soldiers, and I think I speak for the both of us when I say that we will stake our lives for you.' He turned to Delitas and winked at him.

Delitas understood the gesture and replied, 'Aye, if you are truly the nephew of Edgar and crowned Prince of Bolteras, then you are capable of anything! We will follow your lead and give counsel as needed. Rest assured, this is your opportunity to prove your worth!' Tristan looked up and found determination in his heart once more. He was honored to have people put their trust in him.

'Right you are!' he replied with enthusiasm. 'Before we depart, we ought to assemble a few battalions of skilled soldiers! I think it would be best to take forty or fifty of Vallicore's finest. They are the mightiest warriors in all of Bolteras!'

'Whatever you will, it shall be done, young lord,' Gibraltar answered.

'Aye, we offer our services fully to you. I only wish there were more of us from our lands to offer aid,' Delitas added.

'We may save some yet! Fear not!' Tristan said confidently. A strange energy and awareness began to grow within him, and he felt empowered. 'Wait here until I return. Rather, if you wish, you may wait at the pub down the lane and try some of Bolteras' delicious brews! It may be a while before we have time for merriment again, so enjoy it while you may!' Tristan pointed down the way leading north along the walls to a sign that read, 'Marty's Pub.' Delitas and Gibraltar seemed to favor the idea as they strode off down the lane without a moment's hesitation. Tristan called down to them one last time, 'Try some of Borgon's Beer or perhaps some of Mayle's Ale! I will come to you when I am prepared!' After they were beyond earshot, he spoke, 'Thank you for your kind words, my new friends. You have spoken life into me, and I am ever grateful for it!' Then, Tristan sped off at once to the Silver Vestibule to ready a dependable company of soldiers.

Inside the pub, Delitas and Gibraltar met Meridas who was guzzling down his third mug of Mayle's Ale. 'This is the finest beer I have ever tasted!' he shouted as they walked in. 'My friends, have a drink with me! Or three if you like!' he laughed. He then slammed his cup upon the table and belched loudly.

'That sounds delightful! Two pints of Mayle's Ale for me, good sir,' Delitas called out to the bartender, 'one for me and the other for my comrade.'

'Foreigners, eh?' returned the bartender. 'The name is Brunswick, Porty Brunswick at your service! Since you are first-timers, this one is on the house! It is odd to see a Vash'alan soldier in Vallicore, much less in the company of an Alterashian!' he exclaimed with a smile. Delitas and Gibraltar thanked the kind man and then took a sip of their malts.

'My, my, what a fine brew! There is nothing of the sort in all of Alterash!'

'I do not even like the taste of beer,' Delitas added, 'but I love this one! Mayle's Ale, was it? I would like to meet her maker.'

'He has long been dead, I am afraid,' Meridas replied, 'but this was his greatest work! Tell me, when will you two be departing?'

'Today, as soon as the young Prince Tristan returns to fetch us,' Gibraltar said. 'What will you do? Will you go at once to reinforce the borders of the Lonely Forest, archer lord?'

'Nay, I have decided to stay here for a time. Arthur gave me wise counsel. He insisted I send word to my archers in the Lonely Forest while I stay here for a time to learn the ways of Elúvías. After I have learned some of its ways, I will return to my troops and teach them. I merely hope we can be ready in time for war.'

'That is a fine plan indeed,' Delitas responded. After that, the three sat uncomfortably in silence for half an hour sipping their beers. Before long, they had each drifted into a daze of troubling thoughts concerning war. They stirred soon after to the sound of the pub doors crashing open followed by a loud, familiar voice.

'Hull chaps! Come now, good sirs, we have no time to be getting drunk. The king and the White Mage have given us a grand mission! Get up at once I say.' The two men turned and saw Tristan who appeared far more regal than before: he wore a finely designed suit of leather armor underneath a dark green cloak, and he stood tall and proud. Atop his head, he wore a leather helm with gilded edges, and he carried at his side a broadsword resting in a brown sheath of rawhide.

'I reckon the fun is over,' Gibraltar chuckled. 'Meridas, I wish you safe travel and blessed training. Good day!'

'I wish you the same,' Delitas added. 'Farewell!' Meridas wished them good travels and bid them farewell with a wave of the hand before returning back to his beer. The three quickly left the pub, but Tristan seemed to be the only one excited to go. When they came back out into the alleyway, there stood fifty soldiers from Vallicore dressed in elegant leather armors before them. In the group, a few of the warriors carried the Boltian banner on long wooden poles. Gibraltar and Delitas marveled at the sight of them and were encouraged by their fearsome appearance.

'Our trusty steeds are ready for us at the gates. Let us depart!' Tristan spoke now with great authority, sounding more regal even by the tone of his voice. 'How long will the journey take to Kainor, Gibraltar?'

'It will take about four days, traveling swiftly, to reach the borders of Alterash. But we will certainly have to travel slowly once

145

we cross into Alterash or else all the vile wolves of the land will be upon us. At a slow pace, it will likely take us some five days to reach Kainor from the borders. That makes for nine days, perhaps a few more if we are opposed by our enemies. With more than fifty Men, it will be difficult to disguise our presence, but we will find a way!'

'Aye, I have been taught by the wisest man I know! Uncle Edgar is a great king, and I shall be one too some day! I will use the wisdom he has poured in to me, and we will be victorious. Now come; we ride!' The warriors climbed upon their steeds and took flight upon the northern road. They followed by that way until it came to a fork in the road. At that point, they turned east and headed toward Kesh. And so began the journey of Tristan and his company.

* * *

As Tristan and his companions galloped out of the city, Rolo Longleaf and Pakko son of Elko emerged from the stables. They took for themselves two fine steeds from the stables, telling the Head Groom, 'We are members of the Boltian Council. We require steeds for a mission from the king.' The stable master was glad to be of service to the king and lent them two strong horses for their journey. Just as they passed through the gates, the two met their comrades from Treehouse who had finally arrived at Vallicore. The members of the Templar Guard greeted Rolo and Pakko, and the travelers were glad to see their comrades in good health. They greeted each of their kin and bid them farewell, but the weary travelers were confused; so, Rolo quickly explained the decisions made at the council. The soldiers of the Templar Guard became eager to begin training immediately, but Rolo and Pakko's kinfolk were confused and sad to see their beloved Leader depart.

'We will return as soon as we are able,' Rolo consoled them. 'But for now, rest here. Those of you who are able and willing should train in the ways of Elúvías. Do not worry, these brave soldiers will teach you all you need to know. Seek out Arthur Grause. He is living in the King's Hall for now and will teach you all you need to know.'

Rolo inquired of the location of Zoro's fortress, as they nearly left without asking. The soldiers informed them that the location was rumored to be somewhere to the northeast, in the woods between the Lonely Forest and the Grey Forest, called *the Lonely Grey*—it was also known as *the Rebels' Woods* after Zoro and his band claimed it as their own many years ago. The people of Treehouse insistently questioned their departure and begged them to

146

stay, but Rolo simply asked them to trust him; and they did, though reluctantly. At last, Rolo and Pakko mounted their horses and rode away to the northeast, though they did not know where to begin looking for the man called Eagle-Eye. When they had gone, the Templar Guard led the people of Treehouse into the city to an inn where they rested from their long journey. And thus began the journey of Rolo and Pakko.

* * *

The soldiers Paladin, Hauffa and Ragnok withdrew upon the following morning to rally the soldiers of Bolteras with as much swiftness as they were able. And each went their separate ways: Paladin began by calling upon the peoples who dwelt in tents near to the Great Sea to the northwest and then continued to Cayrngras before seeking out further aid from the small villages scattered about Bolteras; Hauffa went northeast to the cities of Bram, Eordil and eventually Balas, calling upon the peoples there; and Ragnok went south through the vast plains of the Weary Vale and sought out support from the tent-dwellers scattered throughout and then continued to Poleden, Carg and Pilias. And thus began their journey to rally the full armies of Bolteras to arms.

* * *

Balan and Langol of the Templar Guard stayed in Vallicore to assist Arthur and Elder Bowman in training the soldiers in the ways of Elúvías. Langol individually trained Meridas, so the archer-captain might return to his people quickly and begin their training. The rest of the Templar Guard, commanded by Balan, trained and strengthened the forces of Vallicore and all the more as Paladin, Hauffa and Ragnok rallied more and more soldiers to arms. Those who were enlisted by the Captains of Bolteras came to Vallicore and began their training at once.

* * *

While the rest of the counselors hurried to depart, Edgar and Grinshawl slowly prepared for their journey and left in the afternoon of the following day. And so, by the middle of the first week of April, all the members of the Boltian Council had disbanded for a time and embarked upon their separate journeys to prepare for the war in one year's time.

Chapter IX

Leaving Bolteras

Edgar and Grinshawl embarked from Vallicore in the late afternoon of April the second as the sun was already passing overhead to the west. Edgar brought with him his mighty war maul, which he called *Earthbreaker*, and two traveler's packs, one with food and the other with spare clothes. Grinshawl carried with him a simple battle axe and mace, though his was much smaller than Edgar's, and he never cared to name his weapons, except for Bolt and Hammer which were his 'favorite arms to bear,' as he so cleverly liked to put it. He brought also with him two sacks for clothes and food, and he burdened his horse further with several flasks of water as well. Both of the men wore simple clothes—tunics, leggings and a cloak—not wishing to be burdened by the weight of armor.

They strode forth along the northern road around to the northwestern tip of Lake Serenity. The path continued due north for nearly eight miles, and they followed it until the road split to the east towards the mighty fortress of Cayrngras. They traveled at a fair pace, merely trotting, for their speed was always slower when Grinshawl rode. He was a great burden to his horse of choice, which appeared to be a pony compared to the stature of the Ogre of Bolteras. Yet, he had found for himself a horse that willingly bore his mighty weight, and the beast proved strong and competent. After they had gone north and left Lake Serenity far behind, Grinshawl decided to name the beast *Able* and deemed him 'the sturdiest of horses.'

Edgar led the way down the main path leading northward. To their right, they passed along the western borders of the Canyon of Gold: it was a large chasm stretching more than fifteen leagues long, and it contained more gold than the Boltians could ever expect to use. For years it existed without any exploring its depths and dark caverns, but the peoples of Bolteras curiously flocked to its underground passages once the corruption of the Alp Greed had spread throughout the land. It was then that the people were consumed with the love of treasure, and some even fought, at times

148

to the death, to mine and gather as much gold ore as they could carry. Thus, the curse of Greed spread all across the lands of Bolteras. The origins of the Canyon of Gold were once remembered in the lore of the world, but its history had long been erased from Bolteras' history. For centuries, it remained a peculiar and mysterious place, yet few ever questioned whence it came.

The main road of Bolteras was stony, and the horses grew tired of it quickly, as was revealed to Edgar and Grinshawl by their lurching gaits; so they led their steeds from the road allowing the beasts to walk more easily upon the smooth grasses to the west side of the road. They followed the main road for a few more miles until it turned to the east. From there, they saw in the distance the fortress Cayrngras, the mightiest of the strongholds in Bolteras not accounting for the glorious capital city. Instead of following the road east, they kept north along a faded, dirt path that continued into the westernmost borders of the Lonely Forest at the foot of the Sage's Mountain. It was three miles from the start of the path to the edge of the woods. By the time they reached the woods, the last light of day had faded. The path disappeared suddenly, but the mountains, illuminated by the light of the moon and stars, loomed high above the tops of the trees, and their way was made clear. They continued, not wishing to halt until they had reached the Sage's Mountain and confronted the mysterious Seymour Gallinger. Thus, they strode forth into the throng of firs and ashes, and slowed their horses to an easy walking pace. They had now entered the Lonely Forest where Meridas' archers dwelt and protected the borders of Bolteras, though they were positioned much further to the northeast.

The king and his companion carefully treaded across the forest terrain avoiding collapsed trees and thick brushes that obstructed their path. The ground rose and fell with many hills along the way, and their pace was slowed further. There were no paths in the woods, so they simply kept straight as often as they could. The way seemed easy enough, but the many fallen trees and other obstructions made their journey difficult. As they strode further into the woods, the darkness of night grew thicker, their vision poorer, and they considered halting for the evening; but they decided, after a brief respite to continue. From there, they dismounted and led their horses by the reins. After a few minutes of walking blindly in the woods, Edgar reached for a lantern that was tied to his horse's saddle. It contained no oil or candle, but Edgar reached inside and made his hand into a fist. Immediately, a red glow emitted from his hand, and a white fire started within the lantern: it hovered and burned all on its own, or so it seemed.

'Elúvías has many uses, indeed!' Edgar exclaimed cheerfully. 'This light shall shine the way before us. I should not like to be lost in the middle of the forest so close to Vash'ala.'

'I feel the same!' Grinshawl replied. 'And night is certainly not the best time to meet Draemhas, or any enemy for that matter!' They paced forth as quickly as they were able, but the lantern's light only revealed a short distance in front of them. Several minutes passed before they emerged from the forest and came upon an open meadow. The forest continued to their east, but they strayed from it for the time being. Just before them was a great lake: it was at the foot of the mountain, its source deriving from the fresh spring waters of the Roaring River. From the edge of the woods, they stood at the southern tip of the lake. Not far from where they stood, a long, wooden pier ran out upon the water, but there was no boat to be seen.

The moon hung overhead and reflected upon the lake's waters. A few stars shimmered brilliantly above as well and were mirrored upon the surface of the water; but clouds began to form and blot out most of their light. Before the sky was fully blanketed by the rapidly forming billows, the two travelers happily gazed at the lake as it flickered from the light of the moon and stars. With no boat to take them across the waters, they proceeded along the eastern rim of the lake, yet they were glad to walk given that their horses could not travel by boat. They peered across the large lake and saw a pathway running down from the mountain: it passed along the northern edge of the lake and continued east where it vanished into the shadows of the forest. As they pressed on, the clouds above gathered so thickly that no light from the heavens could be seen, and Edgar's lantern was their only source of light. After a while, they came to the branch of the Roaring River that poured into the mouth of the lake. The stream was too wide and appeared too deep for them to wade, so they turned east and reentered the woods in search of a ford or a bridge to cross safely to the other side of the river. They had hardly gone two furlongs into the forest when they came upon a narrow, wooden bridge that ran across the breadth of the brook. They crossed it, turned back to the west and emerged once again from the forest.

Once again, the soft blades of grass whispered softly beneath their bustling feet, and they sped forth as the moon began to shine through the clouds once more. Edgar shone the light of his lantern before them to keep from falling into the lagoon at their side. As they scurried onward, wisps of smoke fell from the mountains onto the ground below and their vision was greatly impaired. Edgar's lantern was of no more use in the thick fog, but just then, they caught a glimpse of the dirt path leading to the foot of the peak. Before long and quite unexpectedly, their feet fell upon hard stone. From there, they gazed upon the path to the west as it ran upward into the Sage's Mountain. The fog thinned out just a little, but their vision was still greatly impaired. As they stood at the bottom of the pathway, they suddenly felt an eerie presence like eyes watching them. The feeling sent chills down their spines, and their horses neighed loudly and plodded their mighty hooves upon the stony ground. The noise resonated all around, and Edgar and Grinshawl feared the sound would summon enemies on all sides.

Once the horses were calm, they pressed on and were elated that they were not waylaid by the minions of the Dark Lord. The path before them was carved into the mountain like a brilliantly-fashioned road, and it led all the way up the tall slopes of the mountains in a spiraling motion. 'This path was not forged by Men!' Edgar exclaimed. 'There is some other force at work in the carving of this stone. There is majesty in its making.' Edgar stepped forward and began to climb the slope. Grinshawl followed reluctantly. Oddly enough, their horses were now quiet and appeared rather vitalized. 'This is the second time I have climbed this mountain to seek the aid of Seymour Gallinger. I am amazed that this peak—Elorén after his name—still stands majestically and untouched by the Enemy's hand, though I suppose even the armies of the Dark Lord would stray far from Elorén the Celebhas lest they be brought to ruin. The power of the Celebhas is tremendous indeed! As this is your first time meeting him, I encourage you to remain calm. There is a terrifying presence about Elorén; but I assure you, he is fully good, and we are quite safe.'

'Aye, I sense an eerie presence about this mountain, but it is oddly soothing at the same time.' Grinshawl paused and looked about believing someone had just called his name. 'I hear voices, Edgar. There are voices speaking to me and telling me to ease my mind. Do you hear them, my liege?'

'Indeed, they speak to me as well, but I hear different words. They are saying, "Welcome, King of Bolteras. You are friends, and you are welcome here." Now they are weeping, but I do not know why.'

'Hullo,' Grinshawl shouted, 'who speaks to us?' There was no answer, only the sounds of the voices echoing and fading slowly as they seemed to ascend to the mountaintop. 'This place frightens me, Sire. Are you certain we are safe?'

'Aye, we are safer here than anywhere for the time being. The voices you hear are likely to be those of the dead screaming from the pits of Shaekle. You tend to hear mysterious things in the presence of a Celebhas; but do not fear, for they can do us no harm! Let us not tarry here. Oh, and be warned; you may feel faint in the presence of Seymour, for there is a great aura of power about him that causes weakness in Men. In fact, the first time I traveled upon this path to meet with him, I fell unconscious for a while. The only other time I have beheld the Celebhas was when he delivered Elúvías to the Cathedral of Light during the reign of King Haus. I was only a young lad then, but, ah, those were happier times! I think I was at a safe distance that day in Vallicore, so I did not suffer from his power. Forgive my reminiscing, friend.' Grinshawl felt more nervous now than before, but he followed Edgar all the same.

They traveled further up the spiraling path in silence for a time. A cool breeze blew from the top of the mountain, and the two shuddered and pulled their cloaks about them. Shortly after, the air felt unexpectedly warm and pleasant like the hours of morning when the sun first rises. After nearly half an hour, Grinshawl spoke again. 'After all you have said, I am glad that Elorén is a friend to Bolteras! Yet, if he is as powerful as you say, then why has he not gone to the Eastern Lands to the aid of Sanctum Anthropolis? Surely they need his power more in those lands.'

'He has the power of foresight, and I imagine he saw a greater need here and plans to move east after he fulfills his purpose.'

'Right you are, Edgar King!' a booming voice answered from above them. They stirred in shock, and their horses neighed and tramped about in fear. Suddenly, Edgar and Grinshawl both felt faint, and their legs nearly yielded beneath them. Speaking now in the Celebhan tongue, the voice called out again in a hushed tone, '*Gu, Gu! En Sulia, Irík Helia Seypa 'lo!*' At once, the horses were calm again from the commanding voice of the Celebhas. The Celebhan language was soothing to Edgar and Grinshawl, and it calmed their every fear. It was unlike anything they had heard before. '*Olen, Namaka 'lo!*' the voice called again, but they did not understand. 'Come, friends!' The voice interpreted. They stirred as if waking from a spell or a deep sleep and looked all about, but they were alone.

Continuing onward up the rising slope as if lured by a mighty spell, the horses pressed on with fresh vigor and eagerness forcing their masters to march along with them. Several minutes later, the slope ended at the top of the mountain where it ran into a flat open space encircled by the rising points of the mountain: it appeared to them as a tent hewn from stone, an oddly-fashioned cave. The path ran inside the cave, and it was the only road that ran to the top of the peak. They slowly entered the cave and remained vigilant as if anticipating an inevitable attack.

'Welcome to my home!' called the same voice from earlier, but still they appeared to be alone. 'A sage of the mountains rarely has visitors. I implore you, my friends, to come and sit. And let also your horses rest from their tiresome journey. Rest assured, they will find new strength in my shelter.' Suddenly a hooded figure appeared, like one emerging from a thick fog. He wore a dark cloak and held in his right hand a brown staff that split at the top in two directions: the two branches were finely-crafted into two images resembling the heads of Dragon. He tapped the bottom of the staff upon the rock, and the stone pavilion lit up with colors of greens and purples, blues and reds, and yellows and oranges in a fascinating array of swirls and flashes. It was beautiful to them. The colors flew like birds about the cave and whirled above Edgar and Grinshawl. Their horses calmly plopped upon the rocky ground at the back of the cave and fell fast asleep. 'You must be weary too, friends. Perhaps, you should rest,' he continued. As they marveled at the wonderful sight of the colors, they lay down, as though commanded by an enchantment, and fell asleep.

* * *

Upon waking, the two Men felt greatly refreshed. They expected to be greatly famished as they had not eaten since they left Vallicore but were instead rather satisfied. And they did not even question their contentment, for they had never felt better than they did at that time. Upon waking, Edgar found some blood on his clothes and wiped more from his lips; but he did not recall coughing any up in his sleep. Grinshawl observed with wrinkled brows and sadness in his eyes. They each found a nice rounded stone to sit upon and watched as their horses galloped to and fro about the cavern playing with one another like ponies full of youthful vitality. In the middle of the room, they saw a white fire burning brightly amidst a

153

small circle of stones, and it provided the room with plenty of light and warmth even from a distance. Edgar eagerly looked around the room for the mysterious Celebhas, but there was no sight of him. Looking about, they noticed that the entrance to the cave had vanished and was sealed by a wall of firm stone. Grinshawl rose frantically from where he sat and attempted but failed to break through the wall of stone with his mighty strength. Out of panic, he incessantly and hopelessly beat his fists upon the rock, but Edgar simply watched and laughed.

'Calm yourself, friend!' Edgar said once he calmed his laughter. 'Did I not say that this place is safer than any other? The way has been shut for our protection, and look! there is much light for us to see. I am amazed that our steeds are able to enjoy it so much, yet you ignore all the miracles happening around you.' Grinshawl turned about and sat on the ground, ashamed of his misgivings about the Celebhas. A moment later, the stone wall behind Grinshawl disappeared like a wisp of smoke penetrated by the rays of the sun.

'Top of the morning, young sires,' Seymour called nonchalantly as he entered the room. His hood was lowered now, and he appeared neither young nor old. Rather, he appeared both strong and ageless to the Men as they peered at him with curious eyes. But he took no notice of their interest and continued, 'Elorén at your service, but you may call me Seymour, for that is my name in the tongue of Men. How did you sleep?'

'It was wonderful,' Edgar answered as he stretched his arms high above his head, 'I have not slept so great in many long days.'

'Aye,' Grinshawl added with a yawn, 'it was the mightiest of sleeps until I woke to behold wizardry at work!'

'Wizardry you say?' Seymour laughed. 'Celebhas are not Wizards, simple-minded one! No indeed, that ancient art requires the user to have knowledge of written spells and incantations, which are the instruments of the forces of Dragoth and of Men. Nay I say; we of the Celebhas exercise the ways of Elúvías and nothing more. And there are no incantations or curses or anything of the sort in the disciplines of the Light, for it is an ancient and untamed power, or rather a glorious, living being connected to Vaaspar Himself. It is difficult to explain, but Elúvías is Magic in its purest form, a manifestation of the power that belongs to the Lord of Light. Though Men can utilize the Magic arts of Elúvías, they can never possess it. Men are strong and capable of great things, but their bodies are not

154

strong enough to master Elúvías. In truth, not even the Celebhas can fully master such power! So be wary of your words, Grinshawl former slave of Vash'ala, for one would be careful not to insult one of the Celebhas. But as it is, you are not my enemy, and I am not yours. Be at peace; you are well protected here!' Grinshawl lowered his head meekly in his embarrassment.

'Cheer up, Grinshawl! We are all friends here,' Edgar added excitedly. But Grinshawl still hung his head. 'Well then, what day is it, Master Elorén?'

'Why it is noon already, on the seventh of April.'

'The seventh of April?' Grinshawl asked anxiously raising his head in disbelief. 'How can that be? We arrived upon the evening of the second! Surely we did not sleep for five days!'

'But indeed you did!' Seymour insisted. 'Your bodies were weary, so I let you rest within the shelter of my power. You have awoken now, so fret not.'

'Why, may I ask, are we not hungry if it has been nearly five days since we last ate?' Edgar questioned.

'It has been less than twenty years since you saw me last and you have forgotten much already! It was my power that put you to sleep and kept you safe. I discerned troubling thoughts racing through your minds and distress was written on your faces. You were overcome by anxiousness, so I let you escape from your worries until you could rise anew. Within the borders of my power, if I so choose, time passes as the blink of the eye and your bodies hungered little. And with my power, I satisfied any hunger you experienced.' Seymour saw an expression on Grinshawl's face that seemed to say, '*Is that possible?*' Discerning his thoughts, Seymour walked forward and stooped in front of the giant. 'Yes, such a thing is possible! Do you doubt my words even now after you have already been proven the fool, great Ogre of Bolteras? Or are you simply afraid to trust me?'

'M-me, a-afraid? Never! The Ogre of Bolteras knows no fear! I confess that I might have doubted you for a moment, and though I have my doubts, fear will never rule over me! Still, I beg your forgiveness for my disbelief, great lord.'

'Is that so?' Seymour laughed. 'Very well, then; I am glad to hear it, for it seems fear consumes many these days! Your misgivings are forgiven you, friend, but do not call me a great lord. Truly there is only One worthy of that title: the Lord of Light! Now tell me, with what purpose have you come to an old sage of the mountains?'

'Wise one, you spoke to us upon the mountain pass, did you not?' Edgar asked. Seymour nodded and raised an eyebrow. 'Then you have some greater purpose here that has yet to be fulfilled? Does that mean you will go east when your task is complete?'

'Aye, I have been given a purpose here in the Western Lands that I have yet to accomplish. My mission has become more complicated than I had hoped. Even I did not foresee Abaddon's delay in going to war against Bolteras.'

'What do you mean?' Grinshawl interrupted. 'How has the war been delayed?'

'I see you are unaware,' Seymour replied solemnly. 'The Enemy deferred his plans, but I still do not know what spurred his decision. War was very close, nigh to a month or two, but something held him back. Perhaps the Men of the East proved a greater adversary than the Dark Lord had hoped for, thus forcing him to withdraw some of his western forces. I cannot say for certain, but one of my kin, by the name of Elúndar, has gone to the aid of Sanctum Anthropolis. And I sent with him the Earth Dragon Uras and the Wind Dragon Fujin. With such force, I imagine he dealt our Enemy a powerful blow. The invasion here in the West is feeble in comparison to the trials in the East, but if left unchecked, all the lands of Gaia may fall to the powers of Darkness. That is why I will not abandon Bolteras until Vash'ala and the Draemhas are defeated and the safety of the Western Lands is secured. But that may be prolonged further with the corruption spreading in Alterash.'

'We have prepared a party to handle their situation,' Edgar answered. 'I sent my nephew, Tristan, and a band of soldiers to help expel the Alp known as Gluttony. At the Boltian Council, we received insight from Alastair the White that the Draemhas in Vash'ala would attack in one year's time. He said it was you who informed him of this, yet you say war was closer at once. This is news to us!'

'Aye, I told the White Mage, but I left it to his discretion whether to inform you of that news. The situation has changed, so it was not vital that you know. Now then, if your nephew and his companions succeed—and I hope they do—then perhaps the East will find aid much sooner than I expected. What is it you ask of me then, Edgar King?

'We have been advised by Alastair the White to seek your aid in restoring the Order of the Magus! But I have not come asking anything of you; rather, what is it that *we* should do for *you*?'

'You are a humble man, Edgar King, but this land is under your rule, not mine. As King of Bolteras, you have authority over all those who dwell in your lands, so I am at your service. But alas! I fear I must disappoint you on your mission! Grave news came to me after my meeting with Alastair upon his return to Bolteras,' Seymour responded somberly. 'To his despair he will find that the Order will never be fully restored. A messenger owl sent from my kin, Elúndar, reported many ill tidings to me. Beredor the Black swayed the minds of Maldrad the Red and Raven the Gold in recent days, and they committed their ways to the Darkness. The remaining Magus either disappeared or else died. I am afraid Armand the Blue, convinced that he could change the mind of Leviathan, went upon the waters of the Great Sea and summoned forth the ancient Dragon with his Water Magic. All this happened nearly one month ago. He pleaded with his old mentor to aid Men against the Draemhas, but she rejected his request. He hoped, or so I think, to clear the seas of her threat so Men might freely traverse her waters once more and thus launch an invasion on Dragoth from the seas.

'But alas! Leviathan in her rage called forth a mighty wave, which overpowered the Water Mage and carried him off to his watery grave; and a great mass of land was engulfed along with him. At another time during one of the battles in the Eastern Lands, Maldrad the Red confronted Tiberius the Green, and the two Wizards destroyed one another. In the balance of the elements, you see, water is over fire, fire over wind, wind over lightning, lightning over earth, and earth over water. So neither Maldrad the Fire Mage nor Tiberius the Earth Mage contained Magic more powerful than their opponent. In the end, Maldrad slew Tiberius, but the last of his Mana was consumed and he died as well. Elúndar witnessed the battle between the Mages, but they would not heed his voice when he called out to them. They were consumed with hatred and desired only to pass judgment on the other.

'Regrettably, the two Wizards slew one another and now only Percival the Silver lives. He is the Wind Mage and is the last remnant of the Magus apart from Alastair. And I have yet to locate his whereabouts, but he *has* been spoken of in rumors. At best, Alastair will have one of his old comrades to join him again. But if Percival and Alastair reunite, then the Order of the Magus may

157

withstand Beredor and Raven, or *the Sorcerers of Darkness* as they call themselves. According to the balance of the elements, Percival's Wind Magic can easily overcome Raven's Lightning Magic. And, naturally, Light will always overcome Darkness; hence, Alastair must face Beredor the Black when the time comes. But all told, the Order of the Magus has been shattered, never to return to its former glory.'

'These are ill tidings!' Edgar lamented. He lowered his head despondently and placed his hands over his face. Seymour observed him for a moment and then glanced upon the face of Grinshawl, who seemed lost in thought. A moment later, the giant jumped to his feet; then, he flexed his arms and roared with excitement.

'Fear not, my liege! The Ogre of Bolteras will never fail as long as Bolt and Hammer have strength! Alastair cannot defeat Beredor and Raven alone, so we must find Percival at all costs and help them to bring the Sorcerers of Darkness to ruin! The power of those sorcerers is surely enough to turn the tide of battle in the East, but if we stop them, then perhaps the forces of Light will be able to overcome the armies of Dragoth.'

Seymour chuckled and said, 'Agreed! I see the old prisoner of Vash'ala has become one of Bolteras' mightiest additions and a good friend to the king. Earlier you asked what *you* could do for *me*, but I suggest you consider doing what Vaaspar requires of you. Seek to do justice, show mercy to those of Men who will accept it, and always be humble as you already are. Allow no evil into your hearts and keep fighting until Vaaspar returns!'

'Lawks,' Edgar responded in dismay, 'can it be? Does Vaaspar plan on returning to Gaia? When will all this happen?'

'Indeed! and He always has! This news should be recorded in many annals within the holy city of Vallicore. Did you think all the history of Vaaspar was mere myth? Not at all, I tell you! The Lord of Light will return, but I cannot say when, for I do not know. In fact, none know the time or day but Him alone! But listen closely to me, Edgar King and Grinshawl friend; you must be ready for His return, for when He comes, it will be sudden and terrifying like the flash of lightning. You must guard your hearts and minds against the Evil One, so he will not pass judgment on you when that day comes. Upon His return, all who dwell in Darkness will be filled with many woes. He comes to pour forth His wrath upon Abaddon and any who have obeyed the Dark Lord's will. Again I say it; the Lord of Light will return! Stay vigilant and always pursue good!' There was a long

158

silence in the room for several minutes as Edgar and Grinshawl let the news sink in to their deepest thoughts. Seymour rose and paced about the room until Edgar broke the silence.

'Then how will we proceed? This news is too great for me! I cannot make a decision after hearing such things! Please, wise and knowing friend, what do you ask of us? How can I claim my right to rule when I stand before one of the Celebhas? Please instruct me in your wisdom!'

'I will go with you, most noble king amongst Men,' Seymour responded in a soothing voice, 'to where Percival the Silver resides. But to reach him, we must pass beyond shadows into dark lands stained with blood. We must go to Vash'ala!' Edgar and Grinshawl leapt from where they sat and shuddered from the mention of that barren land.

'Warrior of Light,' Grinshawl added, 'it would require a vast army to storm into Vash'ala seeking a Mage of the Order! Is he a prisoner? And are we to wage war early?'

Seymour laughed hysterically for a moment; the sound of his laugh made Edgar and Grinshawl uneasy. Then he suddenly knocked his staff upon the stone. 'How many times must I repeat myself to you?' he snapped. 'Did you sleep for days, only to return to your worries and fears? Do not be afraid! My eagles have scouted the lands of Vash'ala, and only one of the Draemhas has appeared who can rival my power. Accounting for their many numbers, however, we will pass secretly through the land. Percival now resides in the northeastern region of Vash'ala in a cave nigh to the Great Sea, or so the rumors are told. And where do you suppose such rumors originated? They started from yours truly, but of course!' Seymour laughed again, the same hysterical cackle as before as though he considered the whole journey an enjoyable stroll through a peaceful meadow.

'I do not understand,' Grinshawl replied.

'Of course you do not! You believe there is something to fear, but it is not so with me! There are many ways of going unseen: there are woods, magical cloaks, the shrouding power of Elúvías, and even Dragons!' Edgar and Grinshawl gasped in amazement.

'Wise one, you speak of too great of things!' Edgar exclaimed. 'I cannot contain myself with the knowledge you speak!' Seymour laughed again.

'I see you have had enough of my riddles. I have gained the trust of two Dragons— the Earth and the Wind Dragon—as I mentioned earlier, and I may call upon them whenever I wish. But I will not do such a thing. Such a sight would rouse the armies of Vash'ala to arms, but Bolteras is not yet ready for a war. Furthermore, Alterash is in an ill state and cannot lend us aid; so we must be cautious, for the time being, so as not to attract any unnecessary attention from our enemies. The Dark Lord is dreadfully powerful, and we do not want to taunt him before we are ready. Besides, the Dragons are needed more in the Eastern Lands, so they will stay there. Still, there are other ways of passing safely through Vash'ala; so fear not! Come now, my spies have returned to report their findings.'

They listened closely and heard the cries of eagles in the distance. As they exited the cave, they noticed large aeries on the sides of the mountain, some with eggs and others barren—they had not noticed them on their journey up the mountain, for it was too dark at that time to see. The nests were enormous, and Grinshawl expected the eagles to be of a great, unusual size. Seymour raised his arm, and an eagle swooped down from the air and rested softly upon it. The eagle was not big or small, just the normal size one would expect to see, but it did have red feathers like fire under its eyes. Grinshawl sighed in his disappointment as he had hoped to see something of an anomaly.

'*Gul'Dar Ín Vayne Thrael, Enan*,' the eagle said in a soft, soothing voice. '*Vayne Nap'thar Ireche Ot VexúYahn. Ot Aymorald É Ot Ouchemar 'lo Hagan Mílnk Skrypta.*'

'Speak, my friend' Seymour interrupted, 'in the tongue of Men, so our friends might understand the things you speak.'

'Forgive me, great one,' the eagle returned, its voice now deep and commanding, 'I am not accustomed to speaking in the tongue of Men when I am in your presence.'

'How does it speak?' Grinshawl interrupted in shock.

'I taught it, of course!' Seymour answered. 'Now listen if you wish to become wise and understanding!'

'Ere I continue,' the eagle said, 'allow me to introduce myself. I am Greatwing, leader of the Eagles of the Sage's Mountain. It is a pleasure to finally meet the famous King of Bolteras! My kin and I have long been investigating Vash'ala, even since the war twenty years ago. Vash'ala's power would be nothing if not for the work of those accursed Alchemists and their precious Stone of Power! We have seen thousands of Draemhas roaming freely

160

through the arid lands, and they are welcomed by the evil Men of Vash'ala.

'There were a number who resisted King Marxas and the Draemhas at first; indeed! they even fought back, but to no avail. They were slaughtered and used for an infernal ritual beneath the earth. We saw not what occurred but only heard rumors of it. We were never suspected as spies since we eagles have roamed those lands for centuries. But one day as I was scouting the lands, I witnessed a group of Draemhas carrying a shiny orb, small in appearance, but it emanated a great power. The air about me felt heavy all of a sudden as though the stone was creating a sort of pressure in the air; and it was difficult for me to fly. The demons of Dragoth rose from an underground tunnel with four humans dressed in long, dark robes, and they carried the stone to Osceroth, the capital city. It was there they assembled and built a shrine, placing the Alchemist's Stone at its center. That shrine was later carried away to the king's throne room. A week elapsed and the four humans were introduced as the *Acolytes of Darkness*. They wore dark veils that shrouded the lower half of their faces, so I never learned of their true identity. But there was an unusual presence of evil in the air about them, and they were always protected by a shadowy, sable aura.

'As I watched that day, one of them looked up and stared me straight in the eye. I have never felt more uncomfortable than I did that day, and I will never forget the look in his eye. It was a long time before I returned to that land, but my kin always flew about gathering information as they could. With the Alchemist's Stone, the Dark Lord sent his forces through a portal from Dragoth to Vash'ala. It seems that only about ten or so may pass through the gateway each day, though we have not learned the reasoning behind it. But perhaps the Enemy's power is too weak to summon more, or maybe that is all he can. Whatever the truth is, the Draemhas are gathering in abundance. In our search, we have accounted for the evil Men of Vash'ala, and their armies total to a feeble ten thousand. They are weak if left alone, but with their new allies, they are not to be trifled with. My kin fear many were used in the sacrificial ritual to create the Alchemist's Stone, which would explain their shortage of soldiers.'

'Tell them their odds, Greatwing, and do not give them false hope. They must know the strength of their enemy if they are to be prepared for the coming war.'

'Aye,' the eagle responded solemnly, 'I am afraid, my lords, their numbers are nearing three myriads or more!'

'Thirty thousand?' Edgar questioned. 'Where does such a force come from?'

'It is Abaddon's power,' Seymour answered, 'as it is Vaaspar's. When Vaaspar awoke us from the ground, He taught us to awaken life. And Abaddon has long used his powers to awaken Draemhas and other vile creatures from the depths of Shaekle. If the Dark Lord's armies are this great already, who can tell what will await you in one year. And if he is able to spare such numbers in the Western Lands, then his power in the East is greater than I expected. Certainly all of Gaia will fall beneath his power if his armies succeed here. I advise you to muster your troops as swiftly as you may and do not give the enemy enough time to raise an indomitable force!'

'Aye, my liege,' Grinshawl added, 'I am eager to go on our way and put an end to those fiends of Dragoth! We have already been idle for nearly five days, and this day is already waning. Let us delay our task no longer!'

'Agreed,' Edgar returned. 'Elorén, my friend, can you be ready soon?'

Seymour glared at Edgar harshly, but then replied with a soft voice, 'I am *always* prepared!' He laughed and with a clap of his hands a traveling bag appeared on his back. He pulled his hood up and held his staff by his side. 'My question is, young lads, are *you* ready?' Edgar chuckled with excitement and a large smile spread across his face.

Grinshawl released a mighty roar and exclaimed, 'I have never been more ready in all my life!' He flexed his muscles and then quickly ran to gather their equipment. He called from inside the cave, 'What shall we do with the horses? Will they come?'

'Nay,' Seymour answered, 'leave them. I assure you they will be quite safe here and glad too! There are allies here who will protect them. Worry yourselves with them no more! Let us begin this journey at long last.' Grinshawl said a final farewell to Able and deemed him 'the mightiest of all beasts;' then, he rejoined his comrades.

The three descended the long spiraling slope of the mountain at a slow and easy pace. At the foot of the mountain they traveled east and entered the Lonely Forest along the northern edge of the Roaring River. They traveled abreast for roughly two miles before Seymour turned sharply to his left, unbeknownst to Edgar and

Grinshawl. Edgar turned and began to speak when he saw the Celebhas away to the north through the gaps in the trees. He wavered for a moment and then called to Grinshawl; and the two sped off to rejoin their companion who was whistling blithely as he trudged along.

Onward they traveled, keeping due north for three more miles until they met a great host of archers from Meridas' faction at the edge of the forest. At the forest's end, there was a large bivouac filled with many tents scattered across a wide, flat precipice. The archers quickly identified the group, even Seymour as the Celebhas came to them often and spoke with them of the happenings in the world. The travelers were greeted warmly, but they did not stay long. Edgar stepped aside for a moment to speak with one of the archer-captains, named Genrig, concerning the whereabouts of Meridas.

'Oh, uh, see, Your Highness…Meridas, uh, sent word a few days ago. It seems he, uh, wishes to stay in Vallicore for, ah, a time to learn the ways of Elúvías; then he will, ah, return to, uh, oh yes! He will return to teach them to us, ah, I believe.'

'At ease, soldier. There is no need to be uneasy around me,' Edgar replied.

'No, uh, sir, you mistake me. I, ah, have always talked, uh, like this.'

'I beg your forgiveness! I meant you no insult. When Meridas arrives, listen intently, the lot of you, to all he has to teach you. It is vital to our victory!' The stuttering man nodded, and Edgar reconvened with his party. They left the bivouac and strode north until they came to the edge of the cliff only eight or nine fathoms beyond the last tent of the bivouac. The cliff overlooked the *Valley of Despair* between the borders of Bolteras and Vash'ala at the foot of the northernmost peak of the Sage's Mountain.

'The archers can see a great deal from here,' Edgar said, 'and at this height they have a great advantage against an approaching army. Let us hope, however, they do not need their bows for quite some time.'

After enjoying the view for a moment, they turned right and followed the cliff as it rounded to the northeast for more than a furlong. From there, the path descended down a long hill. The land became grassy again as they strode along the edge of the forest, but the path eventually ran into a rocky bed between two, low stone walls at the bottom of the slope. The three stood now upon the dried riverbed that once carried the mighty, rushing waters of the Roaring

163

River deep into the lands of Vash'ala. Further to the southeast, there was a dam made by the archers of the Lonely Forest that blocked the flow of the river and created a large pond with several small streams branching out to the east and west. They traveled through the dried bed as though it was an open road, and it carried them around to the northwest.

As they went along the path, the stone walls rose higher and higher until they appeared as immense cliffs on both sides. At that point, the ravine became very narrow. They walked one behind the other through the narrow channel for a while until they passed beyond the borders of Bolteras and into the land of Vash'ala. The high wall on their right turned suddenly to the northeast, and they followed a small path that opened up from the riverbed up a tall hill of dirt and ash. They left the dried up riverbed behind them, though it continued further for miles. From the hill, they could see the dried river's end far away to the northwest where the land was full of many cracks and fissures. At the top of the high knoll, the land evened out, and their path continued into the shelter of a long wood of dead trees that rested between the borders of Vash'ala and Alterash, known as the *Putrid Wood*...

Chapter X

The Trial of Fire

Upon the fourth of April, Victor and Alastair arrived at the Boltian fortress of Balas just miles away from the village Kesh. It was there they abandoned their horses and continued the rest of their journey on foot. 'We do not want to attract any attention, so we will not travel nigh the Cold Stone Mountains where our horses' hooves will clatter for vile creatures to hear,' Alastair explained to the confused Keshian boy as they yielded their horses to the Head Groom at Balas. 'Furthermore, I should not like to disturb Asura any more than we already must. Come now; cheer up, lad! It is good for us to travel by foot. Think of it as the beginning of your physical training,' he ended with a wink.

'I think we ought to stray from Kesh,' Victor added. 'Uncle Arthur does not wish for our kin to be involved in this war. And there are few there who could aid us in the war anyhow.'

'Very well then,' the Wizard replied stroking his beard, 'we shall go north from Balas, and then you will lead us through the Grey Forest to the place called Treehouse, if you can remember the way.'

'I think I remember most of the journey,' Victor said doubtfully.

'Nevertheless, we will find our way if we simply head east,' Alastair encouraged him. 'But I should like to travel nigh to where the bandits of Treehouse saw the flying fire. Is Treehouse not close to where you also witnessed the fire?'

'Aye, it is. Surely we can be there in less than three days if we make haste.'

'That is very good. Let us be off then! It will likely be a while before you see a town again, so prepare yourself.'

'I am already prepared. Do not take me lightly, Master White Mage. I have nothing holding me back!' Victor retorted confidently.

Alastair laughed and proceeded out of the stable towards the road leading northwest out of the city. 'You are a bold man, Victor, though a stubborn one you are!'

* * *

165

They traveled determinedly and with few breaks along the way. Two days later, after Victor lost his way a few too many times, they arrived at the place called 'the King's Summit.' Victor led the Mage down the hill to the east, and they continued until they came at last to the foot of the Cold Stone Mountains. The sun had faded in the west by the time they arrived, and the land was grey under the light of the moon. So far, no fire was seen floating in the air, and there were no signs of anything mysterious.

'We will only follow the mountain north into the lands of Alterash if we find nothing here in Bolteras. There are fierce wolves there with a poisonous bite, if you remember. With only the two of us, we would not survive long against such an enemy even with my Magic. We go south!'

They strode southward along the side of the mountain range investigating the walls of the mountain as they paced about. After traveling several miles, they strode to the edge of a tall cliff that formed at the edge of the southernmost peak of the mountains. They stood upon the rim of the precipice and looked out upon the great stretch of land leading to the shore at Bolteras' borders. To the right of the crag, a path led down a steep slope and connected to the plains of the land below. The path bent and turned many times, like a snake slithering upon the ground, all the way to the bottom of the slope where the mountain pass ended at last.

The Wizard saw nothing of importance to him and so decided to turn back to the north whence they came. As they approached the place where they had first arrived, they heard the sound of approaching footsteps accompanied by ferocious groans. They hid as quickly as they could in a nook within the side of the mountain and carefully poked their heads out to see the path. The pitter patter of footsteps fell softly at first but then grew louder suddenly. Alastair and Victor felt as though they had been discovered, and they knew something was headed their way. They were unable to see far as a thick fog descended from the mountains above and fell closely to the ground. 'Curse this fog! This is no time to be blind!' Alastair hissed softly.

He placed his hand upon the hilt of his sword and gripped it tightly. Unsure of what to do, Victor drew his bow and fitted an arrow upon the string. A moment later, a shadowy figure appeared in the midst of the haze followed by several more. They carried long, curved daggers and began to howl and hiss. Alastair stepped back carefully, and whispered to Victor, 'We are in luck! They are not

166

Draemhas, but they are still very frightening foes in large numbers. They are called *Kobolds* here in the West. The Eastern Landers refer to them as *Goblins*. There are many types of Kobolds, but these are amongst the *Lizardmen*, said to be half lizard, half man. Let us be glad they are not *Harpies*, for those are half bird, half human and are adept at ambushing their enemies from the air. As fate would have it, the Lizardmen are fairly weak. But be warned; their eyes are keen, and their agility is great. And never look in their eyes! We will let them pass if we have yet to be discovered. But all the same, I am curious why they have come out of their holes in the mountains. They hate to breathe in the open air, so I am puzzled by the sight of them.'

They waited and watched for any sign of attack, but the Lizardmen simply paced back and forth sniffing the air. Moments later, several more figures appeared, darker and more terrifying than the Kobolds. The Lizardmen cowered before them and groaned loudly. 'My boy, we have stepped into greater danger than I thought!' Alastair whispered in a harsh, panicked tone. 'Draemhas have appeared! Surely they are gathering the goblin-folk for their evil purposes. Be ready and follow my lead! We must stop them here lest the lands of Bolteras are overrun by the Kobolds of the Cold Stone Mountains! But I will leave one alive, though deeply wounded, so we might figure out their intentions. Follow me; we fight!'

Alastair rested his staff against a nearby boulder while Victor raised his bow and pulled the arrow back upon the string. Alastair motioned to Victor with a wave of his hand and suddenly leapt out from the nook with a battle cry: it was intimidating like a lion or a great warrior, and the Draemhas drew their black, notched blades in response. The Lizardmen peered over at the man and charged forth, some scaling the walls of the mountain and then descending upon the Wizard. They leapt in accord at Alastair and swung their blades, but their daggers passed through him like a sword slashing through fog. The figure of the Mage vanished before Victor's eyes, and the boy remained still from fear. The Lizardmen glared at the frightened boy with their yellow, menacing eyes, and he was made powerless to oppose them.

The vile creatures leapt at Victor without a moment's hesitation. Terrified, he released his bow and arrow and fell to the ground covering his head with his hands. 'Never look into the eyes of a Kobold, Victor!' called the voice of Alastair. A white light flashed brightly like the first light of the morning sun and stunned Victor; but the light disappeared as quickly as it came. Victor lay upon the ground for a while expecting a sword to smite him, but he remained unharmed. He raised his head and slowly opened his eyes, for he was still intensely afraid. But much to his surprise, he now beheld the band of Lizardmen slain before him. Standing before him as well was the tall figure of Alastair who was now returning his sword to its sheath.

'Come now, lad,' he said rushing to Victor's side, 'one cannot fight the Draemhas with such fear in his heart. You must be prepared or else it is your life that shall be spent, and not only yours, but all those you fail to protect! Now rise, I have blinded them for the time being, but there are still Draemhas to face. The Lizardmen pale in comparison to them, but even so let us hope we do not meet any more, for my Magic is nearly exhausted. I had the need to protect you, and quickly at that, so I consumed a great amount of my Mana to cast a powerful spell. If there are others, then I will be forced to fight with my sword alone, and you must fight when that time comes! Can I count on you? I cannot do this alone!'

'Y-yes sir...I apologize,' Victor returned still trembling. When he looked into the eyes of the Kobolds, their gaze pierced deeply into his mind and revealed many dark things that deeply troubled him.

Alastair looked at Victor and discerned his troubling thoughts. 'I warned you not to look into their eyes, lad, but have no fear! The Lizardmen have only succeeded in instilling fear in your mind, but the visions they revealed to you were false! Come close, child.' Victor walked forward, and Alastair placed his hand upon the boy's head. A faint light emitted from Alastair's hand and Victor instantly felt at ease. 'Be troubled no more. Alas! I have used too much Magic, but I felt it necessary to cure you of your fear. Now let us strike down the Draemhas that await us and be done with them! I fear my spell on them will be ending shortly.'

Alastair led Victor out of the recess and turned right. The Draemhas looked on from within the fog and laughed as the Wizard drew his sword. He paced forward and whispered into the air, but Victor did not know why. Suddenly, they heard the howling of wolves far away within the Grey Forest. Alastair halted as he felt weak from the use of his powerful Magic and leaned against the mountain wall. 'What was the spell you cast, Alastair? Surely you should have spared your Mana!' Victor stared in horror as the Wizard began to breathe heavily.

'There is some devilry at work here! These Draemhas are using their Magic against me! We have not the time for these useless respites, even more with wolves about! We must find the Guardian of the Fire Stone before it is too late! I pray he is here!' Victor peered at the figures in the fog as they began to stir. Then one of the Draemhas raised his head and roared loudly: the sound of it reverberated and shook the ground beneath the two men.

'But where can we find him? What if he is not here?' Victor called out in despair.

'Then I reckon we will be dead before nightfall, foolish boy! Need you ask inane questions at such a time? Even Wizards tire, and there are those who are more powerful, even than a White Mage! Consider this: the Draemhas were once Celebhas, only now they are perverted by the powers of Darkness! If we cannot defeat them, then we are as good as dead!'

Alastair warily approached the Draemhas, but he unexpectedly heard a noise that troubled him: it was the sound of loud howling and hissing, like that of the Lizardmen. Victor summoned all his courage and grabbed Alastair by the arm and pulled him into the mist to the south. For a moment, they had vanished from the Draemhan's sight. As they waited in the dense fog, they heard voices spoken in another tongue. The words were stifled at first, but Alastair distinctly heard one word: *Nap'thar*. 'They may know our location,' the Wizard whispered. 'I heard them speak the word *Nap'thar*, which means 'Men' in the ancient tongue. I may have heard something about a message, but I am not certain.' Suddenly one of the Draemhas passed beside them on their right, unaware of their presence at first, but Victor saw it and began to breathe heavily. Hearing his panting, the Draemhas turned and thrust his sword into the fog, but the two dodged and slipped away further into the mist. They walked slowly and quietly for a brief moment until Alastair grabbed Victor by the arm. 'We are heading north,' he muttered quietly, 'into the midst of our enemies!'

Then one of the Draemhas called out in the tongue of Men, 'There are Men here! One is a Wizard! Come quickly! I have seen them; there are two at least!' The demon then began to howl and signal for his comrades. Victor summoned all his courage and ran towards his wailing foe. When he could see the demon at last, he bent his bow and loosed an arrow into the enemy's head. The

169

Draemhas screeched and crashed lifeless upon the ground. After that, the ground began to shake from the rustling of footsteps coming from the north. At that time, the fog seemed to thicken, which terrified Victor and Alastair further.

Alastair rejoined Victor; his strength began to return to him. 'Good work, lad! You slew your first Draemhas!' As he spoke, several more shadowy figures appeared dimly from within the smog, and they were sniffing the air for their scent. In an instant, the Draemhas and several Kobolds turned their heads and darted at the two men. While they were still a ways off, the vile creatures leapt forth with violent swings of their blades, but then something miraculous and unexpected happened that saved Victor and Alastair's lives. Almost as though it was a dream, a torrent of wind coiled upward in front of them, and the fog ascended like a pillar of smoke high into the air and then burst into flames. The sky above grew hot and shone a display of reds and oranges. Whatever had just happened, it swept the bodies of the Draemhas high into the air and charred them to the bone. Alastair and Victor looked ahead to the north and saw a small band of Draemhas fleeing in terror, and they screeched and wailed as they ran.

When the smoke cleared at last, Alastair and Victor beheld a small army of Draemhas slain upon the ground, and all of their bodies were scorched and turned to ash. There were also many more bodies of Lizardmen of the goblin-folk scattered abroad. Then a deep voice penetrated their confusion saying, 'O, how the White Mage has grown old, or perhaps he was too comfortable while he rested in the White Land! Has your strength yet to return to you since your departure to Elúne? I am appalled that you let a few pesky Draemhas fill you with fear and exhaust your supply of Mana!' The voice laughed. 'Are you out of breath? I insist you speak now and explain to me why you have come.'

Still breathing heavily, Alastair spoke, 'I have come now to see my old friend and mentor.'

'O, have you now? And why would your old friend wish to see you?'

'Last I recall there was no quarrel or hatred between us! Tell your master that Alastair the White has brought hope!' Suddenly, a flash of light shone before them and a small oval of light, like an egg, rested on the ground in front of them. It began to crack and flames poured out of it like rays of light. '*You,*' the Wizard exclaimed but could not finish his words. When Victor was finally able to see clearly, after the shock of the light had blinded him briefly, he saw a bird of flames flying before him.

'You are a phoenix!' Victor exclaimed excitedly. 'I thought they were only a myth!' He looked at the bird with amazement and wondered if it was the same fire he saw that night on his journey to Treehouse.

'A myth he says!' the phoenix scoffed. 'And who might this human be who speaks so confidently in the presence of one of the Guardians of the Dragon Stones?' The flaming bird peered down at Victor and seemed for a moment to recognize him.

'I am Victor Perigas, son of Valent!' the boy answered boldly.

'Perigas…the son of Valent you say? That name sounds vaguely familiar, though I cannot remember where I have heard it before.' The phoenix turned his gaze toward Alastair, who was still breathing heavily. 'Calm yourself White Mage! Surely you have not become this weak!' As he spoke, he noticed a large group of slain Draemhas to the south, about twenty in all. 'How did you slay so many Draemhas alone?'

'I used the Elúvían power, *Holy Fire*. I acted hastily as a fool, and I did not consider my ways,' answered the Mage.

'A fool you are indeed! That power is difficult to summon even for a White Mage! But I am certain you used it wisely, for you were protecting a frightened *child*,' he scoffed with a sharp glance at Victor.

'I was afraid,' Victor shouted, 'but no longer! And I am no child, arrogant *bird*!'

'Are you fearless or stupid, *child*?' the phoenix snapped back. Victor and the phoenix's eyes were intensely fixated on one another for a moment, and then Victor suddenly laughed. 'What is so funny?' the bird hissed.

'I cannot believe I have actually met a phoenix!' Victor answered merrily; his voice trembled with excitement. 'What is your name, honorable Guardian?' The phoenix was taken aback but then chuckled.

'You are indeed a stupid boy,' he laughed, 'but I think I like you! It is not common to meet one so bold and daring these days. Regardless of how I feel, though, you are clearly not enemies to my master. Come away with me and rest. Surviving a skirmish with the Draemhas is no simple feat! You have done well to come this far without more serious harm done to you.' The phoenix turned and flew into the side of the mountain and passed through as if the wall was an illusion or as though he were a ghost. 'Come now!' he called from within the mountain. 'I have opened the way.'

Alastair paced forward and passed through the wall; it was like Magic before Victor's eyes. Victor swallowed nervously and took a deep breath before running at the wall. Smack! Victor hit the wall and fell to the ground. 'Erg!' he shouted; the two on the other side of the wall answered with loud laughter. 'What did I do wrong?' Victor questioned furiously.

'What did *you* do wrong?' the phoenix answered. 'Nothing at all!' he laughed. 'It is only what *I* did right! That ought to teach you not to disrespect one of the Guardians of the Dragon Stones! You are a thousand years too young to speak so openly before me. Now enter, you fool! I am done having my fun with you.' Victor rose to his feet and slowly pressed his hand toward the wall. He expected to feel solid rock but instead his hands slipped straight through, and he fell to the ground on the other side of the wall. He quickly rose to his feet and stepped forth and saw a long hallway lit with fires that danced and glided across the walls and the ceiling high above. There was only one path. It ran far ahead for a while and then ended at a wall with the image of a red Dragon etched upon it. Alastair seemed healthier and full of great vigor now, even more so than Victor. He smiled at the boy and then laughed subtly with a hand over his mouth as he noticed a large bump on Victor's brow.

'Welcome to the entryway to my master's lair! My name is Kai, which quite literally means "fire," and that is what I am, wrought from the fires of Asura the great Fire Dragon and lord of the Cold Stone Mountains. You two may rest within this corridor until you are ready to go on your way, but I will not grant you more than three days! Rest easily. I give you my word; you are safe here!'

'You know,' Alastair interrupted, 'we came here for more than shelter from the Kobolds of the mountain and the Draemhas who guide them!'

'And I suppose you think I will just hand you the Dragon Stone and let you go about your merry way? I am shocked, Wizard of old! Has your wisdom faded with your youth?'

'You belittle me, Kai! We have come for the Dragon Stone but not by force. I told you already that I have brought hope with me! This boy will bring hope to many. As the last White Mage of the Order, I put my trust in this boy! He is of pure heart and sound mind, though he is still young and foolish at times. If we guide him along

172

the path of Light, then maybe he will be able to change the tide of this war.'

'Do you not remember the sins of Men from ages ago?' Kai snapped.

'That happened ages ago! And I was there in support of the Dragons, and here I am now! I always have and always will fight for good, whether good lies in Men or Dragons or any other creatures of Gaia! You know these things as your master's memories are kept safely within you.'

'Perhaps you are wiser and more discerning than I give you credit, Alastair the wise! There is only one way this boy can be found true. But I assure you, it will inflict a great deal of torture on him. And he must contain a large amount of spiritual energy or he will be consumed by fire. Do you dare risk his life on a game of chance?'

'There is no such thing as chance! And I have faith in Victor as do all those who have known him. Surely he is able to h—'

'Oi,' Victor interrupted angrily, 'I think I shall be the one to decide my own fate! Who are you to tell me what to do with my life? Tell me, Kai, will this power help us conquer the forces of Darkness.'

'Nothing is for certain.'

'That is not what I asked! I, like Alastair, do not believe in chance! By Vaaspar's Light, good will overcome evil! Now tell me; will this power help good defeat evil?'

'Calm down, child; you need not shout when we are so close. It will indeed aid you greatly, if you are able to control its power. But I have good reasons to never release the Stone, even to the strongest and purest of Men. If the five stones were ever united, they could be joined together to make a single Stone of Power equal to that of Elúvías! If such a thing happened and the Dark Lord seized control of it, then he could use it for his evil purposes. That is something we simply cannot risk!'

'If that is the case, then I will become its new Guardian! And I will guard it with my life! The Enemy already draws upon the powers of Vexúvías, yet you will not risk the one Stone to aid Men against the Dark Lord? I will bear all the responsibility and endure the trials if your master will grant it to me.'

'Foolish boy, do you understand nothing? You are far too arrogant!' He paused for a moment. 'What was that?' Kai said suddenly; he floated in the air silent again with his head turned up as if he was listening, but Victor and Alastair heard nothing. 'But Master!' he said out loud. Alastair and Victor looked about but saw only the phoenix. 'It has been decided,' the phoenix said after a long silence. 'Victor shall be put through the *Trial of Fire*! Come with me, to *the Chamber of Inferno*!' He turned without faltering and flew at the wall with the image of the Dragon upon it and passed straight through.

Alastair turned to Victor with a look of despair upon his face. 'It is not too late to turn back, Victor. I have been through the Trial of Fire in my days of training as a young Fire Mage, and it nearly killed me. It is not something you should take lightly! There are many who have gone before you and did not endure its agony. Hundreds have failed the test and died as a result! Choose carefully whether you will continue or a—'

Without a word, Victor paced forward and passed through the wall, and the Wizard reluctantly followed. They passed beyond to another room with a large platform in its center raised extremely high upon a tall dais. There were four sets of steps leading up each side of the dais, and at the top of each of the stairways was an archway of stone with an emblem of fire that burned bright red. Kai was perched upon the archway of the western side facing Alastair and Victor as they stood at the foot of the stair.

'Victor, climb the stairs to the top of the dais and sit in its center. It is there that the Trial of Fire will commence! Alastair, you must wait at the bottom or else you will be caught up in the Trial as well! I imagine you do not want to endure that torture a second time.' Victor did as the phoenix commanded and sat at the center of the platform. 'Be prepared,' Kai whispered to Victor, 'the Trial of Fire is agonizing and will push you to your limits! You may die, but if you happen to persevere, then you shall be made new! Are you prepared?' Victor nodded with gallant confidence. 'Then, let the Trial begin!'

Kai flew up into the air away from the dais and flapped his wings toward Victor. Instantly, the room turned as black as night and a wall of fire encircled the stage. Alastair watched blindly from the bottom of the room and listened to the sound of painful cries coming from within the flames. Inside, Victor sprawled out upon the stone platform wailing loudly, and he rolled back and forth as if on fire. Kai flapped his wings again and chains like fire restrained Victor and held him close to the ground.

174

Fearing for Victor's life, Alastair approached the stairs. 'Go no further, Mage of the Light!' Kai rebuked. 'You cannot help him now! Go any further, and I will not hesitate to put an end to the both of you!' Alastair reluctantly stepped down and sat at the foot of the stairs and began to pray for Victor's safety, but Victor's cries only grew louder for a brief moment and then sounded strained and weak.

* * *

As Victor writhed in torment within the Trial of Fire, he saw many visions and images that were as real to him as the pain he was suffering. Fire was all about him, and his skin seemed to char and turn to ash before his eyes. He saw next to him Uncle Arthur smiling and waving at him, but even as he looked on, Arthur was pierced by many arrows and fell to the ground dead. Victor writhed in anguish more and more as he struggled to draw near to the lifeless man, but the chains binding him kept him away. His vision began to blur and fade to black, but all the while he could hear a faint voice calling out, 'Hold on to your life!' though he knew not whence it came. Suddenly, he seemed to be removed from the Chamber of Inferno and was placed in the midst of a great battle.

He rose with all his might and moved forward to his uncle's body, or so he thought; but in truth, he was still sprawled upon the ground bound by the immovable chains latched to his wrists and ankles, unable to lift even a finger. In his dream, all felt familiar as though it were really happening, and he perched next to Arthur and wept bitterly as he envisioned even more terrors. He watched as all of his friends fought valiantly in a fierce battle against the Draemhas; and one by one each of his comrades fell to their deaths by the weapons of their enemies until at last even Lord Edgar and Grinshawl were slain. Even the thieves from Treehouse were killed by the Dark Lord's armies, and all hope seemed lost. Then he saw something quite unexpected. Hildegard emerged from the ranks of Draemhas wielding his fearsome spear, but his eyes were now menacing and filled with rage. His former friend stepped forth onto the field of battle and slew many great Boltian warriors. Victor struggled to stand and face his former friend but it was all in vain.

At long last, every last Boltian warrior was killed or else fled from battle, and Victor stood alone surrounded by a vast army of the demon-folk. But suddenly a voice spoke to him, 'You can escape with your life or stand and fight. The choice is yours.' And then he noticed a talisman about his neck with a bright red gem fastened to its chain. He found new strength and was filled with rage and spite.

Removing the talisman from his neck, Victor instinctually reached out his hand and fire spread all around the field of battle killing many of the Draemhas. The flames passed over the bodies of his fallen comrades, and he seized his attack, not wanting to bring them any further harm. Hildegard approached him, and he desired greatly, for some reason, to end his life; but he relented and had compassion on his friend. But Hildegard rejected him and thrust his mighty spear at Victor and then disappeared.

The area around him became black as a starless and moonless night except for a dim light in front of him that revealed two hooded figures wearing darkened robes with a crest of the sun upon it like a Magical rune. The figures removed their hoods and Victor beheld the face of his parents. 'Why?' Victor called out. Unexpectedly, a sharp burst of pain shot through his stomach as he spoke, and he fell with his face upon the ground. When the pain had faded, he looked up at his mother and father. 'Why have you done this?' He called out to them, but they would not answer. Instead, they simply looked down at him with a queer, vindictive smile on their lips. Intense ire filled Victor's being, and he despised the very sight of them. A black aura like a shadowy mist encompassed Victor's body, and his entire being began to fade into Darkness. Before he lost all sight, he vaguely saw the image of his parents fading into a black abyss like a deep pit beyond his reach.

* * *

Kai flew anxiously in the air as he observed the Trial of Fire. Victor had stopped moving and his screams had ceased, and the phoenix had almost lost all hope for the boy. He flew down and perched himself upon a step near to Alastair. 'The boy,' he said solemnly, 'I do not think he will last much longer. He is already fading into blackness. I am a—'

'He will make it!' the Wizard interrupted abruptly. 'Do not lose hope, yet! This child is full of surprises!'

Sympathetically, the phoenix remarked, 'He is dying, Alastair. You must be ready to deal with whatever fate comes his way.'

'We are not controlled by fate! There is no fate; there is no destiny! There is a way, and there is truth. He will find that way!'

'You are deaf to my words! Do you not understand what is happening? I have seen his body and mind fading into the black abyss! Soon he will be void of personality, and the Dark Lord will have control of him. When that happens, the fire about him will

176

consume him, for it can allow no evil thing to exist within its walls. He will be engulfed by flames! You know this all too well!' Alastair did not respond but only prayed more fervently for Victor and spoke enchantments of blessings.

* * *

Victor felt his very being fading away and saw everything around him turn to black with not a single trace of light. *What will I do? How will I return now? How can I save my friends and family when I cannot even last through a mere test! I will not give in! I will not be defeated!* Suddenly, his thoughts were drowned out by the darkness all around him; but then a faint light began to shine from within his heart, and he could see once more. He focused all his energy and attention on the light and it grew brighter, and all the more as he dwelt on it. A moment later, the blackness vanished like a fog, and he returned to the battlefield next to the corpses of his friends.

In front of him, a black hole, a deep chasm, hovered above the ground, and he knew his parents were trapped within it; so he leapt forth without a moment of hesitation and entered the void. Inside, the dark was thick, and he saw many evil things: there were vile creatures like the Kobolds and the Draemhas, death, disease, and many acts of malice resulting from the power of the Dark Lord. His parents were amongst them, and he knew not what to do. Confusion overcame him, and his mind plunged into shadows again. He stood there yelling, 'What should I do?' over and over again until he was at last consumed by the Darkness.

* * *

'The Trial is nearly finished,' Kai called from high above the dais. 'Now what will be the result?' The wall of fire around the raised platform vanished at once to Kai's dismay. 'There should have been at least ten or fifteen minutes left in the Trial! This is not good!' Quickly, the phoenix and the Wizard approached Victor, whose body was scorched and lame. He lay flat upon his stomach with his eyes wide open, and he did not move.

'Victor,' Alastair shouted as he passed through the archway, 'wake up, lad! The Trial of Fire is finished! Wake up!' The Wizard carefully shook the boy, but merely touching Victor's body caused blisters to swell up on his hands. Victor lay there still lifeless and unmoved by the Wizard's voice. Alastair released his grip and began to weep bitterly. Victor's body began to turn to ash, and there was not even the slightest sign of life within him. 'Why does he not wake? His heart was pure; so why is he dead?' he cried out frantically. Kai simply looked dolefully and sympathetically at the Mage. 'This is my fault,' Alastair wept, 'all of this is my fault! I never should have brought him here. If only I had minded my own business, he would still be alive!'

'Be silent!' Kai retorted. 'What use is your dismal self-pity? The boy is dead, trapped forever in an endless void of gloom, for there were secret evils in his heart. The Trial of Fire shows no favoritism; indeed, it never lies. It only reveals what is truly in one's heart, and the boy has failed. This is precisely what I feared most, and you fools insisted upon it, the boy included! What I cannot comprehend is why Asura agreed to it.'

'The boy is dead? Alas!' Alastair sobbed. 'How will this old fool share such dreadful news with his beloved Arthur?'

'You must stand up and take responsibility for your actions, White Mage! Be a man! If you had only listened to my counsel, you would not have put the boy through such an impossible test! I knew he would never survive, especially at such a young age. The test reveals troubling things to the one who accepts the challenge. It was a test that boy never should have tried to rival. I pity him, that poor child.'

Suddenly the two heard a loud thud upon the stone of the platform: Victor had slammed his fist firmly and angrily upon the stone of the dais, and the ground cracked beneath it. They glanced over in astonishment as Victor raised himself up on all fours with gritting teeth; his ashy and charred appearance was fading before their eyes until only a few minor burns remained, and he appeared to them quite healthy and strong.

'I told you,' Victor grunted, 'I am not a child!' He raised his head and roared as loudly as he could: it was boisterous like the roar of a mighty Dragon. Kai lowered himself to the ground and turned his head sideways and peered sharply into Victor's eyes. Alastair stood agape and trapped in breathtaking delight as Victor rose and stood erect before him.

'I do not believe it,' Kai exclaimed. 'Indeed, you are no child! Today you have arisen from the ashes a man! You have proven me wrong and overcome all my doubts, young Victor. I am truly sorrowful to have ever doubted you. There is purity in your heart beyond what my eyes can see! You have shown great strength this day by shining your light in the midst of great darkness, and you have overcome hatred and the evil in your heart. Though you were scorched almost to the point of death, you have arisen anew! Therefore, I shall call you *Victor the Phoenix* for surviving the Trial of Fire. Truly you have been deemed worthy and true. And I am amazed as you are the youngest person to ever pass the test! Surely you were born for great things!'

'You have passed the first test, child!' sounded another voice from the shadows below to their right: it was thunderous and unfamiliar and instantly drove fear into Victor's mind. 'My name is Asura, the Dragon of Fire! I am the last remnant of the Fire Tribe of the breed of Basilisks. Very few have ever survived the Trial of Fire, and one of them is Alastair the White. But I doubt he can recall the misery it once caused him since he has died and gone to Elúne where all one's troubles are erased. But perhaps his memory serves him better now that he has returned to Gaia. Ah, my young apprentice, seeing you again makes me reminisce of the olden days! And after all these years, you look the same!' he laughed. 'It is good to see you again, Alastair the Red! O, how I remember those days well! And though you are a White Mage now, I still see that same young Fire Mage who always had that blaze in his eyes, that desire to rid the world of evil.' The Dragon spoke deeply and his laugh was frightening. They saw a puff of fire rise from the shadows below and saw for a moment a large scaly figure of deep red with sharp, jagged teeth and a long, spiky tail; his legs were broad and tall, and his claws were long and colossal in size.

Before they could see any movement, the light faded and the room grew dark again. In the blink of an eye, Asura appeared before them and perched himself on the immense dais spreading his wings high and wide in the air. He raised his head and breathed two streams of fire from his nostrils which turned and swirled into one massive flame. The flames spread all about the room and lingered in the air like torches near the walls and provided efficient light for Alastair and Victor to see. They saw the room clearly now and expected it to be filled with treasures and strange artifacts, but the area was barren, mere dust and dirt with no wealth or weapons or ancient artifacts lying about. There was not even a single carving or rune upon the walls. It was simple, just the way Asura desired it to be.

'I must say, Alastair, I never expected to see you again in my lifetime! But I wonder if our friendship will be as strong as it was before I went into hiding. I have harbored feelings of hatred toward Men and the Draemhas after that outlandish war over a thousand years ago! And after all these years, you bring me this boy, who,

179

though he was tempted in many ways and filled with reasonable anger and hatred, rid himself of his feelings and sought to do good for his friends and family, even of those who betrayed him. At first, I found restless evil dwelling in his heart, but he found within himself a light. In fact, it was Vaaspar's Light that I saw shine within him, and he cast away the evil that tormented him so!'

'Well met, old friend!' Alastair exclaimed. 'I am amazed that you remember me after sleeping for so long. I met this boy in Vallicore, the capital city of Bolteras, if you do not know it yet. New kingdoms of Men have arisen since you went into hiding at the end of the Great Dragon War long ago. Your lair lies upon the borders of the great country of Bolteras. It is a magnificent land, and Vaaspar found favor with its people and bestowed upon them the Orb of Light. I have brought you this boy, so that you might teach him your ways. All who know him boast of his excellence, and I have found him to be a magnificent boy. Though he is young and often times rash, he is truly worthy of your aid. That is why I have brought him to you in hopes that you might instruct him and go with us to war against the Draemhas.'

Asura roared angrily, and Alastair fell upon the ground. 'You would ask *me* to go to war again, furthermore with *Men*?' the Dragon snapped. 'I have the utmost respect for you Alastair, but I have not forgiven the lines of Men. This boy might have passed the Trial of Fire, but I merely wanted to see if good still existed within Men.'

'I know many evils occurred long ago, but this time I would ask that you fight back! Long ago, it was the Dragons' purpose to protect Men, but there are evil Men who seek to do harm to the kingdoms that still hold fast to the Light! It is no longer your aim to save the lives of all Men! Rather fight for those who seek to do good, who seek to put an end to Abaddon and the forces of Dragoth! My friend, Vaaspar will return some day, and then you will be free of all the afflictions that torment you. While I resided in Elúne for nearly four years, He revealed to me many mysteries. His will for you now is to rise and fight! You are among the last remnant of your kin, the Dragons. Do not let their senseless deaths of long ago be in vain! Arise from your lair and remind the Dark Lord why he once lived in fear of your kind!'

Victor gasped. 'He will return? Vaaspar Himself will come to Gaia?'

'But of course!' Alastair responded. 'He promised it to us long ago, and He always keeps His promises. And He has given me the task of rallying all who love justice for the purpose of fighting against the Dark Lord and his armies.'

'Oh, has He now?' Asura answered. 'I believe you, friend, for you have never been dishonest with me. I love truthful Men, but they are rare to find!'

'Indeed they are, but Victor is an honest man as well! Furthermore, he is not to blame for the mistakes of Men long ago. Indeed, he was not yet even born! Will you grant him the power of your Stone for the benefit of good? And I ask, as your friend, for your aid in this war! What say you?'

'I cannot do that just yet.'

Alastair was perplexed and frustrated for a moment but relaxed himself before speaking again. 'And what is holding you back?' he hissed and thumped his staff upon the cold rock of the platform.

'I must test him a second time, and then I will decide whether or not I will give him my Stone. But do not count on my aid in this war. As of now, I have no desire to go to war, if Men are still as evil as they always have been. I miss the days when my kind lived among your people in peace, and I am not quite ready to see dark days again, especially so soon after I have just awoken. Those were better days when I first met you, Alastair, but they are gone forever! And now I will leave you for a while so I can think, but I will return to test the boy again!'

'Friend, wait! I w—' Alastair started, but it was too late. Asura had flown off and vanished through the eastern wall.

'Forgive me, sirs, but I think I need to lie down for a moment,' Victor said after a moment's silence. 'I hope I can pass the second trial. I will do whatever it takes to save those I love.' He ended with a yawn, and then lay down upon the ground with his head propped up on his pack. In an instant, he had fallen asleep.

'Aye,' Kai replied, 'both of you sleep. I will wake you when Asura returns. Alastair answered with a nod of his head and then lay upon the cold stone of the dais beside Victor. Within minutes, he too had fallen asleep. Kai noticed them shiver from the cold air of the mountain and so created a wall of fire around the platform, and it kept them warm during their sleep. They slept peacefully and forgot all about their worries, though only for that night. Even though their relief was short, there were no forces of Darkness that could steal that moment of tranquility away from them.

Chapter XI

Tristan's Master Plan

It was the evening of April sixth when Tristan and his company crossed the borders of Bolteras into the land of Alterash at the northern edge of the Grey Forest. Earlier that morning, they made way across the ford where the thieves of Treehouse had led Grinshawl and the others less than two weeks prior. The day before, they had abandoned their steeds in Balas, one of the defensive strongholds of Bolteras just to the south and slightly west, and continued on foot to remain quiet and secretive as they traversed the vast lands of Alterash. The people of Balas were greatly pleased as they had already received two fine steeds from Alastair and Victor upon the previous day. After hearing of Victor and Alastair's passing through Balas, Tristan was overjoyed and eager to do his part in the preparations for war. But he greatly missed his only friend and wondered night and day how Victor fared in his travels.

On the morning of the sixth, they traveled through the Grey Forest and passed across the fords wetting their feet and cooling their tongues before continuing up the long hill to the top of the Mithras Falls; then they turned left slightly and treaded northeast at a slow and steady pace. They remained on guard and in rank, prepared for wolves and other wild beasts that were known to roam the forest that might attack. But the beasts of the forest were still simple, not yet tainted by the Enemy's power, and they strayed far from the band of warriors. While the travelers were still two miles from the edge of the Grey Forest, wolves began to howl and bark from beyond the woods, but none ever approached their company. As Tristan led them deeper into the forest, a loud noise suddenly boomed from the southeast, and shrill cries echoed throughout the lands. They halted and observed their surroundings but saw nothing of danger. After a while, they decided to stray from the Cold Stone Mountains fearing the Kobolds were coming out of hiding by the Dark Lord's command.

By nightfall, the small band of soldiers came at last to the edge of the Grey Forest. From there, Gibraltar guided them through the night until they came upon a small grove past the woods' end where there were few trees scattered about. 'This is the border of Alterash just beyond these thickets,' he called to the group. 'There is a fine meadow past the border where we can camp for the evening, though I suggest we avoid the use of fire from here on out. But I am not in charge, so we should let Prince Tristan decide upon our actions.'

'Nay, Gibraltar, your counsel is sound. Light no fire tonight and do nothing that could draw attention to us. But I should like to sleep in the woods as I feel we will be more protected and better hidden in case enemies lurk about. And we should establish guards in shifts for the night watch, but it must be fair so that all keep watch at some point during this journey.'

The soldiers were shocked at his response. One soldier called out, 'My lord, I have never seen this side of you! You show great wisdom when it is needed of you!'

'Aye, that he does,' Delitas added. 'I agree with camping within the woods, but let us establish four guards per shift, one to watch each of our sides.'

'Agreed,' Tristan returned. 'Well, you men get some rest! I will keep guard during the first watch.' Three other soldiers volunteered to stay on watch with Tristan, and the rest of the group fell soundly asleep. Nothing disturbed their sleep that night, but they felt uneasy sleeping so near to the Cold Stone Mountains and the borders of Alterash.

The next morning, the sun failed to rouse the travelers as dense wisps of smoke had fallen upon them and prevented the sun's light from penetrating through the trees; but the soldiers on watch roused them after some time. As they rose from their leafy beds, a cool breeze descended from the peaks of the Cold Stone Mountains and came upon them. Afraid they had slept through most of the morning, the company quickly gathered their equipment and continued their journey north. After leaving the shelter of the woods, they turned right and traveled near to the Grey Forest. Many loud howls resonated from the north and others from the west; the sound drove the men forward at a quickened pace. Preoccupied by terrifying thoughts of venomous wolves, they drew closer to the foot of the mountains, much nearer than any had hoped to travel. An hour later, they emerged from the thick fog to find the sun shining down on them from above. They were relieved to find the time was nearing noon, so they halted for a moment and ate a quiet meal.

When they had each had their fill, the party continued more swiftly along the edge of the trees to the east. The Cold Stone Mountains now loomed up ahead, towering threateningly before them. By the time they were about a mile from the foot of the mountains, the sun had moved overhead to the west some, and the air became oddly warm. While they were marveling at the height of the mountain peaks that ascended beyond the clouds above, several figures suddenly appeared from the south—they were fleeing in terror.

'Draemhas,' Tristan exclaimed. 'There are Draemhas fleeing from the Cold Stone Mountains, and lo! they draw nigh!' The entire party jumped and looked to the southeast at the small band of Draemhas approaching—there were twelve in all.

'Perhaps they sought the aid of the Kobolds but failed to earn their trust,' Gibraltar said. 'Our people have long been raided by the goblin-folk.'

'Nay,' Tristan answered, 'the Kobolds are only strong in numbers, as Uncle Edgar tells me, and surely there were more Draemhas than we see now. The Draemhas would not be so easily run off by the likes of the Kobolds. Who can say what power drove them away in fear, but I hope Victor and Alastair are safe. They were to travel to the mountains and should have arrived there by this time. Let us hope no evil has overcome them.'

'Fear not, Your Highness!' Delitas added. 'If the White Mage is there, then I am doubtful any evil will triumph over them. What are your orders, Prince Tristan? Shall we confront the Draemhas?'

'Yes we shall! We must not let even one Draemhas escape with his life! They must all be eradicated lest they return and kill us in our sleep!' Tristan drew his blade and removed his shield from his baldric. 'Subdue the forces of Darkness at once!' From far off, the Draemhas stopped and panted for air. Hearing the shouts of the approaching Boltians, they turned their heads up and drew their notched blades. Tristan led his party closer to their enemy and raised his hand to stop his troops. 'Forgive me. I will no longer act so rashly as your leader. It is better we do not clash swords with the Draemhas if we can help it. Fire your arrows at them from a distance!'

Twenty of the Boltian soldiers were archers, and they drew their bows upon his command and aimed their shots. At Tristan's signal, they loosed their arrows with the sound of many twangs at

185

their frightened enemies. One by one the Draemhan band fell dead upon the ground shrieking as the arrows pierced their shadowy skin. Tristan and his men shouted with acclamation, but their joyous victory was soon brought to an end as the sound of many vicious howls sounded from behind them. A moment later, many wolves numbering twenty or thirty—though it was difficult to count—broke through the thick fog at their backs barking and growling as they darted across the plains.

'We must go at once!' Tristan called sheathing his sword. 'Gibraltar, lead the way! Are there any places of safety?'

'Alas! I do not know of any that still exist! There were once many great refuges and strongholds in the land, but King Bormann laid them to waste during his corrupted conquest of the land. All the fortresses have either been burned or long abandoned, and I fear the enemy may have taken control of them. I dread going near to any of them for fear that they are overrun by the Kobolds or worse!'

'That is ill news. Then we have no choice but to slay the beasts! Do not let them near, soldiers of Vallicore! If these are the same wolves we discussed at the Boltian Council, then their bite is poisonous and deadly upon touch. Ready your bows!'

The Boltian soldiers took aim yet again and faced the approaching hounds. Tristan, Delitas and Gibraltar took the lead with their weapons drawn, ready to slay any that might avoid the volley. Tristan roared and yelled, 'Fire!' at the top of his voice, and the soldiers quickly loosed their darts upon the wolves. The vile beasts were brought to swift justice, save a few that whimpered and fled in horror back into the thick fog to the northwest.

'Well done brave warriors of Vallicore! I suppose we can take on any who attack us!' Tristan laughed with blind confidence.

'But look closely, Your Majesty,' Gibraltar answered. 'Three of the pack have evaded our attack and now flee to the northwest. We may soon have more wolves upon us than we can handle, or perhaps even the Draemhas will be after us in a little while. Do not be so quick to celebrate! We still have a long way left to travel to Kainor, and there may be many more dangers ahead that await us. Furthermore, our presence is no longer secret!'

'Forgive me,' Tristan responded somberly. 'I am still young and make many mistakes. I thank you for your rebuke, Gibraltar. But where do we go from here?'

'We go north. But we must go quickly. I fear the wolves will be upon us ere long. But there is a forest ahead, just across a small stream. Perhaps we can camp there safely for the night.'

Tristan nodded, and the group continued north for several hours until they came upon a stream running down from one of the peaks of the Cold Stone Mountains. It was shallow enough that they strode through the water with ease and came to the bottom of a tall and narrow hill on the other side. Tristan climbed to the top of the hillock to scout the vast land of Alterash to the north and also to the west. He saw many streams and lakes glistening from the sunlight away to the northwest and patches of forests, but he saw no signs of enemies. He turned his gaze to the northeast and saw a thick forest lying beyond the last peak of the mountains. 'That must be the forest Gibraltar mentioned,' he said to himself. Suddenly, the wind blew northward and then turned east carrying along the sound of howling. Tristan quickly turned his gaze southwest and saw a vast pack of wolves approaching. He staggered down the hill as quickly as he could, nearly tripping as he descended. He called out in a hoarse whisper, 'Wolves! I see wolves coming our way!'

'How many are there?' Delitas questioned, 'We can take them! We already slew nearly twenty of them!'

'I saw a small army!' Tristan exclaimed, 'perhaps thirty or forty more than before! I was not able to count them all! We cannot fight them—or rather, I will not risk losing good warriors in a senseless fight against venomous wolves!'

'That is wise,' Gibraltar responded. 'It is not worth our time or our lives. There are many wolves in other lands that I would risk a battle with, but not these. Their poison works quickly and there is no known cure for its sting! We only saw them from a distance before, but they are massive and swift. We must hide from them as quickly as we can!'

'But I fear a forest will not protect us from them' Tristan retorted. 'We cannot tarry any longer in worthless skirmishes against wolves. There must be another way! And look, it is now growing dark!' The sun had only just begun to lower in the western sky but was slowly being veiled by thick, black billows mustering above. 'Where does such darkness come from in the middle of the day? The clouds seem to gather by some Magic!'

'I have never seen such a thing,' Gibraltar answered as he gazed at the oddly forming clouds, 'but I reckon the Enemy has something to do with it. Come now; we must find shelter!' He

187

looked around for a moment and then shouted 'Aha! Follow me!' Gibraltar darted past the hill to another, larger knoll a little further from where they stood. The rest of the party was confused but still followed his lead. 'Trust me; I will show you a secret of our land. Alterash has many secrets, and one of them may still rest in this hill! We have always utilized trenches and tunnels to surprise our enemies during battle.' They proceeded to the hill and stood at its foot, looking out to the west at the approaching wolves in the distance. The beasts flew across the land at a great pace, and Gibraltar bid them to follow his lead. He grabbed the turf at the bottom of the knoll and lifted it up as though it were a blanket of grass. Beneath the patch of grass, a furrow was concealed and ran entirely around the hill. He leapt under the hill to where there were tunnels connected to the channel, and he vanished from their sight.

'Oi,' Tristan called, 'where have you gone now?'

'Down here!' he returned. 'There are tunnels under the ground! Follow me, and we may live through this night!' Quickly the band descended into the narrow tunnels on all fours and hid deep within the ground. The howls drew ever nearer until the travelers heard sniffing and panting just outside the trenches. The beasts barked ferociously and stuck their noses under the patches of grass. One of the wolves even entered the trench; but its body was massive, and it was unable to squeeze through the tight holes of the tunnel.

'How will we get away?' Tristan asked as he stared at the menacing wolf dripping poison from its fangs: the ground beneath it hissed and burned with every drop of it saliva. 'Will we wait until we have suffocated or starved to death? Alas! what can be done?'

'Fear not, there is a way out!' Gibraltar turned about and crawled through a path that ran towards the eastern side of the hill, and the others followed. The wolves darted away at once sniffing about and yelping frantically. The path turned left back to the north, and they passed out of the tunnels at the foot of the hill on its northern side. They marched on as quickly and quietly as they could, frequently looking behind them for any signs of the wolves. Not long after, they came to the woods Gibraltar spoke of, but he led them past it and continued north.

They drew near now to a large river pouring out from the northernmost peak of the Cold Stone Mountains. The dark clouds suddenly ended, and the light of day shone through once again; but it was dim and already fading into the western horizon. Three miles from its source, the immense river branched off into five smaller streams, like long fingers reaching out across the lands of Alterash. They stood now at the widest point of the river not far from where it split into the five smaller streams, which was still a mile away to the northwest. Each branch of the river was less than ten fathoms wide, and all were fairly shallow. Between each stream were vast stretches of land, each one running nearly three miles to the next ford. At the end of their flow, the five small streams emptied into five separate lakes, some far away to the west and others away to the north. 'The only way to cross,' Gibraltar called quietly, 'is to proceed west and pass northward across the five fords of Anagon, the mighty river of Alterash! After we pass beyond the fords, we will be nigh to Kainor, only a three day journey or less!'

'We may run into a few problems on the way,' Tristan shouted. 'Look! the wolves have found our scent!' Away at the top of the hillock, a wolf stood and raised its head high into the air and released a howl that echoed down to the plains below. Many loud barks and growls answered the call, and then wolves fell from the hill like waves of the ocean. 'Run!' Tristan yelled at the top of his voice. 'Run or be eaten!' The Boltian soldiers drew their bows and quickly loosed a flurry of arrows high into the air. The darts whined and killed several of the wolves, but the rest were enraged and poured down the hill more swiftly onto the plains in pursuit of Tristan and his company.

'Fools,' Tristan called, 'This is no time for battle! Hurry lest we all die here today!' They continued with haste westward along the edge of the River Anagon until they came upon the fifth ford of Anagon—as it was counted by the Alterashians—but the wolves were almost upon them; and their ravenous fangs were dripping with burning venom. They quickly darted across the narrow stream onto the small islet between the fifth and fourth fords. A small wood was on their left, and on their right was a long stretch of shoal that ran to the main stream of Anagon where it split five ways. Tristan debated whether to run or hide, but the pressure of the advancing wolves was too great for him to meditate clearly. *Splash! Splash!* The wolves poured across the stream just moments later, and the warriors turned to fight. Suddenly, Gibraltar slammed the butt of his spear upon the ground. 'I will stay, brethren!' he shouted. 'Go now as quickly as you may! You must find shelter and escape with your lives or else this journey will be in vain!'

'No,' Tristan said as he and the rest of the company drew their weapons. 'We will either run together or die together. What can one man do against an army of these beasts?'

'Fool! This is no time to die senseless deaths! Our mission will be futile if we all were to die here this day. Alterash must be liberated from this accursed spell upon the land!' Gibraltar roared with rage. 'Do not interfere with a man's resolve! Go now, Tristan Prince!'

'I c-cannot,' Tristan replied hesitantly. 'We will stay with y—'

'I said go, you fool! I do not belong to Bolteras or to Lord Edgar! I am from Alterash and belong only to myself! This is my stand, my choice, my resolve! I told you, do not interfere!' Tristan looked into the eager yet panicked eyes of Gibraltar and, honoring his decision, took flight to the fourth ford. 'Come at me you devilish hounds! I will be your opponent!' Gibraltar yelled ferociously at the beasts. He aimed his spear, but it became too dark for him to see as the last light of the sun faded in the west. The wolves sprinted across the fifth ford with an untamed frenzy. As they drew nearer, Gibraltar sighed deeply and raised his spear at his enemies. Behind him, Tristan halted and looked back with regret in his eyes; but Gibraltar was prepared to die if it would spare the lives of his comrades, and he had no regrets. He raised a battle cry just before he hurled his javelin at the leader of the pack. The spear struck the beast through its jaw, and the vile creature crashed violently upon the ground. Just before the wolves leapt upon Gibraltar, many loud twangs and whines of arrows sounded from the woods to his right. More than ten wolves plunged headlong into the ground, and the rest reeled and searched about madly.

A moment later, loud shouts reverberated from the woods, and thirty horsemen galloped forth carrying long, silver-headed spears. They flung their javelins as mightily as they could and then fell upon the army of wolves, leaving none alive. Following the horsemen, a small host of archers emerged from the woods and joined Gibraltar. Just then, another pack of wolves from the south arrived at the fifth ford but then fled in terror at the sight of the fearsome horsemen. The riders dismounted and struck the limp bodies of the wolves to assure their deaths. Gibraltar stared at them with joy and alarm, for he recognized by their crests and banners that they were his kin.

'Brethren!' he called out to them, 'how can this be? I witnessed your departure to the Eastern Lands after King Bormann lost his way!'

'Aye, you witnessed correctly!' a familiar voice answered him. A young man rode forth; and he was the only rider who wore a helm: it was silver with a red plume on top. He removed his helmet and let his loose, black hair loll just above his shoulders, and he smiled amiably at Gibraltar.

'Iggy,' Gibraltar shouted, 'Iggy, my friend! I was told you were killed!' At that time, Tristan and the rest of his company returned to Gibraltar very much surprised and elated that their friend was alive and well.

'Nay, I have not been killed; rather they *assumed* I was dead! But I fled many years ago when I first learned of Bormann's treachery, nigh to fifteen years now if memory serves me rightly.'

'Is that so?' Gibraltar stuttered unsure how to respond.

'Ah, I see. So this whole time you were unaware of the truth? Bormann willfully withdrew his support against the forces of Darkness years ago at the Enemy's request. He was promised safety and riches upon the Dark Lord's return, and he is already fattening himself for his royal position. But I took those who remained sane and fled to the Eastern Lands while we still could. Others came after us just weeks ago claiming that Bormann had gone insane, more so than at first. When they had arrived, we knew that someone must have restored the bridge to its former glory, for it was once destroyed by a great spell of the Dark Lord's that was given to Bormann. Our kin reported that many of the villages and towns in Alterash had been laid to waste. I had not heard from you for years, Gibraltar, so I assumed you were dead or else under the Enemy's control. We despaired when we heard our lands were plunging further into Darkness. Many believed us to be cowards when we fled, but we did so to aid the Eastern Landers. And behold! we have returned to save our great land from Abaddon's grip. While we were away, we stayed in Eón Dipheras, the capital city of the Guole Sector of Sanctum Anthropolis, and we held a meeting amongst ourselves and decided to return to Alterash at King Izen's leave. He was rather pleased to see us go…I say there is something rather odd about that man.

'But I stray from the point. We have returned to liberate Alterash. We were roused by the howls of the wolves as you drew near, and we eavesdropped on your conversation—my apologies. When we saw free Men fleeing from the Hellhounds, we were eager to aid you despite your resolve to stand alone. Brother, too many of us have been forced to stand alone in these dark days but no more! Let us stand together!' he paused for a moment and sighed deeply. 'Upon our return, we met a man called Edward Baltheim of the Sigma Cain. He warned us of the dire needs of the Western Lands and bade us to stand and fight. He advised us to stay vigilant and courageous and asked us to restore Alterash for the sake of all the Men of Gaia. He kept saying that grave times were approaching, and he often muttered to himself in secret. He was an unusual man much like King Izen of Guole. Anyways, on our journey home, my men, the last free Men of Alterash, cast lots upon a new king to rule after Bormann is defeated. I have been chosen, though not much to my liking. That is why I have been given this helm to wear until a proper crown may rest upon my brow. I give you my word, Gibraltar; I will rule justly and will return peace and honor to this fallen country.'

Tristan stepped forth with a hand raised in the air. 'Hullo, good sir and well met! I am Tristan son of the late Bristan and Evelia, nephew of King Edgar, and crowned Prince of Bolteras.'

Iggy bowed upon his steed and his company bowed with him. 'It is a pleasure and an honor, young prince. I am Iggor— though my friends call me Iggy—son of Ringor, once a lowly peasant and now marked as the future King of Alterash! We have heard many good things of Lord Edgar the fearless! What is your business in this land, young lord?'

Tristan fell to his knees and bowed before the horsemen and called out, 'Join us! I beg of you, good lords of Alterash, lend us your aid! I know we should be the ones to join your ranks as this is your land, but we have sent soldiers of our own to bring freedom to your people. And I have been placed in charge of this mission. Bolteras has need of an alliance with this land, and it is in our best interest to join forces to expel the influence of evil here. Draemhas are amassing in Vash'ala, and one year from now we will be invaded by the forces of the Dark Lord. Long have Alterash and Bolteras been impartial to one another, but I ask you, future king, to lend us your aid in the war to come. If you do that, you will have Bolteras as your ally for the liberation of your people!'

'If that is all you have to say to me boy, then I suggest you pack your bags and go home; and do not rely on us to save you from the Hellhounds a second time!'

'My friend,' Gibraltar interrupted, 'would you not listen to us?'

'*Us*,' Iggy questioned, 'are you now one of the Boltians? Where has your loyalty to Alterash gone? Though you are my friend, Gibraltar, I will slay you here and now if you have become a traitor to these lands.'

'Alterash is dead, you fool!' Gibraltar snapped. 'Can you not see it? Where are the free riders of Alterash? Why do its people cower in the wooded plains and secret tunnels? If this is truly Alterash, then I gladly declare myself a traitor!' Gibraltar began to sweat and tears streamed forth from his eyes, and he huffed and puffed loudly. 'I will not be loyal to a wicked king! If the day ever comes, you will have my service and loyalty when you are King of Alterash. But until that day, I will still fight as an Alterashian, but one allied with Bolteras!'

Iggy dismounted and approached Gibraltar. He raised his hand as if to hit his friend, and Gibraltar cowered before him. A moment later, Gibraltar opened his eyes was greeted with another amiable smile and a friendly arm reaching out to him. He grabbed Iggy's arm firmly, and they silently formed an alliance. 'Well met warriors of Bolteras! Forgive my sternness, but one cannot be too careful these days. We will unite our forces, but we still have one issue to address: who will be the leader of this force?'

An idea flashed instantly into Tristan's mind, and he began to jump up and down with excitement. 'Aha! I think I have the perfect idea!' he exclaimed cheerfully. 'Oh yes indeed, a grand plan!'

'Let us hear it then!' Iggy replied.

'Wait,' Delitas frantically called out, 'this must wait! Look to the south!' They all turned about and perceived a much larger army of wolves amassing in the distance; they appeared as menacing shadows in the dark. 'Let us hide in the woods! There is no need to risk any of our lives.'

'Aye, tell us your plan when we have shaken off these pesky Hellhounds!' Just as Iggy spoke, the wolves suddenly turned and withdrew to the west as if someone or something was calling upon them. 'Eh, now, what was that all about? That was an odd sight if I have ever seen one! Well, without the threat of the wolves we have time for your plan, Tristan.'

'Right, well I would start by leaving the horses behind. We desired to sneak into Kainor unnoticed so we could slay the Alp called Gluttony. Once we do away with him, we could take flight until the curse is lifted from your brethren, though I am certain not all will return to their old selves. Now that we have more soldiers to utilize, we could do something else!'

Tristan carefully explained in long detail his clever plan to his companions, and he inquired of the layout of Kainor and the resources in the land. The whole group nodded with intrigue and wonder at the intricacy of the plan and the depth of Tristan's thinking; and Iggy carefully answered all of Tristan's questions as he asked them. By the time he had finished speaking, all the Alterashian soldiers were rallied and full of fresh hope for their country.

'So that is your plan, then?' Iggy asked with fascination. 'Marvelous! That idea is absolutely marvelous! And you just thought of that now?' Tristan nodded. 'I think you will make a fine king one day, Prince Tristan! It would be best for us to rally the others of our force. We have camps and hiding places on each of the islets between the fords, so if we encounter enemies along the way we may have the means to evade them or else leave them distracted. Our main force awaits us at the islet between the second and first fords. We traveled down this beaten path to survey the lands as we do daily and I see we picked the best time to scout! I am glad we found your company when we did.'

'We are glad you came at our moment of need,' Gibraltar responded, 'but come now and seize this rambling. Let us talk more after we free our kin! I am eager to free my friends and my family, if they still live.'

'Forgive me, Gibraltar,' Iggy replied, 'I have a habit of speaking too long. We shall ride to our brethren ahead of you. We shall put young Tristan's plan in action after you have taken some time to rest from your travels! I will leave our archers in your company for your protection. Will that suffice?' Gibraltar nodded and waved him off, and Iggy and his company of horsemen galloped away with swiftness and zeal.

* * *

After passing through three more fords, Tristan and his group arrived the following morning at a large encampment with many tents full of soldiers—at least a hundred in all. When they came at last to the first ford of Anagon, Iggy ran out to greet them. He brought them into his tent where a hot breakfast had been prepared. As Tristan and his comrades ate, they shared their tales of the journey thus far. Iggy was elated to hear all of their stories, especially of the Boltian Council and the decisions made there. After finishing their meal, Iggy sat down with his legs crossed and pulled out a relic of a pipe. He tapped it repeatedly on his knee and drifted into deep thought. After a long silence, Gibraltar cleared his throat hoping to stir his friend from his deep meditation.

'Oh, uh, forgive me. I was lost in thought. It has been many years since I have been home in Alterash, not to mention my house in Kainor. I am eager to return, though I am afraid of what I will find when we get there. Regardless, we must depart at once. Now is a better time than any other, as the sun is just beginning to rise, and we will have plenty of light to guide our way. We have nearly thirty leagues to travel by foot, so it will be about a three day journey. We will depart after we have had our lunch. When we arrive, it will be best to carry out Tristan's plan in the evening so the night will shroud our presence. We are truly grateful you have come. I offer you my thanks, Prince of Bolteras! And forgive me for my rudeness yesterday. My people and I are ever wary, and we do not easily trust others. I offer my sincerest apologies.'

'Sir, it is an honor to lend you our aid,' Tristan uttered, 'so apologize no more! But it is as you say. Now is a better time than any other! Are we prepared for whatever might come our way?' The group nodded with determination. 'Then let us reconvene after lunch and depart for Kainor!' For a few hours, Tristan and his companions rested peacefully in the tents of the Alterashians until Iggy woke them to eat. The Alterashian warriors were already feasting gaily throughout the bivouac and were singing war songs telling of the heroes of old.

After they had eaten and prepared their packs for travel, the group left the camp and proceeded over the first ford of Anagon and continued north for several miles. As evening approached, they passed through many grassy meadows and wide, open plains lined with countless flowers but only a few trees scattered abroad. By nightfall, they came upon a series of rolling mounds that continued for many leagues to the north before turning sandy at the shores of the Great Sea, and they camped there for the night.

On the following morning, they turned west and descended down a long, steady dropping slope of grass that leveled out a mile or so later. The level plains continued for two or three miles before they came to a large, steep wold with hundreds of furrows, stretching north and south, filled with decaying plants and vegetables of various kinds, which was an odd sight in the middle of spring. At the top of the hill they halted and beheld a huge fortress resting far away across a vast valley; it was lit with many lamps and stood upon a great, verdant hill with tall stone walls surrounding it. At its foot, though difficult to see from where they stood, there was a large moat dug around the castle walls, but it was quite dry, more like a shallow trench than a defensive system.

'Come now,' Gibraltar called out, 'it should only take another day to reach Kainor. Aye, by tomorrow evening we may have liberated this land from the Enemy's clutches.'

'We can only hope,' Iggy responded, 'and do our part in the matter! At least we have the tall grasses ahead to veil our presence! It seems those gluttonous fools have failed to send servants to trim the lawn of late. Let us use this to our advantage!'

They quickly strode down the western side of the wold as the last light of the sun was disappearing. They marched on at an even greater pace but decided to halt for the night an hour later. Upon the start of the next day, they continued westward and came upon a stretch of land overgrown with tall grass that rose above their heads. But the high lawn shielded them from sight. At Iggy's command, they spread out amongst themselves so the movement of the grass would not expose them to their enemies. They continued through the grass for many miles before the tall grass ended abruptly. Emerging from the high-grown pastures, the company noticed the grass had become brown and wilted as if the sun shone brightly and strongly only in a small area around Kainor.

'This must be the result of Magic!' Tristan called out, considering himself to be quite clever.

'I am not sure,' Delitas muttered. 'The Alps seem to have unique abilities, and I reckon Gluttony dwells here in Kainor. Edgar spoke of one named Greed who influenced the people of Bolteras to horde possessions and wealth, but it had another power. It had the ability to sit upon a person in sleep and trap them in an endless wave of nightmares. He could also change from ethereal to physical upon a whim! It would not surprise me if this particular Draemhas had unique abilities of his own, whether that be Magic or not.'

'Aye,' Gibraltar said in agreement, 'we must be wary until we know the demon's true power!' The Alterashian soldiers stared at them blankly, and Iggy scratched his head in confusion. Since the sun was still in the sky above, Gibraltar took the time to carefully explain in detail the knowledge they gained at the Boltian Council concerning the Alps.

'I see,' Iggy responded somberly. 'We cannot go up against an enemy whose powers are unknown to us.' They all sat there at the edge of the tall grass contemplating, wondering what power Gluttony possessed.

'I think I know!' Tristan exclaimed with much enthusiasm. 'It is poison!' The company gasped and some turned their heads upward as though they had just received a sudden epiphany. 'Yes, I believe that is it, considering the wolves of this land drip venom from their fangs! I am certain none of us have seen poisonous wolves before Gluttony came to this country!'

'I say, Prince Tristan, you are a brilliant lad!' Iggy cried out. 'Where does one obtain such wisdom and insight?'

'I am quite fond of my uncle! I have looked up to Edgar ever since he chose to adopt me after my parents abandoned me. Quite often I make jokes, and I rarely act seriously, for laughter eases my heartache; but I know how to be strong and sober when it matters! Uncle Edgar has taught me everything I know, and I can take no credit for myself.'

'Intelligent and modest this one,' Iggy laughed. 'Edgar, you say? Though I have never met the man, I respect him greatly! Now that we have discovered Gluttony's power, be wary of any Magic or weapon this fiend wields! His arms may be covered in venom, and his Magic may take the form of poison. Let us hope his Hellhounds are far from us!' Above their heads, dark clouds began to form and soon the sky was covered by thick, black billows; and the land turned as black as night.

'Look!' Tristan called, 'dark clouds have fallen upon us, and the sun is veiled. What greater fortune has come upon us! With all light blotted out, it will be rather difficult for our enemies to see us coming. There can be no greater time to attack than now!'

They marched swiftly ahead for another hour before they reached the stronghold on its southern side. The walls of the castle were tall, but Tristan, Gibraltar and Delitas were able to scale them with the aid of Iggy and some of the other soldiers by standing upon their comrades' shoulders and hoisting themselves onto the parapets. After the three had vanished from sight, Iggy led the remaining Boltian soldiers and his warriors from Alterash around the walls of the castle to the main gate on the western wall.

* * *

Inside the castle, Gibraltar took the lead—as he knew the fortress well—and guided Tristan and Delitas towards the king's throne room, where they expected to find Gluttony. They leapt from the parapets to a stone walkway below them and the path split three

197

ways: one path to the left, one to the right and another one leading straight. Gibraltar led them down the pathway to the right for nearly six fathoms and turned left onto a path leading up a short slope. At the top of the hill, there were many buildings and alleys and lamps scattered along the paths. He led them through the alleys always heading eastward towards the throne room. As they snuck through the fortress, they crawled under windows to remain hidden. Moments later, they came to the central path of the fortress.

They halted briefly in one of the lanes between two houses made of stone, for they saw a light flicker upon the road ahead. They quickly pulled their cloaks over them and laid prone near to the building on their right. A soldier wearing crimson armor paced with a lantern in his hand. On his head was a crimson helm with a black plume, and a sheathed blade hung at his side. 'Vash'alans!' Gibraltar hissed in a hushed tone. 'The Enemy has brought our greatest rivals within our glorious fortress! Curse them!' They waited there for several minutes observing the rounds of the guards on duty. They perceived that a guard passed by once every three minutes and were confused as the fortress did not seem heavily defended.

'We have a three minute opening to make our move!' Tristan whispered. 'We must make it count.'

* * *

Outside the castle walls, Iggy and the soldiers readied their weapons and neared the western gate staying as close to the wall as possible. When they arrived, Iggy stood on the northernmost side of the door and beckoned one of the soldiers to stand at the southernmost side. Upon the count of three, they beat their fists violently upon the gates. The rest of the soldiers, those who could, readied their bows and aimed upward at the parapets above.

* * *

Back inside the fortress of Kainor, the guards stirred at the sound of the knocking upon the fortress gates. Many Vash'alan guards emerged from the many buildings in the city and stormed to the castle gates with several Alterashian soldiers at their side, who were surprisingly thin. At that time, it began to rain violently in Kainor, and the water doused many of the lamps that were left uncovered. The inside of the fortress grew black as night, and Gibraltar took advantage of the darkness to the benefit of their mission: by his advice, the three men ambushed a lonely soldier and stripped him of his armor. Delitas quickly arrayed himself in the crimson panoply with the aid of Tristan and Gibraltar.

'It has been quite some time since I wore armor like this,' Delitas said despondently.

'This is no time for reminiscing!' Tristan snapped. 'You know what to do, Delitas. We are counting on you!' At once, Delitas sped off towards the castle gates and fell in line with the enemy soldiers.

After the swarm of the enemies had descended to the foot of the fortress, Gibraltar darted forward onto the main road and turned right. Tristan followed, and they ascended a long slope to a simple throne room with no adjoining chambers. The room was empty of decorations but filled with many tables. On top of the tables were plates full of various kinds of meats and breads, but there were no fruits or vegetables to be seen. Directly in front of them, a fat man sat upon the king's throne, and he appeared to be asleep. Next to his chair, a platinum crown rested on the ground. His royal clothes were stretched and torn due to his size, and he was dirtied with blood and scraps of food.

Suddenly, thunder crashed loudly outside and echoed within the throne room, but the fat man did not stir; then lightning flickered brightly and illuminated the room for a moment, but still the king did not move. Behind the throne, a shadow resembling a man bent and twisted in the light of a nearby lamp. 'Come out, fiend!' Gibraltar called. 'Today you will be judged, and I do not think there will be any who will rule in your favor!'

The figure slowly crept out from his hiding place and moved like a snake slithering upon the ground. He erected himself slightly and threw back his cloak, revealing a staff and a sword at his side. 'I am Gluttony,' he spoke in a frightening voice that switched back and forth from deep to shrill tones, 'I have been expecting you, young prince, and your allies as well, but I must admit that I did not expect so many; nevertheless, I shall slay each of you tonight. I suppose you figured you could sneak into this mighty fortress and slay King Bormann and rescue this land?' He laughed hysterically for a moment and then continued, 'But the king is already dead! And my wolves approach to consume the valiant warriors outside the gates!' He laughed again with the same sinister laugh as before. Tristan and Gibraltar expected Gluttony to be a fat creature, but he was rather thin and sturdy in build.

'Bormann's death was never our goal,' Gibraltar answered. 'We have come for you! And we already considered your precious Hellhounds! They will be burned with fire!'

'In this rain?' the demon laughed. 'The rain is of my making, and it will not cease unless I tell it to stop! The fangs of my pets will seethe as they sink into your pathetic bodies, and you will all die within the hour! Behold! they draw nigh!' At that moment many loud howls, barks and growls echoed from the west, so loudly that Tristan and Gibraltar could hear them from the throne room. 'Victory is ours!' Gluttony hissed. 'And with your deaths, the Dark Lord is one step closer to conquering the Western Lands!'

'You are wrong,' Tristan argued. 'Everything has gone precisely as I hoped it would!' The Alp laughed and peered intensely at Tristan, but something in the distance caught his eye and brought him to despair.

* * *

While Tristan and Gibraltar made their way to the throne room, the Vash'alan guards rose to the parapets and aimed their bows over the edge, but they were shot down by Iggy and his men before they were even able to loose a single arrow. A small host of enemies fell dead from the walls and crashed upon the ground below. But still they laughed and mocked the warriors from within the fortress. 'You will never break down these gates, you fools,' one called out. At that time, several Alterashian warriors appeared on the parapets with tightly fitted arrows at the ready. With a flash of lightning, they beheld the faces of their old comrades who had fled long before, but even the sight of their brethren had no influence on them.

'I am Iggor son of Ringor, though you may remember me as Iggy. Hear my voice and cease this foolishness! Open the gates; take back what is yours, or we will be forced to attack!' His old comrades did not heed his voice but instead proceeded to loose their arrows. A few arrows fell upon Iggy's company, but a bright flash of lightning suddenly hissed across the sky and blinded the archers above. Iggy and his band of soldiers quickly loosed several arrows into the arms of their former comrades—not wanting to kill any of them—and the Alterashians fell back from the parapet. For several minutes, the walls were emptied. From the inside, the soldiers continued to laugh and ridicule Iggy and his men. Moments later, noisy howls and snarls came reverberating over the booming of thunder.

Suddenly the gates flung open from the inside, and a soldier in crimson armor appeared. The warrior removed his helm and revealed himself as Delitas. Iggy and the rest of his company darted within the fortress walls much to the defenders' dismay and slew the horde of Vash'alan troops. As they encountered their corrupted brethren, they disarmed them and knocked them unconscious; but a few of their former comrades proved to be too ferocious and deadly, and they were forced to slay them, though not without regret. The Vash'alan warriors were easily slain as the Boltian and Alterashian soldiers crashed upon them with unyielding rage and fearsome strength.

'Go now!' Iggy shouted, 'the storehouse is to the right in that large shack! Go quickly! I will keep watch over our comrades and strike them upon the head if they choose to wake up.' All of the warriors—nearly two hundred in all—passed quickly one after the other into the gigantic storehouse and withdrew large barrels of oil. At once, they carried them to the castle gates and quickly emptied the oil into the moat at the front of the fortress, and some emptied a few more barrels of oil at the foot of the gate. Most of the soldiers stood on guard behind the walls, but a few rose to the tops of the parapets and aimed their bows at the approaching wolves. When all their preparations were complete, Iggy wrapped a cloth around the tip of an arrow and dipped it into one of the barrels until the cloth was fully soaked; he then climbed upon the walls and aimed his arrow at the pools of oil on the ground below.

More than a hundred wolves poured over the plains from the west only a couple furlongs away from the gates. There was not enough oil to fill the moat entirely, but it was enough for their plan. Moments later, the beasts dipped into the moat below and were doused in oil. The thick grease slowed their run. Most of the wolves had already dipped in the oil when some began to pour into the gates, but Iggy's company formed a phalanx and fired arrows at the scattered hounds. Seeing no greater opportunity, Iggy lit his arrow with a lamp and fired the arrow into the moat below. At once, the moat was brimming with flames that shone with bright intensity. Thick puffs of smoke rose high into the air, and the wolves shrieked in agony. The path of fire traveled to the foot of the gates and burned the wolves that had already passed beyond the moat. In a mere instant, the army of Hellhounds burned to their miserable deaths, save only a few that fled in terror.

* * *

Back in the throne room, Gluttony was astonished and filled with rage. 'Curse you, foolish mortals!' he spat. 'You dare to oppose the Alps? I will not be stopped!' The Alp leapt forth and drew his blade; his body returned to a shadowy form, and he slithered upon

201

the ground toward Tristan and Gibraltar. Gibraltar raised his spear and hurled it at the shadow, but it did the Alp no harm and merely pierced the stony floor. Gluttony slithered toward the defenseless Alterashian, but unbeknownst to him, Tristan had raised his sword in turn. As the Alp reformed into a physical being, Tristan readied his attack. 'Fool! You know not the power of your enemy!' Gluttony hissed as he raised his black sword high above his head and prepared to leap upon Gibraltar. 'I will slay you where you stand!'

'That is where you are wrong!' Gibraltar refuted. 'This was all planned by the Prince of Bolteras!' With those words, Gluttony's face turned sour with fear, and he cowered as Tristan's sword swung through the air. Tristan swung his sword at the Alp's neck, and hewed off Gluttony's head. 'At last we have done it, Tristan! And it is all thanks to you, the wise Prince of Bolteras!' Tristan was full of joy and a bright, large smile extended across his face. Gibraltar and Tristan proudly shouted from the throne room, 'Victory!' and the word echoed many times back to them from the soldiers below.

Chapter XII

The Child of Prophecy

Upon the morning of April tenth, Asura the Fire Dragon returned to the Chamber of Fire where Victor and Alastair patiently awaited him. In the days of waiting, Alastair had begun Victor's training in the arts of Elúvías, and Victor quickly learned leechcraft, though he struggled with the other disciplines. Asura appeared suddenly and descended upon them from the ceiling high above, and the flap of his mighty wings extinguished the fire surrounding the dais. He perched upon the cold stone of the platform and peered at Victor with fiery eyes for a long time and then turned his gaze to Alastair and heaved a sigh of sweltering smoke.

'Why is it you brought me this boy, Alastair?'

'I told you before, Asura. He is an incredible man with a pure heart. I have been amazed by him in the short amount of time I have known him, and we seek your aid in the war to come! We are in need of your Dragon Stone, my friend.'

'Tell me the true purpose you have brought him to me. I have looked hard into your mind and perceived more to your reasoning. I know there was a dream that caught your ear and tickled your mind's eye. Tell me everything.' Alastair breathed deeply and told him of the Boltian Council, and all that was discussed. He omitted none of the details. Asura pondered on all that was said, and when the Wizard had finished speaking, he remained silent for quite some time.

'So it was the dream of the two lambs that captured your curiosity?' he spoke after a long silence. 'And you believe this boy is one of the lambs from that dream?' Victor raised his head curiously yet confused by the Dragon's words. 'Which one do you reckon he is?'

'I am not certain, but I believe he is the second one, the one we have long awaited, the Child of Prophecy!'

'Ha!' the Dragon laughed. 'Many years ago you believed Lord Edgar was the Child of Prophecy, and you held on to that belief until he returned from Vash'ala with a sickness! That day changed your mind, did it not?'

'What sickness?' Victor questioned.

Ignoring the question, Alastair answered, 'How did you know of that? Can the Dragons perceive all things within a man?'

'Aye, it is a gift from Vaaspar that was bestowed upon us. And you are not as complex as you believe yourself to be, Alastair the White! Indeed, you have proven yourself simple, for you have forgotten much of the ways of Dragons and of your old friend. But as it is, I have seen all the memories you hold locked away in your mind, and I see all the good and evil within your heart; and I am pleased to find there is little evil within you!'

'Masters, what is this sickness of the king's that you speak of?' Victor chimed in again.

'Bah,' the Dragon responded in annoyance. 'Have you not seen it?'

'He appeared quite healthy to me, good Dragon. In fact, he appeared stronger than any I know!'

'Ah, but appearances are deceiving, young one! It matters not what is on the outside, but the inside, well, that is a different story. At the Boltian Council you discussed a disease that killed King Aramon, and Edgar mentioned the death of his wife who was with child. To his despair h—'

'Say no more!' Alastair interrupted. 'I gave him my word that none would hear the tragedies that took place unless it came from his own mouth.'

'You are a good friend, Alastair, but I have sworn no such thing. Do you wish to know, lad?' Alastair lowered his head sorrowfully and anxiously stroked his long, white beard.

'No sir, I do not!' Victor answered after a moment of thought. 'If it is as tragic as you say, then I will only know if Lord Edgar tells me himself!'

'That is a fine answer, young Victor,' Asura declared with a happy tone to his voice, 'I believe my ramblings have caused a distraction enough. You have officially passed my second test! I see now that you care more about others than you do yourself or your own interests, and that is the sign of one worthy of honor! Now for your third test, answer me this; what is your greatest ambition, and what will you do with my Stone? Keep in mind, I know your heart and mind fully well.'

Victor meditated on the question for several minutes, clearing his mind and searching his soul for a truthful answer. 'Well,' he spoke at long last, 'I desire to rid the world of the growing

Darkness. When I was younger, I always feared the night. It was always quite dark in Kesh. It terrified me, and I always imagined ghouls and beasts would come after me in the middle of the night. But my Uncle Arthur would always come to me when I was afraid, and he would light a candle and assure me the light would keep me safe. The faint candle light felt warm and soothing during the night. That was when I learned to love Vaaspar's Light.

'I never once enjoyed darkness even after I overcame my fear of the night. It is my belief that I can show others the Light, so that they too may learn to love it the way I do! Perhaps with your power, good Dragon, with that Stone of yours, I can change the world around me; and even if the entire world is swallowed by Darkness, I can still shine some light with the power of fire! Then the Darkness will cower before me, and Men will remember the Light, that is Vaaspar's Light! When I have accomplished my mission, I would gladly return your Stone to you, if that would bring you comfort, wise one. My greatest ambition is to save all those I love from the threat of evil, just as Arthur always rescued me when I was young. Most of all, I want to save my parents, and Hildegard also, from Abaddon's snare. That is my answer, Dragon.'

Asura peered at him sternly and discerned his heart and mind. A moment later, he laughed loudly: it was deep and thunderous like the sound of Deephorn in Vallicore. 'You did not lie when you spoke, child, not even for a moment. Nor did *you* lie when you spoke of this boy, Alastair. Indeed you have passed all my tests, and I deem you worthy of my Stone! Now you see, faithful Kai, why I ordered you to test the boy. But alas! I must interpret the dream you are so concerned about, my old apprentice. The dream does not concern Lord Edgar; that much is sure. There were those who dreamed of him long ago, and one of those dreams came to King Haus during his reign; that is why, I presume, he chose Edgar as his heir. The dream you speak of concerns this boy in part, but he is not the Child of Prophecy!'

'Then is he the first lamb? Who then is the second?'

'That I do not know yet, but Victor is indeed the first, the one with the crown. Though he is not yet a king, I foresee that in his future!'

'I will be a king?' Victor joined in. He paused with no more words to say and stared blankly at the ground.

'Aye and a great king you will be! If you will inherit my Stone, then I will bestow upon you my Guardian as well. From now on Kai will protect you instead of my Stone. Do you consent, my great phoenix?'

'It was you, Asura, who gave me life, so I will honor whatever it is you ask of me, of course!'

'Good! Then, it is settled.'

'Will you join the warfront?' Alastair asked anxiously.

'Do you ask if this old Dragon will fight once again with Men? Nay! I have given you enough aid already, but I suppose I will do one other favor for Victor: I will teach him to control Fire Magic and the power of my Dragon Stone. And you, Alastair the White, can train him in the ways of Elúvías, for I was not made to control such power. But all the same, I will open his mind to the understanding of Mana and the flow of energy in his body! If he is to be a great king in these evils days where Men have obtained and will continue to gain many mysterious powers, he will need a mentor. And I give you my word: I will make him a great warrior and a master of fire before the war in one year. When I am done with him, he will be a king that few will rival, even those of old!'

Victor gasped and squeezed his hands into fists. He then raised his hands into the air and shouted, 'I have heard such good news today!' Alastair chuckled at his excitement.

'After I train you,' Asura interrupted sternly, 'you must leave and never approach me again until you keep your promise and return my Stone to me.'

'I truly wish you would join us, old friend,' Alastair spoke. 'But I am glad for your willingness to help us at all! When will you begin his training?'

'We will start tomorrow! Spend the day peacefully as you would and hunt in the forest to the west if you grow hungry; but return ere nightfall or else you will be locked out of my lair. I will not risk the Kobolds finding their way into my lair. Now then, here is my Stone, Victor son of Valent!' Asura removed an amulet from his neck that hung about a chain of gold and extended his arm out towards Victor. Just as the Dragon held out his arm, something dropped from the air above: it was a shadowy figure with long, blood-stained fangs that drooped past its chin. The creature snatched the Stone away from Asura's grip. Before anyone could act, the being changed into the form of a raven and flew out of the Chamber of Fire. 'Curse the Alps! They have come for my Stone at last! Quickly Kai! Go after him!' The phoenix soared into the air after the

Alp and shot forth fire from his mouth, but his fire did not reach, for the Alp took flight at a greater speed than Kai could match.

Seeing his newly acquired gift disappear from his sight, Victor turned and ran down the western stair of the platform to leave the Dragon's lair. Outside, he saw the large black bird flying above the Grey Forest, and Kai was close behind. The sun was just rising over the mountains in the eastern sky and the light blinded Victor. At that time, Asura stomped out from his cave and called to Victor, 'Get on my back boy! If you are to acquire my Stone, you must take it back from the Draemhas! That form of his must require a great amount of Mana. He must be trying to lose us in the forest! Forgive me, but I fear you must go through one more test to acquire my Stone.'

Asura lowered his body and slammed his spiky tail upon the ground. Victor carefully climbed upon the giant beast using the spikes on his tail to hoist himself up to the Dragon's back. He had hardly settled on top of Asura before the Dragon violently leapt upward from the ground and began flapping his wings. In the blink of an eye, Asura had taken full flight. His speed was incredible and took Victor by surprise—he nearly fell off Asura's back but at the last minute grabbed onto the root of the Dragon's wings. The rush of wind was powerful, and Victor felt a strange sensation in his stomach as they soared in the air. Though he was frightened, he was also rather thrilled.

'Be careful, young one. None can match the speed of a Dragon! You will fall to an unpleasant death if you take me lightly!' He spoke deafeningly loud like a trumpet as the wind blew fervently in their faces.

'You wait until now to tell me!' Victor exclaimed jokingly. 'I nearly died just now!'

'Ha, I am sure you did, but I would never allow that to happen. Now keep your eye on the prize! Behold! the Alp has descended into the forest! Kai cannot follow him in there or else his flames may burn the whole forest down! I will lower you near to the ground. Climb down my tail and hold fast to my spikes; then release yourself and follow the cursed Draemhas. Kai and I will fly above and cut him off from his path. Are you prepared?'

Victor gulped and then took a long, slow breath. He flailed his arms through the air in a circular motion and breathed once more. 'I am ready!'

'It took you long enough to respond! Be wary around the Alp! Long ago they posed a serious threat even to the Dragons, but their power has been fading for many years now and is returning to the Dark Lord to fuel his resurrection. But that does not mean they are to be taken lightly. Here we go, lad!' Asura quickly descended just above the tops of the trees as the Alp passed beneath them and reformed into his physical state. Unable to go further, Kai reeled and flew back into the sky. Asura hovered above the trees as Victor, scared for his life, slowly crawled down the Dragon's tail. He stepped upon the spikes like a ladder and carefully lowered himself to the edge of Asura's long tail.

While Victor was still nearly ten feet from the ground, he held on to the Dragon's tail for a while, too afraid to let go. 'Let go, Victor!' Asura called. 'Release my tail, lad! The Alp is getting away! Go after him!' A moment later, Victor lost his grip. He fell upon a large tree root and collapsed upon the ground. The Alp turned at the sound of Victor's screams and drew his shadowy blade. Victor attempted to stand to his feet and face his foe, but the pain in his legs prevented him from standing up.

'Tell me your name, wretched Alp!' Victor shouted at the creature.

The Alp laughed deeply and then growled. 'You are well informed, boy, though I am not surprised as you were accompanied by a Dragon, a Guardian and a White Mage. I am Envy, the Alp who is responsible for perverting the minds of the Vash'alans. They are my greatest work in this world!' he said with a shrill laugh. 'Long have I whispered to them, and they were easily convinced.' He laughed again menacingly with a peculiar snort. 'And who might you be, lad? I should know your name before I slay the one worthy of inheriting a Dragon Stone!'

'I am Victor Perigas, son of Valent, and it is I who will be slaying you!'

'Perigas?' the Alp replied. 'So you are the son of Valent, eh?' He laughed loudly placing his hands on his head. 'I know your family well, oh yes indeed, very well. Your parents are responsible for the immense growth of Darkness in Vash'ala, though the foolish sun-worshippers would have fallen prey to Abaddon without their assistance. Ironic is it not? You remain good even though your parents have become minions of Darkness!' He followed his speech with a maniacal laugh that made Victor feel uncomfortable. He rose and charged forth at the Alp but stumbled under the pressure of his

208

hurting ankles. The Alp laughed again and then gave a good lick of his blade. 'What a shame to kill the son of the infamous Alchemists! But then again, it matters not to me! If you still cling to the Light, then you are a threat to the Dark Lord's will, and I cannot let you live.'

The Alp raised his blade, but a flash of light suddenly shone forth from Victor's hands. 'I used to fear the Darkness,' Victor said, 'that is, of course, until I learned about the Light! Behold!' He placed his hand over his injured legs and was instantly healed. By the time the light had vanished, Victor's hair and stature had grown ever so slightly, and he appeared older than before. 'My ankle is healed! I wonder who will win now. Will it be Darkness or Light?'

The Alp growled and darted at Victor slashing his sword all about him. The swings of the Alp were so rapid that Victor could hardly see the blade move. Somehow, Victor managed to dodge the slashes of his enemy, and he hid behind a nearby tree. 'You may flee, boy, but you will not be spared!' As the demon spoke, Victor leapt from his hiding spot and charged forward. Victor swung his sword with all his might, but the Alp caught the glint of silver in the light of the sun and blocked Victor's sword with his own. The boy's feeble sword cracked under the pressure of the Draemhan blade and shattered into many pieces. 'The swords of Men cannot withstand the fell blades of Dragoth! Our swords are made of Dragonium, a metal said to be as strong as the scales of Dragons! And with the power of Vexúvías, no human weapon can compare to ours!'

Victor crawled backwards for nearly three fathoms until his back ran up the trunk of a tree. Envy slowly approached him, licking his blade once again, and Victor was terrified. While he was still a couple fathoms from Victor, Asura breathed a large ball of fire that sent the Alp fleeing in terror. The Dragon flapped his enormous wings and the fire on the ground was extinguished immediately. The strong gust of air forced Victor back against the tree even more, and the tree bent under the pressure of the wind. 'Get up, Victor! It is too soon to surrender!' Asura called from above.

'But he destroyed my sword!' Victor replied. 'I have no weapon to fight. I left my bow in your lair.' Asura growled ferociously and flew away after the Alp.

'Victor!' Alastair called from the east. The boy looked all about but could not see where he was. 'Where are you lad?'

'I am here!' Victor answered terrified and pressed still against the tree. Alastair appeared before him in a flash riding a dazzling white horse laden with Victor's bow and his quiver full of arrows. 'But how did you—' Victor wondered. 'Did we not abandon our horses days ago? Where did you find this beautiful steed?'

'It is not a real horse, lad, but a summoned one. Come now and climb atop! We have no time to discuss my Magical arts. We must never allow the Dragon Stone to fall into the hands of the Enemy!' Victor carefully climbed onto the horse fearing he would fall through it.

'Is it a ghost horse?'

Alastair laughed and pressed his heels into the sides of the horse, and it sped off in pursuit of the Alp. 'Nay, laddie; Mage's have many powers, though many of them require a great deal of Magic. This is my spell, and I call it a *Horse Summon*. It is one of many Creation Spells.'

'What is a Creation Spell?' Victor questioned confusedly.

'Ah, there is much still for you to learn, so be patient. There are spells we Wizards cast that can create objects or creatures that have life, though these spells require large amounts of Magic power, and my creations will vanish when I have spent all my Magic, you see. It is a cheap imitation of the *Awakening Magic* used by Vaaspar; but His creations are permanent, and His supply of Mana never runs dry.'

'I see. There are many wonderful things and powers in the world, eh? So did you remake Valor's Bridge with your Creation Spell?'

'Nay, that required a different spell, a permanent one. And yes indeed, lad, there certainly are many fantastic things in this world, but enough of that. Look! The Alp is just ahead. He cannot outrun Lightmane—that is the name I gave my horse. It may be odd to you that I have named him, but this spell has helped me in many ways, even before I ascended to the rank of White Mage. Now prepare yourself! Soon you must face the Alp!' Victor readied an arrow on his bow and aimed it ahead. 'Remember what I instructed you concerning Elúvías. You can cover your arrow with the power of Light thus enhancing its strength. It will be more destructive than a regular dart. Now give it a shot!'

The steed galloped forward at a fierce speed, but it seemed to glide smoothly as though it were standing still. They were now drawing near to the forest's edge at the borders of Alterash, but Envy turned his path left and continued westward toward Vash'ala and remained under the shelter of the trees. Alastair turned his mighty

210

stallion and pursued the Alp to the west as Asura and Kai loomed overhead ever watchful of the Alp's location. 'I cannot do it,' Victor said at last. 'I cannot use Elúvías as freely as you, and I have only just begun to train!'

'Aye, perhaps you would have learned more quickly in Vallicore where the White Stone resides in the Cathedral of Light. But we have no time for regrets! Loose your arrow regardless and bring the wretched Alp to his knees!' Victor inhaled deeply and then slowly exhaled; he then loosed his arrow at the Alp, and it pierced the Draemhas in his back. Envy released a devilish cry and fell to the ground. The shocking pain of Victor's arrow caused him to release Asura's amulet which then tumbled down a steep slope that was just before him. 'Now I shall slay him quickly before he has time to stand!'

'Wait, Alastair!' Asura called from the sky. 'Let the boy deal with the Alp himself! If I am to train him, then consider this part of his training!'

'But he has no blade to use, and this is no time for games!'

'There are no games in war!' the Dragon snapped. 'He must become familiar with killing and facing terrifying enemies now or else he will panic when war comes! Give him your blade if you worry so much.' Alastair reluctantly drew his sword from its sheath and handed it to Victor. The sword emitted a white glow and felt warm in Victor's hands.

'Aye, it is as he says, lad. You must ready yourself for war at all costs. Killing is no easy feat, even if the enemy is the scourge of Dragoth. And it will only be harder if you must face evil Men in the days to come.' Victor nodded nervously. He hesitated for a brief moment and then slid off of Lightmane. He strode anxiously towards Envy with Alastair's sword in his hand. The injured Alp stirred and groaned.

'Fools!' he snorted, 'You are imbeciles sending a young boy to slay one of the Seven Warlords of Darkness!'

'Silence yourself,' Alastair retorted, 'your power has waned greatly since times of old! The Seven were once so great and fearsome. What has become of you now?'

'It is not for you to know! Regardless, no boy can slay me!'

'If you are so confident,' Victor returned, 'then let us test our might with our swords!' Envy laughed: it was the same disgusting, maniacal laugh from before that ended with a snort. He extended his hand toward Victor and small black flames appeared on his finger

211

tips. He grabbed his sword, and the flames shot forth at once and covered the length of his blade in a black, fiery aura.

'Victor!' Alastair called desperately, 'beware the dark flames! They can only be matched by the Power of Light! Hurry and slay the beast before he strikes you down!' Envy did not delay and sprung forth at once with a mighty slash of his blade, but Victor dodged. The blade struck the trunk of a tree, and the black flames spread quickly around it causing it to rot and shed its many leaves. Victor began to breathe heavily in panic, and was unable to calm himself.

'Is this the boy you chose to inherit the Dragon Stone?' Envy laughed with his eyes set on Asura. 'My power has waned greatly but not enough to be stopped by the likes of you! The Dragon is so tamed that he will not set fire to a forest if it will save the lives of many! You cannot defeat me. No, not even you, O great and powerful White Mage, have the power to stop me. Even your Magical sword will not save this boy!' He glared harshly at Alastair, but the Wizard did not stir for a moment. He fixed his eyes on the Alp and great terror overcame the Draemhas. At that moment, Asura crashed upon the ground crushing many trees under him. He perched upon the forest ground with Kai on his back.

'Did you truly believe that I would not crush a few trees to put an end to your pitiful life?' Asura instigated. 'If there is foolishness to be found, it is in you Envy! Of the Seven, you are one of the weakest! And I am already aware that the Dark Lord requires the power of the Alps for his resurrection. Is that not why your power wanes greatly in these dark days? I wonder; what will become of you now?' The Alp growled and gritted his teeth.

At that moment, a strange peace overcame Victor, and he rose to his feet with bold confidence. He stuck Alastair's sword into the ground and drew his bow, quickly loosing an arrow into the stomach of the Draemhas. Envy screeched loudly and a great host of birds flew from the trees in panic. 'I will not be defeated here!' Envy shouted as blood ran from his mouth. He then began to lurch back and forth and eventually stumbled down the hill where Asura's amulet had fallen. He grabbed it and sprinted away as quickly as he could, but Victor had already readied another arrow. He breathed deeply and a surge of energy flowed out of him. Just then, a faint white light covered the tip of his arrow. He drew back his bowstring and fired his shot. The arrow soared faster than the eye could see at the staggering Alp.

212

A mere second elapsed and the arrow struck its target from behind. The dart passed violently through Envy's heart with ease and struck the leafy ground in front of him. The Alp struggled to stand but then fell lifeless to the ground, releasing the Dragon Stone from his hand. Victor dropped his bow and quiver upon the ground and grabbed Alastair's sword. He quickly descended the steep hill and decapitated the Alp. After he had assured the death of his enemy, he stooped down and picked up the Dragon Stone. He held it high above his head with a bright smile upon his face. Alastair, Asura and Kai were atop the hill smiling back at him.

'Good show!' Asura called. 'If that is all the enemy is capable of, then we need not fear this war! Though if this enemy had been at his former strength, then you would have died in an instant! And that is why we must train you well. It was foolishness for the Dark Lord to drain the Alps of their power, even with the day of his resurrection drawing near. Hear me, Victor son of Valent; on this day, you have proven yourself to me and though you may not be the Child of Prophecy, you are most definitely a child of greatness!' Victor ran up the hill with alacrity and offered the Fire Stone to Asura, but the Dragon cordially denied it. 'It is yours now. I have little need for it now. The Last Remnant of Dragons has now awakened and our last days now draw nigh. It is time we pass down our legacy and trust Men once again.'

'It is sad,' Alastair said, 'but I fear what you say is true, and I never wish to see you pass from this life.'

'All must die, good friend; the only question is when and how, though it is not our place to know such things. I have foreseen many events that lie ahead, but never once have I seen the last of my days or any others' for that matter. You should know that Vaaspar has hidden these things from us as you have seen him face to face.'

'Oi,' Victor shouted. 'I would like to think of life rather than death! I have all my friends and comrades to think of who have yet to die. And I still hope to rescue my parents and Hildegard—wherever he may be—and his parents too. There is life all around us, and it saddens me to think of dying. It is for our friends, nay, for all our loved ones that we must work hard and do our part if we are to save the world from eternal Darkness!' His voice was low and solemn, and the others took pity on him.

'Aye,' Asura said somberly, 'shall we return to my lair? We have much work to do if we are to prepare you for the war, and you are ill-prepared as you are now.' Victor nodded. Alastair climbed down from Lightmane and placed his right hand on the horse; instantly a light flickered like a flash of lightning, and the horse disappeared before him. Alastair lurched after releasing his spell and rested himself upon his white staff.

Noticing Alastair's fatigue, Asura spoke, 'After all these years, I see you still exhaust unnecessary amounts of Magic, Alastair. You have changed little since I trained you during the Dragons' Reckoning,' Asura laughed. 'It seems not even a thousand years can change you that much; but I am grateful that little has changed about you, for that makes things still seem quite familiar and full of promise.'

'Very little has changed,' Alastair returned, 'for you left long ago when the world was full of great evils, and you have returned during another evil age of Men. But there was hope then, and there is hope now! We survived that wicked age, and we will survive this one too! So what will you do now that you have witnessed the evil at work?'

'The Draemhas only move about Gaia so freely since we Dragons went into slumber long ago; and none of them dared to search for us for fear that they would wake us. The wretched Draemhas, and even Abaddon himself, fear our power! We were the reason Abaddon's plan failed during the First Age of Kings, and he has feared and resented us since. But now our numbers have dwindled to a meager five, one from each of the original tribes, and Abaddon is confident that he can destroy us. Furthermore, he has already swayed the mind of Anu the Lightning Dragon, as told by my spies. And cursed be Leviathan, my lover of old! She has hardened her heart; aye, her heart has become as cold and hard as the stone of my mountains! She hates Men; yes, she despises them. Kai reported to her on my behalf—as I have kept my whereabouts secret—and she nearly drowned him in the sea. Curse her I say! What will become of the great Dragons of old?' The Dragon shook his head in disappointment, and Victor swore he saw tears running down the Dragon's face, though they were of bright yellow and red hues and shimmered like fire.

'I wish that I could be reunited with Leviathan, my love, but I fear she will not remember me and will resent me for cowering through the ages in deep sleep. If you did not know, she stayed awake all these years and refused to sleep. She has long since caused chaos in the seas and destroyed many good ships, of both Men and Draemhas. And now the age of shipwrights has passed, and Men now dread her waters. But I will stay true to my purpose, to the one given me by Vaaspar Himself. Even if I die, I must protect Men. Now I only wish I knew what became of the other two tribes. There is a prophecy of my kin that speaks of these days. It goes like this:

In a world of evil wrought from malice old:
The Last Remnants of Light stand and oppose
The armies of Dragoth, their ancient foes.
The Last Remnant of Dragons awaken anew
To combat the Dark Lord, of him to subdue.
The Last Remnant of Wizards return to the fight
Against their brethren who strayed from the Light.
The Last Remnant of Men their last tales now unfold
In the struggle against Abaddon and his malice of old.

That is why, after I train young Victor, I will join you in the western war and seek out the Last Remnant of Dragons! Abaddon will pay for the misery he has caused my people!'

'Did I suddenly fall asleep and wake in a dream?' Alastair responded in wonder. 'What a glorious opportunity for you, Victor; you will have the joy and honor of fighting alongside a Dragon of old!' A bright smile shone on Victor's face, and he clapped his hands with excitement.

'Do not celebrate war, child! War is never a celebratory occurrence. Over the course of my many years, I have seen large numbers of my kindred slain before me, and I have seen countless Men kill and be killed. It is sad and disheartening. Cheer not unless you rid the world of war and evil for all eternity. That will be a day worth celebrating!' Victor hung his head and sighed deeply. 'Forgive me, child. I do not mean to scold or pester you with an old Dragon's memories. I merely wish to warn you of the future that lies ahead of you. It is a gloom future that awaits you, and it is full of troubles and trials far worse than the ones I presented to you. Be cautious, lad; I foresee you playing a large role in this war.'

Asura carried them back to his lair and passed once more into the Chamber of Fire. From there, he flew to the top of the room, and by his Magic they passed safely through the ceiling and appeared atop the peak of the mountain on a flat portion of land. The top of the Cold Stone Mountains was icy and deadly, but Asura surrounded the flat with a thin dome of fire that protected them from the piercing cold of the mountains. It was not long before they decided to sleep and recover from the excitement and danger of the day. Upon the following morning, Asura and Alastair worked together and began Victor's training. They taught him many things concerning the Dragon Stone as well as the many uses of Elúvías.

Victor worked endlessly and with little rest, for he was eager to be of great use in the war. Determined to grow in power, Victor trained every day and pushed himself to his limits and beyond. With the power of the Dragon Stone drawing out the latent spiritual energy within him, he learned quickly and his capacity for Magic increased greatly. They toiled day after day for many long months, and Victor forgot what it meant to relax and enjoy the simple peace and quiet of his old life. But he had made his resolve and beat every part of his being into discipline until he could learn no more from the Dragon and the White Mage.

Chapter XIII

Eagle-Eye Zoro

The day was April the fifteenth and Rolo and Pakko were passing through the Lonely Grey in search of Zoro of Fort Leaf, the named king of the bandits in Bolteras. The two travelers had already gone to the mighty fortresses of Cayrngras, Bram and Eordil and passed daily into the woods north of the strongholds. For many long and tiresome days, they knocked upon the doors of every house in every stronghold and village near the woods inquiring of Zoro's whereabouts, but they only discovered rumors which proved useless in their search. Some of the villagers and city folk laughed and sneered upon their inquiry which forced Rolo and Pakko to withdraw in disappointment far more times than they liked. A few more villagers glared at them angrily and rudely slammed their doors in the two travelers' faces.

The journey thus far had not been kind to them as rain fell in abundance and the woods were muddied from the downpour. A woman in Bram giggled and mocked them for their dirtied appearance. She stood in the town square and shouted, 'I see a couple of Zoro's companions got lost from the pack!' She spoke loudly for many of the townsfolk to hear, and others joined in to mock them shouting, 'Only filth would look for more filth! Leave our city before you get dirt everywhere!' The people gathered and jeered at Rolo and Pakko, and the two became frustrated and stormed out of the fortress angrily. They passed several villages smaller than Kesh inquiring of any clues but to no avail until at long last, in a village called *Oga* to the northeast of Bram at the edge of the Lonely Grey, an old man called to them to speak in private.

'Hullo fair travelers,' he said cordially, 'be cautious of speaking the name of Zoro in these parts. His group has plundered great loot from many villages and strongholds in northern Bolteras, and many are bitter towards him and his people. Needless to say, he is quite unpopular amongst the people of these parts. And though he has not looted or appeared anywhere for several years, the people still despise him and cannot let go of their grudges. There are rumors here in Oga that he was last seen in the Lonely Grey, the area of

217

woods between the Grey Forest and the Lonely Forest. Luckily for you, the forest is just ahead to the north from here. But be wary; some have traveled through the woods and returned claiming to have seen ghosts! Others still have claimed to see a large fortress within the woods, but we have deemed them all to be myths. It was decided after some time that none should speak of Zoro or investigate those woods, for several have gone searching and never returned! Let us just say that it is an unwritten law in Bolteras to shun the name of Zoro and stray from the Lonely Grey. It is my advice that you boys go home now and drop the matter. I assure you, none will give you the answers you seek!'

'But we have been ordered by Lord Edgar himself to investigate this man and call upon him for war!' Rolo returned.

'Lord Edgar calls upon such a wicked man as Eagle-Eye Zoro? Nay, I cannot believe it! And what war do you speak of?'

'We wished not to reveal our purpose, but we are growing weary and desperate. I speak of the war against Vash'ala and the Draemhas!' The old man looked at him with a raised brow. 'Many of the smaller villages have been kept in the dark, for the king does not wish to disturb the simple life of the villagers. But we shall go to war in less than one year! And Lord Edgar requires the aid of all who are willing, even Zoro if we can find him. He may have been a wicked man at once, but he was being controlled by the Dark Lord Abaddon. His deeds are unforgivable, but he will atone for his sins by joining in this war.'

'I see,' the old man replied solemnly. 'Forgive me, young ones. You must have endured much ridicule along the way, but I am glad you trusted me with your mission. I do not wish to insult you further, but you two resemble bandits yourselves. What business, might I ask, do thieves have with the King of Bolteras?'

'Lord Edgar is a gracious king,' Pakko intervened, 'and he has looked upon the wood-folk with favor. He came to us in our fortress in the Grey Forest and earned our trust. He is honest and true and has chosen us, though I myself do not know why. But we beg of you, by order of the king, to tell us where we might find Zoro! Time is of the essence!'

'Lower your voices now,' the old man urged. He looked about to see if they were alone and then whispered, 'Come with me to my home. I feel uneasy talking about this in the open. It is more quiet and private at my house, and we can be away from eavesdroppers.' He turned around and led them down a path that ran north to the end of the village where a lonely house of stone stood: it was a small, simple house with a roof made of straw, and there were only two windows, one near to the entrance and one at the back of the house. 'Welcome to my lovely abode, gentlemen!' Entering the front door, Rolo and Pakko saw a young man who appeared badly disfigured and lame; he did not move or stir in the least the whole time they were at the old man's house, and Rolo pitied him.

'This is my son, Alfred. Oh yes, and I am Winslet Grammog. What were your names?'

'I am Rolo Longleaf and this is Pakko son of Elko.'

'Did you say the son of Elko? It cannot be! Come with me, laddies.' Rolo and Pakko were alarmed and quickly followed Winslet to a door with an iron latch in the floor of his kitchen. The old man reached down and grabbed the handle and pulled it up, revealing a short narrow stairway that descended into a cellar beneath his house. Winslet lit a lantern and led them down the stairs and through a small corridor to a room beyond. The passageway led to a small storage basement filled with many old, dusty artifacts. 'Never did I imagine I would actually meet the son of Elko!' Winslet called excitedly.

'It happened five years ago,' Winslet continued. Rolo gasped and listened closely to the old man's words. Winslet cleared his throat and continued, 'As I was saying, five years ago I was sitting in my house when I heard loud screams from the forest to the north. I went outside to investigate the matter, but I could not see a thing. I then heard noises like the whining of arrows and the wailing of women and children. I waited with my sword at my side to defend my home until I saw a lonely man emerge from the woods: that man was Elko. He was struck with two arrows and blood poured from the wounds. He called out in a loud and angry voice, "Zoro, that accursed tyrant! May a curse be on his head!" Then he saw me.' Rolo and Pakko's ears stood up at the mention of Zoro and Elko's names, and they were eager to hear the rest of Winslet's tale. 'He staggered over to me as quickly as he could and spoke again saying, "Good sir! Lend me your ear quickly!"

'He fell to the ground and muttered several things. He strained to talk for some time and began to mumble words so quietly that I could not comprehend him. A moment later, he untied a pouch full of coins from his belt and handed it to me and said I could keep the money if I would just pass on his bow to his only son. I told him, of course, that I did not know his son and reminded him that I was quite old already. Furthermore, I informed him of my son's illness which prevented me from leaving his side. He ignored me, and the last thing he spoke to me was this: "I am Elko. Find my son and give him my bow. Tell him I wished that I could give him all the treasures in the world, but alas! I have only my lonesome bow and not even an arrow to fit the string. It is a good bow, sturdy is its make and powerful is its shot. I beg of you, this is my dying wish. Tell him I loved him and make sure he knows that I regret not being able to see him become a fine, young man." There was more he said to me, but my frail mind has forgotten the rest.

'And when he passed, I gave him a good man's burial and sung a dirge for his passing. I do not know what became of the others, and I did not investigate out of fear of entering those dreadful woods. But I found it fitting to give him a proper burial seeing as he was all alone. And I deemed him an honorable man, so it was the least I could do. That is my tale and now here is your bow!' He walked to the wall across the room from the doorway and removed a brown bow from a hook. There was nothing unique about its look, but Pakko was pleased to see it despite its plain appearance.

'So it was Zoro who slew my father?' Pakko said after a moment's silence.

'I cannot affirm that. Those were simply your father's last words. I witnessed no murder that day.'

'I should like to have the bow he left for me, and then we will be on our way.'

'Though your father passed before I could give him my word, I swore to pass it on to you if ever I met you. And see what fortune brought you to my doorstep! All this time I believed I would die and never meet the son of Elko, but here you are now!' Winslet began to tear up and then said, 'Truly miracles still exist! All things happen for a reason, of that I am convinced!'

'Aye, you speak the truth!' Rolo joined in. 'Few of us escaped that day, but we made a new home in the woods and called it Treehouse. You see, we were amongst the survivors of Zoro's attack, and I became their leader; but we were few and poor and my leadership was meager at best. It was Elko's sacrifice that saved us that day.' Pakko glared at Rolo with a look of confusion. 'Aye, forgive me for concealing this from you all these years, young Pakko, but your father was a hero.'

'Come now, young master!' Winslet interrupted. 'I am sure you were a fine leader. I can see it on young Pakko's face. Now then, take your bow, son of Elko; but you need not leave in a hurry. Stay as long as you need before going on your way.'

'We greatly appreciate your generosity, Master Winslet, but our mission is urgent so we must go at once,' Rolo answered. They returned up the stairs and Pakko requested to see his father's grave. Winslet went to the window at the back of his house and pointed to a large mound of dirt. Pakko went out at once and knelt down on the ground by the mound that was made for Elko. 'I am quite curious, good sir, what became of your son.' Rolo continued after a while.

'Alfred? Oh, well—' Winslet said with sadness in his voice. He took a seat in an old wooden chair and remained silent for a while. 'I am afraid he was born that way. He rarely moves, and he only lives because I tend to him. I have spent many long days and nights praying over him, asking Vaaspar to heal him of his infirmity, but alas! my prayers remain unanswered. I had stopped believing in miracles until today when Pakko son of Elko arrived at my home. But I am a quickly aging man, and I fear what will become of my son when I have passed from this world. And I doubt that I will ever see the miracle I pray for the most. My wife abandoned us some time ago, and I have no other children. My dear wife simply could not handle the sorrow of seeing her only son suffer so much. I do not blame her, but now I am all alone; and I fear he will starve to death when I am gone.'

Rolo felt great sadness overcome him. He bowed before the old man and walked back to the front room where Alfred sat still quiet and unmoving. Rolo placed his right hand on Alfred's left shoulder halfway expecting some power to flow out of him and cure the lame man, but nothing happened. He hung his head sadly and wished he had knowledge of Elúvías to cure him. He turned and called, 'We thank you, Winslet, for your time and hospitality. Pardon our intrusion and any trouble or grief we might have caused you.'

'Wait, lad!' the old man answered and came hobbling back to the front room. 'I believe Zoro still resides north of here through the woods! I was sworn to secrecy, but I see that you are honest men. I often hear the voices and cheers of men in the distance, and I have once seen an archer of the wood-folk to the north if that aids you in any way. Now whatever happens, I will take responsibility if any evil befalls you; may a curse be on my head if harm is done to you! And may my son find healing after I die so that I may not be able to celebrate with him.'

'It does more than you know, kind sir! But wish no such evils upon yourself, for on this day you provided aid for your king and country. Thank you, Winslet. May Vaaspar's Light shine on you and pour forth many blessings unto you. I will pray for healing to come to your son, so do not lose hope, for in this world, hope is all we have!' Winslet wept and fell to his knees in prayer as Rolo left the house. He prayed fervently for the traveler's safety and for his son to be healed. Though it was faint, he had found hope once more, and he gave thanks to Vaaspar for the seemingly random encounter with the two travelers.

* * *

Outside, Pakko was crying at his father's grave with his face upon the mound. Rolo approached and placed his hand on his comrade's back and shared the knowledge of Zoro that Winslet passed on to him. Pakko was filled with rage and eagerness at the same time, and he greatly desired to ignore Lord Edgar's request and avenge his father by killing Zoro. Rolo saw the anger and sadness in Pakko's eyes and solemnly vowed to protect both Zoro and Pakko if ever they were to meet each other.

The two companions bid Winslet farewell and strode on to the north into the shelter of the Lonely Grey. They paced several furlongs into the forest and came upon a net hanging in the boughs of the trees: a deer was trapped in it and was writhing wildly in an attempt to free itself from the snare. They heard a noise far away that seemed to them to come from the northeast. It sounded like a loud snap followed by a booming crash, so they left the deer and headed towards the noise. The forest terrain remained flat for most of the way with only a few minor hills for them to cross, and it was easy to traverse even without a path to follow. Two hours later, they came upon the Roaring River rushing loudly through the middle of the woods, but it was too wide and violent for them to pass. Rolo decided it would be best to travel east and look for a ford or a bridge to cross. An hour more passed, and the light of the sun was beginning to fade; so they halted and made camp for the night.

On the following morning, they traveled further east along the edge of the river and continued for eight hours before they came to a portion of the river where several trees had either collapsed or were chopped down—which it was, they could not tell—and formed a bridge across the stream. The trunks were swathed in moss and were wet and slimy from the rushing and splashing of the river, so they crossed slowly and warily. When they had finally reached the other side of the river, they stopped for a minute and ate a late lunch before heading further north. The land ran before them down a steep slope. They considered traveling another way, but everywhere they looked, the land fell steeply at some point or another. Rolo reluctantly led the way down the hill and Pakko followed. The land was muddy and slippery, and within seconds, both of the men clumsily slipped and tumbled violently down the length of the hill. They each crashed into trees at the bottom of the slope and received many bruises, cuts and aches. Pakko screeched upon colliding with the tree, but Rolo was too shocked to even make a noise. For a while, they sat upon the wet ground rustling in the leaves with large roots digging into their backs. Unable to stand, the two sat on the damp land and tried to recover their strength. Suddenly, two arrows whined through the air and struck the two trees just above their heads.

Pakko flinched and fell face first upon a bed of leaves. Rolo forcefully moved to the other side of the tree and called out, 'Who is there?' but there was no answer. A few minutes later, the trees around them shook and leaves rained down upon them. They looked up and saw two figures looming above in the trees with bows in hand. 'Who are you?' Rolo asked again. A moment later, two thick wooden sticks appeared in the corner of their eyes and struck them violently upon their heads, and they both fell unconscious. Several mysterious figures appeared all about them. Rolo and Pakko were bound and blindfolded and then led deep into the woods of the Lonely Grey.

* * *

They awoke the next day bounded and trapped in a dirty prison with stone walls and a gate made of sturdy wood. There were no lights inside the prison, and it was hard for them to see; but a slight glimmer of sunlight poured in from a door above them and revealed two guards stationed outside their cell. They could hear outside a host of voices chattering noisily as though there was an ongoing debate. Rolo and Pakko sat uncomfortably upon the dirt floor of the cell and attempted to wiggle out of their binds but it was in vain, for their injuries proved too much for them to struggle any further. They looked out at the door above them as a figure appeared followed by three taller figures. They descended a nearby stairway of stone and came before Rolo and Pakko's cell. The smaller man cleared his throat; the three large men then unlocked the gates of the cells and lifted Rolo and Pakko from the ground. From there, they were led up the stairs through the door which ran outside into a large

223

village surrounded by large wooden walls. It reminded them of Treehouse. As they emerged into the village, the sun shone brightly in their faces and blinded them for a moment. They squinted and lowered their heads and were unable to see another man approaching them from a walkway made in the trees.

'Welcome,' the man said, 'to Fort Leaf, the fortress of trees where the great Zoro resides! Forgive our rudeness yesterday, but we can never be too careful when it comes to looking after our own. We are not so popular with the Boltians these days.' The man had a deep, familiar voice, but his face was shrouded by the blinding sun. Rolo and Pakko squinted to make out his face but their eyes had not yet adjusted to the intense sunlight. 'Tell me, travelers, where do you come from and why are you here?'

'Who speaks to us?' Rolo answered. 'We are on an urgent mission sent by Lord Edgar, King of Bolteras. Release us!'

'Bah!' the man scoffed, 'Edgar King of Bolteras fails to keep his promise!'

'What promise do you speak of, and what is your name?'

'He promised us long ago that he would leave us in peace. But I will not answer your second question; it is rude to ask a man his name before one first introduces himself!'

'I am Rolo Longleaf, and this is Pakko son of Elko!' Many voices rose in whispers all around them. The mysterious man grabbed a nearby rope and swung to the ground where Rolo and Pakko stood. Rolo and Pakko tried to make out the man, but he wore a mask that shrouded all his face save only his eyes to be seen.

'It cannot be,' he exclaimed with widened eyes. 'If those are truly your names, then you are our kin!' Then something happened, like in a dream, which greatly puzzled Rolo and Pakko: all the wood-folk about them fell to their knees and bowed before them as though the two were royalty. 'Forgive us, young lords! Men, release them and bring them to my courts at once!' The man withdrew at once to another portion of the fortress away to the north. Their binds were cut, and their guards led them away to an open space of land free from trees with a large, solitary edifice in the middle of it. Along the way, their captors held their heads low as though they were greatly shamed.

'Welcome to the house of Zoro!' one of the guards muttered. Anger welled up inside Pakko, and he clenched his fists tightly. He desired vengeance at that moment, but he failed to notice that their weapons had been seized. They entered through a tall archway and

224

many rows of seats rested before them with an aisle in the middle. The room looked more like a cathedral than a leader's hall, for there was an altar upon a dais at the back of the room. The man from before sat on a chair to the right of the altar with his head held high: his mask was removed and he wore a brown leather patch over his left eye. There were many others in the room with him sitting in the chairs along the aisle, each of them clothed in rags.

'Welcome kin of the wood-folk! We have much to discuss. I w—'

'Stay your tongue, knave!' Pakko shouted. 'I know who you are! You are Zoro the Eagle-Eye, the man who killed my father!'

'Calm down, Pakko,' Rolo pleaded. 'Lower your voice! We are here on peaceful terms.'

'Nay,' Pakko snapped. 'I swear on this day that I, Pakko son of Elko, will avenge my father at long last! And I will set free the ghosts of our tormented kin with the death of this man!'

'I urge you, be silent!' Rolo yelled as loud as he could. 'Listen to this man!'

Pakko crossed his arms, sneered and muttered a distasteful, 'As you wish.'

'Do not be harsh with the boy, Rolo. He has enough reason to hate me. I once was a man of great evil. Let me tell you, Pakko; it all began nearly twenty years ago, just after the war with Vash'ala, when an evil creature came upon the land. Before I was aware, I had been trapped in a spell wrought by one of the Dark Lord's minions, and he troubled me with great nightmares and visions. I was tricked into obeying his will and soon my sanity faded away; then I became the evil man I was revealed to be in my dreams. I became a cruel man, heartless in fact, even though I was once a respectable citizen of Bolteras like any other.

'This creature called himself an Alp of Darkness; Greed was his name. Along with those dreadful nightmares, I was filled with a great yearning for riches and possessions. I was foolish and weak, and that demon took advantage of my frailty. With his influence on me, I led many others astray, and we became bandits roaming the lands of Bolteras. We plundered and killed as we went, but, oddly enough, we never went outside our own borders—I think the Enemy planned to use us to weaken the forces of Bolteras. This pattern continued for many long years, and we carefully evaded the Boltian army with each attack. We were mere thieves at first, but then Lord Edgar placed a bounty on our heads when he learned of our betrayal.

225

That was when we retreated to this place in the woods. We horded our goods in the shelter of the forest and called this place Fort Leaf. But our hunger for wealth was never satisfied, and we grew even greedier. We often snuck into villages and fortresses in Bolteras near to our borders and stole away with many treasures. But suddenly we became careless or else Edgar became wiser, for our numbers dwindled with each looting. Guards were prepared for us at every turn, and many were killed.

'While all these things took place, the Alps' grip on me increased by some vile Magic of the Dark Lord. I could see all and hear all that happened, but I was unable to stop myself. Greed revealed everything to me during that time. Aye, I knew all that the Dark Lord was scheming, and I could do nothing to stop it. After five years, the Alp left me and roamed all of Bolteras swaying the minds of many. I hoped to find freedom, but his spell upon me lasted through his absence. Eventually, my selfishness grew so large that I desired to be ruler of all our wealth. I chose from our midst a few companions to accompany me in my conquest for riches, and they were to be my loyal servants for the rest of their lives.

'My son—who was always selfless and free from Greed's curse—came to me and for years urged me to put away my foolishness, but I banished him from Fort Leaf and disowned him. He took a great host of our people with him, and I was overcome by my selfishness once again. I was filled with anger, for he had swayed some of my people to follow him. On that dreadful night, I ordered my followers to pursue and kill them, even my own son. I watched as my own flesh and blood was struck with two arrows, and I stared on as he crawled away crying out many curses. On that same day, Rolo Longleaf and Pakko son of Elko stole away with a small band of thieves far into the east where my warriors would not travel, for fear of the Cold Stone Mountains and the dangers in her depths.' Zoro saw Pakko's face light up with awe and rage and continued, 'Yes, son of Elko, it was I who slew your father. You were still young then, only eight or nine I imagine. In those days, I always wore a mask; my identity was hidden from you, for your father was ashamed of me. The truth is, I am your father's father, Pakko. Indeed! I am your grandfather!'

'I do not believe you!' Pakko shouted. 'I think I would know if you were my grandfather, and you are not! I was old enough then to know you!'

'Unless your father spared you the troubles of knowing,' Rolo snapped. 'And I swore also to protect his identity from you! No one wanted you to learn who he was, Pakko, not even your father Elko! But this man is indeed your grandfather. His name is Zoro Windleaf!' Pakko was amazed and frustrated at the same time; he clenched his fists and paced forward. He stood before the hunched form of Zoro and struck him with as much strength as he could muster, and Zoro fell to the ground bleeding from his lip.

'Do you think the power of the Alp excuses your crimes?' Pakko shouted with spit spraying from his mouth. 'I will never forgive you! No, even if we are forced to fight alongside each other, you will always be my enemy! And I will never recognize you as my grandfather!' Pakko turned and found a seat in one of the nearby rows of chairs and wept bitterly.

'I know this is difficult for you to hear, child, but I w—'

'Be quiet! I do not care what you have to say!' Zoro's heart welled up with sadness, but he fought back his tears.

'I killed your father, Pakko, and I have never expected you to forgive me for that. But my life changed forever on that fateful day five years ago. I saw your father talking to an old man at the edge of the woods. Some of his last words were, "Zoro, that accursed tyrant! On his head be a curse," but I was spared from his dying wish. Instead, I was blessed, and I felt heartache once again. That night, I wept bitterly for the loss of my son, and the destruction of my people, knowing I could never repair the damage I had caused. But after nearly fifteen years, my heart softened again. And as every day passed, I slowly returned to the way I was before the Alp overpowered me.

'And after that night, we have not raided any towns or villages since. But some of the greed remained in my heart, and I was deeply troubled by its presence. I cannot explain it, but I knew at once when the creature was killed. I felt a weight lifted off of me. It is as though he was a part of me for a time, and, by the end of January, the curse was lifted from me. I felt completely free for the first time in twenty years, but now I want to use my freedom for good instead of evil. For a brief moment, I was filled with joy until all the awful realities of those twenty years returned to me; then I was filled with overwhelming grief.

'To this day, I remember every awful deed I committed, every house I looted and every person I wronged. I remember the death of your father and the deaths of many others also. Those painful memories caused me so much anguish that I thought I would die! In fact, I was bedridden for two weeks as a result of my grief. I only just began to move about on my feet again. All my kin had regained their sanity as well, and we began to live again. All we can do now after all our sins is beg for forgiveness, knowing we do not deserve any such kindness. So I leave the decision in your hands to kill or spare me, grandson! What will you do?'

Zoro fell to his knees and began to weep. He then bowed before Pakko with his hands and face pressed to the ground. Rolo paced forward and said, 'Have you not suffered enough, Zoro? Stand up; the king calls upon you!'

'Is that it?' Pakko interrupted angrily. 'Are you just going to forgive him and forget all the awful things he has done? What atonement is there in that?'

Rolo grinded his teeth and turned to Pakko and shouted, 'Do you really think I could forgive or forget the things this man has done?' He turned back to Zoro, and his eyes shone brightly like fire. 'This *is* his payment! He will atone for his sins by living and fighting for the king and his army!' Pakko was not aware of it, but Rolo secretly smiled—the sort of forgiving and warm smile exchanged between friends—at Zoro; and Zoro was filled with astonishment. 'So rise to your feet Zoro Windleaf and begin to atone for your sins at once! Lead your people to Edgar's aid and die for him on the field of battle!'

Pakko suddenly felt compelled by Rolo's words, and his heart softened for the pitiable man kneeling before him. He forced a grin upon his face and chuckled. 'It will take years for this fool to atone for his sins! Join Edgar's ranks but do not die! Live and fight until there is no more fighting to be done! Then, and only then, will you atone for your sins!' Rolo laughed and ran a hand through his long, grimy hair.

Zoro raised his head and tears began to pour out from his eyes. He wheezed and cuffed his hands together as though he was praying and said, 'Vaaspar has shown me great mercy in letting me live, but now my brethren, though I deserve their hatred, have shown me such immense kindness! I cannot bear it! Please, slay me; end my life, for I cannot live it anymore!'

'That would be too easy,' Pakko replied. 'And you will not take your own life or else you would have done so by now. You believe you should die by the hands of the ones' you wronged, and that may be true; but you will be spared and forced to repay your debt, you and your kin. Therefore, you will come to Vallicore with us and enlist in the king's army to fight in the war against Vash'ala and the Draemhas in one year's time. That is your punishment, and that alone will bring penance for your wicked deeds!'

'Aye, I could not have said it better myself,' Rolo replied. 'But I will say this: I have carried anger and bitterness for many long years and have hated you, but no longer will I allow myself to be laden with such troubles. I was spared from my hatred by Lord Edgar. I would even say he saved my life.'

'What do you mean?' Zoro replied, tears still flowing down his cheeks.

'I mean that I have forgiven you, Zoro Windleaf! All things pass, but I learned from Edgar King of Bolteras that love always remains. Out of my hatred of heart, I led my people from Treehouse to an old man's birthday party to steal food from their feast. When I learned the food was gone and the tables were cleaned, I ordered Pakko to kill the innocent man. I am just glad Pakko was more kindhearted than I was, for he secretly spared the man. And I learned also from our king to never have regrets or wish your troubles or mistakes away. "It is the hardships in life," he told me, "that make a man who he is, for a true man will embrace his pain and use it for good! A man's true character is tested when the evil and cruel happenings of life come his way." This Edgar taught me many things, and I know now why his people support him the way they do. My crimes were meager compared to yours, but I was still glad to receive the king's mercy.

'Remember this, Zoro: the greater the crimes you have committed, the greater the mercy bestowed upon you will be. Mercy was shown to me by Lord Edgar himself, and I now extend it to you! What kind of man would I be to receive such kindness, from a king no less, and then make you pay for similar crimes? We did not become honorable and honest people when we left Fort Leaf. No, in fact, we became greedy as were you. We pilfered and sabotaged at times and, yes, we even killed! We became desperate thieves no greater than you were years before. This is why I do not condemn you!'

'Nor do I,' Pakko added with calmness in his voice. 'Though anger still dwells within me, I choose to forgive you. In these dark days, there is no room for grudges and bitterness. If we fight amongst ourselves, then the Dark Lord has already won! We must unite against the forces of Darkness and keep the flame of Light burning bright. So what say you, Zoro Windleaf? I suppose I ought to call you grandfather now, but tell me how you came to be a man of great evil, grandfather. I would like to know the origins of this tale.'

Zoro wiped the tears from his eyes and rose to his feet. He stared at them with his good eye and bowed before them. 'I will do as you ask of me and join this war if that is how I may begin to atone for my sins. It may surprise you, grandson, but I fought alongside King Haus in the war against Vash'ala twenty years ago, and we were close friends. I saw many die upon that field of battle. Aye, there was Haus and Groffa and Threngol and Bolos and hundreds of others, all good soldiers of Men. I returned to Bram—that was my hometown then—after the war and mourned their losses.

'When I came to my home, I learned my wife was with child. I was filled with joy, but she died not long after during a cold winter's night. A great fever overcame her, and I lost both wife and child; but Elko, my firstborn, was already eleven years of age and had been away training with the archers of the Lonely Forest. It was always his dream to join their ranks. And he joined their group quickly, for he was an excellent bowman. So with Elko's absence, I was left alone; and during all my sadness, aye, through my great depression that cursed Alp came to me in the appearance of a man. He comforted me the way a friend does, all the while my mind was being poisoned and my heart filled with deceit. It was not long before I was under his spell! During the day, he came as a friend, but during the night, unbeknownst to me, he was tormenting me in my dreams. For five years, he was both friend and enemy, all for the purpose of using me for the Dark Lord's will. I was always lonely and I coveted those around me who still had many friends and healthy families.

'I had received word that my son married young at the age of seventeen and bore a son the next year; that child was you, young Pakko. But I had already been corrupted by the Enemy, and I did not care. Your father cared deeply for me, but it was my leadership that drove a wedge between us and brought him to ruin. He was always such a loving and caring man, the best soldier I ever knew. Eight years ago, he brought you with him when you were still young and desperately tried to change me, but I was stubborn at first. Rolo was a good friend of your father's and traveled with his company. After three years, I began to see the Light once more, but Greed returned and enslaved me again! It was then that I banished your father from

Fort Leaf and had him killed. I wore a mask in those days to intimidate any who dared to oppose me; but it was your father who first gave me the mask, for he was ashamed of me. That is why your father kept my identity a secret from you, and Rolo agreed to keep it a secret as well. That is the origin of my story in short. There are too many things I wish not to discuss. With all my past, I am eternally grateful for your forgiveness, lads. Certainly my kinsmen and I will join you, so what would you ask of me?

'There is much you have to learn I am afraid,' Rolo answered. 'The king held a council in Vallicore and we learned many things, of Elúvías and other forms of Magic and things of that sort. We will return to Vallicore to learn the ways of Elúvías, so we might be prepared for war.' Zoro suddenly began to laugh hysterically.

'Elúvías you say? After all these years Lord Edgar now uses its power as King Haus did long ago! O, how we would have thrived if we had not forgotten its ways! If it is Elúvías you must learn, then I will teach you!' Rolo and Pakko were shocked and doubtful.

'You know the ways of Elúvías?' Pakko questioned skeptically.

'Indeed I do, and you would do well to mind your cheek, laddie! Did you not hear me earlier? I was close to King Haus who was given the Orb of Light during his reign. It was given to him by one of the Celebhas. He is known in Bolteras as Seymour, but that is a false name given by Men. Elorén is his true name, if my memory serves me well. We were the first generation of Boltians to freely use Elúvías. If you do not believe me then come and observe!'

At once he rose from his seat and walked outside. Rolo and Pakko followed out of curiosity. They paced back to the crowded area of Fort Leaf near the prison, and Zoro picked up a bow and an arrow. 'Now look!' He pulled the arrow back on the string and fired at a tree maybe four fathoms to the west. The arrow pierced the trunk of the tree and hung there; it was nothing impressive to Rolo or Pakko. 'That is the power of a regular arrow, good friends. Now observe my second shot!' He fitted another arrow to the string and a small orb of light appeared around the tip of the arrow. The bowstring twanged, and the second dart whistled as it soared towards its target. In an instant, the arrow struck the same tree, only this time it passed straight through and vanished from their sight; and it left in its wake a large hole in the trunk of the tree.

Pakko and Rolo both rubbed their eyes as though they were dreaming. When they opened them again, they still beheld the tree with a large gap in the middle of it. 'You really are well trained in the power of Light!' Rolo exclaimed joyfully! 'Do you happen to know leechcraft?'

'Leechcraft you say? Of course I do! It is not difficult to use once you understand the flow of energy within your body. Here I will show you!' He placed one hand on Pakko and the other on Rolo, and instantly they felt a surge of energy flowing through their bodies. 'All this energy has slept dormant inside of you all these years and you knew it not!' Zoro laughed. 'It will take some time to learn it well enough to control, but you will learn with my help. Now, do you know why they call me Eagle-Eye?' Rolo and Pakko shook their heads. 'Bah! I shall tell you! It is because my eye was blessed with sight that can see further and wider than any in all the lands of Gaia. And there is none who can rival my aim with a bow because of it! I was one of the rare warriors blessed with the power of the Light Gates!'

'We heard of those powers for the first time in Vallicore but only vaguely,' Rolo answered. 'Can you tell us more about it?'

'Aye, it is quite simple. There are some who have been blessed with unique powers, and we believe them to be special gifts from Vaaspar. When we use our ability, our eyes emit a light, though the color of the light is different with every person. It is an odd occurrence, but all things are odd these days! I am afraid you will just have to see it for yourselves one day!'

'Can you not show us now?' Pakko responded eagerly.

'I refuse. The power of the Light Gates requires a great amount of Mana, and my supply has dwindled with age. I shall only use that power if I have no other choice! Come now and get some rest. We will begin your training tomorrow!'

* * *

Their training began the next day after a much needed rest and their fill of food. The hours of training during their days with Zoro were extensive and grueling, and the disciplines felt tedious at times; but they eventually understood the flow of energy within their bodies and used Elúvías freely. They trained their bodies more than their Mana in order to control the Magic fully. After many long days of practicing, their supply of Mana grew, and their bodies became strong.

232

Several months passed and Rolo mastered the arts of healing with Elúvías, and his body was strong enough that the Magic had no effect on his body. He left Fort Leaf for a few days and eagerly returned to the village Oga to meet with old man Winslet, who was very pleased to see him again.

* * *

'Master Winslet,' Rolo said huffing and puffing. He was tired and out of breath. He had not stopped running since he left Fort Leaf, for he was eager to fulfill his purpose. 'How is Alfred?'

'Alfred you say? Well, his condition is worsening. I fear my final days draw nigh and his with me! Woe is me!' he said despondently.

'I have brought good tidings, nay, a gift!' Rolo passed by Winslet and placed a hand on Alfred's body. 'I will heal Alfred now, so never stop believing in miracles, Winslet!'

'I have no money to pay you for such a thing!' Winslet remarked.

'It would not be a gift if it cost you something! Behold!' A bright white light surrounded the body of Alfred and all his deformities were erased like dirt washed away by water. His body appeared more youthful and vibrant, and he stirred in his seat. Rolo turned and smile at Winslet who was frozen in awe of what he saw. After a moment, the old man fell to the ground gripping at his heart. Alfred leapt from his chair and for the first time in his life moved on his own. He held his father in his arms and kissed him.

'Father, stay with me! All these years you have cared for me. It is time I return the favor!' Alfred spoke hastily for fear that his father would die soon.

Winslet smiled and said, 'My son, this is the greatest day of my life! You owe me nothing.' Turning to Rolo, he spoke, 'I thank you; now I can sleep at long last.' In the blink of an eye, Winslet breathed his last breath with a bright smile upon his face in the arms of his beloved son. Alfred wept bitterly, unable to celebrate his recovery. After he had grieved for a time, Alfred buried his father next to the grave of Elko Windleaf, and Rolo helped.

'I am grateful to you, Master Rolo. I have watched my father for years, but I was never able to speak to him. I mourned for him as I was trapped in my mind for so long, wishing only for him to abandon me and live a happy life. I had lost all hope of seeing him smile again, and yet he smiled in his last moments! I thank you for healing me. I am forever in your debt!'

'Do not thank me, Alfred! If not for Vaaspar bestowing his powers upon us, I could not have done such a thing! Go and enjoy your life; move about and be free for as long as you live!'

'I will not. I shall go with you wherever you go.'

'Then you shall go to war, for that is my destiny in this life.'

'Then it will be mine too! Take me with you, good sir! I am weak now, but I will become strong and devote my life to repaying my debt to you.'

* * *

Rolo agreed and returned with Alfred to Fort Leaf, and they stayed there for many days to train. Alfred learned archery and practiced Magic with Rolo and Pakko after building up his strength. Together, they grew strong and forged a bond of friendship that would be their greatest strength in the days to come.

Chapter XIV

Beyond the Desolate Plains

On the night of April the twelfth, Edgar, Grinshawl and Seymour camped within the shelter of the Putrid Wood. Resting on the eastern border of Vash'ala, the rotten forest ran for many miles from north to south and separated the vile country of the sun-worshippers from Alterash. The night of the twelfth was their last night within the shadows of the forest before voyaging into the arid, desolate plains of Vash'ala. Along the way, the three travelers never made fires for fear of being exposed, and even still they were nearly discovered upon several occasions; but Elorén provided them with magical cloaks that used Mana to keep them hidden from the Enemy's spies: they were mainly birds and tiny, evil creatures, but some of the wild wolves of Alterash roamed the lands as well. At other times, Draemhas would emerge from the fissures in the ground to the west, but they never traveled near to the Putrid Wood.

In the days of their journey thus far, they had made much progress, but their only shade and protection, the forest, was at its end. Elorén was reluctant to leave the shelter of the woods, but there was no other way to reach the cave where Percival the Silver resided. As they rested for the evening, they looked out upon the vast, deserted lands with despondent eyes, for it seemed an impossible journey was before them. They saw all across the valley below burning rocks and lava glowing from within the miles of fissures that were formed by the many volcanoes scattered throughout the land. And in the vast barren wastelands of Vash'ala the light of the sun could not be seen, for the volcanic ash created dark billows in the sky overhead. Thus, the land was always encompassed by darkness as if surrounded by some Black Magic.

They slept little that night constantly roused by the cries of the tormented and the wails of the devilish folk. Many sounds of beasts echoed from the scorching gorges below and disturbed them further. There seemed to be such a strong force of Darkness at work that Edgar and Grinshawl were afraid even the decaying trees would come to life and attack them in their sleep. In the end, the constant noises and eerie presence of evil about them kept them from sleep, and so they rose before the rising of the sun and descended westward into the rocky vale known as the *Desolate Plains*, leaving the Putrid Wood behind them.

The land was vast and blistering. As they journeyed onward, intense heat rose from cracks in the ground as though many more volcanoes resided directly beneath them. Each of the travelers began to sweat and grow weary as the land stretched endlessly before them; and a mere hour of travel felt like days to them. At the end of the slope leading out of the woods, they turned due north and walked cautiously along the large fissures in the land. The last stretch of the Putrid Wood continued northeast above them and ended in an incredibly tall cliff at least a thousand feet above the Desolate Plains.

Many leagues away to the west amidst a small range of mountains rising high in the air, a dark city rested upon the rocks with dark clouds looming over its head. Seymour glanced to his left every so often with an anxious look upon his face. Suddenly, he increased his pace. 'That is Osceroth, the dreadful capital of Vash'ala. Let us stray far from it lest we fall under the scope of Korvash the manslayer. Even I, as I currently am, would not stand long against such a fearsome foe! Indeed, I was surprised to hear he had come to the Western Lands, for he wreaked much havoc in the Eastern Lands; but the Dark Lord must have seen it fit for him to stir up further chaos here in the West.'

'What do you mean, fair Elorén? The last time we fought together, none could rival your strength!' Edgar remarked.

'Yes, that was true of my power twenty years ago against the might of Men, but the longer I am away from Elúne, the weaker I become. Now our enemy belongs to the Draemhas—my former kin—and they can certainly rival my might. My power is fading from this world, and I fear it will not be long before I fade entirely from Gaia and my spirit returns to the White Land. When the time comes for battle, I will release my true power against the Draemhas, but Korvash still has the upper hand. The longer the Draemhas reside in Gaia, the more powerful they become as they draw power from the endless wellsprings of Vexúvías, but the opposite is true of the Celebhas. We were meant for Elúne and Elúne for us. The Holy Land is our source of power. Since ages past, the Celebhas have been sent to Gaia in the form of Men only to return to the White Land when our task is complete or when the last of our life force is depleted. But it always happens that our Mana is depleted at the time we accomplish our mission, just as Vaaspar plans.'

236

'I do not understand, old friend,' Edgar replied. 'Why were you sent in the form of a man? Would that not weaken your power?'

'It is not for you to understand. There are many things Men do not comprehend, but it is only their place to trust and believe in Vaaspar's greater plan. I do not understand all things either, but I go where I am sent and accomplish what I was sent to do as Vaaspar commands me. That is all you need to know. Come now; let us travel closer to that cliff. If we use our cloaks any longer, we will all exhaust the last of our Mana and be revealed to the Enemy. It is best we conserve our energy in case battle comes upon us. Perhaps we will be well hidden under the shadow of the cliff.'

Along the edge of the stone wall of the cliff, shadows veiled their presence for many miles until the cliff ended. Then, they were exposed once more, surrounded by nothing but the foul smell of sulfur and the open tracks of stony land; but every so often, they would pass decayed trees that were blackened with ash. Continuing north, they stayed near the eastern edge of the land; but they could travel no further east, for the land fell hundreds of feet below into the deep dells and grassy plains of Alterash. Hoping to remain out of sight, Seymour never led them more than a few fathoms from the cliffs unless the road became too perilous. After several hours, they halted to set up camp, for they were fatigued and parched in the dry and weary land of Vash'ala where there was no water to be seen. They thirsted greatly during their journey and decided to only drink water from their flasks once every two or three hours as they had no means to replenish their containers; but it proved a difficult task, for their throats were dry, and they yearned for cooler air. They woke the next day thirstier than before and were greatly discouraged.

'What will become of us if we must fight the Draemhas in this scorching heat?' Grinshawl asked. 'We will surely die of thirst before our enemy lands the finishing blow!' He wiped the sweat from his brow and plopped down; the weight of his body shook the ground. 'Where is the result of the Alchemists' *hard work* in this forsaken land?' he commented sarcastically looking all about the seemingly endless miles of rocky land with no clear roads. 'And not a single path exists in these lands! What kinds of barbarians live here? Even when I was a prisoner in these lands long ago, it was much fairer than it is now, if fair it ever was! But I suppose I only saw a portion of the land when I was imprisoned far away to the south.'

'Aye much has changed,' Edgar answered. 'But keep in mind the Alchemists came for a good cause but finished with evil in their hearts, and the land now reflects their evil purposes.'

'If I were with you in my original form, Grinshawl, I could conjure the water your dry throats so desperately long for,' Seymour added. 'But I can do no such thing in the body of a man. But Edgar speaks truthfully. For many years, the land was growing greener; in fact, I saw trees in full bloom nearly thirteen years ago. It was marvelous what I could see from my home in the mountains, and my eagles reported more of its increasing beauty. But five or six years ago, Korvash was first spotted in Vash'ala; it was then that the land became putrid and full of death. The Vash'alan King, Marxas, who now calls himself Sol'Czar the Sun King, greeted Korvash, according to my spies. Originally, Korvash and an army of Draemhas lived safely in deep, dark caves beneath the ground. It was easy for them to dwell there since the Draemhan Alp Envy had already poisoned the minds of the Vash'alans. I believe Korvash must have been in Vash'ala for several years mustering an army. Sadly, it was the power of the Draemhas combined with that of the Alchemists that turned this land dark and miserable.

'While the Draemhas dwelt in caves, the Boltian aides were using the Alchemist's Stone to summon Draemhas daily, but there is a limit to how many may pass through the portal. You see, the world used to have many Alchemists and though they are scarce now, they were once very powerful. The Alchemist's Stone was created many centuries ago and was used by the Draemhas and evil Men to transport their forces across the lands of Gaia in an instant. But opening the portal requires a great deal of Mana, and thus, it can only be opened for short amounts of time. With rest, I reckon the Alchemists from Bolteras were able to open the portal two or three times a day, but at their level of spiritual awareness it seems that only ten Draemhas passed through the portal each day. I reckon this has been going on for nearly eleven years now.

'Now I fear their numbers are more than forty thousand strong!' Edgar and Grinshawl stirred and clenched their fists angrily. 'And there are many lesser minions, indeed thousands of them, wrought by the power of Vexúvías; they are known as *the Imps of Darkness*. But there is strength yet in Bolteras! And perhaps the Men of Alterash will be liberated and join the fray! So do not give up hope, for you are Bolteras' strongest warriors. Aye, you two have come to be nearly as strong as I am, and if you have no hope, then who will? Listen closely now; I believe they will commence their attack once their forces are at least fifty thousand strong, which is why they are waiting for one year to attack. Perhaps they think Bolteras will crumble under such a force, and indeed it may! Furthermore, they have ten thousand or more Vash'alans in their midst. This news may be troubling to hear, but you must know your enemy's strength! It will take great courage and unity for Bolteras to stand against these odds, but it can be done!' Seymour halted suddenly before a pathway that descended downward into a lightless ravine. He then turned around and looked up into the air. 'Aha! One of my messengers has arrived!'

Edgar and Grinshawl turned about and saw an eagle swooping down upon them, and as the bird flew closer they recognized him as Greatwing, for he had distinguishable red feathers like fire on his face below his eyes. 'My liege,' he called, 'I have urgent news!' In his talons, he carried three flasks full of water tied together by a thick string. 'Firstly, accept these gifts as a token of our friendship. I imagined you would run out of water quickly in this land.'

'It is most appreciated, Eagle-King!' Seymour returned happily. 'We are quite parched indeed. Though the sun is trapped behind thick clouds of smoke and ash, it is hot enough here to kill a man! You have my undying gratitude.'

'As always, I am pleased to be of service to you, Master. But I have news, both good and evil. Which will you hear first?'

'It is only right and common to go with the bad news first, of course!' Edgar answered.

'Not one for being unique, I see,' Greatwing remarked sarcastically. 'For the ill news, a certain young boy has been found amidst the evil Men of Vash'ala wearing the crest of Bolteras. It is as you foresaw Elorén: the boy is Hildegard Gruff! The last we saw of him, the Acolytes of Darkness were greeting him with open arms; and his appearance was…sinister I would say.'

'Alas!' Edgar cried, 'young Victor will be greatly troubled to hear this news.'

'How was the boy so easily swayed?' Grinshawl asked.

'I am not so sure he needed to be swayed. I can only say that he appeared very happy to see his parents once again. Even with young eyes, he cannot see! He still believes his parents are good, the blind fool!'

'Is there any more of this evil news?' Seymour questioned.

'Aye, there is more. We have seen the Men of Vash'ala assembling towards the south of the land. I believe the enemy seeks to send us a message and to leave a scar upon the land of Bolteras before the Draemhan assault in a year. I fear the crimson army may assault Bolteras before long!'

'Then you will inform the archers of the Lonely Forest when that day comes,' Seymour commanded. 'Meridas is a capable leader, and his archers are vital to our victory. Do not let them be caught off guard! Meanwhile keep your watchful eyes on the borders at all times in my stead. Now tell us the good news.'

'I am afraid I misinformed you before. This is not good news; it is excellent news! Some of my kin scouting in Alterash discovered something very interesting. They were perched within the trees of a small wood nigh to Kainor when a fire blazed in the east and howls resonated across the land. There had been much commotion in the land as of late, so my kin were investigating its cause. They took flight to the castle and were greatly alarmed at what they saw next: in front of the fortress there were hundreds of the brown wolves of Alterash slain before the gates, burned with oil and fire. On the ground around the walls near to the gate, there were many slain Vash'alan soldiers. They were sent to keep the Alterashians in line no doubt.

'Inside the citadel a large host of Alterashians and a small band of Boltians stormed the city. In moments, they had slain all of the Vash'alan guards, but they spared those of Alterashian decent. In the throne room of the late King Bormann, two men emerged shouting with much merriment: they were recognized as Gibraltar of Alterash and the Prince of Bolteras—aye your nephew Tristan, Lord Edgar. And it seems they had slain the Alp Gluttony and had recaptured the fortress of Kainor. Though they subdued as many of the Alterashians as they were able, others were stubborn and died by their hands. It was a glorious victory for the forces of Light, and the people boasted of "Tristan's master plan."'

Edgar jumped to his feet excitedly. Grinshawl smiled brightly and then roared with a flex of his muscles, as is his custom when he is elated. 'My lord, your nephew really has outdone himself this time, but not in the way of his expected tomfoolery! The little pest has some fight in him I see and intellect too! I am overjoyed; perhaps he will be a great and mighty king after all!'

Edgar laughed and said, 'All this time he has acted the jester and deceived us all! It appears he has listened to my lessons after all

240

and can be quite capable when it counts. I have never been more proud of him than I am now. Tell me Greatwing, were many of our allies injured or slain?'

'That is the most miraculous part of the tale! Only five warriors suffered injury and of those five, only two died, may they rest in peace. It seems Tristan devised a fine plan and accounted wisely for the enemy's strength. The Enemy counted on the hundreds of venomous wolves—the Hellhounds of Gluttony—to destroy their forces, but Tristan had considered them as well! By the time the wolves neared the gates, Tristan's soldiers had already filled the moats with oil and doused every last one of the beasts in it as they passed through. And one of the Alterashians sent a flaming arrow into their midst and set them all on fire! It was a marvelous tale my kin returned to me.'

Edgar clasped his hands over his mouth and wept joyfully, and Grinshawl roared again, louder than before. With all the exciting news of Tristan's victory, they had nearly forgotten where they were, and their cries of delight were heard by a band of Vash'alan troops marching through the fissures below. Suddenly, they heard a loud horn resound below them and, for the first time since they entered the land of Vash'ala, they noticed roads and tunnels below them within the fissures. Sounds of clanking armors and noisy footsteps echoed beneath them. Enemies were drawing near.

As the sounds of approaching soldiers grew louder, a massive gale from the north unexpectedly appeared and headed straight for Edgar and his companions. The whirlwind carried great wisps of dust and dirt and many rocks were swept up in its spiraling winds. 'With your leave, I should like to depart, Master Elorén,' Greatwing shouted. The noise of the approaching army grew even louder and many more horns sounded below. Seymour waved his hand, and the eagle took flight leaving the flasks of water on the ground next to the travelers. They attempted to flee back to the south, but the windstorm overcame them in an instant and they were swept into its current.

Just as the Vash'alan soldiers emerged from the passages below, the typhoon vanished, and the travelers disappeared along with it. The air had cleared, and the dust and rocks returned to the ground. The enemies looked about curiously and scoured the land for hours, but they did not find Edgar or his companions. After desperately searching for the source of the noise, the sun-worshippers returned to the tunnels below and sent word of the strange voices to Sol'Czar and Korvash the manslayer. After the Draemhan leader heard the news, he commanded his Draemhan minions, the Imps of Darkness, to roam the borders of the land at all times.

* * *

Edgar awoke beside his two companions three days later to the sound of dripping water and a soothing noise like the rush of a waterfall. He woke suddenly with a scream as one does from a nightmare; his yell woke the others. Looking around, they saw nothing but stone and water and discovered they were in a cavern. There was a strange light of a cool blue tint flickering on the walls, and it reflected off the surface of the pools in the cave. Water was dripping from the many spikes along the roof of the grotto and splashing into a small, stagnant pool to their left; its sound was tranquil to them. They were relieved to be alive, but they did not know how they arrived at the cavern.

'Where are we, my liege?' Grinshawl said breaking the silence. 'The last I remember we were nearly swept away by a windstorm!'

'Aye, that is all I remember as well,' Edgar replied placing his hands on his head. 'And now my head is throbbing with pain and my chest too!' He looked down at his tunic and saw blood stained upon it. He then touched his face and wiped fresh blood from his mouth. After cleaning his lips he said, 'And other problems have returned I see.'

'It has happened again, I see,' Grinshawl said forlornly. 'This is grave news!'

'Well now, this was a twist of fate!' Seymour laughed, ignoring Grinshawl and Edgar's concerns. 'Nay, it is Vaaspar's providence, a godsend! We have arrived at the cave of Percival the Silver and several days earlier than I imagined! I nearly asked Greatwing to fly back and forth refilling our flasks with water!' He laughed again. 'I am elated that we have left that dry land and have come to a place of peace and comfort. And lo! there is plenty of fresh water to drink here.'

'You are as keen and discerning as always, Elorén,' a voice called from a marble throne at the top of a short stony stairway to their right. The figure's speech was rather queer: he paused briefly every so often between words and overly stressed certain sounds. For him to say anything took longer than it ought, by Edgar's reasoning. 'Welcome to my home of late, though it once belonged to my late

242

brother of the Order, Armand the Blue. I heard you approaching my cave days ago. Ah, let me explain to the simple-minded; the wind is my messenger you see, so I hear many things. Anything the wind carries, I can hear if I so choose. I just happened to discover you on your travels as I listened intently to the lands nearby my home. You see, I find enjoyment in listening to the happenings of the world, especially when I am able to hear the Dark Lord's inane plans. But as it happened, my listening gave me the opportunity to save you from the wretched Vash'alans.' He paused with an odd smile on his face which turned suddenly to anger. 'Now get out!' he hissed. The old Mage was now hunched over, and his silvery locks lolled atop his face.

'That was a mighty harsh response, Percival,' Seymour retorted. 'You ought to know it is quite rude to get rid of your guests so soon when they have just awoken. And you are quite bold to speak thusly to one of the Celebhas! Your manners have diminished of late, I must tell you.'

'Bah!' he hissed once again. 'I have given you shelter for three days already and spared you also from the armies of the Enemy! And now what would one of Vaaspar's beloved, the King of Bolteras and the so-called Ogre of Bolteras want with an old, forgotten Wizard?'

Grinshawl let out a loud roar that made the walls of the cavern tremor. 'I cannot stand this man's disrespect! Let me teach him wisdom through a good beating! Then, he will know a thing or two about manners!'

'Calm yourself, Grinshawl,' Edgar replied. 'There is no need to fight with an ally. I am not offended, so ease your mind.'

'But, my liege, I—'

'Now, now, loyal dog,' Percival remarked, 'listen to your master. You would not want to stray far from your leash!'

'That is enough out of you, Percival!' Seymour snapped. 'You may be the Silver Mage, but your tongue is anything but silver-tipped! Stay your uncouth tongue and keep it sealed behind your teeth lest you bring yourself to ruin! I am weak now as I am, but I have power enough to silence the likes of you!'

Percival raised his hands and waved them up and down mockingly. 'I understand. I understand. No need to be hasty. Yes, yes, do not be so rash! I have saved your lives and that is more than I owe any of you. Please leave me for I desire solitude.' He spoke mockingly and sarcastically, and Grinshawl grew more and more irate with every word.

'We left Bolteras with the purpose of restoring the Order of the Magus,' Edgar replied. 'That was our initial task, b—'

'The Order?' Percival laughed and suddenly halted his odd speech patterns. 'Wake up, Boltian King! The Order has passed from this world! Beredor withdrew from the Order after killing Alastair and took with him Maldrad and Raven, and together they betrayed the sanctity of the Order and our friendship. Then, Tiberius and Maldrad slew each other in a senseless fight. Armand was foolish enough to summon Leviathan from her depths and too has perished. And now Beredor reigns in Scipherius and controls the Dark Guild that rules over the Unsentane of the Eastern Lands. And Raven the Gold lives on as Beredor's most trusted apprentice. So tell me, O you among the wise and knowing, what Order is there left to restore? I am the last of the Mages who still belong to the Light!'

'Knave,' Grinshawl shouted, 'perhaps Edgar can overlook your snide remarks, but I will not. The king is my greatest friend, and I will not allow you to speak to him thusly. I am not called the Ogre of Bolteras for nothing! My strength can bring the roofs of this very cave crashing upon your head! Do not underestimate the power of Bolt and Hammer!'

'I see the fool has named his precious arms. Are you proud of your physical strength, Ogre?'

'I have no pride in what has been given unto me. My strength is a gift, and I use it to aid my friends, most of all Lord Edgar. I would not be alive this day if not for Edgar's kindness and bravery. From the day I was saved from the prisons of Gorgonash, I dedicated myself to learning the mysteries of Elúvías and thus my strength became what it is today! I will show you your foolishness, Percival. Alastair the White lives! Kneel down before the king and beg forgiveness for your trifling words!' The cavern trembled at the blaring sound of Grinshawl's voice, and Percival rose from his seat in shock.

'Alive you say? It cannot be! I witnessed his death four years ago in Portrinath.'

'I say he is alive you accursed dotard!' Grinshawl barked. Percival looked to Seymour for affirmation, and the Celebhas nodded with a smile. Percival plopped down in his marble chair and placed his hands over his face. A moment later, he began to weep.

'Three days,' the Silver Mage spoke removing his hands from his face, 'for three days, I allowed you to rest safely in my abode, and it took me all three of those days to recover my Mana from using the overwhelming spell that saved your lives. And now you come to mock me by speaking of the restoration of a broken band of Wizards and claiming a dead Mage has come back to life?' He paused and then moaned bitterly. Then he was filled with rage and rose again from his seat again. 'Get out! You cannot force me to aid you in a meaningless war! Even you, Elorén, as you currently are, cannot do me harm! With my Wind Magic, I have the power to destroy you all!' He stared at them threateningly and then continued calmly, 'but I desire no such thing. Just leave me; I beg of you. Leave me to die alone!'

His voice echoed through the cave, and no one dared to say another word. They gathered their belongings and left the cave of the bitter, old Wizard. They strode out onto a beach at the northern tip of Vash'ala and stared out at the vastness of the Great Sea. The land there was entirely different from the rest of the country: there were palm trees and white sand, a beautiful view of the sky and also of the vastly stretching waters of the Great Sea. They decided to soak their feet in the coolness of the ocean and enjoy the coast for a while. But they were greatly discouraged, for it seemed their mission had failed.

Grinshawl removed his tunic and boots and dove into the ocean waters, but he did not swim far and returned to the beach shortly after, for fear that Leviathan and her offspring would arise and kill them. Edgar paced along the edge of the coast for nearly a mile to the west; meanwhile, Seymour sat sorrowfully on a dune of sand and looked ever so often to the entrance of the cave. After his swim, Grinshawl joined the Celebhas on a dune of sand and reclined backward to stare at the beautiful sky above. For the first time since they left Bolteras, he saw a blue sky with white, fluffy clouds, and he felt a peace come over him for a time.

'We would be swept away in an instant if Leviathan knew I waded in her waters,' he laughed after a drawn out silence. 'That would be quite a vain end for the King of Bolteras and Elorén the Celebhas. Ha!' Seymour smiled for a moment but then appeared again downcast. 'What troubles you, warrior of the Light?'

'Men experience many troubles,' Seymour sighed. 'I am saddened to see Percival in agony from the loss of his friends. He has witnessed the deaths of those closest to him and even betrayal from others who were closer—one could say they died in spirit. And after

245

all his sad times, he wishes only for solitude. It is no longer necessary to restore the Order as it has been greatly shattered, but Alastair's desire was always to be reunited with his old friend, to bring him some comfort in his time of grief. Aye, Alastair knew the Order was dead. I imagine that is why he wished to seek out Percival himself in the beginning, and he knows now that his powers are unnecessary. It used to be that only a Wizard could defeat another Wizard with a few exceptions, namely the Dragons and the Celebhas, but those days are dead and gone. Men are rising up now to rival the power of Wizards, and yes, even that of the Dragons and Celebhas; but that is the way Vaaspar always intended it to be. He has desired for a long time now to have his children return to Him, to call upon Him once more. That is why He gave Elúvías to Men. Though Men are responsible for killing Vaaspar, He wanted to impart a gift before He returned to Elúne. The days are changing now and rapidly too, but pain and sadness still remain. I merely wish to see the days when Men unite under the banner of Light and fight together for justice. As it is now, I feel useless. I know how to heal many diseases and injuries, but what can I speak to Percival to heal him of his sadness, to show him there is still value in living?'

Grinshawl lay there silently for a moment contemplating the Celebhas' words, but he could not find anything to say in response. After a time, he rose and sat beside Seymour on a rock jutting out of the sand and stared at the rolling waters of the ocean. Edgar returned an hour later and joined his comrades upon the beach. No one spoke for many more hours. Feeling restless, Grinshawl found a soft patch of grassy ground to the south to lie upon and fell asleep. Seymour stared away into the distance, never blinking but ever thinking. At long last, Edgar rose and grabbed his war maul and turned towards Percival's cave.

'Before we depart tomorrow morning, I wish to speak with Percival alone,' Edgar called to the Celebhas. Seymour said nothing but only continued to stare off into the distance. As Edgar approached the cave, a wall of spiraling winds encompassed the cave blocking the entryway. He stooped down low and grabbed a stone from the sand and then hurled it as hard as he could at the tempest. The winds sliced the rock into pieces too small to be seen. 'Do you think this will keep me out, coward?' Edgar shouted. Edgar spread his feet apart and raised his mighty war maul over his head. He exerted his Mana, and the energy ran down the length of his weapon and into its head; he then swung his weapon down at the vortex of cutting wind. Covered with the power of Elúvías, the king's weapon crashed upon the wall of wind as though it was made of hard steel; but Edgar's attack broke through the current and formed a small opening for him to pass through. Edgar entered the cave safely, and the winds around the cave subsided at once.

He returned to where Percival sat upon his marble throne, but the Wizard appeared to be asleep. Edgar approached the stair of the dais and bowed his head before the Silver Mage and waited for several minutes without saying a word, but the Wizard remained quiescent. After a while longer, Edgar's patience expired, and he rose with a thud of his hammer on the ground. The Wizard stirred.

'Who goes there?' Percival spoke alarmingly. 'Oh, it is *you* again. I told you to leave me. How did you pass through my defense? Was it the Celebhas? Curse him!'

'Nay, it was I who cleared the way,' Edgar snapped. 'I have something I must speak with you about.'

'Well I shall not hear it,' the Mage retorted in his queer manner of speaking. 'Now go away. I shall not warn you another time!'

'You are powerful, Percival the Silver, but I am certain you can do me no harm.'

'Would you care to test your theory, Lord Edgar? I know of your sickness. Do you think I only listen to the winds of Vash'ala? Bah! I hear anything I want to hear, and I know well of the dreadful disease that plagues you. It is like a shadow always looming over your head, and I even hear the frail pitter patter of your heart as it beats slowly like the drops of water falling from the ceiling of my lair. I wonder: how would the King of Bolteras fair against a Mage of the Order with such a dreadful condition? Once you exert too much Magic, will you even be able to stand firm on your own two feet, or will the disease in your body prove too strong? I am certain you would die attempting to overcome me. But I am not a cruel man, so do not anger me Edgar King!' Edgar stood shocked and frustrated, for the Wizard anticipated his ruse.

'You are wise and powerful Percival, but hear you me: those who refuse to fight for evil are not necessarily good, but those who do not fight for good are always evil. There is only good and evil, Silver Mage; there is nothing in between! You believe you can sit upon your throne in isolation and avoid war; and since you do not aid evil, you think you are good. You tell yourself lies to ease your guilt! You remain passive and that will be your downfall! We all have a choice to make, whether for good or for evil. But by sitting idly in your solitude and loathing your life by living in self-pity, you have more than given your soul over to the Dark Lord! Which side will you choose when the time comes? Will you betray your comrades who went before you? Know this: Abaddon will come for you if he wins against Men. Your place of comfort will not keep you safe for long, and then you will have no place to hide. Beware of daydreaming when you have already received the call to do what is right!'

Percival laughed at Edgar. The laugh was exasperating to Edgar, and he could not stand it any longer. He ascended the steps of the dais and stood next to Percival, who did not seem to notice the king's presence but simply continued to laugh. Edgar raised his fist and hit him as hard as he could, and the Wizard's eyes grew several sizes. Percival sat agape and silent on his throne, unable to move.

After a moment, he spoke at last. 'I will die alone here,' he wept. 'This world is dying, and I am prepared to die with it! I will ask you no more. Leave me or else suffer my wrath! Can you not see my despair? Will you not spare me any further burdens? Speak to me no more; I beg of you!' At his last word, torrents of wind surrounded his throne and Edgar was hurled violently to the floor. From Percival's throne, he rolled down the stairs and his war maul fell far away near the entrance of the cave. When he had settled on the ground, he spat out blood and felt extremely faint.

* * *

Grinshawl awoke as the sunlight faded in the west and stars appeared in the sky. After looking around for any sign of Edgar, he went to Seymour who was pacing back and forth near the shore of the beach. 'Where is the king? Has he gone away again?' At long last, the Celebhas stirred to the voice of the giant.

'Aye, he left to talk with Percival while you were asleep. I reckon he will return soon.'

At that time, Edgar emerged from the cave and returned to his companions. As he walked, he dragged his hammer on the sand behind him. 'Well,' he called, 'let us find rest in this peaceful place while we still can, and we will depart tomorrow at the first light of day. I have seen enough of this country for now and yearn to return to Bolteras.'

'What happened with Percival?' Grinshawl asked as he noticed a drop of fresh blood on Edgar's lip.

'Some words were said, but he refused to awake from his stubbornness. Other than words, not much happened.' Edgar spoke unflappably and guardedly, and it appeared to Grinshawl that he was keeping some truth from them. He stared at the king with an investigative, piercing glance, but Edgar would not look him in the eye. After a moment, Grinshawl bellowed and laughed loudly.

'Did you strike him, my liege?' Edgar looked suddenly alarmed, and his face confessed that he had. Grinshawl laughed even louder. 'I suppose he had it coming to him!'

'It was a blunder of mine and no laughing matter, Grinshawl! I lost my temper, but I think he understands me better now.' Seymour chuckled softly. 'Do you find this amusing as well, great Celebhas?'

Seymour paused for a moment and then whispered, 'Only slightly.' The three of them laughed for a moment, but Edgar felt a slight remorse for hitting the Wizard. Unbeknownst to them, Percival peered out of the doorway to the cave observing their joy and laughter at his own expense. A part of him longed to share in their laughter, but he quickly and silently withdrew back into his cave and was filled with bitterness once again.

'As I was saying,' Edgar continued, 'let us sleep well tonight. We will have many days of journeying before we reach the borders of Bolteras, and it may be more perilous backward than it was forward!'

They listened to the soothing waves of the Great Sea as they rested, and it was not long before sleep overtook them. Upon waking the next day, they looked beyond the lushness of the area about them to the dark wasteland to the south and were saddened to begin the next part of their journey.

Chapter XV

The Clash of Brews

Since the day following the Boltian Council, the two elders left in charge of Vallicore and the armies of Bolteras, Arthur Grause and Tom Bowman, were hard at work: they slowly learned the ways of Elúvías from the Templar Guard and aided in instructing the masses of Boltian soldiers as they worked hard to prepare for war. They spent many days training under the instruction of Balan and Langol and then tried to aid their teachings; but as time elapsed, they came to find their abilities faired better in wisdom and counsel. Elder Bowman was officially in charge of Vallicore as steward in the king's stead, but he was quite fond of Arthur's counsel and called upon him daily as he considered Arthur 'a wise and noble man.' And so the two governed the peoples of Bolteras and checked often on the affairs of the many fortresses and villages in the land.

At the onset of their cooperation, they were more of acquaintances than anything, and their relationship was strictly business-oriented; and Elder Bowman wanted it that way, for he refused to befriend any whom he worked alongside. He would often say things to Arthur such as 'leave your rebukes and personal matters at the door; they have no place here!' or 'come now, wise Arthur, you are my advisor in these military matters. There is no place for friendships these days. If we lose ourselves in the enjoyment of one another's company, then what will become of Bolteras and its people? There are many relying on us, and I cannot be distracted by the burdens of friendship.' But Arthur desperately pressed all the more to befriend the old man. Since he was separated from Victor and his old friend Edgar, Arthur became lonelier with each passing day. It was now the third of May, and the two men sat in the council room discussing their strategies.

'What advantages do Men have against Draemhas?' Bowman asked frustratingly; he was rubbing his wrinkled brows and combing his long, white beard with his fingers. 'Are not their bodies more capable, their weapons more deadly and their Magic more potent?'

'Aye, they have many advantages as I have heard, but I do not know such things personally,' Arthur replied. 'But I imagine, good friend, t—'

'Eh, eh, eh,' Bowman interrupted. 'Bah! I say, there is that word again: *friend*. You always say *friend* as though we were…well, friends! Let us set the record straight. You are wise and thusly I call upon you for counsel, and that is all. You are my advisor, and I am the Steward of Bolteras until the king returns. There are no friendships or anything of the sort. Now stop wasting my time with such sentiments!'

'I should think we would spare more time if you quit making such long speeches every time I said the word friend! Are we not allies?' Bowman nodded. 'And are we not comrades and fellow citizens of Bolteras?' Bowman nodded again saying, 'yes, yes.' 'And are we not fellow lovers of the Light and also of Vaaspar's greater will?' Once more Bowman nodded in agreement. 'Then we are friends I say!' Arthur said it with such exaggerated excitement that Tom's face suddenly appeared ten times more wrinkled than it had ever appeared before. Arthur laughed cheerfully. 'I only jest with you, fr—I mean, Tom. I have a few strategies that you may be interested in.'

'Aye let me hear them already!'

'One was favored by my belated son Threngol. He used to read war stories about Men from the ancient days. Though many of them are said to be rumors, there was a group of Men, only thirty or so, who survived many battles with a single strategy. Though it is a common idea, it is rarely seen these days. Perhaps it will aid us in the war.'

'Yes, yes, go on! You keep talking, but I have yet to hear your proposal!'

'Moats,' Arthur remarked.

'Moats you say?'

'Aye…moats or rather trenches I should say. In this particular story, these wanderers always positioned themselves on high land and dug trenches down below them that were very deep and wide and long. Thus, when their enemies approached, they would form a phalanx about each other with mighty shields to stay the darts of their enemies. Meanwhile, the enemy was exhausting themselves climbing in and out of the trenches. When the enemies' darts seized, they would fire their own arrows upon them and bleed them dry. It was an old legend we knew very well in Kesh called *The March of Nine*.'

'That is a fine tale, but it is only a tale, is it not?'

'Some would say that it is. But we called it *The March of Nine* for a particular reason: from that group, nine survived after fighting hundreds of battles and marched from the Eastern Lands to the West, and they found a lovely patch of land and claimed it their own. These Men found for themselves wives and started a small village away in the eastern parts of Bolteras and called it Kesh. Aye, this is the tale of the famous Bradeur family who founded my hometown, and thus Mayle Bradeur was born from their line. And it is due to those brave thirty that he was able to rebuild Kesh out of fine cedar and finish his legacy with the finest ale ever brewed!'

'So that is the history of Kesh is it? Very well, I rather enjoy the sound of that idea! But I must disagree with you on one point.'

'What is that, wise steward?'

'Mayle's Ale is not the best brew. Nay I say; Borgon's Beer conquers it in every way. Its color is darker, its taste is sweeter. And its strength is...how should I say it? it is stronger!' Hearing Tom Bowman's words, Arthur angrily beat his fists upon the table.

'Fool of a steward,' he said in rage. 'You would compare that awful, bitter beer to Mayle's Ale, the sweetest drink of them all? You are foolish like the king! I see Vallicore breeds a horde of dotards! Your words are blasphemous I tell you! That is a cruel and wretched thing to say, *Older Bowman*!'

'You misspoke, you decrepit halfwit!'

'Nay, I said what I meant, and I meant what I said, old man!' Arthur snorted.

'It seems we have a rather unpleasant disagreement between us, and there is only one solution that can put this matter to rest.'

'*A Contest of Champions*,' both Men exclaimed in harmony as they placed their hands upon the table and rose from their seats, staring intensely into each other's fiery eyes. Both Men scurried out of the council room and strode abreast throughout the city, pushing upon each other as they strode along. They went from pub to pub in search of a barkeep who was a seller of both brews. It took several hours of searching but they finally found a solitary pub in the southwestern quartern of Vallicore; it was called *High Spirits* and was owned by a man named Borgy Hamtrotter. It was located in a drab area of the city and was full of roughnecks, ruffians of various peoples of all kinds and shapes, from thieves and ex-soldiers to mysterious wanderers.

'Welcome to the merriest pub in all of Bolteras!' Borgy announced as the two old fellows entered the room. Tom and Arthur quickly darted to the counter, and both placed a small bag of coins on the table. 'What will it be, good and generous sirs? These are many coins for a simple drink.' At that moment, all the gathered ruffians were observing as the well-dressed old codgers huffed and puffed in their anger.

'Do you keep Mayle's Ale at this pub?' Arthur asked anxiously.

'But of course I do!' the owner replied.

'And do you keep also Borgon's Beer?' Tom added.

'Why yes I do! Calm down now, old timers! There be plenty of beers to go around.' He began to push the bags of coins back towards the old men, but Arthur quickly placed his hand on top of Borgy's arm. He leaned in and carefully explained their intentions.

'By my graying beard,' Borgy shouted. 'Roughnecks and strangers, the whole lot of ya, clear me some tables and give these codgers some space. It has been many years since we have been honored with such an event. Make way for a Contest of Champions!' Instantly, all the Men in the bar began to shout and clap and beat their mugs upon the table, some shouting, *'Here, here!'* The pub was incredibly noisy, and many who were sleeping in the upstairs inn came down to witness the competition.

'These two fellows will be competing in a drinking contest. Here are the rules: each of you will drink until you can drink no more! You see,' he turned to the crowd, 'these men cannot agree on which is the finer brew: Mayle's Ale or Borgon's Beer!' Some of the people roared with shouts of *'Mayle's Ale is the best'* while others shouted, *'No, Borgon's Beer conquers all!'* 'Calm you down now,' Borgy continued. 'There is plenty of time for hollering and noise making. The last man drinking wins the contest, and their favorite beer will be deemed the mightiest of brews! This will be the way to settle the manner. And each man must drink the favorite beer of his opponent to see which is strongest.'

'Let us add another rule if I may, good sir, and if Tom agrees of course,' Arthur said gaily. Both Tom and Mr. Hamtrotter turned their ears to listen. Arthur grinned and raised an eyebrow. 'Let each man drink in turn, but after we have finished each mug, let us each sing a drinking song in honor of our preferred beer! If the man takes his turn and cannot hold his own or cannot think of a song to sing, then he will lose the competition, so long as the next man can successfully complete his turn, unless he had already drank for that round. What say you?'

'That is a fine proposition, Arthur, and I shall drink first!' Tom replied eagerly. 'I will be drinking the dreadful ale passed down from the Bradeur family known as Mayle's Ale to prove it is the lesser of beers, kind sir, and the fool across from me will be drinking the delightful Borgon's Beer.' Arthur frowned at Tom, and Tom answered by pointing his tongue at him.

'Aye each must adhere to the rules and I will judge the competition as this is my tavern. Come to me, my sons!' Borgy snapped his fingers and two lads ran out: they were no older than thirteen or fourteen, but were very large in size, liking to Mr. Hamtrotter. He turned and spoke to them, and they sped off at once and returned with trays carrying mugs nearly three sizes larger than the average drinking vessel. The two boys sat the mugs on the table and sped off again to prepare more drinks. Mr. Hamtrotter raised both his flabby arms in the air and shouted, 'Let the competition commence!'

Tom took up a mug of Mayle's Ale and guzzled it down rapidly, with a sour expression on his face. Some of his beer spilled into his beard, but he finished it quickly and slammed the mug on the table. Then he opened his mouth and began a song:

> O, Borgon's Beer it tastes so sweet
> From the hairs of me head to my hairy feet
> Drink it slow or drink it fast
> It does not matter how long it lasts!
>
> It conquers all, both big and small
> Like Vallicore it will never fall
> So bring your liquor, wine or ale
> But in the presence of Borgon's all will pale!
>
> O, Borgon's beer it is the greater
> I pity all the knaves that hate her!

He ended his song, and the pub roared merrily and turned their gaze to Arthur who was reaching for his cup of Borgon's Beer.

He drank it slower than Tom and peered intensely at his opponent. When he had reached the bottom of the mug, he belched and sang:

> *All along this beaten path I think,*
> *There is no greater a brew I drink*
> *Than Mayle's Ale, the mightiest of beer*
> *So good it is; it wipes away fear!*
>
> *Skillful Mayle of carpentry olden*
> *Your greatest skill is one now golden.*
> *All throughout the vast plains I will hail*
> *So that all will know of Mayle's great ale!*
>
> *Borgon's is fair but I do not care*
> *For to Mayle's, behold, it will never compare!*

There was much laughter and clapping as the crowd eagerly anticipated each drink and accompanying song. More people curiously crept in from outside the bar to witness the event. Tom quickly drank again and began:

> *O Borgon, fair Borgon, I revel in your brew*
> *A jolly heart I have, aye, it is never blue*
> *I sing a song and clap my hands and feet*
> *I dance and whistle to the sound of my own beat*
>
> *I am shameful not to drink of your beer*
> *For from west to east, aye, either far or near*
> *All know of Borgon's, the rich and gold*
> *To compete with her, aye, you be mighty bold!*
>
> *But none will beat her with whip or lash*
> *For she carries a kick that will inspire a dash!*

The crowd cheered on the jolly, old codgers and beat their mugs on their tables. Arthur took a drink and began his next tune:

> *Borgon is famous and heard all about*
> *For she is odorous and fills Men with shameful doubt*
> *She promises happiness but fails to deliver*
> *If she were an arrow, I would refuse her my quiver!*

255

Arthur ended his short verse and glared fiercely at Tom who was quite irate at Arthur's insulting song. The crowd laughed and clapped louder than ever. Tom now feared he would lose the game, but he downed another drink and began his next verse:

Listen now to the wails of the bewildered dead
The ones trapped in mounds and filled with dread
They cry and whine and gnash their fangs
Cursing Mayle for their eternal pangs!

Many lawks were heard from the crowd and laughter all the more. At this point, unbeknownst to the cheerful group of merry-drinkers, several Boltian soldiers entered the pub to enjoy the competition. With them was Meridas, the archer-captain, who entered silently and crept away to a quiet corner of the room. Arthur reached for another cup of ale and drank. Then he opened his mouth to sing:

Along the length of a mountain I saw heaps
Of bodies piled high and graves dug deep
What, I asked was the cause of their death
But none could speak, not even a breath

I lamented at first for their deaths were unclear
But then saw amongst them large barrels of beer
Written on them was 'Borgon's Beer, it conquers all'
And indeed it did, it was the cause of their fall!

And then it was said in the legends of old
That vile creatures arose from origins untold
But to explain the Goblins I have a reason;
They were wrought from Borgon, her dreadful poison!

Once again, the crowd cheered, but at that moment, Tom reeled and fell to the ground; and Arthur, feeling he had won the competition, began to laugh at his rival. Suddenly, Arthur swooned and fell off his stool to the ground beside Tom. Both of the old codgers fell from the table, bringing the remaining mugs of beer crashing upon them. The crowd looked to Mr. Hamtrotter with anticipation awaiting his conclusion.

He stroked his ashy beard and grinned deviously. 'And the winner is…' he paused with a smile on his face that grew larger with every passing second and then continued, 'me!' He grabbed the two sacks of coins left by Arthur and Tom and sped off into a room in the back. The crowd sat there agape and highly disappointed at the bizarre close to the contest. A moment later, Borgy Hamtrotter popped his head out from the back and shouted, 'Wake those poor galoots up and get them off me floor! I will bring them good food to eat. Aha! You soldiers there in the back, come and help the old-timers. I wish the competition ended differently, but ah, I cannot complain,' he said with a large, queer smile on his face and gold coins in his hands.

The Boltian soldiers obeyed the owner's orders and sat Tom and Arthur side by side upon a bench across from Meridas. They shook them for several minutes before the two men roused from their drunken slumber. Borgy reappeared with steaks and taters for the old men. Both hung their heads and whined for a moment but then sat up and gratefully ate their meal.

'What happened?' Arthur questioned. 'Who won the competition?'

'You both passed out!' a soldier exclaimed. 'But it was a fine contest up 'til that point! Here now, eat some food before you pass out again!'

'Thank you kindly, good soldiers,' Elder Bowman added. 'Well then, how will we now decide which *beer* is the mightiest, Arthur?'

'I think the *ale* that is victorious is Mayle's, of course.' Once again, the old men glared at one another, but then their heads began to throb so they rested their heads upon the table.

Thirty minutes later, they awoke once again. Meridas was still sitting across from them tapping an old pipe on the table. The other soldiers had departed, and most of the ruffians had cleared out as well. Mr. Hamtrotter was behind the counter cleaning his mugs and tidying up the place with his two sons. Arthur and Tom placed their elbows upon the table and leaned their chins upon their hands with a few moans. Meridas cleared his throat, and the old men reluctantly looked up, rather annoyed by the sudden interruption.

'How do you gentlemen fare this fine evening?' Both of the men groaned and snickered. 'That good, I see,' Meridas said with a smile. 'As a member of the Boltian Council, I wanted to inform you of my departure, as you are my superiors while Lord Edgar is away.

Tomorrow morning I will return to the Lonely Forest and begin training my kinsmen.'

'You are leaving already, lad?' Elder Bowman declared with a huff. 'It has only been a month since you began your training! Surely you have not mastered the arts of Elúvías.'

'Aye, you speak truth. But in such a short time, I have learned enough for the archer-folk to fare well in the war. The Templar Guard called me a prodigy, and said they had little left to teach me. The flow of Mana within me is great, and I feel it easily. It appears that the Stone of Power in the Cathedral of Light quickly drew out the latent energy within me. I do not comprehend it fully, but I suppose I have been given a gift. Whatever the reason, I will reconvene with my soldiers at once, with your leave of course.'

'That is a fine idea,' Arthur answered. 'The sooner you teach the archers of the Lonely Forest, the better our defenses will be.'

Tom coughed forcefully. 'Excuse me, Arthur,' he said scornfully. 'As steward, *I* will be making such important decisions.' He cleared his throat and gawkily looked about for a moment, forcing Arthur and Meridas to wait for his answer with much anticipation and annoyance. 'Upon *my* leave, you may go. But you must go under one condition.'

'And what would you ask of me, good steward?'

'There is a plan master Arthur proposed to me earlier today. I would have your people fulfill his wishes by digging deep trenches wide and long, as much as you are able.'

'And where would we dig such trenches?'

'That is a fine question. Let us ask Arthur.' He turned his gaze to Arthur who had a perplexed look upon his face.

'I do not know,' was all he could say. He blushed and felt embarrassed for proposing the plan.

But Tom had compassion on him, and cleared his throat again. 'Well then, I suppose we shall leave that up to you, archer-captain! Are not the archers the most sensible when it comes to such things since you must be able to see far and discern the advantages of the land even at a distance? If our enemies attack before we have assembled the armies of Bolteras, then perhaps such a defense will delay their march.'

'Aye, we will devise a strategy if we can. If trenches will aid Bolteras, then I reckon we ought to dig upon the borders of our lands at the Valley of Despair. I suppose we can handle setting a trap for the Draemhas and lure them to a field of battle where we will have our trenches as an advantage. Regardless, we archers will see to it that your wishes are accomplished.'

'Obedient folks you are!' Tom exclaimed. 'To help you in your endeavors, you may take horses and oxen from Vallicore to dig the trenches. Put the beasts to the plow and tear up the land. But be certain you train your bowmen first.'

'I will do as you have said. I thank you, wise counselors. With your leave, I will retire for the evening.' Both men nodded and Meridas departed.

Tom turned to Arthur and rose from his seat extending his hand to his fellow drunkard. Arthur rose and shook his hand. 'Well tonight was the most fun this old man has had in years!' Tom exclaimed. 'Thank you, friend, for this joyful evening and fun competition.'

'The pleasure is mine, for I am a fan of all kinds of competitions. I assure you—wait, did you just say *friend*?'

'Eh? I suppose I did.' He paused for a moment with his eyes opened widely and then his face suddenly turned sour. 'Now look what you have done! You are a cunning one Arthur, and you have tricked me into a game of friendship. This is the reason I do not have friends, for they always distract me from what really matters: my duties!' Tom paused again and sighed deeply. He then raised his head and smiled at Arthur. 'It has been many long and lonely years since I have had a good friend or anyone persistent enough to desire my friendship. Getting old, you watch many of those closest to you pass away while you continue to live a gloomy and forlorn existence. It is rare indeed for someone to come along who is worthy to be called a friend! But when you find him, he is worth keeping. The last friend I ever had was my wife of late. She passed several years ago. I have been bitter ever since.'

'I see,' Arthur said quietly. 'It would be an honor to call you my friend, Tom!'

'Who said you could call me friend? Nay we are not friends!'

'But I—'

'Let me finish!' Tom interrupted. 'I do not see you as a friend but more like a brother! Yes, you are closer than a friend to me, Arthur.'

'Brothers can also be friends,' Arthur retorted. 'I will never replace the friendship you had with your wife, but we could both use friends, for our last days are drawing to their end.'

259

'Perhaps you are right, you stubborn, old fool! Since I will never hear the end of it, I suppose we are now both friends and brothers!'

From that day on, Arthur and Tom cheerfully spent the rest of their days as friends, and they worked closely together to govern the lands of Bolteras. And they never quarreled amongst themselves again, except for once during another Contest of Champions. In the end and after a few unkind words, they agreed to favor the other's choice of drink. And they never fought again after that day. Since the passing of his wife, Elder Bowman had finally found joy in his heart once more. He was so happy that he shared the title of steward with Arthur, and they both held great honor and respect for one another from that day forth.

The day following the first Contest of Champions, on May the fourth, Paladin, Hauffa and Ragnok returned with good tidings. They had successfully recruited Hombag of Poleden, Teles of Carg and Enren of Pilias and brought them before Tom and Arthur. The three new recruits stayed in Vallicore for several weeks and trained in the ways of the power of Light before returning to their fortresses a month later to begin training their soldiers. But Paladin, Hauffa and Ragnok, after presenting their news, continued their mission imploring all capable Boltians to rise to arms.

On the fifteenth of May, Rolo and Pakko returned to Vallicore with Zoro and his men from Fort Leaf. They presented their tale to the two stewards of Vallicore—much to the old men's delight—and requested to be sent to join Meridas and the archers of the Lonely Forest, to which the elders were thrilled to permit the request. During the month of May, the people of Bolteras were pleased to hear the good reports from the many members of the Boltian Council returning from their journeys. And the people were even more thrilled when a messenger arrived and presented the news of Tristan's victory in Alterash; and there was much merriment in Vallicore that night.

But then the month of June came upon the people of Bolteras, and no word had been received from Lord Edgar or Alastair. The stewards were growing more and more anxious with each passing day, for fear that great perils had befallen their comrades, and the warriors of Bolteras were beginning to regret their decision to go to war.

Chapter XVI

Percival's Decision

Edgar and Grinshawl continued south along the eastern edge of the borderlands of Vash'ala with Seymour in the lead. They left the cave of Percival regrettably and strode away from the beaches of the coast. The land continued for several miles maintaining a lush, hopeful vitality before it returned once again to the dark and blistering territory of charred rock and fissures of fire that was far too familiar to the downcast travelers. Hot steam rose periodically from the fissures below forcing the travelers to elude the gusts as they shot forth. A shrill whistle rose upward just before each puff of smoke ascended high into the air above, so they knew when to expect it. Grinshawl was nearly burned badly as he felt his arm tinged by the scorching heat. The land appeared endless once again, and it was not long before their bodies were covered in ash and their clothes were tainted with the smell of sulfur.

On the way back, the Desolate Plains proved to be more fiery and arduous than their first adventure through the land. Miles from the serene shores of the coast, the path ran into a steep, rocky slope descending far into the fissures below. They pressed on to the bottom of the hill where the path broke in two: one path led straight and returned to the Desolate Plains above to the place where Percival's Magic had saved them days before, but the other led to the right and continued the length of several furlongs. They peered down the path to the right and beheld a bright red light like fire flash upon a wall at the end of the passageway. The light continuously appeared and disappeared every so often. Curiosity overcame Seymour, and he proceeded toward the red light as it flashed across the tall, jagged wall in front of them, only this time it lingered for a while. Edgar and Grinshawl followed reluctantly.

'I believe we have reached a unique area of the Gorgonash prison in the north of Vash'ala,' Seymour whispered as they pressed forward. 'Perhaps there are captives that we can save. If we liberate enough people, we may be able to strengthen the forces of Bolteras and thus weaken the Enemy's force.'

As they drew nearer, they heard unpleasant cries of anguish as though someone was being tortured in the levels of the dungeon beneath them. The path split again, one to the right and another to the left. The path to the right descended another long slope; the left path was level and curved around a bend leading west several fathoms from the split. It seemed to Edgar and Grinshawl that something was beckoning Seymour to follow the right path that descended into inevitable terror, whence the awful cries of torment reverberated from below.

'Elorén,' Edgar called nervously, 'where are you taking us?' The Celebhas ignored him and continued along the path down to the bottom of the slope. Suddenly, the pained cries faded and were replaced by the laughter of small, piercing voices. It was clear to them that the laughter came from creatures that delighted in the agony of the tormented. The path split again at the bottom of the slope, one straight and another left down yet another incline. 'Never have I heard such dreadful, wicked laughter in all my life. Tell me Elorén where you are taking us!' he said in a harsh whisper.

Sweat was falling off of their brows and their bodies were growing famished, but they pressed on, their thoughts now distracted by the mysterious laughter. None of them knew the day or the hour as the dark clouds of the land veiled any sign of the sun and sky above, but they were almost out of food and were growing weary. Seymour stopped suddenly, about six fathoms from the split in the path, and turned about. 'We must get a better understanding of the horrors that await us. Forgive my silence, but this place holds an eerie yet familiar sort of power, one I have not felt for a very long time.' He reached for his flask and took a sip of water to satisfy his thirst. 'I do not believe it! In all the confusion of things, I never realized that our flasks were filled with fresh water! Percival must have filled them whilst we slept in his cave. Bless that man, though he is a stubborn fool.' Edgar and Grinshawl reached for their flasks and gratefully sipped on the water; it was still cold and soothed them greatly.

'I do not like the looks of this place,' Grinshawl called. 'It reminds me all too well of my captivity in Gorgonash many years ago!'

Seymour gasped and quickly clasped his hands over his mouth. 'I recognize this feeling,' he whispered. 'This power is the source of the evil that is plaguing the lands of Vash'ala, and I believe this place to be where Greatwing and his scouts first noticed the

Draemhas. We have stumbled upon the Sacrificial Catacomb! We must leave at once. This is a place of great peril!' Suddenly, a flash like lightning flickered from a room adjoined to the pathway ahead, and Seymour, drawn by some great power, desired to know its cause. 'Come with me quietly,' he whispered to Edgar and Grinshawl. 'Let us take a quick look and then leave this place for good!' They proceeded as quietly as they could along the edge of the wall until they came upon an opening leading into a large room. Seymour pressed his back against the hot stone and peered around the corner. He saw many terrifying sights in the large chamber.

The Celebhas, using a special power of Elúvías to see far and wide and even around corners, beheld gibbets all along the edge of the room surrounded by lit torches with fresh corpses hanging upon them; the blood of the deceased Men poured like streams into trenches carved in the stone below. The furrows ran in a circle around the room with four pathways leading towards its center. He saw also in the very middle of the chamber a pit. Leading down into the hole was a stairway that led to a platform below and an ominous aura poured forth from its depths. The blood in the trenches flowed into basins on each side of the crater's edges before emptying into channels that ran to the platform below. At the center of the platform was a pedestal holding a stone of dark, shifting colors, and the blood poured all around it. As the blood ran close to the pedestal, it was mysteriously drawn to the stone and absorbed into it.

Seymour turned back quickly, his face as white as snow. Inside the chamber, many voices began to chime in harmony, '*Mak mak pele ine futal.*' The chant continued for several minutes and then ceased suddenly, and another flash like lightning emitted from the chamber. Cold chills ran down the spines of the three companions as horns sounded from within the chamber followed by the sounds of boisterous footsteps and clanking armor.

Roars came thundering from within and many creatures began to whisper in the ancient tongue. The shrill laughter returned for a moment, which made Grinshawl terribly uncomfortable. He anxiously looked all about and then removed his axe and mace from their holdings on his belt. After seeing Seymour draw his magical blade from its sheath, Edgar reluctantly raised his war maul and readied himself for battle. Then they heard the voice of a man saying, 'The preparations are nearly complete, masters. The Alchemist's Stone has served the Dark Lord well, but its full use has yet to be seen. The last days of the Western Lands are but moments

263

away. We have deceived them,' the man laughed. 'They believe we will wait a full year before our assault on Bolteras,' he scoffed. 'But that was all part of the Dark Lord's plan!'

'When will you send your armies to do battle with the Boltians?' a deep, menacing voice called out in response.

'If all goes well, then we will assault them in a month's time. We only require the Imps of Darkness to strike a devastating blow to the feeble Men of Bolteras!'

They heard the slash of a sword resonate in the air followed by a faint thud and a crash. Seymour glanced around the corner again and beheld a decapitated Vash'alan soldier upon the ground. Several other soldiers drew their weapons and pointed them at a small band of Draemhas—ten in all—rising from the pit below. He noticed a dark glowing portal emanating from below, but it soon vanished from sight. He turned back to Edgar and Grinshawl and whispered, 'This is the place where Vash'ala and Dragoth are connected! We have found where they are summoning the Dark Lord's minions, and thus, we have found the Alchemist's Stone! We do not have enough strength to combat them all, but it seems as though the Draemhas and Vash'alans will fight one another. Let us wait but a moment and then counter their evil!'

As Seymour predicted, the two forces—twenty Vash'alans and ten Draemhas—lashed out against one another. During the brief skirmish, the shrill laughter from before returned, and it echoed menacingly to the ears of Edgar and his company. The Draemhas slew all of the Vash'alans swiftly and discarded their bodies in the pit. 'What ill news!' Seymour exclaimed in a soft voice. 'Not even a single Draemhas was slain! That is a pity, for I would have liked to do battle with my evil brethren, but there are far too many for us to fight.'

'Then now is the time,' Grinshawl said with authority. Edgar and Seymour stared at him with astonishment in their eyes. He erected himself fully, and a light sparked within his eyes. 'If this is the portal, then we have a duty to seize the Alchemist's Stone from our enemies! Let us claim it as our own lest they summon more forces to Vash'ala!' Edgar and Seymour smiled at the Ogre of Bolteras and nodded in agreement.

'Today, Grinshawl, you will witness the might of the Celebhas!' Seymour said confidently. He then roared loudly. The Draemhas stirred and brandished their weapons once more. A bright light suddenly surrounded Seymour's body and manifested itself into a strange, white suit of armor that covered him from head to foot. Then his sword turned white and swayed like fire. Two large wings grew from his back a moment later, and he stretched them as far as they would go—about twelve feet from one end to the other. He halted before his wicked kin as Edgar and Grinshawl joined him on either side. They were amazed by the sudden transformation.

'Well, well,' one of the Draemhas spoke, 'Elorén has finally revealed himself after hiding for so long! Who would have known that I would be the first to encounter him?' The voice belonged to the same Draemhas that slew the Vash'alan soldier. He appeared to be the leader and the strongest of the group, for he had solid, black skin and was brawnier than his kin; the nine behind him had ghostly bodies like shadows or wraiths.

'Many of your kin have encountered me before, Kraerik, and all have fallen to my sword. And you shall be no different!'

'You might be one of the mightiest of the Celebhas, but your power is diminishing in this world. But mine grows ever stronger! Certainly my power is equal to that of Korvash.' Edgar and Grinshawl grew uneasy at the mention of Korvash's name, for Seymour had spoken of him as a fearsome foe.

'You have grown strong, but you are weak compared to Korvash! You shall fall this day, you and your brethren.' Kraerik growled and leapt upon Seymour, but before Seymour or Kraerik could strike the other, Grinshawl dashed forward and struck the Draemhas in the head with his mace; and with the power of Elúvías strengthening his weapon, he quickly laid waste to the Draemhas. Edgar and Seymour's eyes grew wide with astonishment.

The remaining nine Draemhas rushed the group, but they were quickly defeated with one attack from Seymour. He spread his wings wide once more and seemed to vanish, but he reappeared behind the band of Draemhas as quickly as a flash of lightning; then the Draemhan warriors mysteriously fell dead upon the burning stone of the dungeon floor. Edgar lowered his war maul and appeared gravely disappointed, for he did not slay even one of their enemies. Grinshawl stared at Elorén in shock after witnessing his fearsome attack, and then spoke, 'What is that armor you wear? And what Magic did you use against them?'

'Ah, this is one of the powers of the Celebhas. We use Elúvías to form what we call *Holy Armor*. It is one of the many uses of Elúvías, but it uses a great amount of Mana; thus, I use it only upon necessity! It is not a discipline that you can utilize at your current level, so wipe that look off your face! You still require much more knowledge and training to delve deeper and attain the higher arts of Elúvías. As for slaying our enemies, I used a power of the Celebhas called *Light Step*. It allows my speed to increase to that of light, and I struck the Draemhas where they stood without them ever knowing it. Again, this is a discipline beyond your level. And now I am greatly exhausted, and my Mana is well spent. Come now and follow me.' The three had hardly taken a step before dreadful shrieks of laughter echoed in the chamber once again. None of them could tell who or what made the noise even as they looked about frantically for its source. Suddenly, many lights flickered upon the walls and the ceiling of the chamber: they were eyes gleaming with a mysterious light like fire. Suddenly, they saw many shadows of tiny creatures scaling down the walls of the chamber, their eyes burning with malice.

'At last, they show themselves!' Seymour shouted. One by one the pairs of eyes crept downward until their forms could be clearly seen in the light of the torches about the room. In a swift moment, hundreds of small, nether fiends surrounded them.

'What are they?' Grinshawl cried out in despair.

'They are the Imps of Darkness! Do not be fooled by their size; they are not to be taken lightly! The Dark Lord commands thousands of their kind. They are weak creatures alone, but they feast upon blood and have the power to drain the Mana from your body. In large numbers, they are nearly impossible to defeat! Do not let them near you! Escape with your lives!'

'But we have no place to run!' Grinshawl cried out again as the Imps drew closer and surrounded them. Seymour looked about to find a solution, but it was too late: the Imps had already seized them, and their strength began to fail. As they fell to the ground, their sight grew black, but they heard suddenly a loud thud echo from the entrance of the chamber. Edgar smiled as a gust of wind swept through the ranks of Imps and carried them upward. The ceiling creaked and cracked, and the hundreds of Imps poured out into the foul air above and came crashing down upon the hot rocks of the Desolate Plains. Only a few survived the mysterious attack, and they withdrew swiftly, laughing as they fled.

The force of the tempest was so powerful that the ceiling split all across its length and came crashing down upon the chamber floor, and many of the gibbets within the chamber were crushed beneath the large boulders; but the three men were kept safe by a

266

sphere of spiraling wind surrounding them. Edgar rose to his feet and raised his arms up, as though he was waiting to embrace someone. 'I am glad you came, and not a moment too late I should add.' The others rose to their feet and beheld Percival the Silver Mage, staff in hand, and the hood of his cloak pulled over his head. 'Did my words reach you at last?'

'Words you ask?' he questioned in a deep, riddling tone, 'Words—ah—yes, it was words that brought me here; but they were not yours, Edgar King. I hear everything carried by the wind as you know, for that is my dominion. I heard the many voices of evil folk laughing and screaming and scouring the borders of Vash'ala. I am afraid there is no place of refuge in this wilderness. I came quickly, so as to save you from your imminent deaths.'

'What do you mean?' Grinshawl questioned. 'Are you saying they were aware of our presence?'

'Aye, the moment you entered the Desolate Plains, the Enemy knew, for his spies were watching for you. The Imps of Darkness were sent by Korvash to search about the edges of this land for "the intruders," as I heard him speak. They are swift-moving, crafty little creatures, constantly hiding in cracks and fissures in the land and acting as spies for the Draemhan forces. And they never sleep. They do not require sleep. They are wrought from the very power of Abaddon and the Draemhas, simply Mana given an evil form through the power of Vexúvías. Surely you know of them, Elorén?'

'I have known of them since before you were born,' Elorén snapped, 'but I was unaware our secrecy had been exposed. Let us be gone from this place as quickly as we may before more return. Leave the Stone lest they hunt us down and reclaim it; we must not risk dying here.' Ignoring Elorén's command, Edgar quickly descended the stairway leading to the Alchemist's Stone. Reaching out, he grabbed the shimmering orb, but a sudden pain spread through his chest as he touched it. He struggled to stand for a moment, but then crashed upon the ground, spewing blood from his mouth. Grinshawl heard the sound of his body falling to the ground and ran to his aid as swiftly as he could. He knelt down beside Edgar and shook him, but the king remained silent and unmoving.

'He is not well, as you may know!' Grinshawl cried. Seymour approached the foot of the stair and peered down at Edgar. 'He has been this way ever since he rescued me from Gorgonash twenty years ago. That dreadful curse still holds on to his body, and I reckon the Alchemist's Stone is worsening his condition!' Grinshawl raised his mace high into the air and struck the Stone violently, but it was unharmed and his mace shattered into many pieces.

'You cannot break the Alchemist's Stone with brute force!' Seymour rebuked. 'Give it to me! I shall carry it until we are free from danger. Grab the king and let us depart quickly!' Grinshawl lifted Edgar upon his shoulder, and the company exited the labyrinth and returned to the ground above. As they stepped upon the Desolate Plains once more, the Imps of Darkness revealed themselves, only now they were snarling and yelping like slaves pressed forward by the whips of their masters. There was frenzy and exigency in their voices as if their lives depended on capturing the intruders. A myriad or more came pouring across the plains, and the ground trembled beneath the travelers. Even amidst all the noise and howls of the enemies, Edgar remained still, his life hanging by a thread.

Grinshawl shook Edgar fervently, but the king continued to sleep. 'What should we do? Edgar will not wake up! We shall not get very far carrying a man upon our shoulders, and we have not the might to defend ourselves.'

'It is odd,' Percival called out, 'that a portal was opened from Dragoth without the Alchemists using their power to hold it. And it is odd that the Alchemist's Stone was so poorly defended, though its importance is great. I believe you were led into a trap, drawn by Abaddon's will to your deaths. Surely this Stone before us is a false one! Go now while you still can and spare your lives. I will delay them until you can enter the Putrid Wood. But do not follow the way you came; go east to the land of Alterash! You will be safest there for the time being.'

'No, this Stone is very real,' Seymour exclaimed solemnly. 'I have held one before in the days of old and felt its power. It is all too familiar to me now. But perhaps they have other means of opening the portal from afar. I am afraid I have no explanation for its light defense; perhaps, the Draemhan force is strong enough now that they no longer require the Stone. Whatever the reason, I cannot allow you to die for our sakes. Capturing the Alchemist's Stone is not more important than your life. It is my sworn duty to protect you; flee with us or else sweep us away with your Wind Magic!'

'I cannot! I used too much Mana in the summoning chambers below. And if I go with you, we will all surely die! You drained all your Mana in the fight against the Draemhas, and the king has been put to sleep by the Enemy's power. Furthermore, the Ogre of Bolteras must carry Edgar and hence cannot fight. We do not have the means to oppose them, and their numbers are too great! Go now! Whatever the reason, they have poorly guarded the Stone, and it is best for them not to have it. Hearken to me, friend of old; this is my decision, my resolve. Do not gainsay me, Elorén! My death shall not be in vain if you three survive.'

'Now in your last hours you decide to be brave? Or else you are a fool; which it is I am not certain!' Grinshawl retorted.

'I have lived a rotten life cowering in my cave away from all the pain and suffering in the world. But the greatest suffering has been mine, of not being there to offer my aid, especially to my brethren of the Order when they needed me most. I fled long before Armand and Tiberius fell when I first learned of Beredor's betrayal and Alastair's death. I had lost hope and had become a coward, but now I must atone for my selfishness. Go now or else die here with me!'

Grinshawl gnashed his teeth and bitterly turned his back on the Mage and darted away. Seymour reached out and grabbed Percival's arm and gave it a shake. 'I will return for you, if you still hold on to your life. I give you my thanks. And I commend you for your courage!'

'It may be that my time has come to pass from this life, but I cannot tell. I just know it is right for me to stay for your sakes. Perhaps Lord Edgar's words reached me yet! But this is my duty as a Mage of the Order and a protector of peace amongst Men; so do not thank me, warrior of Light, unless you come back in victory! Go now!'

Seymour hesitated for a moment but at last turned and darted away behind the Ogre of Bolteras. They ran to the south for a mile with the threat of death still breathing down their necks before fatigue finally overtook them. Upon halting, Grinshawl knelt upon the ground and laid Edgar down, for he could carry the king no further. Seymour turned around with haste to oppose their enemies, but none had followed them. He stood there and watched as the masses of Imps withdrew to the western corners of Vash'ala, toward Osceroth, and he perceived Percival in the midst of their ranks with his far-seeing eyes.

* * *

As soon as Seymour turned to leave, Percival confronted the army of Imps with his staff raised above his head, and the winds were summoned to strike his foes. Hundreds were slain by his violent Magic, but still they poured upon him with great swiftness. His Mana had been greatly drained in the Sacrificial Catacombs, so he fell to his knees, unable to cast another spell to attack his enemies. Knowing he was nearly drained of his Mana and was unable to secure safety for his comrades, he used the last of his power to form the image of a stone in his hands. It felt and looked like the Alchemist's Stone, but it was forged by a Creation Spell of his making. Just as the last of his Mana was spent, the Imps quickly surrounded him and drained him of his last strength; and as he fell, he intentionally dropped the false Alchemist's Stone so they would see it. The Imps cheered loudly and chuckled as they bound Percival with tight, black ropes that sealed the Wizard's Magic and continually drained him of his strength. Believing they had achieved victory and seized the Alchemists' Stone, they dragged his limp body behind their immense force back to the mighty city of Osceroth and ignored the three men fleeing to the south.

* * *

'Lo! they are departing, but why?' Grinshawl panted as he beheld the Imps retreating in the distance.

'I do not know,' Seymour returned, 'but we need not question this blessing. Let us rest for a moment and pray for the safety of our friend, Percival. His sacrifice was one that few in Gaia would dare to risk.' They sat one on either side of Edgar and took a drink of water and said a prayer for Percival. Grinshawl then took his flask and poured some water into Edgar's mouth, but he coughed it back up as soon as it went down his throat. Grinshawl watched eagerly as he hoped the king would awaken, but still Edgar slept. 'We have already stayed in this land longer than I hoped, but we would not have gotten so far without the aid of Percival. Let us keep on, lest we are ambushed by our enemies and Percival's sacrifice is in vain. I agree with the Silver Mage; Alterash is the safest road for us to follow now. But if war is nearer than we anticipated, then we have no time to spare. Perhaps we should just continue south until we reach Bolteras.'

'The king is not fit for travel, and I am certain we will not be able to return to Bolteras as easily as we came. For the time, we must get Edgar to safety, and the borders of Alterash are nigh. I fear Bolteras is too far off for us now, so let us travel there by a safer way. And perhaps we shall meet with young Tristan as we pass through the lands—only time will tell.'

270

'Ah, it is as you say. The woods are still nearly a day's travel from here, so let us not tarry.' Grinshawl picked Edgar up once more, and they treaded on for another hour until they were too exhausted to continue. Sleep evaded them during the night, for the air was stifling and the scorching rocks of the Desolate Plains provided no further comfort. After an hour of attempting to sleep, they were overcome with impatience, and so they grabbed their belongings and continued on. They arrived at the Putrid Wood several hours later, not long after they had exhausted the last drops of water in their flasks. It was dark still but the gloomy clouds above were ending, and they could see the moon and stars above the tops of the trees that were before them. As they neared the edge of the woods, a shadow suddenly passed through the air and perched itself upon a branch of one of the nearby decayed trees.

'Who is there?' Seymour called out, troubled by its abrupt appearance. It looked to them to be a man hunched over, but it was still too dark for them to see clearly.

'Have your eyes grown frail of late? What happened to you these few days since I saw you last?' Seymour exhaled a sigh of relief and wiped the sweat from his brow.

'Greatwing, my friend, you have arrived at no greater a time.'

'Do you think I would forget about you? It took me a few days, but I flew all about the northern borders of Vash'ala near the cave of that dotard searching for you! It was only after I heard loud noises from the south and saw a massive whirlwind of dust and rock that I located you at last. And I saw that fool of a Mage being dragged away by tiny, dark-skinned menaces.'

'He may be a dotard, but a brave one is he,' Grinshawl interrupted. 'He sacrificed himself for our sakes and was captured by the Imps of Darkness.'

'Ah, did he now? Bless his soul! Well I am glad to learn you are safe, but what has become of the king?'

'His sickness worsened in one of the Gorgonash prisons,' Seymour replied. 'But come now; I know you well enough to discern that you have more important matters to speak of.' Grinshawl snickered at the Celebhas' remark and mumbled, 'What is more important than the king's health?'

'Yes, yes,' Greatwing answered, 'but I wish to speak in secret…away from this wretched wasteland. Come with me Elorén, for this is a matter that does not concern Men.'

Without a word, Seymour followed Greatwing deep into the woods and vanished into the shadows of the trees. Grinshawl laid Edgar upon the ground and sat down next to him. For nearly half an hour, he stared despondently across the Desolate Plains; then Seymour returned and beckoned for him. Placing Edgar on his shoulders once again, the giant staggered forward and entered the shelter of the Putrid Wood.

'I must leave you sooner than I originally wished,' Seymour declared suddenly.

'Leave us?' Grinshawl questioned with frustration. 'Where are you going? And when will you go?'

'I must return to Elúne,' he answered solemnly. 'And I must go without delay.' Grinshawl had no words to say, but Seymour discerned the thoughts of despair running through his mind. 'Do not fret! I will not leave you without relief. The Enemy relied too much on the power of the Alchemist's Stone, and now that we have obtained it, it is they who will despair! The Stone had enough power to provide an endless supply of Mana to its wielder, for it uses the blood of sacrificed Men to fuel its evil purposes. It is an ancient Stone of evil origins that requires Alchemists to make, and it is only wrought by the spilt blood of thousands of sacrificed Men. With the lives of thousands running through it, it would take many years— perhaps forty or more—before its power fully waned. For that reason, Aramyst, the first Black Mage, desired to wield the Alchemist's Stone so greatly that he forced his friend Elric to create the Stone. He desired that endless pool of Mana so much that it drove him mad.'

'Then why do we not wield the Stone and use it ourselves?' Grinshawl stammered. 'An endless supply of Mana would benefit our army! You could wield the Stone and be unstoppable!'

'Fool! You do not know what you say! This Stone's essence is evil, for it contains the spilt blood of countless sacrifices that willingly devoted themselves to the Stone's evil purposes and also to Abaddon's will. The Stone was forged by the Alchemists who now dwell in the Darkness, and its wielder must be evil in order to use it. Anyone who tries to use the power of this Stone will succumb to the power of the Dark Lord. It is destructive in the hands of both good and evil, so it must be destroyed. Even if there were no consequences, I would never wield such a shameful Stone of Power! Elúvías is all I need, all any of us need!'

'Forgive me for speaking so rashly. So why then must you leave? Can you not sink it into the ocean and be done with it?'

'Must Men always think so imprudently? If it was that simple, then I would hand it over to Greatwing and let him release it into the depths of the Great Sea. This Stone has an aura of evil about it. Even in the depths, it will call and draw some vile creature to seek it out. The Dark Lord speaks through it, bending the minds of weaker beings to do his bidding. It must be destroyed and only Vaaspar has the power to do so. The only other way to destroy the Stone is to exhaust it of its power. Since that is not an option, I must return to Elúne.' Grinshawl opened his mouth to speak but Seymour interrupted him saying, 'Speak no more. I know the confusion going through your mind. I just ask that you trust me.'

'Will you ever return? I have grown fond of your company,' Grinshawl said glumly with his head lowered.

'I may, but that is not for me to decide. Do not act as though all hope is lost! You are a strong warrior, and I can see that you will not be so easily defeated. After all, you defeated Kraerik with a single blow! Irrefutably, that is a remarkable feat!'

'But what will we do without you? I was only strong before because your presence gave me courage. So how can I protect Edgar single-handedly?'

'That is a part of this painful parting. Come with me.' They proceeded deeper into the forest for two hours before they reached the edge of the woods at the border of Alterash. Midway through their journey, the trees became suddenly—as if by Magic—vigorous and full of life. They stood a few fathoms from the forest's edge as the sun was beginning to rise before them. 'I want you to lay Edgar near the edge of the woods in a place of your choosing; but you must remember your location and never forget it. Is that understood?' Grinshawl nodded and laid Edgar on a bed of leaves near the forest's edge. 'Then this is where we will say farewell. Do not be afraid, no matter what may come your way. You will be safe here. But remember to never forget where you have placed Edgar, not even for a second. He will need to borrow your strength when he awakens. I hope to see you soon. Farewell, my friend.'

Grinshawl watched as Seymour gradually faded like a mist before his eyes along with the Alchemist's Stone. Greatwing peered down from a branch above and hollered, 'I will be taking my leave as well, Ogre of Bolteras. Keep the king safe and always stay on guard.' With a mighty flap of his wings, Greatwing flew off and disappeared in an instant from Grinshawl's sight; and it was odd to him as the eagle had barely left the branch before suddenly vanishing. In order to investigate the matter, Grinshawl ran outside the forest into the lush land of Alterash and gazed into the morning sky. Just above the tops of the trees he beheld the figure of Greatwing soaring towards the heavens; then the mighty eagle swooped to the south, and he saw him no more. Turning back to the forest, Grinshawl strode forward and sat down next to Edgar and fell asleep.

Several hours passed before Grinshawl roused from his sleep. The sun's rays were intensely bright and warm, but he was glad to wake to its friendly light, for its warmth was much more satisfying than the hot air of Vash'ala. Edgar lay still on the leafy turf, and he had not stirred since he coughed up water the evening before. Grinshawl strode forth onto the plains of Alterash to enjoy the warmness of the land and lay upon the grass for a time. After enjoying some relaxation, he rose and turned around to keep an eye on Edgar, but the king was no longer there. Frantically, he darted into the woods, but there Edgar rested before him. It appeared now that the king had never moved. Grinshawl scratched his head curiously and muttered to himself, 'You are seeing things, fool! Yes, that is it. I was imagining it! Bah-ha, I say! Perhaps all this recent excitement has driven me a bit mad, or perhaps I rested in the sun too long.' He roared and laughed at himself, but he soon became sad, for he felt lonely and troubled.

He began to mutter some more under his breath and paced once again onto the turf beyond the woods. Turning back again, he looked amidst the trees, and once more Edgar was nowhere to be found. 'I understand at last! That Seymour must have used his Magic to protect the king whilst he sleeps. Yes, that must be it,' he said rubbing his chin. He was bemused but also glad as he felt Edgar was safely out of harm's way. After carefully examining the area near Edgar and marking his location, Grinshawl withdrew to investigate the land to the east. He descended a long slope a few furlongs from the edge of the forest and followed it into a long open valley that had only a few trees scattered throughout. He continued due east for several hours and then heard the sound of rushing water faintly in the distance. The valley met a steep wold, and at the top was a road that ran from north to south. On the other side of the road, the land fell and rose many times like green waves rolling across a vast ocean.

Grinshawl stood upon the roadway and peered out across the land to the east and spotted a body of water in the distance.

'I say, that looks to be a large lake! It may not be the cleanest of water, but perhaps I can find a fresh spring nearby,' he thought aloud. 'But I cannot leave Edgar alone for so long. What will I do? Woe is me! What will I do?' He stood there for a moment and began to cry, for he did not know what to do. He was all alone now with no one to help him figure out his way. 'I feel so lonely. O how I yearn to see my friends again!'

Grinshawl returned to the woods and tested the range of the protective spell to ease his boredom for a while. After he grew tired of doing so, he decided to search for food, but there were no fruits or vegetables, and he saw no animals to hunt. Upon his return he heard the rustling of grass behind him. 'Who is it?' he shouted in a commanding voice, but he received no response to his liking. Instead, he heard a vicious snarl followed by a strained yowl. He quickly jumped back and faced his foe: it was one of the wolves of Alterash still corrupted by Gluttony's power. Its hair was black and its body was frail; it appeared starved to Grinshawl.

'I am not afraid of a starving, mangy cur! Even if you are hungry and desperate, I will not spare you if you decide to attack me!' The wolf hissed and growled and revealed its teeth dripping with venom. Without hesitation, the creature leapt at Grinshawl, but he drew his axe and hewed off its head. 'A wolf with poisonous fangs, eh? What a barbaric creature!' At that time, two more wolves appeared at the top of a hill in front of him; they were starved like the first. At once, Grinshawl darted back to the woods with the wolves in desperate pursuit. He entered the woods slightly north from where Edgar lay and hid himself in the throng of trees. He awaited the wolves behind an old sycamore with his axe in hand listening as the sound of their feet rustled across the leafy terrain of the forest. The pitter-patter of their steps seemed to be in perfect tune with Grinshawl's beating heart. One of the wolves drew near to the sycamore tree; it sniffed the air searching for the man's trail. Grinshawl moved rapidly from behind the tree and swung his axe with a mighty slash that struck in between the eyes of the wolf, and it fell dead at once; but Grinshawl's axe sunk too deeply into its skull, and he could not remove it.

Before he could pull the axe from the dead wolf's head, the second wolf pounced upon him and began to snap at his face. Desperately, he pushed his predator's head away; then, summoning all his strength with the power of Elúvías, Grinshawl heaved the wolf against a tree, and it whimpered loudly. The Ogre of Bolteras hunched over the wolf and slammed his hand into its head, and the creature's skull cracked and yielded under the mighty blow. Exhausted, Grinshawl returned to the south to the place where Edgar rested and fell asleep under the protection of Elorén's spell.

* * *

For many long days, Grinshawl fought for survival, eating mainly deer meat as he found it, and drinking from the fresh springs of the five streams of the River Anagon. Often, he went days with no food and simply drank his water with gratitude, but one day he came across a grove of trees to the south with fruits of various kinds and was very pleased. Before long his strength returned to him as well as his hope; but the days were long and mundane, and his loneliness grew heavier with each passing moment.

Quite curiously, Edgar never appeared starved or in any danger at all, and his breathing continued peacefully. Moreover, his body appeared healthier than ever before, and at times Grinshawl returned from his journeys to find a white aura about him. Even still, he was confused and worried, so every few days he would force some water and mashed fruit down Edgar's throat. But his attempts to feed the king made no difference in the end; for unbeknownst to Grinshawl, Edgar was protected by Elorén's power, and the white aura about him was suppressing the effects of the deadly disease that plagued his body. Edgar was quickly finding new strength, and it was only a matter of time before he would wake from his troubled sleep.

Chapter XVII

Shadows of the Enemy

The month of June came quickly and peacefully to the archers of the Lonely Forest, except for Meridas who was hard at work instructing his soldiers in the ways of Elúvías. He seldom found peace during the long hours of the day. Since his return from Vallicore, Meridas was burdened with the task of teaching the archers the power of Light, and he had none to help him with his mission. Furthermore, the archers had received word from Greatwing—leader of the eagles—that Seymour had departed from Gaia; and he informed them of the possibility of war coming soon upon Bolteras. So Meridas sent word to all the neighboring towns and toiled endlessly to train his soldiers, and the work was taxing. But with much discipline and patience, the archers learned to use some of the powers of Elúvías, and they favored a certain ability called the *Light Arrow*: it was a power that allowed them to coat their arrows in a shroud of white light, and it made the darts strong enough to penetrate any armor. They trained night and day in shifts and most had mastered the Light Arrow by the end of May, but there were some who struggled and did not master many of the lessons. Meridas tried as he could to teach those still lacking in understanding; but there were too many and he could not train them properly.

Then the seventh of June came to the archers of the Lonely Forest, and they had the honor of greeting a group of unexpected recruits. Rolo and Pakko had returned to Vallicore with Zoro and his men from Fort Leaf during the month of May. After meeting with the Stewards of Bolteras, they departed with the archers from Treehouse to join Meridas and his faction in the Lonely Forest. With them also came Alfred son of Winslet. The bitterness the archers of the Lonely Forest had once felt towards Zoro—for he was the cause of their beloved Elko's death—melted away when they met, and there was a warm welcome given to him and his comrades. They feasted for many hours that night and began their work again the next day. Zoro and Rolo worked closely together with the soldiers who were still lacking and trained them successfully in the arts of Elúvías. Meridas

277

observed Zoro and his teachings in admiration and named Eagle-Eye his new captain under Genrig. Rolo was made a leader of a smaller unit of archers and was once again addressed as *Leader,* for he was greatly respected by those under him. Pakko worked hard to help as he could, but he was often ignored or given menial tasks for he was still young in the eyes of the older men. As a result, he worked even harder to earn his recognition. After two weeks of living amongst Meridas and his kin, all the newcomers were gladly welcomed as fellow archers of the Lonely Forest.

Peace was in all the land of Bolteras during the month of June with not a single disturbance that was any cause for alarm. But the quiet provided them no comfort as the tension of the impending war grew with every passing moment. With the extra help, Meridas commanded some of his archers to ascend the Sage's Mountain and scout the land from its high peaks and to give and receive reports from the eagles of the mountains. Rolo led his division to the northeastern border—where Edgar and Grinshawl began their journey with Seymour into the land of Vash'ala—and kept watch over the land near the Roaring River. With the eastern and western borders now heavily guarded, Meridas was able to station most of his bowmen at the cliffs overlooking the Valley of Despair. There was no border between Bolteras and Vash'ala that was left unguarded by the archers of the Lonely Forest.

In the mundane hours of the day, they whittled many arrows of wood even though they already had a large supply delivered to them from Cayrngras. It helped to pass the time at first but the days passed slowly, and they grew weary and anxious waiting for a war they were reluctant to fight. Arthur's plan for trench warfare had failed, for the stony ground of Vash'ala was too sturdy to dig. Even with the oxen and horses put to the plow, there was no way to carry out the plan, so Meridas sent the creatures back to Vallicore with a messenger to deliver his report to the stewards. Upon receiving the news, Tom and Arthur hastily began to devise new strategies. In the end, they failed to find a new tactic; and so they prayed for the warriors, all the while hoping that Elúvías would be enough to bring them victory.

As the days elapsed, Meridas focused more of his watch upon the Valley of Despair—the vastly stretching gorge of stony land where many Boltians fell during the war with Vash'ala twenty years ago—that rested at the foot of the Sage's Mountain within the borders of Vash'ala, as an uncanny feeling roused him from his sleep. Not long after, dark clouds began to form in the distance and lightning hissed all throughout the arid lands of the Desolate Plains; the booms of thunder that followed were deafening and often kept the Boltian archers awake at night.

A few weeks passed before the approaching billows reached the lands of Bolteras, and it was at that time that the land began to tremor beneath the archers' feet. Then, in the last week of July, the sun was completely blotted out, and their only sources of light came from the violent streaks of lightning flickering from the dark clouds above and also from their lanterns. The archers stationed at the Sage's Mountain returned to Meridas' bivouac as they could no longer see from the mountain's peaks. Restlessness and panic filled their ranks. Meridas tried to console them but to no avail. Then during one night, or day—which it was, they could not tell—they heard a sound in the distance that troubled them greatly: it was the sound of many footsteps crashing upon the ground and the loud clanking of armor. They peered into the seemingly endless mass of shadows, but it was too dark to see the source of the noise. Moment's later, horns blared from the midst of the chaos. Meridas and his men watched vigilantly and with great anticipation, but still the lands were too dark to see. Then, lightning branched out across the sky, and they could see many forms illuminated in the Valley of Despair below them.

'The day has come,' Meridas shouted through the ranks. 'An army approaches! Send word to Rolo and his division to return here quickly!' Genrig volunteered to deliver the report to Rolo and took with him a small battalion of archers. 'Stay vigilant!' Meridas shouted to his frightened comrades. 'Light torches! See if you can spot the enemy!' Fires sprung up all throughout the ranks with no delay, and the soldiers held them near the cliffs overlooking the Valley of Despair. Still all was pitch black from the dark clouds passing overhead, and there was a strange feeling amongst the Boltian archers that made them feel as though they were being watched. Suddenly, lightning hissed and crackled above and for a moment they could see the approaching army once again; but none could see how many their numbers were or how close they were. Meridas fitted an arrow to his bowstring and released his Mana onto it, and the dart shone a bright white. He loosed the arrow and observed as the light grew ever fainter as it flew through the air. By the time the arrow had struck the ground, Meridas could see nothing.

'I cannot tell how far away they are, but my arrow has struck only ground,' he called with a wavering voice. 'Wherever they are, my arrow cannot reach them, so we still have some time!' The lightning crackled once again, and the archers saw strange shadows amidst the trees: they did not belong to the trees but rather to creatures, tiny ones at that.

'What are they?' a voice hollered from the ranks. Suddenly, several voices whined and wailed in agony. Lightning crashed again, and the soldiers found several of their comrades dead upon the ground. The light faded and more screams echoed in the darkness. Fear and anxiety overtook the soldiers of Bolteras and many fled in fear to the south, some stumbling as they ran. At that time, Genrig returned with Rolo and his group of archers, and several cries echoed throughout the woods once more.

'Retreat,' Meridas hollered, 'Retreat and find light! We cannot see our enemy. Retreat to the south or we will all be killed this night!' At once the archers fled in panic, and there was much chaos. Many crashed into their comrades; some into trees; and others still tripped upon roots as they fled for their lives. Some panicked and abandoned their bows to save their lives, carrying only their swords now at their sides. Shrill laughter echoed all around them, and the Imps of Darkness poured upon them like waves crashing upon the shore. Many cried for help as they were brutally beaten and stabbed to death, but their comrades ignored them and wept with regret as they escaped. The remaining archers emerged from the forest by the dozens and were relieved to see the light of day before them. The dark clouds of the Enemy seemed to stop mysteriously over the edge of the forest.

Meridas darted forth into the light and rallied his troops with the help of Genrig. Rolo and Zoro joined them quickly, and the rest of the troops fell in line. 'Where is Pakko?' Rolo cried. 'Pakko, where are you?' There was no reply; Pakko had never emerged from the woods. He searched for Pakko throughout the ranks for several minutes before a shadow crept out of the woods: it was an Imp, and many of its kin soon followed. Rolo was filled with rage and loosed an arrow into the head of the first Imp, and it vanished like a wisp of smoke caught up in the wind. He continued to fire without orders until all his darts had been loosed at his enemies.

The Imps continued to emerge from the woods in large numbers, and the clouds began to move in front of them as if they were meant to protect the Imps by veiling their presence. The archers who fled without their bows stood at the front line with Meridas at the lead. 'Ready your bows!' he shouted with fresh sweat falling from his brow. 'Attack,' he called as the Imps began to advance. Hundreds of bows twanged as the archers loosed their darts, and a horde of Imps were slain in that instant. But still the enemy emerged from the forest, and they screeched and snarled with their jagged daggers in hand. 'Keep up the attack!' The archers attacked until every arrow had been used from their quivers, and the Imps fell by the hundreds. Then, they drew their swords and prepared for the waves of approaching enemies.

The Men swung in rhythm and slew the first and second waves, but the rest of the creatures halted at the edge of the forest. Meridas and his men watched anxiously, but the enemy would not advance. Then, a single Draemhas emerged arrayed in black armor tainted with the stain of blood. He raised his head and roared loudly before charging at the cowering Men, and the Imps followed at a swifter pace. Meridas answered with a battle cry that was deep and strong, and his comrades felt empowered with courage. The Men raced forth and met the approaching enemy with many clashes of swords. They fought with great zeal as they carried the anger of losing their friends and slew the enemies quickly, all but the Draemhan leader who sneered and scoffed at the Men.

The dark clouds above began to grow lighter as if a curse had been broken with the defeat of the Imps, and thin rays of light poured through the dense shroud of gloom. The Draemhas leader swung his large sword violently, and the Men of Bolteras shirked and shrunk back in fear. Meridas stepped forward to face the demon, and his sword met the Draemhas' with a loud clink and many dancing sparks. The Draemhas kicked Meridas, and the archer-captain fell dazed upon the ground. As the enemy raised his sword for the kill, the Men of Bolteras summoned their courage and surrounded the monster. They quickly grabbed hold of its arms before it could attack and forced it to the ground. Rolo came forward with anger and sadness in his heart and beheaded the Draemhas as it struggled upon the ground; he then held its head high for all to see. The archers answered with boisterous shouts of joy to accompany their victory.

'The Draemhan force has been vanquished!' Meridas shouted proudly. 'But many have fallen because of them,' he continued in a sad voice. 'We must signal for the forces of Bolteras to assemble or else the Vash'alan warriors will destroy us all! Leave the forest for now. I promise you, we will return to bury our dead!'

But the victory was insignificant to Rolo. Instead of obeying Meridas' order, he darted forth back into the forest without a word. As he disappeared into the shadows of the woods, he shouted, 'Pakko! Pakko! Where are you?' Meridas turned about in panic as he heard the voice of his companion fading in the distance. Then a noise rang in their ears and sent chills down their spines: it was the sound of deep, bellowing horns sounding from the woods to the northwest.

'That horn belongs to the Vash'alan scum!' Meridas hollered. 'Genrig, where are you now?'

The archer captain quickly presented himself before the archer-leader and bowed humbly. He then said in his stuttering speech, 'Here I am, sir, alive and well.'

'Good, good. I need you to lead our forces to Cayrngras. That will be the first fortress the Vash'alans will assault, so we must warn our brethren! Surely they will not lead a senseless attack upon Vallicore lest they all die in vain. Inform Paladin and the forces of Cayrngras to rise to arms and assure the preparations for battle ere the enemy falls upon them.'

'I will not l-leave you, s-sir. S-send s-someone e—'

'Fool! I will not argue with you. Go at once. Those are your orders. And send messengers to Bram and the other nearby towns and call for aid! Eagle-Eye Zoro, I have need of your assistance. I will need your eyesight!' Zoro stepped forward willingly with his sword at his side. Meridas sprinted forth into the woods in pursuit of Rolo with Zoro at his heel.

As Genrig led the remaining archers to Cayrngras, he counted their losses: two hundred and twelve were missing from their ranks. 'We have lost many. Only four hundred thirty-two remain that I can count,' he spoke quietly to himself. Another echo of horns sounded, and the Vash'alan troops began to emerge from the woods; the ground quaked beneath them once again. A volley of arrows whined through the air, but they fell short of the Boltian archers. 'We must hurry!' Genrig shouted. At once, the Boltian archers withdrew to the mighty fortress as quickly as their tired legs could carry them.

* * *

In the woods, light was returning and Rolo beheld the disturbing sight of his slain brethren, some belonging to his tribe from Treehouse. He wept as he ran and continued to cry out Pakko's name. The bodies of his dead comrades were bloodied and maimed, and his mind was filled with discouragement, for he feared he would find Pakko dead. With one last desperate ploy, he raised his head high and shouted out his friend's name. He wished so greatly to know Pakko's fate that he did not care if the Vash'alan soldiers discovered him. Several fathoms to his right, he heard a faint cough and a panicked whimper respond to his cry. Rolo sprinted towards the sound and found Pakko lying against a tree. The boy was beaten and covered in blood.

'Pakko, wake up, lad! Speak to me, friend!' Pakko squinted at Rolo and smiled weakly but then fell unconscious. 'Stay with me, Pakko! Hearken to me!' Suddenly, an arrow whistled through the air and struck the tree where Pakko rested. Rolo leapt backward in fear. Again, an arrow whined at him from the west, but he evaded and then pulled Pakko behind the tree. He peered about whence the arrow came and saw many Vash'alan troops—twenty-five in all—marching towards him. Five of the soldiers darted ahead of the others with swords drawn, and Rolo drew his sword to meet them. He stepped out from behind the tree to defend his fallen friend and roared loudly. He was blinded by his rage. An arrow soared at him, but he parried and the dart toppled onto the ground behind him.

The enemies had nearly overtaken Rolo when Meridas and Zoro arrived and ambushed them. They slew two before they were noticed, and Rolo leapt forward to slay a third. Without hesitating, Meridas and Zoro continued their attack and disposed of the last two. 'Did you find Pakko?' Meridas asked.

Forgetting about the enemy archers, Rolo answered, 'Yes, he is behind that tree. I do not know if he is alive. He fell unconscious but a moment ago.' Suddenly, several arrows flew through the air and struck the ground near the three Men. 'Quickly, get behind the trees!'

'We have no time to wait,' Meridas called as they jumped behind the trees for protection. 'Grab Pakko and let us leave this place as quickly as we may! If we hurry, then perhaps we can still reach Cayrngras before it is overrun.' The Vash'alan bowmen halted several fathoms away and sounded their horns. Moments later, many more soldiers appeared in crimson armor with swords drawn and advanced upon Meridas and the others. Zoro peered at his wounded grandson and bit his lip angrily until blood seeped out of it.

'Go,' he shouted. 'Get Pakko to safety. And do not think for a moment of arguing with me! I may have never been there for the lad before, but I am here now. I may never atone for all my sins, but I will protect my grandson with my life! This will be my last stand and my reparation for my evil deeds! Now go before they finish what they began! The others need you. I still have some fight left in me! Let me slay as many as I can and buy you enough time to escape.' After hesitating for a moment, Meridas picked Pakko off of the ground and placed him over his shoulder. Rolo knelt beside Zoro and embraced the man before pursuing Meridas and Pakko.

'Do not die yet!' Rolo called as he ran. 'I have not given you permission to do so!'

Zoro chuckled. He raised his sword before him and took a deep breath. He spun around the tree and drove his sword deep into the chest of one of the Vash'alan warriors. His blade stuck deep in his enemy's armor, and he was unable to remove it. Without a moment's hesitation, he released his sword and grabbed the blade of his enemy. Lunging forward, he slashed at another, but his attack did not end there. He raised the sword over his head and slung it at his next foe as an arrow whistled and struck him in his leg. Zoro moaned and crashed upon the ground grasping at his leg. His enemies slowly approached with weapons pointed at him.

Zoro blinked and softly said, 'So this is the end, is it?' He accepted death and closed his eyes as he anticipated his enemies' blades piercing his skin; but at that moment, many arrows screeched past the layers of trees and struck the Vash'alans where they stood. Seconds later, many more arrows whistled through the trees and struck the Vash'alan archers in the distance. One of the enemy swordsmen had survived the first volley, and he leapt upon Zoro; but a spear flew through the air and struck him before he could land the final blow. Zoro opened his eyes in his confusion and beheld many soldiers in crimson armor slain upon the ground. 'I am saved!' he panted. He rolled and looked about for his rescuers and was shocked by who he saw: there before him stood Tristan the Prince of Bolteras with his band of Boltian warriors and Delitas, the former Vash'alan soldier. Delitas was looking down and sneering at his once-brethren who were now slain upon the forest ground.

'Hey, ho, how do you do?' the vivacious prince exclaimed. 'I always arrive on time, unlike my uncle. That is why I will be a better king one day,' he said arrogantly. 'I do say that is a nasty wound you have there, good sir. Come brave soldiers and help this man! Break the arrow in his leg and relieve some of his pain.' Two soldiers assisted Zoro as Rolo and Meridas returned with Pakko.

284

'Ho, hey, who is t—' He paused not expecting to see Pakko so wounded and near to death. Great sadness overcame him, and his lively conduct turned to gloom. 'Is young Pakko alive?'

'Aye, Sire, he is,' Meridas replied, 'but only by a thread does he hang on to his life. We must have his wounds tended to or else he w—'

'That is enough out of you,' Tristan snapped. 'I have gone through far too much excitement to be distraught over this! Place him on the ground; I will heal his wounds.'

'Tristan, there is a cost to using the healing powers of Elúvías,' Meridas returned.

'Do you think I am ignorant of the cost?' Tristan snapped. 'If there is a price, I will gladly pay it! He is my friend, and that is all the reason I need to save him.' Meridas laid Pakko on a bed of leaves, and Tristan scanned the boy's battered body: there were gashes and bruises across his torso and teeth marks in his neck. He rested his hands above the wounds in Pakko's chest and stomach and calmly closed his eyes. A warm, white light spread out from his palms and covered the boy's body. To the amazement of those watching, the wounds miraculously sealed leaving only scars as evidence of Pakko's injuries. Being drained of his Mana, Tristan swooned and fell to the ground. He appeared now slightly older—but only if one looked upon him closely. He had become much stronger in his time away, so the use of leechcraft had little effect on his body. Rolo and Meridas came to his aid and sat him upon the stump of a collapsed tree. Tristan did not mind its discomfort as his fatigue was great.

'Someone bring me something to eat. I am famished and must replenish my energy.' One of the Boltian soldiers withdrew a bag full of food and handed it to the prince. Tristan ate a slice of bread gratefully and guzzled down some water to quench his thirst. Several minutes after being healed, Pakko coughed and opened his eyes. He was rather perplexed by his sudden rousing. He quickly examined his body and was alarmed to find his wounds were healed.

'W-where am I? And what happened to me? Last I remember a great darkness overcame me. I remember seeing Rolo coming to my aid just before I closed my eyes.'

'You are well now, lad,' Rolo answered him. 'Prince Tristan has rescued you from the clutches of death.'

Pakko looked upon the face of the worn out prince: his eyes were closed and his head hung tiredly as though sleep had evaded him for days. Delitas approached Tristan and gently lifted him from the ground. 'Wake up, Tristan! There is not a moment to spare. Lo! My former kin march along the road to Cayrngras! Alas! I rue the day that I was born under the flag of the sun-worshippers! Their hearts are filled with great evils, and they will destroy everything in their path. I beg you, Prince Tristan, wake up!'

Tristan stirred and lifted his head and gave it a good shake. His long locks fell upon his shoulders, and he stood. His regal appearance had faded, but he still spoke with great authority. 'I will go,' he said as though a question was posed, 'I will go to Cayrngras. Delitas, I would have you go with me, for I trust you greatly, but I shall not take any others. This will be a mission that requires secrecy, and we cannot accomplish it if we all go together. If they see all our numbers, then they will certainly take notice and kill us before we arrive. I know of an escape route in Cayrngras; its entrance is at the bottom of an old wine cellar in the fortress and leads to an old mining route nigh the Canyon of Gold. I believe we can evacuate the city safely if we hurry, but there is no time to spare. I will make certain that we put up a fight in Cayrngras, as best we may, until we can fight no more, and I will assure the safety of as many as I can manage. Then, I will be certain to lead them to Bram, where the rest of you will be waiting for us. That is where we shall take our true stand against them! I leave it in your hands, Meridas, to lead the rest of these brave soldiers until I arrive. Tend to the wounded here in the forest and transport them safely to Bram if you are able. But do not draw the enemy's attention. And take this injured man with you and tend to his wounds; remove the arrow if you are able and see if he can still fight.

'If we arrive safely, I will make certain our stand in Cayrngras lasts no longer than the night; I give you my word. And these are your orders as soldiers of Bolteras. Until my uncle arrives, I will temporarily assume control of the armies of Bolteras. Are there any objections?' None opposed Prince Tristan; instead, they appeared quite pleased to listen to his commands. At once, Tristan's guard began to scour the forest for survivors—those who survived numbered four counting Pakko. When they had gathered their belongings, they traveled to Bram in a slow and desperate procession, but they were out of harm's way, for the armies of Vash'ala had their eyes set on the mighty fortress of Cayrngras.

Before Tristan and Delitas had gone far, Meridas returned with downcast eyes. 'Sire, my archers have retreated to Cayrngras to defend the city. I am afraid I made a poor decision by sending them there. Please, rescue them at all cost! If you will not take me with you, at least give me your word that they will live on.'

'Aye, Meridas, I give you my word. You are a great leader. I will honor you and do all I can to save every last one of your archers.' Meridas bowed and darted away after the company departing to Bram.

* * *

Tristan and Delitas darted southwest out of the forest across the plains of the dale towards Cayrngras. In the distance, they saw the stronghold under siege with soldiers of Vash'ala on all sides. 'How will we make it past so vast an army?' Delitas asked doubtfully.

'We will find a way. Believe in the soldiers of Cayrngras. There is a reason their refuge lies so close to enemy lands. They are strong, but pray still that Vaaspar's Light will shine upon us. We will need His blessing if we are to make it safely into the stronghold.'

The two proceeded closer to the fortress with caution, but there was no sign of hope for their entry into Cayrngras. The way was blocked by thousands of Vash'alan troops surrounding the bastion. To make matters worse, the dark clouds of the Enemy spread across the sky above the city, and the last light of the sun was fading within the shadows. Tristan knew his opportunity would be lost if no light remained to guide their way. 'What can we do, Delitas? This is hopeless! I was not expecting all sides to be overwhelmed so soon!'

'You are a clever man, Tristan. Hold true to yourself. You will find a way!'

He thought for a moment but nothing came to mind. He watched as the Vash'alan armies raised ladders upon the fortress walls and began to ascend onto the parapets above. Loud bangs of the enemy's battering rams echoed from the doors of the citadel as the Boltian forces desperately loosed arrow upon arrow to push back the advancing force.

'I have one idea, but it is risky,' he said at last. Delitas looked up with hope. 'We could sneak upon them and climb their ladders quickly. Perhaps we can take advantage of the chaos and reach the top of the walls before they realize we are enemies. Otherwise, we must travel to the far end of the miner's tunnel leading to the wine cellar in the city. But I am afraid we will arrive too late if we follow that path. So what say you?'

287

Delitas was not pleased with Tristan's plan, and his displeasure was revealed by his wrinkled brow. 'That is madness! Forgive my rudeness, but a plan of that intricacy will never succeed. Cayrngras is lost to us! Let us flee to Bram and rally the other strongholds to arms.'

'That will simply not do! I cannot abandon these good people. Uncle Edgar would never abandon his soldiers, and I will carry that honor through the generations! Fear not, good Delitas. Look now to the southern wall. The forces are weakest there. Surely the soldiers there are only meant to be a distraction. And see now to the north! Hundreds, no, thousands wait at the gates of Cayrngras for entry, but it seems the gates have not been breached yet. The soldiers will not be able to hold the fortress for long, so let us go to their aid! And let us use the hills of the land to veil our presence as we draw nearer. When the forces at the rear have been reduced, we will call upon our soldiers and identify ourselves. They will allow us quick entry through the back door or else we will climb upon the enemy's ladders and lead the people through the mines. Cayrngras will surely fall, but we must not let its people fall with it!'

'You never fail to impress me, good prince. You are both droll and stupid; but you are also brave, so I must commend you for that. I suppose that is our only chance, if chance we have. If you lead, I will certainly follow wherever you go.'

'I am glad to hear that. You are a good friend, Delitas. It is a surprise that you are a former soldier of Vash'ala. I commend you for leaving your wretched country for the good of all Men. On my honor, I will not let you die this day. Better yet, I will not let you fall until you have seen your country liberated from the threat of the Draemhas and restored to a land of honor and glory. I give you my word.'

Delitas bowed graciously before Tristan. 'I will serve you as either servant or ally to the end of it all. And if we survive, I will make Vash'ala an honorable land that will never trouble Bolteras again as long as I rule. Of that, you have my word. Shall we?'

'Indeed we shall!' Tristan said eagerly. They descended down a long slope towards the besieged city's southern end, ever warily but fully ready for whatever evil awaited them. They passed behind many small knolls along the way and arrived at last behind a large hill just a furlong away from the southern wall. They looked on with anticipation as the Vash'alan troops to the south were slain

slowly by the archers on the parapets within the city, but there
seemed to be no way for them to enter.

Chapter XVIII

One Worthy of Kingship

Tristan and Delitas waited patiently at the bottom of the hill only a furlong from the southern wall of Cayrngras. An hour had passed since they arrived, and they watched as the mighty warriors of the city gallantly defended against the Vash'alan assault. But Tristan could tell the soldiers were growing weary, and their hope was beginning to fade. The volley of arrows from the defenders had ceased, for they had no more darts to loose upon the wicked Men from the north. The Vash'alans, however, still had a large supply of arrows, and they loosed them in great numbers upon the defenders. One by one the protectors of Cayrngras began to fall; even some of the civilians within the walls fell by the enemy darts. At last, Tristan could bear it no longer. He rose and sprinted towards the wall, and Delitas sprung forth after him. Nearing the gate, Tristan waved his hands and shouted, 'Champions of Cayrngras! Hearken to me! It is I, Prince Tristan. Hearken to me!' The guards on the wall looked and beheld their loveable prince. 'I have come with my friend, Delitas! Let us in through the back gate!' At the sound of Tristan's cries, the Vash'alan troops turned and set their gaze upon the Prince of Bolteras.

'We are doomed, Tristan!' Delitas lamented. 'They have turned their eyes upon us! There are too many for us to fight alone!' Tristan looked about with uncertainty as the enemy withdrew from the southern wall and advanced upon them. But suddenly, the back gate of the fortress flung open, and a hundred strong Boltian warriors fell upon the Vash'alans. Several more stood on the parapets above and hurled their spears at the enemy troops. Soon, the fields to the south of the city were blanketed by the bodies of their enemies. At that moment, many of the Vash'alans fell back, and a path was cleared for Tristan and Delitas to pass safely into the fortress. The Boltian guards slammed the doors behind them and barred them quickly just as the Vash'alan reinforcements arrived. The wicked Men beat angrily on the gates and continued to raise ladders onto the fortress walls, but the Boltians were quick to knock them down. Tristan and Delitas hurried to the aid of the defenders, and within minutes, all the ladders were removed from the castle walls. The Boltians began to rest and recover, for the Vash'alans' attack was delayed for the moment.

'By Vaaspar's great white beard,' a soldier exclaimed as they came into the light, 'it really is you! What are you doing here, lad? You should not have risked your lives coming here!'

'I only did what Uncle Edgar would have done! But never mind that; this is not the time for explanations! Who is in charge here?'

'Paladin is our leader, of course.'

'Paladin is here? I thought his orders were to round up the armies of Bolteras.'

'Aye, those were his orders, but he returned to his hometown to find rest for a while. Already he enlisted the troops of Poleden and Carg, where Ragnok and Hauffa had failed. Hauffa and Ragnok gained the loyalty of Pilias, but Balas still remains unspoken for. And there are still many smaller villages scattered about who refuse to join our cause. I am afraid that is all I know, Your Highness.'

'Very well, soldier, back to your duties. Keep these ladders from the walls at all cost; burn them if you must! But tell me first, where is Paladin?'

'He is at the northern wall aiding the defense of the gates. With your leave, Sire, I will return to the battle.'

'Yes, I thank you, good soldier. Go at once!' Tristan led Delitas through the middle of the city and pressed on with haste toward the northern wall. The dark clouds above grew wider and thicker, and lightning began to hiss within it once again. As the darkness spread beyond the fortress walls, rain began to fall, and the water quickly doused the torches of the defenders. The soldiers had hardly prepared their torches before the rain quickly extinguished the flames. Tristan looked back and shouted, 'Push the ladders down! Pour oil upon the ground below and set the ladders ablaze in the fields! That will keep them at bay! Do not let them overcome us!' At once, the soldiers obeyed, and they poured large barrels of oil onto the grass below. Moments later, large fires ignited along the west, east and southern walls and the Vash'alan armies retreated back to the north. Their ladders were set afire, and the Boltians were greatly encouraged, for their enemy had been delayed once more.

'Who gives orders to my troops?' a voice called from the northern gate.

'It is I, Tristan Prince of Bolteras. Tell me your name soldier!'

'You are mighty arrogant these days, Tristan fool!' the voice answered. Tristan recognized the voice at once. 'Get down here, lad, and help me hold these gates.'

'Paladin, I am glad you are safe!'

'Safe you say? I may be alive, but safe I am not! Save the reunions for later, laddie. We barely cling to our lives as we speak! If not for those brave archers from the north, we would be overrun!'

'Archers you say?'

'Aye, they belong to Meridas' faction. But all our arrows are spent, and they grow weary from battle. They were led here by Genrig their captain, and it is only by their bravery that we have lasted so long. They are resting in the western courtyard now.'

'I will go to them, but I shall return quickly. Delitas, my friend, assist Paladin and his men in the holding of the gates while I am away.' Delitas nodded and quickly ran forward and joined the ranks of defenders with Paladin at his lead. Tristan made his way to the western court where Genrig and his soldiers rested. 'Oi, Genrig! I have come to you by Meridas' command to bring you to safety. I will need your help to bring all the peoples of Cayrngras safely to Bram.'

'Your Majesty,' Genrig said in his usual speech as he rose from his seat. 'Sire, it has been many years since I saw you last, and it is a pleasure to stand before you now. Meridas bravely risked his life for our brethren, and I am relieved to hear he is alive! I would very much like to see him again.'

'Still you stutter after all these years, Genrig? I have no time for your delays in speech!' Tristan snapped. At that moment, Tristan peered intently into Genrig's eyes and perceived something evil in them. 'What have you done, Genrig? Your eyes reveal the powers of Darkness at work. Tell me snake!'

'Sire, I assure you, I know not what it is you speak of,' he said still stuttering.

'I know you have done something, and I will figure it out. Why have the Vash'alans attacked us so soon and how were we caught off guard? Have you betrayed your country? Answer me!' Genrig began to laugh queerly: it was deeper than his manner of speaking and vile in nature.

'Betrayed my country you say?' he said without a falter in his words. His stuttering speech had ceased, and his voice was now clear and sharp. 'I would *never* betray *my* people! Bolteras is not my country, Tristan Prince! I was born in Vash'ala and have been living amongst you repulsive Boltians for all these years. I was sent to deceive you all, and I have accomplished my goal!' He laughed again more maniacally and harshly than before. 'And now I get to see the glorious day of my people overcoming your frail kingdom!'

Tristan gritted his teeth and scoffed. 'What reward did they promise you, Genrig?'

'For all my faithful years of service to the Dark Lord, I was promised that I would be made king of any land of my choosing when the strength of Men has failed at last! And all I had to do was deceive you and pretend to be your ally. When I learned that the Celebhas of the Sage's Mountain had discovered the Draemhan's course of action and passed it on to the rest of Bolteras by word of his scouts, I informed my brethren. From time to time, I would slip away from my station in the Lonely Forest, and the Imps of Darkness would meet with me in secret. I passed on my report, and they were quite pleased to hear of the Celebhas' discovery!' He laughed again and Tristan grew very irate. The archers of the Lonely Forest were troubled and heartbroken by this sudden news, and a few rose and drew their swords. 'It was I, Prince Tristan, who suggested this assault. All these things occurred to weaken the forces of Bolteras! The real war has yet to be waged on this accursed, greedy land! And when all my kinsmen are dead, I will be crowned King of Vash'ala with a legion of Draemhas under my command!' Some of the archers under Genrig raised their blades to strike him down.

'Stop,' Tristan intervened. 'I will handle this traitor. I have had enough out of you, Genrig! You have betrayed those closest to you and have deceived those you falsely called friends. As Prince and acting King of Bolteras, I hereby sentence you to a painful death!'

At Tristan's declaration, Genrig grinded his teeth and several of them cracked from the pressure. He drew his blade and leapt upon Tristan, but the prince eluded his attack and swiftly sliced at the traitor's arm. Genrig wailed in agony as his hand and sword crashed upon the white stone of the courtyard in a pool of blood. 'You are a foolish orphan!' he snapped as he writhed in anguish upon the ground. 'You are not worthy to be a king; nay, you are not even worthy of being a prince! Your father and mother hated you and left you for dead! You are scum, a worthless worm! And you will not steal my inheritance away from me!'

293

'My father and mother may have abandoned me and I may be a worthless worm, but I pity the vile creature that bore you into this world! Snake! You shall be punished for your treachery.'

'Do your worst, foolish prince. Meridas gave me orders to send word to the surrounding fortresses, but I ignored his command. No reinforcements will come to you. And soon, my kin will pour through the gates and end your miserable lives! Then I shall be saved and gain all the favor of the Dark Lord!'

'What kind of death shall I give you, knave?' Tristan asked ignoring Genrig's babbling. 'Aha! I know the perfect punishment!' Tristan grabbed Genrig by the hair and dragged the wretched man behind him into the central courtyard and then led him beyond to the northern wall. Hearing the screams of Genrig behind him, Paladin turned and beheld the ruthless scene.

'Tristan, what are you doing with Genrig? Release him at once!' Paladin called anxiously.

'I am not a cruel man, brave Paladin! A traitor simply gets what he deserves. Indeed, he shall reap what he has sown!'

'Genrig is a traitor?' Paladin replied sadly. He followed Tristan as he led Genrig up the stairway onto the northern walls. From the walls, Tristan saw the vast armies of Vash'ala stretching far and wide. The fires around the castle had been put out, and the fortress was bombarded on all sides once more. The Vash'alans beat fervently and ferociously on the gates with their battering rams, but the sturdy doors held with the aid of the defenders of Cayrngras.

Tristan turned his eyes back on the pitiable man beside him and said, 'Well, Genrig, what are your finals words?' Genrig opened his mouth to speak but Tristan interrupted, 'Fool! I do not care what you have to say!' and he pushed the disloyal man over the edge of the parapet. Genrig crashed upon the ground below and was violently trampled under the feet of his alleged allies. Tristan spit down at the body of the crushed man and then returned to the foot of the gate.

'Sire, I had no idea,' Paladin said with regret.

'None of us did. Do not blame yourself. Let us be thankful that his treachery did not cause more harm! There is still hope, Paladin. The time has come for us to evacuate the city through the tunnels!'

'I cannot, Sire; you ask too much! This is my hometown and I cannot a—'

'Enough!' Tristan retorted. 'Be brave, but be not foolish! We must abandon the city for now. I need you for this mission, Paladin.

The people of this city respect you greatly. Go to them and lead them to safety! I give you my word, we *will* reclaim this city! It will only be overrun for a short time. Trust me and do what I ask of you.'

'I will abide by your orders, Your Highness, but how will we get my people to safety and still defend the gates?'

'I will have you lead your people through the abandoned mines adjoined to the old wine cellars in the southwest sector of the city. We will appoint some to hold the gates until all the people have escaped safely; then we will pull back as quickly as we can. There may be some losses, but we must save as many as possible.'

'Aye, I know the way through the tunnels well. I will go and gather the civilians of Cayrngras with your leave, Your Highness.' Tristan dismissed the man with a wave of his hand and then climbed upon the walls once again. He gazed out upon the armies of Vash'ala just as a cascade of arrows fell upon the city. Tristan hid himself behind the parapet and evaded the attack, but ten of the defenders were not so blessed. *Bang. Bang.* The enemy continued to strike the gates with their wooden rams. The defenders toiled endlessly to hold the gates, but the doors began to crack; and the Vash'alan warriors thrust their spears through gaps in the broken frames. Still the warriors of Cayrngras refused to relinquish their defense, and they countered their enemies with many thrusts of their own weapons.

'We cannot hold the gates much longer!' one of the warriors called. Tristan leapt from the walls into the marble courtyard and sought out Paladin, who had withdrawn to the southwest corner of the fortress with the civilians to the basement of a pub where the old mines connected to the city. When he arrived, there were hundreds of people waiting patiently to pass down the stairs and through the passageway below.

'Paladin,' Tristan called, 'get these people through the passage with haste! We need to evacuate the soldiers before they break through the walls!'

'Yes, yes, I am aware! But we must guide the people carefully lest we bring the old walls of the mines crashing down upon us! Go and assist my men. I will rejoin you when I am able.'

'I am counting on you. Do not fail me!' Paladin nodded and returned to maintaining order as the masses of people slowly passed from the city down into the mines. Tristan returned to the western court where the archers of the Lonely Forest sat; they appeared dejected and confused. 'Rise men! Your captain was a traitor, but you are still honorable people. You must evacuate the city with the civilians at once. We will retreat to Bram and make our stand against the Vash'alans there!' The archers remained still, and Tristan pitied them. He pleaded with them for several minutes more but to no avail and then withdrew in intense anger and sadness back to the aid of his comrades.

'Tristan,' Delitas called from the northern gates, 'we cannot hold these gates any longer. We must flee ere they break through to the city!'

Tristan quickly helped with the fortification of the gates. 'It will not be much longer...I hope.' Suddenly, several cries of alarm echoed from the southern wall.

'They have brought rams upon the southern gate!' a soldier cried in distress. 'The door is breaking!' At once Tristan sped away, and the archers of the Lonely Forest met him in the central courtyard. He stared at them for a moment and then smiled, for they were all armed and ready for battle.

'You may be archers, but I have heard great stories of your skills with a sword. Your Meridas is a man of great talent and has trained you well. I will trust you with this task so go now and hold the gates! Do not let them within these walls!' The archers sped off without a word.

'Prince Tristan,' Paladin cried from behind the group of passing archers, 'the last of the civilians are proceeding through the mines as we speak. I have sent many of my soldiers to guide them to safety, and they have lit torches within the tunnels along the way. But the light will not last for long, so send these archers through the mines at once. They are of little use to us without their arrows.'

'You are wrong,' Tristan answered. 'They are mighty warriors even with the sword!'

'Be that as it may, send them at once lest we are overrun by our enemies! Now is the time to evacuate!'

Tristan clenched his fists and yelled, 'Oi, archers of the Lonely Forest! Return to me! We must evacuate the city at once before both gates are destroyed and we all perish!' The archers reeled and rejoined Tristan in the central courtyard. 'Paladin, ready your soldiers. It is time we withdraw to Bram.'

'Sire, there is no time! The moment we release the gates, they will fall upon us like the rain from these cursed clouds! There will be no place to hide from them.' All of a sudden, lightning hissed and crackled across the sky, and one of the bolts struck the roof of a nearby house and lit it with fire. Before long, the dark clouds of the

296

Enemy returned to the land and covered the city in darkness. As their vision began to fail, the last defenders of Cayrngras were overcome with strife. 'Tristan, we have no time for idle chatter!' Paladin continued. 'Take your men and leave this city. One day, you will be King of Bolteras, so I cannot allow you to die here. I take my final stand this evening with those of my men who would fight with me. The mighty fortress Cayrngras has not been overtaken for many long years, and I will not let it fall easily under my watch! So go now and lead the people to safety.'

'No, there must be another way!'

'There is none!' Paladin scolded. 'I will not argue with a foolish prince whose mind wanders after wild fantasies! If I am to die, then I wish to die with honor for my country. This is my final wish!'

Tristan grinded his teeth and wrinkled his brow in annoyance. 'Then, I have failed! If I cannot even save my countrymen, then how will I be a worthy king? It is I who should stand here and die! What fool would choose me to rule?'

'Nay, Tristan!' Paladin retorted. 'This loss is not your mistake. There are times you have to live to fight another day. And besides, I am the one who failed to defend my people, so do not be so hard on yourself. If it were possible, Your Highness, then I would have followed you to the very end. If not for your bravery, then more of my people would have died this night. I owe you my undying gratitude. I tell you the truth, Tristan: the only man worthy of succeeding Lord Edgar is you! You have surprised us all with your recent deeds. I am honored to have known you, and I know you shall be a great king like Lord Edgar one day. Go to your people and guide them to safety. Defend them in the stronghold at Bram and win against Vash'ala; then they will follow you forevermore! You will be hailed as one worthy of kingship, and tales of you will spread all throughout the lands of Bolteras. Your Highness, you are a capable leader! Never doubt that.' Tristan began to cry, but he wiped away the tears and turned his back on Paladin. 'Prince Tristan,' Paladin called out in a softer, sadder tone, 'promise me you will reclaim my precious hometown and restore it to glory!'

Turning back, Tristan vowed, 'Not only will I do as you have asked of me, but I will tell of your bravery. You will be known as a hero by all who know your name. But do me one favor, brave knight.'

'Anything you ask of me, Sire, that I will do.'

'Slay as many of those wretches as you can!'

'Aye, milord, we will not be defeated until we have taken many of them with us to the grave.' The sound of gates creaking reverberated from both ends of the castle. 'Go Tristan! Live and succeed your uncle when the day comes. Always remember that I would have followed you proudly for all my life, if I could have lived to see that day. But alas! This is my final hour.' *Bang.* The rams crashed upon the gates and the last defense of the city began to fail.

'Delitas,' Tristan shouted at the top of his voice, 'come with me! We must leave at once!' Delitas wished good fortune upon the brave defenders of Cayrngras and then joined Tristan. The prince turned his back on Paladin one last time and said, 'I wish that I could defend this great city with you, but I know the wise decision calls for survival. Thank you for your selfless sacrifice!' Tears welled up in Paladin's eyes, but he hardened his heart and gave Tristan a good nudge in the direction of the pub.

'Farewell, friend,' were the last words Tristan ever heard from Paladin. Tristan stood his ground, but Delitas grabbed his arm and forcefully guided him towards the pub. They found their way to the entrance of the caverns, and the way was still lit with torches on the wall. Shadows from the convoy of civilians fell upon the walls as they slowly advanced forward. Before long, Tristan and Delitas joined the group and urged them to move forward at a quicker pace.

* * *

Back in the central courtyard, Paladin beckoned his soldiers to join him in arms for one final stand. Now that they were alone, some were frightened and reluctant, so he addressed them sternly. 'Those who wish to be with their families, I give you leave to go to them. Do not delay!' Several soldiers hesitated for a moment and then left eagerly, but there was one man, named Laman, who halted at the doorway to the pub and watched curiously from a distance. Paladin shook his head in disbelief, for he had only a small band of warriors remain at his side. In all, there were one hundred and twenty-three defenders left to fight the assailants, including those who barred the northern and southern gates. The walls and courtyards of the citadel were emptied now, and the city was quiet, except for the incessant banging of the battering rams. The remaining warriors gathered around Paladin and formed a wall of defense, their swords and spears aimed all about. 'Upon my order, release the gates,' he shouted. He took one final breath and exhaled slowly. The troops that fled to be with their families passed out of sight at last into the shelter of the pub. Bright bluish-white bolts of lightning shot down from the sky several times and set fire to many of the city's structures. The lord of Cayrngras wept as he saw his hometown emptied and ruined. 'Release the gates! Fall back to the central courtyard at once!'

Paladin's loyal men obeyed his command and released the gates, and the doors collapsed from their hinges almost instantly. The front line of defenders was crushed under the northern gates, and others were quickly filled with the darts and spears of their enemies. Thirteen fell at the northern gates and only ten rejoined their comrades safely at the fortress' center. Twelve more returned safely from the southern gate as it maintained its defense; but it was soon broken and the armies of Vash'ala advanced from both flanks. Within a swift moment, the last defenders of Cayrngras were surrounded, but the enemy halted and lowered their weapons. The crowds of enemy soldiers parted down the middle as a tall figure approached from the ranks to the north. A man appeared dressed in an eloquent, crimson suit of armor that was different from his companions, for there were spikes upon the pauldrons, and the helm contained horns that turned inward and held aloft at the tips a yellow, shimmering orb liking to the sun; and rather than a plume being on top, there were two snakes of black metal that seemed to slither from the back of his helm. His look was frightening to the Boltian warriors, all the more as he carried an enormous, jagged sword.

'To what do we owe the honor of being face to face with Marxas King of Vash'ala?' Paladin inquired.

The figure laughed and removed his helmet. There stood the King of Vash'ala peering down upon the Boltian regiment with vicious, yellow eyes full of hate and evil intent. 'You are mistaken. I was once Marxas King of Vash'ala, but I have been given great power from the Dark Lord. I have become a god! In your last hours, you will know me to be Sol'Czar, the Sun King! Do you fear me, mortals?' he asked in a deep, hoarse voice.

'You are a fearsome king,' Paladin answered. 'There are few, a foolish few, who do not hold you in dread.'

'You have good reason to be afraid, for soon you will know the true meaning of despair. First, we will disarm you; then, you shall feel cold steel piercing every limb of your bodies; and after you have died, we will certainly maim your bodies and hang them as a warning to all of Bolteras. None will ever desire to return to this place once they see how we have desecrated it with your blood and limbs!' He released a roaring laugh that revealed unreserved, contemptible pleasure.

Paladin clenched the hilt of his sword tightly and focused his gaze on the fearsome foe before him. Marxas met his glance and grinned terrifyingly as though the Boltian warrior posed no threat to him. The brave knight hurled his sword at the Vash'alan King, but it shattered suddenly and fell in pieces to the ground. Marxas laughed uncontrollably as a peculiar, reddish-black fog appeared around him like a protective shield wrought from the power of Darkness. Paladin stared hopelessly and fell to his knees as the leader of Vash'ala raised his mighty spear to strike.

'Alas!' Paladin cried out in despair. 'What can Men do against such untamed hatred?'

The defenders of Cayrngras tried as they could to spur their leader to battle, but he would not stir. The spear fell upon Paladin, but one of his comrades intervened with his life. Blood ran from the soldier's mouth and he spoke, 'Will you die without a fight? Show them the might of Cayrngras! Die with honor!' The captain of Cayrngras stared in horror as the body of his companion was lifted high into the air. The Vash'alan King swung his spear with ease and threw the warrior's body high and far into the midst of his army.

Paladin rose and picked up the sword of his fallen comrade. 'Attack,' he shouted, and the host of Boltian troops charged forward without delay. They battled with great ire and slew many of the Vash'alans, but the numbers of their enemy only seemed to grow as the fight waged on. Paladin charged toward Marxas at full speed, but the King of Vash'ala was quickly surrounded by a large host of his countrymen and faded from Paladin's sight. By the end of the hour, the last remnant of the forces of Cayrngras was defeated, and Paladin alone remained. As Marxas declared, the defenders were disarmed and pierced in every limb with swords or spears, and their bodies were mutilated. But the army died with honor and slew nearly a hundred enemies in the process—Paladin alone slew fifteen. Cayrngras was lost and brought to ruin, and fires raged all throughout the city. Even in solitude, Paladin continued to defend his beloved city with great courage; but the enemy grabbed hold of him and he was beheaded. Then his severed head was placed upon a spike on the northern wall just above the gates for all to see. And so Cayrngras fell under the enemy's control, but Marxas was not satisfied.

'We are not finished yet! Once the Dark Lord's clouds reach the city of Bram to the east, we will attack the Boltians once more! Rummage around. Salvage as many arrows as you can and make ready. Search every house and corner of this city! There were others here, and I will not rest until they are all dead!' Laman continued to watch and listen from the door of the pub but fled into the tunnels as the Vash'alan army began to scour the city. The great host of Men from the north ransacked the fortress, breaking and smashing as they went. Soon the whole fortress was laid to waste, and Laman heard from the tunnels the sounds of the enemy roaring, destroying and blowing their shrill horns in victory.

* * *

The path through the tunnels of the mine was long and darkening: the refugees' supply of oil was gone and only a few of the torches maintained a flame to guide them. As they strode through the corridor, Tristan and Delitas removed several unlit torches that hung on the walls of the tunnel, as many as they could carry. They trudged along tiredly until they came at last upon grassy ground. They stood now at the top of a hill at the cave's end looking down upon the legendary Canyon of Gold—named for the vast amounts of gold within its depths—below them to the south. The vast chasm extended for many leagues in between the glorious city Vallicore to the southwest and Poleden to the east. The dark clouds of the Enemy were behind them, but they remained in deep darkness for nightfall had come upon the land. Not long after emerging from the tunnels, the last light of their torches failed, and some of the people began to cry out in sorrow.

Before the company, a single path ran down the hill to the southeast and then diverged into two separate roads: one ran south to the edge of the immense canyon while the other turned about to the northeast and met the main road of Bolteras. Tristan and Delitas emerged from the tunnels and passed torches around to the travelers and urged them to light them. Tristan wanted the Vash'alans to see their torches in hopes that the light would beckon the enemy army to Bram where the Boltian warriors could stand and defeat the invading force. But the people had no oil left in their company and many were glad, for they did not desire to have the Vash'alans following them. Tristan took for himself a few of the torches and released some of his Mana over the tops of them, and orbs of light floated and shone like fire to light their way. He then strode with haste to the front of the pack and led them up the northeastern path towards Bram. Of the

301

host, there were four hundred that belonged to the archers of the Lonely Forest and another two hundred or more soldiers belonged to Cayrngras. The warriors led the group of civilians—some three hundred of women and children—just behind Tristan and Delitas. As they climbed to the top of the hill and drew near to the main road, seventeen more soldiers ran out of the mine. One shouted, 'Wait!' and the company halted. Some of the women in the caravan recognized the soldiers as their husbands and dashed to greet them with warm hugs and kisses.

'Come now,' Tristan called irately. 'You are reunited for now, but do not let that console you yet. Let us arrive safely at Bram first, and then we may have a little peace.' The party moved on reluctantly and continued on their way. The path met the main road through Bolteras and leveled out, much to the travelers' delight. There before them to the northeast was Bram standing gloriously across a vast dell. 'Continue on this path to the east,' he beckoned to the group. 'It will meet the southern road from Bram. Go at once!' Tristan then whispered to Delitas, 'Come with me for a moment, my friend.' The two left the pack and began to walk on the grass to the right of the road. 'I need a few envoys to help me with something.'

'I would be glad to help, if I may. What is the task at hand?'

'That is kind of you to offer, but I would like for you to stay with me at Bram. If I am to be king one day, then I must keep as many people safe as I can. I need you to find me messengers, light-footed ones at that. Poleden is to the south of us. We were told that Paladin had successfully recruited them to bear arms in this war, so we will call upon them. But I need a second runner to go to Vallicore and report to Elder Bowman, and another still to travel to Eordil. Since the traitor Genrig failed to obey Meridas' order, we will have to carry out the call for reinforcements. We will hold off the forces of Vash'ala in Bram until our help arrives.'

'That is a magnificent plan indeed! I will go at once.' Delitas ran to the front of the group and raised his hands. While his friend spoke to the crowd, Tristan plopped down upon the grass, for he had used too much Mana and was now exhausted from travel.

'Halt good people,' Delitas called. 'The Prince of Bolteras seeks a brave few to come forth for a special purpose. He calls for three swift-footed men. Who will go?' Two archers of the Lonely Forest stepped forth. 'Hullo, archer-folk. What are your names?'

'Engel,' said one. 'And I am Gerrin, Engel's brother,' said the other.

'And you are swift runners?'

'Aye, sir, and twin brothers too!' the two exclaimed in unison. 'There are none we have ever met who can rival us in a footrace!' Engel concluded.

'Which of you is the quickest?' The twins looked back and forth with uncertainty. 'Forget I asked that silly question; I do not wish to start a quarrel amongst you. Engel, by order of the prince, you are to go to Poleden to the south and inform them of the assault on Cayrngras; inform them also of Paladin's death and bring them to our aid in Bram. Tell them Prince Tristan calls upon them. And Gerrin, you are to go to Eordil and do the same. Is that understood?'

'Aye sir,' they answered in unison once more. Delitas gave them both a shake of the hand and sent them on their way, and the two darted away with great swiftness.

'Now who will be the third to aid the prince?' Delitas asked with his eyes set on the crowd.

'I will go,' said one of the soldiers from Cayrngras; his wife cried and begged him to stay, but he would not listen to her. 'I abandoned my brethren to be reunited with my family, and I must make amends for that. They died honorably, and I will not allow Vash'ala's evil scheme to continue.'

'Tell me your name, soldier.'

'Peri is my name. And you are?'

'I am Delitas, servant to the prince. Well met sir! Go to Tristan and seek the quickest route, for tonight you will go to Vallicore!'

Peri hugged his wife and found Tristan who had fallen asleep on the ground. He cleared his throat loudly, and Tristan stirred. 'Excuse me, Your Majesty. I am Peri, the messenger who will go to Vallicore with your leave. What would you ask of me?'

'Hullo, Peri, it is a pleasure to meet you. Go with haste to Poleden. Delitas should have sent a messenger there by now. It will take a moment for the soldiers there to rise to arms. While the herald calls upon them, take for yourself a horse and ride swiftly to Vallicore. Your quickest route is to go south from Poleden around the Miners' Ravine. Ride westward through the Weary Vale until you arrive at a bridge; cross said bridge and climb to the top of the hill there. From there, you will be able to see Vallicore in the distance. Go and give word to Elder Bowman and Arthur Grause. Report to them the events at Cayrngras and the attack on Bram. Ask if they will send aid to us, and go with haste!' Peri bowed and ran off after the form of Engel who was now nearing the bottom of a very steep slope.

Tristan rose and staggered back to Delitas. The caravan continued onward, slowly at first, but a moment later, Laman appeared on the road behind them. He was shouting and running as fast as he could. 'Prince Tristan! Where is Prince Tristan?'

'Continue to Bram, good people,' Tristan called. 'I will meet with you shortly.' He took off immediately with Delitas by his side and met Laman down the road. 'What is it soldier? Are you from Paladin's ranks?'

'Yes sir. My name is Laman. There were others who came before me, but I stayed behind for a while to witness Paladin's final stand. It was brutal and sad to watch, but that tale can wait. I bring ill news!' He leaned over and panted frantically to catch his breath.

'Forgive my rudeness, Laman, but I must hear your news without any further delay.'

'My apologies, Sire, I have been running for half an hour,' Laman replied with one last puff of air. 'I heard the Vash'alan King speaking. They are salvaging arrows for another assault. And I heard something about the Dark Lord's clouds.'

'Clouds,' Tristan mused. 'What more do you know?'

'King Marxas said to his armies, "Once the Dark Lord's clouds reach the city of Bram to the east, we will attack the Boltians once more." And then his armies proceeded to wreck our great stronghold! Alas! what more can we do?'

'You have done well to report this.' Tristan looked away at the sky above, and the clouds were slowly creeping towards the fortress Bram. 'The clouds seem to be moving slowly, so we will have time to catch our breath before the enemy arrives. But I fear there may be some evil secret to those clouds. I cannot imagine why they would delay their attack. But come; let us tarry no longer. We must first secure the safety of the townsfolk.' They rejoined the caravan and saw Bram in the distance still many miles from their position. Tristan informed them of the enemy's delay, and the townsfolk were greatly elated by the news. The civilians scurried along slowly, for many carried with them infants and small children. The soldiers moved now to the rear of the party and were ever watchful of the clouds and the lands between Cayrngras and Bram. They strode forth with swords drawn and were ready to lay down their lives to defend their people if the need arose. 'Delitas,' Tristan called after a long silence, 'I ask just one more favor of you.'

'Forgive me, my liege, but I am doubtful this will be your last request of me,' Delitas laughed.

Tristan shrugged his shoulders and glared at him whimsically. 'You are swift by my knowledge. Go ahead of the people and call upon the soldiers of Bram; ask if they would send aid until we have reached the city.' But just as he spoke, the voices of the travelers rose with shouts of joy. Tristan turned his eyes up and peered out into the distance to the northeast. Far off, many horsemen bearing torches approached on the southern road from Bram, and the people shouted in accord, *'We are saved!'*

Chapter XIX

The Battle of Bram

The moon was resting in the eastern sky, covering all the rolling fields south and east of Bram in a shade of grey, but the western sky was mostly shrouded in darkness by the thick billows approaching from Cayrngras. There were thirty or more horsemen riding on the southern road from the city to meet the refugees, and to them the people ran as swiftly as they could, up and down the tall hills of the country, crossing the plains between the two roads. Far behind and to their left, the dark, ominous clouds inched across the sky and fires flickered in the distance as the evil Men of Vash'ala emptied the fortress of Cayrngras.

The riders halted upon the southern road, save two who came galloping swiftly across the grassy land. Tristan and Delitas sprinted to the front of the caravan and descended down a long slope where they met the two riders, whom they recognized as Hauffa and Ragnok. *'We are saved!'* the people shouted again as they followed after the Prince of Bolteras. Just then, horns blared from the west and the two captains halted, turning their eyes upon the gloom to their right. Hauffa drew a horn from his pack and gave a good puff, and it echoed long and loud. Behind them, the other horsemen turned and galloped away back to Bram. The travelers' joy quickly turned to despair, and they began to panic. *'Save us! Save us!'* they shouted as they dashed closer to the knights.

The dark clouds inched ever closer, and several more horns blared from the west. Lightning hissed and cracked within the clouds of the Dark Lord, and the Vash'alan army advanced towards Bram, following the northern road out of Cayrngras to the east. The people began to cry out in desperation. Moments later, the stars in the western sky were veiled behind the immense billows, and great darkness began to fall upon the horrified host. As the people drew nearer to the knights, Hauffa raised a hand and silenced their chatter.

'Come now, good people of Cayrngras! The Vash'alan army moves quickly. Go to Bram at once and do not tarry! Lo! The enemy draws nigh!' The people halted and gazed upon the vast army beneath the darkening sky behind, and many cried out in anguish and began to weep. Annoyed by their incessant moaning, Hauffa continued, 'We have no time to spare! Go now or be left to die!' Tristan ran to the side of Hauffa and bowed before him, and the knight lowered his torch to behold the face of the young prince. 'My liege, Vaaspar's hand must have been upon you! Not long ago your companions arrived safely in Bram. Many believed you to be dead, but I am pleased to see you alive.'

'I live indeed, but not for long if we do not move these people quickly. I grow weary of these delays! March back to the city and ready the defenses; we will guide the people behind you.' Hauffa bowed upon his steed and turned about. The two captains rode forth carrying the hopes of the people with them. Once more, the caravan was overcome with grief and despair, but Tristan consoled them. 'Go at once! The captains are leading the way to safety. Follow the torches to the city!'

None delayed. They ran swiftly after the lights before them, ignoring their fear and fatigue. They scurried up and down the hills weeping as they ran. The archers of the Lonely Forest strode forth and led the pack, but the remaining soldiers from Cayrngras fell back to assist the civilians, for the children were too tired to walk. Tristan and Delitas provided them aid as well and carried a child or two in their arms, which caused them to fall far behind the rest of the host. But still they pressed on. Fear drove their feet forward. Another flash of lightning flickered in the west; then the sound of thunder rumbled in their ears, and some fell upon the ground in terror. The banging of thousands of plated feet came next, and the noise roared across the plains. The ground trembled as the massive horde of Vash'alans approached Bram. Hauffa and Ragnok arrived at the fortress and waited patiently for the people. Anxiety overtook them as the clouds seemed to roll more quickly towards the mighty stronghold. Half an hour passed before the frontrunners of the caravan arrived at last in Bram, and many knights emerged to lead them to shelters within the city. But Hauffa and Ragnok awaited the laggards, every so often peering despondently to their right as the hammering of feet banged against the road to the northwest.

The approaching army began a lengthy climb up an extended range of knolls along the road to Bram. They had only just left Cayrngras in full force and still half their journey was before them. At length, the Boltian refugees had withdrawn behind the walls of the fortress in full. As they entered the city, the women and children were filled with joy. They felt safe, for the walls of Bram were

307

carved purely from ironwood and rose some twenty feet or more high. Four towers rose from the four corners of the stronghold's walls, and archers were stationed within its shelter. Footmen and archers lined every inch of the walls and many more soldiers stood guard within the courts of the city. Masses of troops ran throughout the city preparing for combat, and the people of Cayrngras began to find hope once more. A few catapults were wheeled into the front court near the gates and loaded with large boulders. Bram was a mighty fortress and had never been conquered, despite its wooden defense, but the credit belonged to the warriors of Bram, for they were wise and skilled beyond all reckoning. Even still, the wooden enclosure filled Tristan with great anxiety, for he feared the enemy would burn the fortress to the ground.

Inside the citadel, the knights dismounted and returned their steeds to the stables. Hauffa rejoined Tristan at the foot of the southern gate while Ragnok equipped the archers of the Lonely Forest with fresh quivers full of arrows—they carried nearly thirty arrows each as far as there were provisions. The city was exceedingly crowded now with all the newcomers; but room was made as the civilians hid in the many shops and houses of the town and were safely out of the soldiers' way. Delitas withdrew to the top of the wall facing west and watched as the Vash'alan troops marched thunderously loud across the rolling knolls. To his delight, they were still far away.

'Since you have come, Prince Tristan, I shall grant you full command of my forces,' Hauffa declared.

'And it is greatly appreciated. My only fear is the wooden framework of the city. Surely the enemy will set fire to the walls if the lightning from those dreadful clouds does not do it for them.'

'The walls may be wooden, but Bram has never been conquered. We will hold them, and we will defeat them. Be at peace.'

'I hope with all my heart you are right, but I have had little peace since I returned to Bolteras. Tell me something; where is my uncle now? We only just returned from Alterash, and I have not been informed of his whereabouts. And if Ragnok is with you, then where are the forces of Eordil?'

Suddenly, Hauffa appeared deeply troubled. Lowering his head, he spoke, 'I do not know of the king's whereabouts. He departed to the Sage's Mountain more than three months ago and has yet to return. That is all I know. Regarding Ragnok, he was here delivering reports to me of his soldiers' progress in their training. He knew nothing of this battle, I am afraid.' Tristan was overcome with grief, and he shook with sadness and doubt. At that moment, Meridas appeared before them.

'I know where the king is,' he interrupted, 'or at least where he was headed. I was informed of much when I returned to the Lonely Forest. And there is more I am afraid.'

Hauffa cleared his throat and said, 'Pardon me, but I must return to my duties. I go with your leave.' Tristan waved him off quite annoyed by the sudden interruption. Hauffa bowed respectfully before Meridas and Tristan and withdrew to the northern wall.

'Tell me everything,' Tristan insisted, 'everything you know!'

'He sought out Percival the Silver in a solitary cave in the far northeastern tip of Vash'ala, as reported by the eagles of the Sage's Mountain. But in all the time leading up to the enemy's attack in the woods last night, Edgar King never returned. But days before Vash'ala assaulted us, the eagle leader known as Greatwing came to me. He reported that Seymour the Celebhas was returning to Elúne for a time, though I know not the reason. He said not to worry about Lord Edgar. He was heading to Alterash, and that is all he said. I have no knowledge of his location now. I hope that brings you some comfort.'

'Even with all you have told me, I still fear the fate of my good uncle. I pray the enemy did not capture him. I could use his wisdom at a time like this. Is there nothing else you know?'

'I am afraid there is not, Your Majesty. But many know you to be a capable leader. Take charge and lead the forces of Bram to victory!'

'Tristan,' Hauffa interrupted with a shout from the northern wall, 'the enemy draws nigh! Come hither!'

Tristan sprinted forward at once to the top of the walls and looked out upon the horde of enemies still several miles in the distance. The Vash'alans halted their march along the road northwest of Bram, and King Marxas presented himself at the head of his army. Nearly every Boltian knew the armor of the Vash'alan King, for it was frightful and well spoken of in many tales. Above the heads of the enemy force was the edge of the dark billows that guided their way. The army stood and waited as the clouds inched ever so slowly toward the city. Tristan smiled as he looked upon the image of the self-proclaimed god leading the waves of Vash'ala and then scoffed.

'I want that man dead,' he shouted to his brethren. 'Destroy him! I will not rest until Marxas is filled with arrows from head to foot!' The Boltians bawled and sounded their war horns. They were ready for battle, but to their surprise, the soldiers of Vash'ala sat upon the ground and lingered. The land grew unusually quiet, and it was unsettling to them. Delitas ran across the walls to the northern gate and stood beside the appalled prince.

'Tristan, this is an opportune time for us! They are waiting for the clouds to reach us before they attack, just as Laman has told us. Although we do not know the reason they wait, this will surely give us the time to rest. We will need to be at full strength to win this battle, so let us find sleep.'

'Aye, you have spoken wisely. Hauffa,' he called out, and the lord of Bram turned about. 'The enemy has halted. They will only advance under the shadow of the clouds. Position some of your soldiers to keep watch on the land, but let the rest of us sleep now lest we exhaust our strength from keeping our eyes open!'

'Yes, Sire. That is an excellent plan.'

'The credit belongs to Delitas. Inform your guard to signal us if the armies begin to move. We must be ready when they come upon us.' Hauffa nodded and ran about the lengths of the walls shouting Tristan's instructions. No more than half an hour elapsed before most of the soldiers found rest. A few of the archers in the towers kept watch in shifts, but the Vash'alan army remained still for many long hours. For some four hours they watched, but still the Vash'alan army remained unmoved. The slow night waned on with not even the slightest disturbance or need for alarm. But by the fifth hour, the clouds had inched across the sky and passed over Bram, and soon the night sky above was shrouded by endless darkness. The archers in the towers could barely see the ground below. The Vash'alans were hidden from them for a time, but then they heard the sound of the enemy's march ring thunderously across the plains.

'Arise Boltian warriors,' said one of the archers, 'the enemy advances on Bram! Look now; the clouds have blinded us!' At once, an outburst of noise rang throughout the city as the soldiers awoke and made way to their posts. Then the clouds released their rain, and it dampened the Boltians' spirits. Tristan took his stance upon the northern wall just above the gates and peered out to the west, but the gloom was too thick for him to see. The sight of the good Men failed. Out of the darkness, arrows screeched at the defenders of Bram. Several were struck and fell from the walls. The Boltians quickly loosed a stream of arrows that vanished into the shadows before them; none could tell if they hit their targets. The banging of feet grew ever closer, the darkness growing ever deeper. Lightning hissed again and branched across the sky, and the host of Boltians saw for a brief moment the vast armies of their enemies stretching far and wide about the city. The Vash'alan army was at their doorstep now. Anxiety overtook the defenders, and a great many fired another volley of arrows. The sounds of arrows clashing against the enemies' armor resonated below. But the clouds grew darker still until all of Bram was shrouded in endless blackness.

Delitas staggered along the walls and found Tristan at the northern gate; even at a close range and in the light of torches and lanterns, he could hardly tell who was standing before him. 'Tristan, I do not understand! We were just at Cayrngras yesterday, but these wretched clouds are infinitely darker now than they were then.'

'Yes, I am confused myself. This must be the full strength of our enemy. Be wary and do not relent. Fight on Boltians! Do not lose hope!'

One by one the Boltians loosed their arrows over the walls, not knowing if they struck enemy or ground, for the rain and thunder drowned out the sounds of their arrows clashing against the metal of the Vash'alans' armor. The fight seemed endless and impossible to win. 'We are doomed!' cried one of the soldiers; his voice came from the western wall. The ranks of soldiers began to mutter and moan words of hopelessness, and Tristan was losing confidence in his ability to lead. Following another flash of lightning, terrifying noises echoed to their ears: it was shrill laughter coming from creatures with the sound of malice in their tiny voices. 'Enemies! There are enemies on the western walls,' cried a panicked soldier.

'How can that be?' Tristan mumbled under his breath. 'Look for ladders! Cast them down!'

'There are none,' another voice answered from the western wall. Shrieks followed his voice and several warriors cried out in pain.

'Delitas, come with me!' Tristan struggled forward to the western wall feeling the wood of the parapets as he trudged along, and Delitas followed closely behind.

'They are in the city!' a man shouted from below.

'Find some torches and carry them with you,' the prince shouted. 'We must expose them!' Suddenly a hand grabbed Tristan, and he leapt in alarm.

'Fear not, Tristan! It is I, Pakko.'

'You gave me a quite a scare, lad! Should you not be resting still? You have only just been healed.'

'I cannot rest while all my comrades are fighting. Moreover, Zoro is still fighting, and he was struck in the leg with an arrow just yesterday.'

'So that man in the forest was the one they call Eagle-Eye?'

'Indeed it was! But listen closely; these are the same creatures that attacked us in the woods. They are fearsome, for they hide in the shadows. Though you healed me, I feel pain in my neck just being near them. We must slay them quickly, for their touch will drain you of your strength.'

'If what you say is true, then they are fearsome indeed! Let us slay them quickly!' They parted ways and carried torches with them. The Imps of Darkness were soon exposed, and the defenders of Bram slew them in an instant. But more came pouring over the walls, now on all sides. 'Do not relent! Keep up the fight!' Tristan hollered as loudly as he could. *Bang. Bang.* The doors of the castle creaked. The rams of the enemy were crashing upon the northern gates. 'Hold them! Archers to the gates! Do not let them through. Bar the gates and hold them at bay!'

The battle continued in the Boltians' favor for a while, but the Imps' numbers only seemed to grow. Men fell by the tens, but they relented not. Tristan fought ferociously and slew some twenty Imps, Delitas another fifteen, and Pakko some ten. Meridas joined the fray with Rolo and Zoro, and together they slew another thirty. Hauffa came up the rear with Ragnok and killed some twenty more. Half an hour after the Imps had scaled the walls, the clouds began to grow lighter. The defenders of Bram could see again, and it elated them greatly. Thunder boomed and the gates creaked again under the pressure of the battering rams, but the noises did not worry the Boltians. The defenders now beheld the plaza filled with tiny, evil creatures as the dark clouds turned from a deep black to a dark grey.

'Archers of the Lonely Forest,' Tristan called, 'destroy them at once!' From the walls, the archers aimed their bows and attacked. The arrows whistled as they fell upon the Imps below, and most of the force was slain—the remaining fled in terror and disappeared over the walls. Moments later, a larger host ascended to the tops of the western wall. Tristan observed the ambush from the southern wall and hurried to oppose them. The bowmen from the Lonely Forest emptied their quivers and quickly drew their swords against the tiny demons. The Imps' numbers had dwindled greatly. In a final and swift charge, a band of soldiers from the courtyard occupied the walls with drawn swords; they fell upon the tiny devils with great vengeance, and the Imps retreated yet again. Suddenly, the clouds changed to a pale grey, and the rain ceased. All the walls were secure, and the northern gates still held strong. The archers of Bram continued to attack the main force of the Vash'alan army for several minutes, but their darts ran out at last. From the west arrows shrieked through the air and fell upon the Boltians. 'Fire the trebuchets,' Tristan yelled. The massive boulders were hurled over the walls and crashed upon the battlefield. The soldiers quickly loaded the catapults one last time and fired the last of their stones. The rocks slew many of the enemy troops, but still hundreds advanced on Bram.

'Fall back from the walls!' Tristan shouted. 'We have no arrows left. Fall back to the plaza and regain your strength!' The soldiers fell back to the square, and the city was crowded from north to south and east to west. *Bang.* The rams crashed once more on the gates. 'Hold the doors. We must hold out for our reinforcements! Fortify the gates!'

Suddenly the banging of the rams seized, and the area was quiet. The defenders quivered in fear and waited with anticipation. A moment later, the gates dissolved before their eyes like a smoke blown away by the wind, and there stood King Marxas encompassed by a bubbling mist of red and black. The Boltian warriors at the gates hurled their spears at the Vash'alan King, but their weapons failed and shattered before him. Marxas laughed savagely as the forces of Vash'alan slowly crept into the city, slaying the twenty who defended the gates.

'He is protected by the Magic of the Dark Lord!' one of the soldiers shouted. 'We are doomed!'

'Silence,' Tristan retorted. 'Slay him and crush their morale! He must be dealt with quickly! Do not fret in the face of his evil! We have the strength of Elúvías, and the enemy will cower beneath its power. Now attack!'

The Boltians charged forth at the enemy king and coated their weapons with the power of Light, but Marxas withdrew and vanished amidst the throng of crimson armors. All the same, the soldiers kept on and slew many of the Vash'alans with the power of Elúvías as they desperately tried to reach the Vash'alan King. Just then, a flurry of arrows whistled over the walls and fell upon the

313

Boltians. They quickly drew their shields and defended against the assault, but the attack had slowed their advance. Now Marxas was too far for their reach. The battle waged on, and the enemy refused to yield. The Vash'alans poured through the gates and climbed the stairs to the parapets. A mere minute or two passed before they lined all the walls of the fortress. Desperation overcame the forces of Bram. The city was overcrowded and none could move freely. 'What shall we do now, Tristan?' Delitas shouted from the ranks of soldiers. Tristan turned this way and that searching for a solution, but he was trapped in an endless sea of troubling thoughts and could find no answer.

As the Men of Bolteras met swords with the Men of Vash'ala, the clouds above grew dark and heavy again, and the rain returned. The Imps of Darkness attacked once more, but their numbers were few. Leaping from the wall, some fifty or more came crashing upon the heads of the Boltians, but the Men worked together and slew the last of the tiny devils. Almost at once the rain ceased, and the clouds above turned to a soft grey. None knew the hour of the day, but, much to their delight, the sun was beginning to peer through the billows. The champions of Bram felt renewed and encouraged and fought back with more fervor. But still the battle continued on slowly, for the Men could not move about easily. Only a few soldiers fought at a time, and it was beginning to burden them with annoyance and fatigue.

The Boltian warriors attempted to run the enemy out of the city, but the push was risky and claimed many lives on both sides. In retaliation, the Vash'alans hurled their black spears upon the defenders and regained their lost ground. Soon after, Ragnok and Hauffa pushed to the frontlines with fearsome attacks, and the enemy cowered before them. Meridas climbed onto the southern wall with his kin from the Lonely Forest and fought back their enemies there. In the skirmish, the archer-captain received a stab wound in his left shoulder and fell back, but his host continued the attack. Rolo took Pakko and Zoro and a host of Boltians upon the eastern wall and began another battle there. Alfred son of Winslet took charge of another band of soldiers and rose upon the western walls and drove back the enemy. It was their last resort, one last attempt to reclaim the city. But the armies continued to push their way into Bram and forced their way onto the walls of the stronghold. After examining the battle for a time, Tristan and Delitas led a battalion of men to the frontlines to aid Hauffa and Ragnok; and with the power of Elúvías,

314

they drove back the forces of Vash'ala. The city was emptied of their enemies at last, and the vile Men of Vash'ala fled across the rolling fields to the north. They made way for the shelter of the Lonely Grey.

But at that moment, a horn sounded from outside the walls; it appeared to come from the southwest. Then another answered from the northeast. The ground began to tremble, and the defenders of Bram watched and listened with curiosity. Like leaves blowing swiftly in the wind, horsemen galloped thunderously loud to and fro across the plains and past the road. Some rode east, others went west. The tired troops looked through the open entryway of Bram as a great host of horsemen darted into the throng of the enemy. Tristan quickly climbed onto the northern wall and gazed out upon the plains to the north. Some two thousand horsemen galloped about smiting the Vash'alans as they rode. Others ascended the stairs to the parapets with the prince, but the rest proceeded out of the city and onto the northern road to witness the end of the battle.

The riders sped by with their banners waving in the air; the mark of Alterash waved dimly amidst the gallantly flowing masses of Boltian banners as the horsemen trampled upon their enemies. Red covered the battlefield with the many scattered armors of the enemy and the pools of blood beneath them—the battle of Bram became the bloodiest battle in all of Bolteras' history. King Marxas scurried along until he was the last man standing. He was surrounded now by the vast armies of Bolteras and her allies. Tristan peered across the plains before him and began to weep as he beheld the figure of a large, black man riding upon one of the steeds: it was Grinshawl, the Ogre of Bolteras. And none other than Lord Edgar was at his side, alive and full of vitality. The King of Bolteras had returned and his people were never happier to see his face.

The entire host within Bram—not counting the women and children—emptied the city and ran to hail their saviors, but Tristan stared on from a distance with a large smile upon his face and great relief in his heart. Pakko and Zoro could not bear to walk any longer, so they limped slowly to the top of the wall and stood proudly next to the prince. Pakko had a large smile of his own stretched high upon his rosy cheeks. At that time, some of the riders lifted their heads and blew mighty, resonating horns that chimed inspirationally with the sound of victory. The defenders of Bram cheered as they ran forward and hailed their honorable king.

Tristan gazed out in awe and joy, for there amongst the armies was Hombag of Poleden with Engel the messenger, the messenger Gerrin with the forces of Eordil, and Gibraltar with the riders of Alterash. The envoys had accomplished their mission, and the forces of Bolteras answered with haste. But the true victory came with Edgar King of Bolteras, for it was with his return that the dark clouds of the Enemy shrunk back and the light shone through once more, thus sending the reinforcing Imps of Darkness whence they came. This was due to the power of Elorén the Celebhas, for he imparted his authority to the king upon returning to Elúne. In Edgar's presence, the power of Marxas faded, and his protective aura was destroyed. The King of Vash'ala, hailed as Sol'Czar the Sun King by his people, appeared now old and frail as a slave mistreated by his cruel master. And that he was, for he belonged to Abaddon, the cruelest master of them all.

The army of riders encircled the Vash'alan King until he relented and fell to his knees in surrender. Edgar dismounted and drew near to the feeble king with eyes full of compassion. He looked upon the pitiable man as he recoiled upon the ground and whimpered in fear. Tears were in the eyes of the King of Bolteras. He knelt down beside Marxas King and spoke with a soft voice, 'Why have you done this, Marxas? Did we not have peace, a treaty, for nearly two decades long now? What happened to the pact we made, you and me?'

'Forgive me, Edgar,' the man cried as he threw his helmet upon the ground in defeat. 'I never wanted any of this to happen. I wanted to be set apart from all the kings before me, especially Ramox my predecessor. That man was said to be the cruelest in all the history of Vash'ala, but as for me, I wished to be known as a kind, gentle king full of grace and mercy. Yet, I was never given power before my time as king, and the Great Council of Osceroth tainted my mind, filling it with their vile, poisonous ideals. Their words had power over me. Yes, I was trapped by their spell. Yet the fault is my own. I listened, Edgar, oh alas! I listened to those decrepit parasites.' He began to cry and beat his fists violently upon the ground in his torment. 'And only now in my defeat do I see clearly! It is I who now knows the true meaning of despair!' He fell with his face on the ground and wept bitterly.

At that time, Tristan and Pakko made their way to the gathering to hear the conversation, and Zoro hopped along beside them. As they neared the crowd, Tristan saw Delitas at the rear and began to call out his name, but the former Vash'alan pushed his way through the crowds toward King Marxas. Edgar now sat beside the humiliated king and slammed his mighty hammer onto the ground; the land caved slightly beneath the blow. Edgar appeared now angry. 'Do you know how many brave soldiers are dead because of you, including those of your kin? You have brought great evil upon your land and mine as well. And now the lines of Vash'ala will be cut off, perhaps forever!'

'You are wrong,' Delitas shouted as he emerged from the crowd, 'the people of Vash'ala will not fade from this world until my life fails me. Forget not, Edgar King that I too am of Vash'alan blood. With the death of Marxas, I will be the last remnant of the once great country of the sun-worshippers. But I will remake it! No more will Vash'ala bow before false gods that bring only misery and vile contempt! I will become King of Vash'ala, and the country will follow the path of Light under my rule. I have already discussed these things with your nephew, Tristan, and he has sworn allegiance to my ideals for when he becomes King of Bolteras. As long as I draw breath, Vash'ala will be an honorable land, no matter how long it takes to reestablish it. My country will no longer submit to Vash'alari god of the sun or to Sol'Czar the Sun King; my allegiance is now with Vaaspar, the Lord of Light! I give you my word, the great and noble of Bolteras that I, Delitas Crux, heir to the line of Ramox, will forever be an ally to Bolteras and to the great Ruler Vaaspar.'

The gathered crowds began to whisper amongst themselves, many gasping at his words. There was great awe throughout the host of Men, and many glared angrily at the heir of Ramox. Until now, none knew of Delitas' heritage, for he had never before mentioned it. Edgar rose and stared Delitas in the eyes. 'How can it be that you are the heir of Ramox's line? And why have you kept your name hidden all this time? I thought you were raised as a servant to the king!'

'Aye, that is what I told you, but I did not tell you everything. Forgive me. I was foolish to hide this from you, but I felt disgraced being born the son of that dreadful line. Furthermore, I never wished to be called by his name again. But now that the armies of Vash'ala are defeated and her king awaits death, I stepped forth to reveal my lineage. I came to you as nothing more than an ignorant soldier thrown into the armies of a father who never loved me. I was indeed raised as a servant. My father forsook me before I was old enough to know who he was. My mother, before she died, told me that my father never once held me as a baby. I was rejected, and I despised Ramox for that. It was his dying will for me to become a great warrior and be a king like him: a man who is cruel and full of malice. As I got older, his advisors carried on his will. I was trained as a soldier and taught the ways of kingship. But I never believed his ideals, so I turned from their teachings. Every day the Great Council of Osceroth tried to sway my mind, but I would not listen. I hated my father more than I cared to be king. Then evil Men and Draemhas alike came to murder me, but I fled to the lands of Bolteras. I sought the good Men of Light and so came to you, Lord Edgar. I have been honest with you from the beginning, as much as I could. It was not my plan to deceive you. I merely hoped to earn your trust if ever this day came upon us. That is why I withheld the truth of my lineage, though regrettably now, for I see you are an honorable man. So what say you, Edgar King?'

'You are a brave lad, Delitas. It must have been quite the burden keeping your ancestry secret. If we are indeed victorious in this war, I will gladly forge an alliance with you. I understand your reasons for concealing this great truth, so apologize no more!'

'And when I am king,' Tristan shouted from the middle of the crowd, 'I will gladly keep my promise to you!' The people cleared a path, and Tristan shook arms with Delitas. All who heard were filled with relief and applauded for the hopeful alliance. But Edgar was merely relieved to see his precious nephew still alive.

'But let us not be too hasty,' Edgar interrupted. 'We still have matters to attend to,' he said as he turned back to his enemy. 'Marxas, long have I yearned to have good relations with your people, but you and your kin ever hardened your hearts against us.'

Marxas began to laugh. Edgar replied with a confused and angry glance. 'Forgive me; I laugh only for irony's sake. We have long envied the people of Bolteras, caught up by the curse of that despicable Alp. And yet, our spies reported months ago that the Alp Envy was slain by a boy accompanied by a Dragon and Alastair the White.' Edgar's face lit up with delight. Tristan too was happy but sad at the same time, for his desire to see Victor again grew ever stronger. 'I laugh because the curse should have been lifted from us. But we had already willingly given ourselves to the Dark Lord, so we could not return to the Light. Alas! The curse continued in a new form, and we were bound to a fate we despised. Instead of envying the wealth of the Boltians, we envied all Men who belonged to the Light. So we continued on the path of Darkness with anger still in our hearts, and the Evil One used our hatred for his selfish purposes. And now I have seen my wicked deeds and hate myself more than anything else in this world. Kill me, Boltian King. Kill me and let my spirit pass from this life to the pits of Shaekle where I belong. I beg of you!'

Tears formed in Edgar's eyes and then ran down his cheeks and onto to the grass beneath him. He was filled with sorrow, for he hated killing Men above all things. Many were surprised to see Grinshawl crying as well and some even took it to be mere banter, but the giant cried with genuine grief for his fellow man. Edgar paced to the Vash'alan King's side and drew his sword. 'I wish that I could avoid this part of my kingly duties. It is my least favorite part of being a ruler.'

'I always heard that without killing, kings could never be great,' Marxas replied. 'And yet you have always maintained greatness through your character alone. I have always envied you for that and with good reason! Even now you weep for your enemy, a wretched man as me. You are the image of a true king, the prime example of lordship! I do not deserve to be honored thusly by you; but I must admit that for the first time in my life, I have truly been shown a brother's kind of love through your acts of compassion. I will now die a happy man, and the Dark Lord will never steal that away from me. Farewell, Edgar the benevolent! I beg of you; do not let this happiness depart from me.' He closed his eyes and breathed out heavily, but Edgar hesitated.

'How do you wish to die?' Edgar said softly after a long pause.

'A clean stab in my heart is what I desire. All the evil that I allowed in my life dwells within my blackened heart. I want all the hatred and wickedness of my heart to die with me. It has been cunningly deceiving me all these years, and I want to have my revenge for its tyranny in my life.' Edgar nodded and swiftly, though reluctantly, thrust his sword into the chest of the Vash'alan King. 'At last,' he panted, 'the curse is lifted. I am free!' The Vash'alan King breathed his last and fell dead to the ground. Many wanted to cheer for their victory, but no one was able to speak. Sadness silenced them, and their feelings of merriment were replaced by great remorse. The crowd bowed their heads in reflection of the dead. Moments later, the silence was interrupted by the sudden movement of Lord Edgar. He rose with fresh tears upon his cheeks and withdrew to Bram without a word.

Inside the city, the civilians emerged hesitantly from their refuges and beheld Lord Edgar in all his royal glory. They cheered and applauded, and for a moment, the king smiled for their joy. Peace and hope had returned to the city of Bram as well as to the rest of Bolteras, but Edgar felt none of it. His mind was set on what waited in their future: the war against the Draemhas. The people's joy quickly turned to grief as they scoured the city in search of their loved ones. Mourning filled the air for hours, and Edgar mourned with the people. He withdrew to a quiet corner of the city in the southeastern square and remained alone for several days.

After an hour of searching the city, the townsfolk gathered and commenced a ceremonial procession for the dead—at that time the Alterashians returned home. The civilians chose a lush field full of many flowers to the east of Bram and buried their loved ones. Many aided in carrying the dead, but it took hours to transport them all, even with carts pulled by horses. Hauffa ordered his soldiers to number those amongst the Boltian dead, and there were three hundred forty-three counted in the battle at Bram. There were many more unaccounted for in Cayrngras, and none desired to count the losses there. The Boltians had suffered a mighty loss, but victory belonged to them. Others were found wounded within the city walls, but they were cared for by the tender loving women of the city. The remaining soldiers from Cayrngras approached the king in hopes of returning to their beloved city, but he urged them to stay. Reluctantly, they agreed to help at Bram, but Edgar promised they would be allowed to return home soon. After the commotion and mourning of the grief-stricken people had ceased, food was prepared. The Boltians ate quietly that night, despite their inspiring victory. When it was time to sleep, after all the work of burying the dead was complete, it was near midnight. Some of the warriors slept within the city, but the most of them found beds upon the grassy plains about Bram. They slept peacefully that night knowing the threat of war was far from them.

The next morning, every able-bodied man was at work removing the cadavers of the enemy to outside of the city walls. Bodies were piled in numerous heaps and burned. There were no respectful graves given to them. The men toiled all the day long, pausing seldom only to eat, and then went quickly back to their work. More than three thousand were numbered among the enemy, but the soldiers eventually lost interest and stopped counting. Later in the evening, they ate a quick and quiet meal and fell asleep shortly after.

Upon the following morning, Edgar allowed the people from Cayrngras to return to their homes and promised to come to them soon. The forces of Eordil returned home with Ragnok at their lead, and so did the soldiers of Poleden led by Hombag. Several days passed, and the people of Bram found gladness in their hearts once more. They began to laugh and play and, most importantly to them, sing and drink; and they honored and celebrated their fallen heroes. But Prince Tristan found little joy in those days. He recalled the envoy he sent to Vallicore and felt shame for sending Peri on a needless adventure. Furthermore, he feared Elder Bowman's anger and was certain he would see it soon enough. And for a few days, he even avoided his uncle, for he felt he had failed in the battle at Bram. Above all his, Tristan was afraid that Edgar would scold his leadership for allowing so many to die. Grinshawl could not locate Edgar or Tristan during those few days and so spent his time in Bram with the archers of the Lonely Forest and listened day and night to their tales.

* * *

When August the third had arrived, Edgar found peace anew in his heart and eagerly sought out Tristan and Grinshawl. The three found shelter in a tent outside the city and talked for the entire day. They had hardly begun their chatter when Rolo, Pakko and Zoro joined them. It was the early afternoon, and they shared their tales over a warm meal and were greeted by Meridas shortly after, who brought drinks for their enjoyment. Edgar wept upon receiving the news of Paladin's heroic death and Genrig's betrayal, and he required, or so he said, several mugs of Borgon's Beer to ease his mind. When evening came upon them, all withdrew upon the king's request, leaving only Grinshawl and Tristan to speak more privately with him.

'Why have you not spoken to me sooner, my dear nephew? I have yearned to speak with you since I heard of your heroic deeds in Alterash.'

'Forgive me, uncle. I feared that I had failed you. And besides, *you* are the one who disappear for several days,' Tristan answered cynically.

'Ah yes, I most certainly did. It is not easy killing Men. I dread it, though at times it is necessary. But I do not understand your other point. How have you failed me? I have only heard good reports

321

regarding you since I left Bolteras. I have nothing but happiness in my heart because of you.'

'But I was not able to save the people of Cayrngras, and many died under my authority. And many more fell at the battle of Bram! Our forces are weak now, and I fear that we will not be able to withstand the Draemhan army! I w—'

'That is enough out of you!' Edgar snapped. He rose from his seat and wrapped his arms around his nephew. Pulling back, he said, 'All of this is my fault, lad, not yours. Had I been here, perhaps none of this would have happened the way it did. But lo! I will have no more of this foolish talk. We must not question what could have happened. All things happen for a reason, though we may not understand it at the time. Bolteras' armies have certainly weakened with the losses at Cayrngras and Bram, but we are not weak! I will stake my life upon another victory, even against the wretched Draemhas. Bolteras must not fail. It is vital that we win for the Eastern kingdoms are in great need of our aid, and our families and friends are counting on us. Use their feelings, their dependence on us, to give you strength, and trust always in the power of Elúvías. We will not fail!'

'Forgive me for not seeing you sooner, uncle. I thought you would hate me or else deem me unworthy to be your heir. I have simply wanted to please you, to be the son you never had, one you could be proud of. You have been like a father to me, and your opinion of me matters most. I was a coward who wished to avoid another scolding.'

Edgar fell upon his knees at the feet of Tristan. 'My boy, I could never hate you even for a second. You are young and yet you helped liberate an entire land from an evil curse with but a few soldiers at your side. I have always believed in you, but you have surprised me still. There is greatness in you, lad, and I would be honored for you to inherit the throne of Bolteras after me. You are indeed the son I never had, but I love you as much as I could my own flesh. I am proud of you, Tristan, and I consider you worthy to be my heir!'

'Thank you, uncle,' Tristan wept as he embraced Edgar, 'I will make you proud! I give you my word!' He wiped his tears and sniffed. 'Tell me, where have you two been for so long? I heard briefly from Meridas that you had gone to the lands of Alterash. But how did you come to lead the Alterashians to battle? When last I

322

spoke to them, they refused to return with me to Bolteras saying they had too much work to do. So how did you persuade them?'

'We came looking for you after some time,' Grinshawl interrupted, eager to speak. 'But that was at the end of our journey. I am afraid we have failed our mission for now...' He informed Tristan of all the events he and Edgar had endured since they left the land of Bolteras. The prince was amazed and terrified, all the more upon hearing of Percival's captivity, but he found comfort in knowing that his uncle had received great power from the Celebhas. 'When Seymour had departed, a mysterious power shrouded the body of Lord Edgar. I could travel ten feet in every direction and be covered by the spell, even ten feet upward! He was made invisible by Elorén's protection, so I had to mark his location well. I lived upon the land for nearly three months, toiling endlessly to survive. But Edgar rested peacefully, and his body became healthier as the days elapsed. He received little nourishment from me, but the spell seemed to keep his body fed. I cannot explain it, but he was cared for by the Celebhas' Magic. It appeared that the Celebhas bestowed upon him the very essence of his power, and Edgar was aware of it the moment he roused from sleep.

'When he awoke upon the eve of July the twenty-third, we began our journey to the mighty stronghold of Kainor. The warriors were training vigorously when we arrived. A few in their midst were, shall I say, stout individuals, but they too worked hard. We were welcomed cheerfully, though they were quite surprised by our coming. They spoke highly of you, Prince Tristan, and claimed to be forever in your debt. When we asked to see you, they said you had returned to Bolteras just days before we arrived. We stayed with them two days before urging them to return with us, for Edgar had a strange feeling come over him—I reckoned he had inherited a power from the Celebhas that allowed him to sense approaching danger, but that is only my suspicion. At first, the Alterashians refused but then, on July the twenty-sixth, we saw dark clouds looming in the sky to the southwest. We managed to persuade a small company of them to escort us to the borders of Bolteras. When we drew nigh, there were large, dark billows beyond the forests, and an eerie feeling overcame our company. Fearing the worst, we rode forth, and that is how we came upon the battle of Bram; and not a moment too late I should add.

'We passed the borders of the Lonely Grey in the coolness of night just as the forces of Eordil were emptying, and we rode forth to meet them. Hardly had they mentioned the Vash'alans and the fall of Cayrngras when Edgar sped away in great haste. At once, we all followed in full pursuit. Edgar was full of rage knowing his people were under attack during his absence. We rode forth and fell upon the Vash'alan army, hacking and slashing as we went, and we met the forces of Poleden riding to us from the west. In a swift moment, we defeated the last of the enemy. We merely finished off the stragglers, but it was you, Tristan, they feared most. You might have won the battle with out us if not for the Dark Lord's protection about Marxas and the returning Imps of Darkness. It was Edgar's newfound powers that cleared the Dark Lord's clouds and dispelled the shield around Marxas. But truly, you won the battle without our aid, Prince Tristan. That is our tale.'

'Thank you, Grinshawl,' Tristan said with a yawn, 'but now I am quite sleepy. I will retire for the evening, but I wish to speak more with you both in the morning.' Edgar smiled and waved his hand, and Tristan withdrew.

'He will make a fine king,' Edgar declared, 'and a much finer one than I ever was.'

'Sire, Tristan will surely make a fine king one day, and I will follow him as devotedly as I have you; but there is no king as magnificent as you, save Vaaspar Himself. You are strong but also full of mercy and grace, and you have a heart filled with compassion and love that has long been forgotten by the kings of this age. There could be no greater king amongst Men. The world will know it when you are gone, but I see it now. Do not forget how much the people need a king like you and pass that legacy down to your nephew. He will need someone to be his aspiration. You must be that example to him, Edgar. But, well, I have said too much for one evening. I bid you goodnight, my liege.'

Grinshawl rose and sought out a place to lay his head for the night, but Edgar stayed awake for many hours reflecting on his life and remembering the times he spent with his belated wife. That night, he wept himself to sleep crying out, 'Amelia!'

Chapter XX

The Armies of Bolteras Assemble

Edgar awoke the next morning from a frightening nightmare recalling the death of his wife. He rose from his bed with tears in his eyes, and Grinshawl came running at the sound of the king's screaming.

'Sire, what is the matter?' the giant hollered as he entered the king's tent.

'It is nothing, friend. I just had that dream about Amelia again. I keep seeing her death. I wish she could be here with me again. I yearn to hold her in my arms just one more time. Woe is me!'

'Do not let it trouble you, my liege. Her death was not your fault. Yearn for her as long as you wish but shame yourself no more!'

'You are right, Grinshawl, as you usually are. Come now; let us move on from Bram. The people of Cayrngras await us.'

They left the shelter of his tent and rallied the troops. By the early afternoon, the land was cleaned of the many tents, but the stain of blood was still upon it. The air was distasteful for quite some time, but the farmers of Bram quickly went to work pouring fertilizers and seed upon the tainted ground, hoping for something new and pleasant to spring up from the soil. But even still, it took many months for the tainted land to be free of the stench of death. The bodies of the burned Vash'alans greatly displeased the people of Bram and many began to wheel the remains into the forest and dump them far from their sight.

After the hard work was done, Edgar called together Grinshawl, Tristan and Delitas to depart to Cayrngras. Meridas followed after him. 'Sire,' he shouted. The archers of the Lonely Forest were at his heel. They halted before the king and bowed. 'Sire, what are your orders?'

'For the time being, take your men and return to the Lonely Forest. After hearing your tale, it is only proper that you go and bury your own dead. Take some time to mourn but keep watch on the borders for our enemy. Prepare fresh arrows and be ready for war. Until then, await my call.'

'We shall do as you wish, Your Majesty. I am glad you are alive and well! We hope to see you again soon.' Meridas strode forth to the north leading his archers into the shelter of the Lonely Grey. Rolo came up last with Pakko at his side.

'Lord Edgar, what would you ask of us? Is there to be another gathering of your counselors?'

'Aye, we will return to Vallicore to discuss our next course of action, but I would have you go with Meridas. You have suffered losses as well. Go be with your friends and bury your kin. We will meet again soon.' Rolo nodded, and Pakko bowed; then, the two sped off after the host of archers now heading westward through the forest.

Edgar led his small company—Grinshawl, Delitas and Tristan with his men from Alterash—on horseback to Cayrngras. A sort of gloom seemed to hang over the once mighty fortress. As they drew nearer they saw before them a small bivouac to the north, and there were many soldiers scurrying about bearing the dead in their arms. As done in Bram, many of the fallen Vash'alans were already gathered into large piles and burned. To the south of the city, there were many mounds of fresh dirt containing the bodies of their comrades. Edgar wept as he beheld the misery of the people. They arrived at the fortress in the late afternoon as the sun was westering in the sky, and they were saluted by a host of the Templar Guard from Vallicore under Arthur's command—there were a hundred or more gathered. Edgar rode forth to the gates of the city to greet his troops and was bewildered to see so few. Arthur galloped forward on his steed and met the king. The two locked arms and shook with great excitement as they were glad to see one another. Behind the elderly man, thousands of bodies were thrown into piles, but there were still many more scattered about the field of battle. 'Even amidst a field of defeat, such joy fills the heart of this old man today!' Arthur cried. 'Tom and I were dreadfully worried all this time that you had died, Lord Edgar. Where have you been for so long?'

'There will be time for reunions and stories later. But tell me, why have so few of my soldiers come to the aid of Bram?'

'It was a decision made by Tom and myself. You did leave us in charge after all. Elder Bowman would have come with me if his frail limbs allowed him to rise from his bed, but alas, he has been quite ill these days. We would not risk emptying Vallicore of all her troops for fear that the Draemhas would attack while we were away, so I was sent with one hundred of the Templar Guard to the aid of Bram. But as I neared Cayrngras, the dark clouds above began to retract and within its shadows hundreds of tiny lights—they were eyes as I deduced—flickered throughout and faded away to the north. We meant to come to you sooner, but the tragic fate of the warriors of Cayrngras delayed me for a time. We kept watch in case the Enemy's armies returned to our lands. But as it was, we saw the forces of Poleden riding to the aid of Bram, so we felt no shame in lingering here. I suggest you go into the central courtyard now, Your Highness, but expect to see nothing pleasant. The city is in ruin, and the people need their king.'

Edgar slid from his horse and proceeded through the gates into the once mighty fortress, and Grinshawl followed. Tristan did not go in but simply sat on his horse looking in through the gates: his shame prevented him from entering. Inside the city, the smell of death lingered, and the city was covered with gnats and flies, for they were drawn to the corpses all about the city. 'We have been toiling since we arrived,' Arthur said from outside the gates, 'to bury the dead, but we were too few to get the work done before you arrived.' Edgar was filled with heartache. Hundreds of cloven shields lay scattered about amongst the bodies of the dead. He came at last to the central courtyard where a small host of Boltians lay dead in a pile. Edgar then turned about and saw on the northern gate the head of Paladin placed upon a wooden spike. At once, he darted back to the gates and climbed upon the wall to remove the head of the captain from its disgraceful position. He then carried the head of Paladin to the courtyards below and placed it on the ground and covered it with a cloth. He lowered his head in silence for a moment before withdrawing back to the gates. Grinshawl perched himself upon the walls and looked forlornly upon the ruined city. All the buildings were either burned or broken, and the city was layered with corpses and stained with blood.

'Arthur,' Edgar called, 'I wish to bury these men by tonight.'

'Sire, there are many dead, and it would take hours of grueling work to accomplish that in one night.'

'Please, friend,' he said with reddened eyes full of tears, 'I hate seeing the death of my soldiers. They deserve to have a proper place of burial. This reality torments me more than anything else in this world. I want to show them proper respect even now in death. Let us all work as hard as we may.'

'Aye, I understand.' Arthur returned to the small host of Boltians who waited patiently for their orders. 'Soldiers and civilians, hearken to me. Lord Edgar is overcome with grief for the death of his people. Let us put aside our mourning for now and work hard to provide these brave people a decent burial. We should honor our dead, for they died with honor.'

The horses would not go near to the city, so they led them to the forest's edge and tied them to the trees. Every able-bodied man went to work while the women kept watch over the children. The corpses of their enemies were brought out in large numbers to the north and piled beside the other mounds to be burned. With a little oil and a few torches, the Vash'alan cadavers were set ablaze. Smoke ascended, and the air became heavy. The sun had vanished into the west by the time they had finished dragging the last of the Vash'alans to be burned, but their work did not end there. For some three hours, they toiled harder to carry their fallen brethren out of the city to be buried. The work lasted much longer than anyone hoped for, but it was finished at last. The people were glad to bury their loved ones at last but soon their grief and mourning returned to them. The graves of the dead were soon covered by the bodies of the living as the people wept for the departed. The sky yielded no rain that night, but the people's tears were enough to dampen the ground.

The streets of Cayrngras were cleaned of the dead at last, but they were anything but clean. The survivors of Cayrngras returned to what was left of their homes and began purifying the city of the filth left behind; they were unable to find rest that night. But Edgar and his companions withdrew to the plains to the east and easily found asleep.

Upon the following morning, Edgar began his journey back to the capital city of Vallicore with his companions. Already, the scars of war were across his kingdom, and he dreaded returning home only to prepare for further battles. The journey to Vallicore lasted fewer than two days at a slow pace. With them also were the Templar Guard and those left from Tristan's band—one hundred and forty-three in all. They rode silently. Along the way, they peered every so often to the north. The shadows of the Enemy were far away now, but that provided them no rest.

At long last, Edgar returned home to Vallicore, and he and his company were greeted by thousands of soldiers who stood on guard upon the walls of the city. Many held poles bearing the banner of Bolteras in their hands while the rest held their weapons lifted high. They hailed the king with a mighty shout as he drew near. But Edgar and his company were full of gloom and not even the warm welcome was enough to cheer their hearts on that day. Edgar entered the city and was greeted by the masses of civilians within the city. They lined themselves all along the path leading to the Silver Vestibule and cheered incessantly. At once, the company dismounted, and their steeds were taken to the stables by a host of soldiers. Edgar waved at the people and forced a smile upon his face; but he did not linger and quickly led his advisors to his throne room.

* * *

For three days, not a single person outside the Silver Vestibule saw or heard from Lord Edgar or his companions. The king and his counselors spent the three days in deep debate over their next course of action. The same words were spoken each day, but Edgar could not figure out what to do. Elder Bowman wished to join their discussion, but he was confined to his bed and moaned in agony, for he was extremely sick. Quite often, Arthur slipped away from the council room and sought Tom's advice; but the old man was nearing his last days, and his voice was failing. On the third day of council, Arthur did not leave Elder Bowman's side out of fear that the old man would die at any moment. When evening came, he slipped away to the outside of the Silver Vestibule and stared off into the east, hoping to see Victor returning with Alastair. But Victor never returned. After a time, Arthur slipped back into the council room. The men were still discussing, and they still seemed far from making their decision.

'Consider this, my liege,' Grinshawl spoke. 'Our defenses are much greater if we fight here in Vallicore. This city has never been defeated, and few even dare to stand against it. In all your time as king, none have come to wage battle here.'

'That may be, but we cannot simply wait for them,' Edgar snapped. 'When we left the lands of Vash'ala, we were saved by Percival the Silver, and he was captured by the Enemy's minions; or have you forgotten? It is only right that we rescue him.'

'But, my liege, we have no way of knowing if he lives! And b—'

'How many times,' Edgar interrupted, 'how many times have others sacrificed themselves for us to live on? I wonder. All the same, it is too many by my reckoning! And now it is our turn to repay the debt we owe them. We have been given many opportunities to live and fight another day, and that day has come!

329

Furthermore, we from the Boltian Council each went our separate ways with a mission. But each of our missions failed to some degree. Grinshawl and I failed to return with Percival, and Elorén has withdrawn to Elúne to make matters worse. Alastair and Victor are unaccounted for. Tristan succeeded in liberating the peoples of Alterash, but those stubborn fools refuse to lend us their aid. Paladin and the other captains succeeded in enlisting my armies for war, but Paladin is dead; and the forces of Cayrngras and Bram have suffered great losses. Furthermore, we still have not received word from Balas. And the watch along our borders is feeble as Meridas and his archers suffered many losses as well. This seems hopeless.'

'That is all the more reason to take our stand here in Vallicore,' Tristan added. 'You must consider this, uncle!'

'We cannot take our stand here! Percival changed his mind and heart and chose the path of Light. He came to our aid only to be captured by the Enemy. Even if there is only a glimmer of hope of rescuing him, then I must consider marching upon the Draemhas. What would you have me do as your king? Should I cower behind my fortifications and let a friend die? Or should I stand against the armies of the Dark Lord and do all I can to rescue the one in need? We may have failed our missions initially, but we must not give up!'

'If I may,' Delitas spoke, 'I have something to say.' Edgar waved his hand and plopped down into his chair. He was exhausted and annoyed. 'I agree with Lord Edgar. We simply cannot ignore the Draemhas in my lands. If we allow them to muster a greater force, then we will surely lose this war. I fear the Dark Lord will send more troops, and we will be overrun. What will happen if they swarm the lands of Bolteras, burning and pillaging as they go? Will not all of Bolteras fall to ruin? And what then will become of Gaia if the Western Lands fall?'

'That cannot happen,' Grinshawl replied. 'We have captured the Alchemist's Stone, and Elorén the Celebhas has returned it to Vaaspar in Elúne to be destroyed. The Draemhas can no longer open a portal from Dragoth. They cannot increase their armies any further.'

'That has been troubling me,' Edgar added, 'ever since we found the Stone in the prisons of Gorgonash. It is odd, is it not?'

'What do you mean?' Delitas questioned.

'What I mean is that it was far too easy to capture the Stone. Elorén said it was the real thing, but I wonder if there is another.' The crowd looked doubtfully at Edgar, and he chuckled. 'I know what you are all thinking, but consider it. If the Alchemist's Stone is such an important piece of their plan, then why were there not hundreds or even thousands of Draemhas guarding it? Furthermore, I believe the Enemy was aware of our presence in Vash'ala since we entered the land. When I touched the Stone, I was struck with pain in my heart, and my sickness of old returned to me.'

'What is this sickness you speak of?' Delitas inquired.

'Ah, I forget you do not know. It is the same sickness from Vash'ala wrought by the power of Envy. It plagued many good soldiers in the war twenty years ago. I was stricken by the disease as well, and it took all my Magical power to suppress it. I only sit before you now by the blessing of Elúvías.'

'I am confused,' Delitas answered. 'At the Boltian Council, you said it was your wife who was struck with the disease. Did she not die from it, taking your unborn child with her?'

'Watch your tongue!' Grinshawl snapped.

'Calm yourself, friend,' Edgar interjected. 'He meant no harm. Let me ask you something Delitas, how do you suppose my wife became sick?'

Delitas thought for a moment and then a look of dismay shone upon his face. 'Your Majesty, forgive me for prying!'

'It is forgiven. It was I who caused my wife and child to die. When I returned from war, I was ill, struck by the curse of Envy. We believed the disease belonged only to us who went to war and could not be passed on to others, but we were gravely mistaken. The disease caused me to wake from sleep many times, and I would cough up blood violently from my mouth. One day, nearly six years ago now, I woke with a violent cough. At one point, I coughed up blood and it fell into the mouth of my wife, Amelia. Within days, she became sick and died. I have carried that burden with me for all these years, knowing that both my wife and child are dead because of me.' Edgar began to weep. None said a word. A moment later, he spoke again. 'The Dark Lord and his armies have taken too much from me. They have taken my wife, my child, and many of my friends; they have even stolen the happiness of me and my peoples. I cannot stand for it anymore! As I was saying before, I think our enemies presented a false Stone before us as an attempt to strike me dead. Or maybe his goal was to strike down Elorén. Either way, I suspect there is a second Alchemist's Stone. I may not know for certain, but we cannot wait for the Dark Lord's armies to come upon us! No more will we allow the forces of Darkness to rule over us and threaten our peoples. I have made my decision. We go to war!'

'Agreed,' all the advisors but Arthur answered in accord. As the counselors withdrew, Arthur asked to speak with Edgar in private.

'Sire, Victor has not returned. We cannot advance on the enemy yet. Why are we not waiting for the Draemhas to come to us where our defenses are greatest?'

'We can wait no longer, Arthur. And you have heard my decision. You are one of my oldest friends, and I need you to trust me in this. We must take the fight to them while they think we are recovering from our losses.'

'But our forces are weakened severely!' Arthur snapped. 'And Seymour has departed back to Elúne! Furthermore, Paladin is dead, and Alastair has not returned with Victor. We do not even have the White Mage to aid us. Why do you not care about my son's fate?'

'Of course I care about Victor's fate!' Edgar hissed. 'Did I not ask you to trust me? We will not fail, and Victor will return to you. Now are you going to come with me, or will you go to him?'

'Forgive me, friend. I merely yearn to see my boy, and I fear I will never get to see him again. I will go with you, of course.'

'I thank you. Go now and get some rest. I will send word to our armies to gather in Vallicore at once!'

Edgar went out from the throne room and climbed to the second floor of the citadel. There he found a lonely soldier and called upon him.

'Soldier, I need you for a special task. Go for me and call upon my armies. I grant you authority to take other soldiers from Vallicore to aid you in this matter. Go now and do not tarry! You have one month to accomplish this task!' The soldier obeyed without a word and darted down the stairs and out of the Silver Vestibule. The man called upon others, and they departed—one hundred and thirty went out.

* * *

In the first week after the heralds went out, the soldiers from Cayrngras arrived in Vallicore. Following them were the tent-dwellers hailing from the coasts to the north and the lands from the south. They were free Men, not belonging to any town or village, but still devoted to serving Lord Edgar. In the week that followed, the forces of Bram, Poleden and Eordil arrived in full force headed by

332

Hauffa, Ragnok and Hombag. Another week elapsed, but no more arrived. Edgar was growing impatient, for he needed a larger force to go to war. But during the last week when the messengers had returned, the forces of Balas, Pilias and Carg arrived, much to Edgar's surprise and delight. All the while, the archers of the Lonely Forest stayed vigilant near the borders of Vash'ala.

As the mighty forces of Bolteras assembled, Arthur kept count as the leaders of the strongholds delivered their reports to him. At that time, there were nearly twenty-two thousand warriors residing in the glorious city of Vallicore. There were another four thousand of the elite soldiers of the Templar Guard. Several Keshians had arrived numbering thirteen in all—they had heard news of the approaching war and decided to join the fray. Ten came from Oga. And of the tent-dwellers, there were nearly three hundred. Of Poleden, there were twelve hundred twenty-one led by Hombag; of Bram, there were nine hundred thirty-three led by Hauffa; of Carg, there came a pleasing twenty-two hundred strong less one led by Teles—many had believed a much smaller force would arrive, for Teles was a stubborn man. Of Eordil, there were thirteen hundred twelve led by Ragnok; of Balas, eight hundred and fifty answered the call led by Bory and Grob; and of Pilias, there were three thousand led by Enren. In all, the armies numbered near to thirty-six thousand soldiers, excluding Meridas' faction.

After numbering the troops, Arthur reported the news to Elder Bowman, and the old man coughed and exclaimed, 'I never thought I would see such a glorious day! But alas! I still do not see it!' Arthur aided his friend to the window of his bedroom, and Tom looked out upon the vast armies of Bolteras congregating at the gates of Vallicore. He felt great joy in his heart and was proud of his country. 'I thank you, Arthur. Help me to my bed. I have seen the armies and am quite happy now.' Suddenly, Tom felt sharp pains throughout his body and writhed in agony on his bed. Arthur tended to him and sat by his side until the hurting ceased.

'I am better now, Arthur. Thank you for staying by my side.'

'What should I do, Tom?'

'Whatever do you mean, you old fool?' the codger snapped.

'My son has not returned, and Alastair is not here either. I wish to go to him, to my boy that is.'

'Do not be a fool. He will come. Just believe he will and he shall!' Bowman coughed.

'Then, perhaps I should stay here with you.

333

'Bah!' Tom answered angrily. 'Are you trying to avoid war again? What would Threngol think of that if he were alive today?'

Arthur chuckled and shook his head. 'You are right, as you are often. I pray that I get to see you again, Tom. I have become fond of our conversations. Do not tell the king, but you have become my closest friend.'

'Aye, I feel the same of you, Arthur. I will at last die knowing I had a friend in this life. But whether we see each other again is not up to us! Go now and join the ranks. I will await your return as long as I can.'

'Farewell, Tom.' Arthur embraced his friend and then withdrew to the gates of Vallicore.

'Farewell, you old codger,' Tom replied with a laugh. A mere four days later, Tom Bowman was found dead in his bed with a smile on his face. Beside him was a note addressed to Arthur. It was sloppily written but read:

Dearest Arthur,

I tried to hold out for your return, but I fear I can hold on no more. Thank you for befriending a petulant, old man as me. I never thought I would have a friend after my wife's passing, but you were eager to call me your friend. I am quite happy now, and I owe you my gratitude. I have lived a good life, but my time has come. My only regret is not being by your side in this war. Forgive my fragile body. Fight with courage. Make proud your belated son Threngol. Believe in Victor! I believe with all my heart you will see him soon. Slay a few Draemhas for me in my stead. And do me one last favor; come and visit me at my grave when you return.

My sincerest apologies for passing too soon,
Tom Bowman.

* * *

The day was September the fourth. Arthur descended the slope to the gates of Vallicore. In the distance, Edgar climbed upon the walls over the mighty gates and examined the ranks of his armies. He smiled proudly and shouted, 'For too long the armies of the Dark Lord have challenged the strength of Men. But lo! Men still live on! And we will continue to exist, for whenever the armies of Darkness rise to test our valor, we will stand to face them. And we will never fail, for we carry with us the power of Light! There is no army or Magic greater than the might of Elúvías. This is why we will

334

take the fight to them! We must defend our borders and protect those we love. The Draemhas scum are mustering their forces as we speak, but we will not back down! Nay, we will march upon them, and they will answer. Hearken to me warriors of Bolteras; many of us may die in this war, but if we are to die, then let us die with honor. Let us sacrifice ourselves for the good of our families just as our brave brethren of Cayrngras fought to the death to keep our freedom alive.

'As your king, I will not cower behind the ranks of my soldiers. I refuse to be so cowardly. I will lead the march and fight on the front lines of battle, whether my end is death or life. Together, we will rid the Western Lands of the corruption wrought by the powers of Darkness and drive the forces of Dragoth whence they came!' The forces cheered loudly, their voices carried in the wind like the sound of powerful thunder. 'I do not have a lengthy speech prepared for such a day as this, but I have one thing to say to you: you have all made me proud. I am honored to be in the presence of so many faithful people under one banner. I see there are some before me who are friends, and others are amongst my family. But regardless of status, you are all my brethren. I give you my word that I will as much risk my life for any of you as I would my nephew Tristan. I thank you my beloved brethren for showing me respect. Now let us go together whether we meet our end or begin a new chapter of life! We all have loved ones waiting for us at home, and none of us wish to see their freedom taken from them. And so now...we go to war!' The host shouted as Edgar raised his mighty hammer high into the air. He turned about and ran down the stairs to the foot of the gates. There awaiting him were Tristan, Grinshawl, Arthur and Delitas.

'Ah, my good advisors!' the king called enthusiastically. 'Come, I need a word! Something very important has slipped my mind. We need a man to stay in Vallicore in my stead. I know this is sudden, but I would like that man to be you, Arthur.'

'Absolutely not,' Arthur barked. Edgar's brow wrinkled at the sudden outburst. 'Do you think I will sit back during another war while my kin go off to die? I did that once, and a messenger returned to me the news of Threngol's death! I shall not stay behind a second time.' He crossed his arms stubbornly and released an angry groan.

'Then who will stay?' Edgar answered plainly.

'I know a man,' Arthur responded. 'He helped Tom and me a great deal during our work as stewards. I speak of Langol of the Templar Guard! He would make a fine leader in our absence.'

335

'Grinshawl, call for Langol to come to me,' the king responded with a smile on his face. He seemed quite pleased by the suggestion.

'Yes, my liege,' Grinshawl answered. He sped off and the other four waited patiently for his return. Some twenty minutes passed before he returned with Langol.

'You called for me, Your Highness?'

'Indeed I did. I need a man to stay in Vallicore while we go to war. The people will need a leader while I am away. I am calling upon you to do this for me. What say you?'

'I wish to fight with my brethren, but if the king asks me to stay, then I shall stay.'

'It is much appreciated, Langol. You are an honorable knight. This is an unfortunate request, but I assure you the people will need a capable leader. You are well spoken of, so I have chosen you.'

'Your words are kind, Edgar King, but I would be a liar if I said this decision pleased me. Still, I agree that the people will need a leader. I will stay. Take courage knowing your people will not be abandoned to their confusion.

'May Vaaspar bless you!' He placed a hand on Langol's shoulder and smiled tenderly. Turning to a guard to his right, he said, 'Bring me my horse! We leave at once!'

'Pardon me,' called a soothing voice from behind them. It belonged to a woman. 'Might I speak to the prince for a moment?' The company halted. Turning about, Tristan beheld Naomi, the girl who was quite fascinated with young Victor.

'Hullo, Naomi. Why the last time I saw you, you were quite rude to me! What words would you have with me?'

'Forgive my rudeness from before, Your Highness, but I thought you wished to court me. You see, I have been waiting for Victor to return. He has been gone for a long time, and I am growing more worried with each passing day. How does he fare? Where is he now? I should very much like to have a word with him.'

'Ah, well, I am afraid it is rather difficult to say. He has not returned. But fear not! He is traveling with Alastair the White, and he was found in the company of a Dragon. Whether or not he is alive, I cannot say, but I am confident in Victor. He is strong. I believe with all my heart you will see him again. Worry no more!'

'If you see him,' the girl continued with downcast eyes, her face reddened with embarrassment, 'tell him I await his return.'

336

Before Tristan could speak another word, the girl had turned and darted away. Tristan smiled and mumbled, 'You have my word.'

A moment later, a soldier approached the company with the king's steed: it was a gallant, dazzling stallion with white hair and a mane of brighter white. Edgar was the only one to ride on horse, but he did so simply to stand out to his men. His advisors followed on foot, but he marched at a slow pace and led them east out of the city and then north. As Edgar emerged from the city gates, he placed a regal helm upon his head: it was a silver barbute with gold trim about the edges, and a thick white plume like the mane of his horse ran from the top of it. Attached to his pauldrons was a long cape of white that seemed to blend in with his horse's hair. Emblazoned on his breastplate was the same image borne on the banners of Bolteras. Over his breastplate he wore a baldric with a steel shield fastened upon it. On his hands and feet, he wore finely crafted gauntlets and greaves of steel. And ever at his side was a short-sword and Earthbreaker, his trusty war maul.

It had been many years since the warriors of Bolteras had seen Edgar arrayed so gloriously, and it was his appearance that drove them forward with fresh courage in their hearts. Next to the king were the Ogre of Bolteras and his nephew the prince. Grinshawl roared loudly, as is his custom, and an expression of eagerness and contentment shone upon his face. Edgar smiled, but his eyes were focused on the road ahead. Tristan placed his own helm on his head and stood upright as he walked. The armies of Bolteras prepared the way for the king. He rode straight through the middle of his army and came to a halt at their end. He looked back and observed his countrymen. There were thousands before him. Some wore full suits of metal armor; others wore leather. All in all, they were magnificent to behold.

Edgar gazed all across the ranks of his armies and smiled. He raised his head and shouted with authority, 'Onward to Vash'ala!' All the soldiers roared. Their battle cry signified their approval of going to war. As Edgar turned and began the long march to the north, he led the Men in a battle song. The hordes of Boltians sung merrily as they went; some even played music. The Boltian warriors were happy now, but great terrors awaited them in the lands of Vash'ala.

www.ingramcontent.com/pod-product-compliance
Lightning Source LLC
Chambersburg PA
CBHW050921250626
47155CB00001B/319